Reluctant Rebel

Reluctant Rebel

by

FREDERIC F. VAN DE WATER

Duell, Sloan and Pearce
New York

****

To

Judge Edward J. Shea

in long-term friendship

Chapter 1

HE ALREADY had learned that in this strange, new land reticence provoked endless questioning and, though he spoke to the man who came forward, he actually addressed the entire company. Their faces, to sun-dazzled eyes, were pale ovals in the taproom's gloom.

"Adam Corlaer, at your service; lately from England and bound on private business from York province to Canada by way of Panton town."

The fulsome announcement, he hoped wryly, might save him later interrogation. Meanwhile, standing stiffly in the doorway, he suffered scrutiny that was like the intrusion of bold hands.

Drinkers had halted their tankards, half raised, to stare. Before the fire, a young man stood clasping a punch bowl and gaped while others at the chamber's far end rose to peer at Adam over neighbors' heads. He almost could feel the penetrating regard delve beneath his cloak to estimate the English-made blue broadcloth and dusty riding boots. He half expected the company to inquire in unison the price of each item.

"Sarvent," the man who had advanced now told him. "Stephen Fay, innholder."

He wore a deerskin jerkin over a butternut-stained linen shirt and the nap had been worn from the knees of his brown-plush breeches. In a face of kindred sad hue, gray eyes were alert. His manner was so barren of landlordly fawning that Adam hesitated, "Is there bait and bed for my mare and me?"

"Ehyah. Joe!"

The young man at the hearth thrust a loggerhead into his bowl and bore it to a table before he followed Adam out into the bleak

1

brilliance of the afternoon. He blew upon the nostrils of the tethered mare, Allegra, and inspected her teeth while the traveler unstrapped his saddlebags. With their burden over his arm, he paused and looked about him.

Low sunlight stretched crooked shadows of bare trees along the road and gilded the roofs of the prim houses and the barnlike church. In the stillness, Adam could hear, far away, a sawmill's whine. There was frost in the air and, once again, he fancied he could sense a further something, tingling and undefined. This might be the not yet encountered danger of which James Duane, his father's friend, had warned him; it might be only an invigorating quality belonging to land as young as this unruly precinct of New York.

The sun was leaving the Green where a few stumps still moldered. Oxen came lurching uphill from the valley and the logladen cart they drew cried mournfully for grease. The driver stared as he clumped past, and Adam, to avoid his questioning, turned and considered the gaunt bulk of the hip-roofed tavern and the effigy that served as signboard.

A scaffold, high on the wall, bore an ineptly stuffed panther, squatting in an attitude more sacklike than defiant. The cracked lips, the black mouth snarled toward the glowing west. Adam grunted as the symbolism struck home. This was Bennington town, in what the rebels who now were afflicting York's new governor, William Tryon, and already had caused James Duane much pain, persisted in calling "The New Hampshire Grants," and Adam had found lodging in that notorious hotbed of revolt—the Catamount Tavern.

Joe still waited at the mare's head and a semicircle of soiled children, materialized from nowhere and still barefooted in late November, considered Adam with similar gravity. It was plain that in The Grants guests bore their own luggage. Adam asked the young man:

"You've oats?"

"Ehyah. Prime."

"Bait and hay her well, then. She's come a long way."

Stephen Fay stood with an air of illimitable patience where his patron had left him. Adam, now more inured to mass observance, drew comfort from the warmth of the taproom. Tallow dips were beginning to shine like faint stars through the smoke, and more men than he would have thought so small a town could supply perched on settles against the pine-sheathed walls or sat together on benches beside long tables. Great logs on the hearth were wrapped in yellow flame that fondled a black pot steaming on the crane. Blue haze moved over ceiling beams where dried herbs hung. Wood and tobacco smoke, scents of liquor, men, and barnyards were pleasant after the austere outer air.

He followed the landlord across the sanded floor and up a flight of narrow stairs. He had found, neither below nor in the dim upper hall, warrant for Duane's warning.

"Bed single, if you've a mind," Fay suggested and, at Adam's nod, opened the door to a chamber where a bed and bench shared imprisonment. His long nose twitched in the cold and he looked doubtfully at the small black fireplace.

" 'Tain't London, I mistrust. Send ye up a fire if you're minded to bide here."

"Later will serve," Adam replied, setting his saddlebags astride the bench. He ordered trout, venison, Indian pudding, and a bowl of rum flip before Fay went silently away.

Adam's breath steamed as he bent to inspect the bed. The mattress was of cornhusks but the blankets were clean. He moved half aimlessly about the room and paused at the window. Dusk was creeping in upon the settlement, though on the far, tall hills sunlight still dwelt. He found no cheer in the distorted prospect the flawed panes afforded. The mountains' aloof splendor abased the little village. Its grim dwellings and disheveled clearings were proper haunts for the rebels whom Duane had denounced. Adam felt the room's chill heighten his fatigue and loneliness.

The weight beneath his ribs was heavy and blank as the still unlettered slab upon his father's grave in the crypt of Albany's English Church. This was all that remained of the kind, the quick man who had been ambitious for his only son. His father's insistence had sent Adam to Oxford; his father's death had called him home.

The last tarnished glow was fading from the distant ranges. Two riders drew rein before the tavern and, dismounting, led their horses toward the stables. Adam wondered drearily whether, by civilization's measurement, any place on earth could be further

3

from Oriel College than this Bennington in the year of Our Lord, 1771. He shivered. Already he was regretting a mission that, if Duane had not opposed it, he never would have undertaken.

Mr. James Duane, executor of the estate of Gerardus Corlaer, had rendered an accounting in his usual precise fashion, deliberately choosing item after item from his orderly mind and presenting each neatly. There was money enough here in Albany, Duane explained, seasoning his announcement with snuff, to warrant Adam's return at once to Oxford and when James Morrison of Montreal, Gerardus Corlaer's agent, had made his final accounting there doubtless would be more.

"I shan't go back," said Adam huskily. "If I'd stayed here—"

"The lamentable conclusion," Duane completed and flicked a grain of snuff from a knee, "would have been equally inevitable. Your father also owned, my dear boy," he pursued, clearing his throat, "rights under a New York patent to wilderness land on Otter Creek in the territory Governor Wentworth of New Hampshire has tried to steal."

"The Grants?"

"The New Hampshire Grants." Duane's voice was rising. "So called by ruffians who make mock of York law. Benning Wentworth, the damned, fee-pocketing thief, established scores of towns on what he knew in his black heart was New York soil. These have been peopled by a most pestilential banditti who swear they will maintain their fraudulent titles, at need, by open civil war."

He swallowed his anger with an effort, sat the straighter, and pursued in a determinedly calmer voice, "Your father purchased the rights of which I speak from me. Because they have been incompletely surveyed and because of the riots that endure in that wretched district, their value is dubious, but I shall be willing to buy them back from you and I urge you to sell them. I also counsel that you go to Canada and confer with Morrison."

"Visiting this Grants property on the way?"

"That," Duane said hastily, "I should not advise."

He leaned back in his chair, a silk-stockinged leg dangling over a black-satin-clad knee, a composed and impeccable figure that, as he justified his counsel, gradually was disorganized by emotion.

4

Adam, with mounting relish, observed how Mr. Duane's face grew crimson as he told of Benning Wentworth's unscrupulous granting of territory that His Majesty later had proclaimed York property. The narrator's hand shook so violently that he spilled snuff while he described the original settlers' refusal to surrender the land they had occupied. His wig was slightly awry and the anguish in his speech revealed personal deprivation when he recited the burnings, the beatings, the brawls, and evictions with which the pestilential banditti of The Grants had resisted New York's attempts to acquire what was legally hers.

"And now," Mr. Duane shrilled in conclusion, "what should be a united province is torn apart by rebellion that assumes the proportion of war. Thank God that His Majesty at last has sent us a governor who will deal with such ruffians. William Tryon may be harsh, but he is thorough and a sound drubbing—"

He became aware that Adam was amused and paused, readjusting his wig and slapping at snuff on his waistcoat.

"That," he resumed in a calmer voice, "is why I advise you to go direct to Canada. Sell me the rights, my dear boy, but don't venture into The Grants."

His air was so patronizing that Adam replied, "Men must come and go from there unharmed. If I ride as a traveler, why should there be danger?"

"Why have they chased my surveyors out of the region? Why does John Munro, my agent in Shaftsbury, go in daily fear of his life?"

"Because they are your agents. Isn't that so? Suppose I go, as a neutral traveler? There should be no danger then."

"Well," said Duane, and thoughtfully tapped his snuff-box lid, "perhaps you are right. As your father's friend, I oppose it. As a patentee under York law such a journey of inspection recommends itself, for you will have unclouded eyes and an open mind. What you learn may be of advantage to us. I have a surveyor in The Grants now. He should be able to help you locate your land in what the rebels call Panton town. I'll give you letters to Munro and to Cockburn, but again I warn you that the enterprise holds dangers."

The condescending concern, the well-turned, silken calf, the reopened snuff box with the twin doves on its cover, the lately ruffled, now restored sleekness of look and manner, all prompted Adam's sudden determination. He would dare the reputedly perilous region, inspecting the rebellion's interior, seeing for himself the Panton land his mentor disparaged yet offered to buy. The venture, whatever its outcome, would be anodyne for bereavement's weight and the daunting sense of aimlessness.

Adam had ridden from the Hudson ferry toward distant hills that, each time he glimpsed them through gaps in the forest, rose higher in the diamond-bright air. The wilderness was fair country, ripe for settlement, rich in timber, but his body had found a danger in the stillness and had grown tautly alert before his mind recognized it.

The greedy curiosity of the few travelers he encountered did nothing to dispel this nameless distress. None of them was willing to let Adam pass with a brief greeting. Each demanded news from overseas, from Albany, New York, and Boston towns, and, finally, more insistently of Adam himself.

He tarried at noon in a log tavern, rank with the smell of spruce beer, and dined on journeycake and pork that swam in grease while the frowzy landlord hovered about him and slyly tried to extort Adam's politics.

Later, he was cross-questioned by two lank horsemen who suddenly appeared on the road before him with muskets across their saddle bows and comported themselves more like a military patrol than the deer hunters they professed to be.

He was weary of interrogation and nervously spent when at last he passed cabins where dry cornstalks still stood about the clearings' stumps, crossed a log bridge, and rode uphill into Bennington. He had grown less scornful, too, of Duane's vaporings.

As he stood by his bedroom window, he wondered whether memory of the older man's warning was not all that kept him from abandoning his enterprise at its outset.

He was weary and downcast, but cold was his chief immediate affliction. Food and a hot draught could remedy this. He was angry to find as he went downstairs that his palms grew moist and his breath came quickly.

The blaze on the hearth and the candle flames warred with the taproom's shadows. The chamber was even more crowded now and murmurous with low-pitched speech. Adam sought and found an empty space at a table's far end. He was heartened and then ashamed of his relief to see, lounging beside the fireplace, two young men in yellow-faced scarlet uniforms. If The Catamount Tavern tolerated His Majesty's soldiers, rebellion was more limited than Duane had alleged and a mere traveler could discard his girlish fears.

The young man called Joe came at once and placed a fragrant pewter bowl before Adam. The rum was raw and stingily spiced, but it lifted his spirit and untied a hard knot in his belly. He ate with good appetite the plain fare Joe served and, when the table was cleared, ordered a fresh bowl of flip.

Adam relaxed in the rigid pine chair and considered with amusement his late dejection. A voice, close to his ear, said, "By your leave, sir."

A plump man in a decent suit of gray homespun stood, tankard in hand, and indicated the empty place on Adam's right. The stranger's swarthy face was bland and his hair, worn clubbed and unpowdered, was black and shining as his eyes. He took the seat with an indrawn hiss of appreciation.

Adam, still looking about the shadowy chamber, again marveled idly at the patronage of Landlord Fay's hostelry. It was odd that one wilderness settlement could furnish so many tavern loungers in fustian, homespun, leather, and towcloth. They were decorous revelers. As the taproom had become crowded it had actually grown quieter. The patrons, as though under some spell that imposed decorum, sat together, drank gravely, and talked in wary voices. It was, Adam appreciated suddenly, as though they had assembled here, not for revelry, but for some still unperceived event. At his elbow, the plump man offered, "A large meeting tonight, eh, sir?"

Above the rim of his tankard, the black eyes were bright.

"Yes." Adam shrank from renewed questioning but his brevity did not daunt the other.

"You are attending, if I may make so bold?"

Adam looked away from the round, wheedling face. Down the long table, a rawboned man peered too intently into the mug he

7

held. Above a grimed, brown frock, the long face wore the look of a drowsy horse, but Adam knew it was vigilance that had half closed the humorous eyes.

Something was astir that a stranger could not fathom; something undiscerned, furtive, and best left alone. His questioner still waited for reply with alcoholic patience. Adam's brief gesture included the whole taproom.

"If this be the meeting you mean, plainly I am attending."

The drowsing horse-faced man stirred and batted his eyes. Adam's questioner squirmed and dropped his voice still lower.

"I mean, sir—upstairs."

He drank again and leered.

"In the council chamber—no less."

Adam said coldly:

"I am not good at riddles, sir. I travel to Canada by way of Panton town."

"Panton," the other repeated, and in a half whisper, "but why to Panton?"

"On business." Adam stressed the next word. "My personal business."

He thought for an instant that this had won him relief, for his unsought companion washed the information down with a long draught and tabled the empty tankard before he resumed, "No offense, sir. Yet it is strange that one of the gentry, for your clothing so proclaims you, should tour The Grants in late November, or indeed"—sinking his voice still lower—"in any month during these desperate times."

The horse-faced man seemed wholly asleep now. Adam deliberately withheld reply. His companion wiped his mouth on the back of a plump hand and pursued, "Now I, sir, am of humbler station and must go as my employers bid. Benjamin Buck, sir, at your service. An agent for Albany merchants. Are you acquainted perchance in Albany?"

"I was born there."

Buck ignored the hostile brevity. The sigh he uttered was a release of pent suspicion. He leaned closer, blowing a malty breath.

"I thought so," he wheezed. "And yet your English clothes

8

puzzled me, sir. If you are from Albany, then you are of the right party."

A hiccup shook him and he blinked brilliant eyes. Adam spoke loudly enough to reach the ears of the ostensibly slumbering man.

"I am lately returned from England—too lately to know aught of parties or politics."

Buck peered reprovingly into his empty tankard and then beat it lustily upon the table until Fay took it away. The horse-faced eavesdropper roused, hauled himself up, and followed the landlord. His departure and drink's waxing valor removed Buck's discretion.

"Parties and politics," he echoed, wagging his head. "You'll learn of them, sir, tonight."

"Tonight?" Adam sought for threat or warning in the voice. Buck blinked like an owl.

"You know nought of parties," he confided, "yet the leaders of one are all around us. The Bennington Mob, sir, is here tonight, to meet upstairs in what they call 'The Council Chamber.' "

He misunderstood Adam's stare and leaned closer, boozily patting the other's arm.

"Have no fear, sir. It is not their habit to assail in forthright fashion. A skulking, rick-burning, ambushing pack of rascals. Governor Tryon, G'bless him, will teach 'em to dance to the measure he played for the Regulators in the Carolinas."

Another hiccup jolted and hushed him. Adam said, "You are scarcely discreet."

"Discreet? Pah! I'm for York. I care not who knows."

He hiccupped again, looked uphappy, rose with an indistinguishable mumble, and went hastily away. Adam turned quickly as another voice spoke behind him. The youngsters in uniform whom earlier he had seen at a distance bowed in unison. The slighter recited, standing ramrod-straight, "Ensign Jocelyn Feltham and George Wadman of the 26th and much at your service, sir, if they may have the pleasure of your company."

He was blond and spoke with the faintest lisp. His lips, barely meeting over the prominent teeth, gave him a look of permanent scorn that pale blue eyes and cropped, downy hair belied. Wadman bowed again as Adam named himself and lowered his thick

9

body into the chair Buck had occupied. Feltham sat down across the table with a sigh.

He and George, the light voice resumed, were grateful for Mr. Corlaer's company. "Corlaer" was right, wasn't it? They would become used in time, he fancied, to these outlandish names. George and he were on their way from Boston town to join their regiment in Canada and already were regretting their decision to cross the wilderness to Crown Point instead of following the military road from Number Four. It was unexpectedly pleasant to encounter in this savage land someone who did not smell of the barnyard.

"Or even more damnibly of himself," Wadman amended, the solid bar of his black eyebrows twitching. His brown eyes seemed to seek offense even when he was begging the privilege of ordering a bowl of punch.

"Jocelyn," he accused, "was for roaming the wilderness. He prated of Indians, moose, and bear. Folk like these"—he waved toward the company—"are the sole wild creatures we've seen. Lord, sir, Boston seems a proper town, but we have found no other in a week of riding. A desolate, damned unpleasant land."

"England," Adam said, curbing an impulse to more violent defense, "was much the same a thousand years ago."

"A thousand years," Wadman jeered, "would be too short a space to breed gentility into these sorry folk. They do not like Englishmen. Then, damme, sir, they should be taught to fear us."

Joe approached and set a large punchbowl on the table. His face was wooden. Feltham grasped and raised the brew.

"A toast," said he, "that all true Britons can drink! To—"

The tavern door burst open. A gust of cold air shook the candle flames and bore a strong voice, crying, "Greetings, the whole!"

Chairs rumbled, feet tramped as most of the company rose. Wry voices shouted, and above the confused acclaim someone raised the high, keen howl of a wolf. The intruder laughed.

His bulk filled the doorway. His harsh face shone against the night. He swung his gilt-bound hat aloft in acknowledgment and shrugged off his cloak. Epaulettes stressed the vast shoulder breadth of the green and golden coat. A gorget gleamed below a massive chin. Scarlet waistcoat and buff breeches further encased the stranger, and on tall boots immense spurs jingled as he strode forward. Light found the hilt of a mighty saber and gave it brazen shining.

Feltham sat with the bowl half raised and his toast unuttered. While men pressed about the giant, his intense blue eyes searched the room, and Adam, meeting them for an instant, felt an odd shock at the contact.

"Lord," Feltham tittered uneasily, "have mercy! What is this?"

Wadman glowered as the apparition raised again that trumpeting voice.

"I would have the folk of Bennington to know that I bring reproof, nay, judgment, upon them from the seat of the mighty, even from Governor Tryon. Repent ye, repent ye, turn from wickedness and cast out the sinners among ye, saith Butchering Billy."

He shook a placard in a gloved hand and grinned at the yelp of delight his mockery roused.

"And where else should this testament be posted than in this nest of rebellion? Stephen Fay, bring hammer and nails that I may set a sign afore ye all."

The landlord advanced with his sharp eyes twinkling. The giant, trailed by the crowd, clumped to the taproom's far end and with a thunder of hammer blows fixed the placard to the wall.

"By the hindparts of Jehovah that fired the face of Moses," he proclaimed, turning with hands on hips, "heed the words of our good Governor Tryon. Tryon, forsooth! Try on, then, Billy, you dog, and be damned to you."

He led the responsive guffaw and then stepped aside, searching among the men who clustered about the placard. He reached to tap one on the fringed shoulder of a buckskin hunting shirt and draw him aside. While the rest milled and muttered before the proclamation, the giant and his companion spoke briefly together. The smaller man nodded his sandy head, drew thin lips tighter still, searched the crowd with sour eyes, and called, "Olin."

A blackhaired youngster in a butternut frock freed himself and approached. The pair moved softly away, chose fur caps from pegs and firelocks from the many that stood against the wall, and with weapons trailing slipped out through the door.

The giant dealt the horse-faced man, Adam's late neighbor,

a clap on the back and with one great arm across his shoulders moved toward the stair. The crowd about the placard spread and followed. Great boots pounded on the treads. The sword clanked, spurs jingled, the ceiling beams quaked. A leaf from the dangling herbs dropped to the table before Adam. Overhead, they heard the blaring voice raised again, then laughter, and, once more, scaling high, the long wolf howl.

The almost empty taproom was silent. Feltham atoned for his awe by an uneasy snicker.

"And who," he demanded, "is Sir Pomposo Furioso?"

Wadman, glowering, snorted. "A damned insolent mountebank."

Adam held his peace. The intruder, he felt, was something more. He had a force, an elemental power, that his companions overlooked, however much they despised his trappings and his bawling gusto. Dust had blinded Wadman and Feltham to a tempest's passage.

"By your leave, gentlemen!"

The familiar voice oozed into Adam's ears. Buck had returned, shinier and more ingratiating, tankard in hand.

"Perhaps," he ventured, seeking no more permission than the others' regard, "you are not familiar with that great soldier."

He licked his lips as though his sneer had left a pleasant taste.

"That, sirs, was a greater rascal than you will see again in your travels, go you ever so far. That, gentlemen, was Ethan Allen."

Chapter II

BUCK leered expectantly, in his excitement slopping beer from his tankard, but his tidings produced less sensation than he had hoped. Adam alone showed interest. Feltham drawled, "Ethan Allen?"

Clearly, the name meant nothing to him. The scowling Wadman demanded:

"By what right does he wear a colonel's epaulettes? What are those fantastic regimentals?"

Buck addressed Adam, deeming him the most receptive hearer, while Feltham drank deeply from the punchbowl and passed it to Wadman.

"Ethan Allen, no less, and with him upstairs his fellow bandits —Peleg Sunderland, Seth Warner, Robert Cochran, Sam Herrick, and lesser villains, with Remember Baker and that dark lad gone forth on fresh deviltry. Sir, if the Council Chamber and those within should burn tonight, we should have peace in The Grants."

He blinked and, lifting his tankard, swigged loudly. The ensigns, unwilling to include him even in talk, looked inquiringly at Adam, who explained with care: "There has been trouble here over land titles. Most of the settlers hold, under New Hampshire, land that New York province claims."

"Claims!" Buck repeated indignantly. "New York holds the land rightfully by charter and by His Majesty's own confirmation."

"Oh, tally!" Wadman drawled with heavy distaste. "Are all the provinces peopled by damned rebellious yokels?"

Adam lifted the bowl and drank, resolutely swallowing indignation with punch before he replied, "That was scarcely so when I sailed for England two years since. I have but lately returned."

"Perforce, I trust," Feltham smirked. "Otherwise I should deplore your taste. And these unwashed oafs, this Bennington Mob?"

"I believe they call themselves 'The Green Mountain Boys.' "

"And, by God," said Wadman, "a martial array! A company of the 26th could disperse them all."

"A half company," Feltham amended and picked up the bowl. Adam said nothing. It was Buck, still lingering, who supplied:

"York has a stronger governor now, gentlemen. The Mob's time is short. His Excellency William Tryon is not one to trifle with treason."

The name pricked his recollection and his wet eyes slid away to rest upon the placard on the far wall. He tiptoed off and stood squinting before it. A handful of patrons who had sat by the hearth rose and went noisily out. The landlord and Joe bore in a great log and laid it on the fire. They and Adam and his companions, and Buck teetering before the poster, were the taproom's only occupants.

"Said I not," Buck demanded thickly, "that our new governor was of sterner stuff? Hear this, 'Now therefore do I, William Tryon, by His Majesty's grace governor of his province of New York, call upon all liege and faithful subjects of George III forthwith to apprehend the said Ethan Allen, Remember Baker and Robert Cochran and do hereby offer twenty pounds reward for the capture of each of these rebels and miscreants.' "

"By God," he exulted. "They've been outlawed; all three of 'em. Outlawed!"

He turned again to the placard and silently reread it with relish so complete that he was heedless of the tramp of boots, the chime of spurs on the stair.

"Captain Fay," Allen cried, "the council doth protest that it cannot legally be called to order nor legitimately assemble itself together while one prime requisite is lacking. Wherefore, good Captain, bear to us forthwith in a proper bowl that punch rightfully known as The Colonel Commandant's Particular."

Buck had turned from reading and Allen marked him. He moved across the room with light speed startling in one who lately had tramped so ponderously, and loomed above the suddenly quailing man. The brazen voice rang muted through the still room, "Greetings, friend. It is in my mind that we know each other."

"I have not the—honor," Buck faltered, dwarfed in person and presence by the looming giant.

"Then, friend, it would seem that my memory is better than yours. Benjamin Buck is your name; Buck, the Yorker; Buck, the spy."

His last words clanged and Adam, watching the suddenly suffused face, thought of molten metal shivering and twitching. Buck croaked, "Colonel, that is a—misapprehension."

A big hand shot out, grasped him by the coat lapels. The startling voice now blared, untrammeled, "The truth," said Allen and shook the man as though the coat he grasped were empty fabric. "A sneaking, peering bastard of old Munro, the Yorker. By the toes of Agag, we shall make a hell of his house and burn every son of a bitch within it. Bear him that message, Master Spy. Captain Fay, this man saddles his horse and departs at once."

The landlord hesitated, then nodded. Buck, released, shook his head, wheezed, and pleaded for delay.

"Colonel," he begged, " 'tis a cruel cold night to be abroad."

"I promise you instant passage to a warmer place if you are here when I return," Allen retorted and tramped upstairs. Buck hesitated, looked appealingly toward Adam's table, and then disconsolately followed Fay from the taproom. Wadman's bleak laugh broke the silence, "Gad, sir! What a people—mountebanks and spies, oafs and hobbledehoys! The bowl, Jocelyn; let me wash away their taste."

He drank deeply and handed the vessel to Adam who, recoiling from the ferocity he had seen, ventured doubtfully, "It was shameful—and yet—"

"Shameful!" Wadman picked him up. "Ours is the shame, Mr. Curler. We trim and wheedle and placate this rabble. Their need is the fear of God, sir; put into 'em with foot, horse, and guns."

In the brief stillness a loggerhead hissed loudly as Joe plunged it into a vast bowl. Feltham looking askance at Adam, ventured, "Now I'll wager my breeches, George, that Mr. Corlaer does not agree with you."

Adam struggled with his temper. He said, at last:

"It is not so simple a disease and remedy. Even louts and mountebanks might fight for their own land."

"Oh, tally!" Feltham waved the doubt aside. "Can you fancy that vast popinjay leading a charge or storming a fortress?"

"Lord!" Wadman scoffed as Joe, heavily laden, passed them and climbed the stair. "Even heroes would scarcely fight for a land like this. Stab me, sir, if since we left Boston town we have found a meal worth eating, a draught worth drinking, or a maid worthy an officer's favor."

"That," Adam told him, "is women's misfortune," and withstood blandly the ensign's stare. In the pause they heard the clink of hoofs on frozen ground as Buck rode away.

"No maid, wife, or widow," Wadman reiterated, hoping by insistence to drive Adam to plainer speech, "befitting the embraces of one of His Majesty's most tolerant subalterns, which I proclaim myself to be."

Feltham giggled convulsively.

"George is a famous swordsman. Lord, the tales he tells!"

The door opened. Adam sat with his mouth ajar and his comment unuttered. In the world he knew, only loose women ventured into taprooms, but the girl who had entered clearly was not of their sisterhood nor did she seem conscious of impropriety. She hesitated an instant, a slender, vivid figure in the hooded red cloak, and searched the chamber before she advanced. The dark face framed in the bright fabric was inquiring rather than embarrassed.

Wadman's truculent eyes were fixed on Adam.

"Mr. Curler," he challenged, "was about to make an observation."

Adam rose and the ensign, misunderstanding, lurched to his feet. He wheeled as the girl said quietly:

"Your pardon, gentlemen. I am looking for my brother Justus —Justus Sherwood."

She was younger than Adam had thought. Her soft prettiness and the unformed brightness of her mouth were still childish, yet her smile stirred him. Wadman had reeled as he turned and, before he could recover, Adam said:

"We are strangers here. Perhaps your brother is upstairs. Shall I escort you thither?"

"No," she said and shook her head, smiling. "But if later you could tell him I shall await him at Parson Dewey's—"

Wadman had tugged at his waistcoat and run his hands over his cropped, tight curls.

"Brother! Fie, Chloe! Nymphs of the night must not seek brothers. A toast to this meeting."

He held the punchbowl toward her. Her laughter was unfeigned as she pushed the bowl away, but broke off sharply as the ensign set down the bowl and fumbled with her cloak.

"Now surely so fair a face reigns over a fairer form. Tarry with me, Amaryllis."

"Please," the girl whispered and looked toward Adam as Wadman tried to draw her down beside him.

"Good old George," Feltham giggled. Adam bade quietly: "Have done, sir."

Wadman seemed deaf. Adam caught his shoulder, spun him away, and stepped between him and the breathless girl. There still was mirth as well as fright on her face. Her innocence was fuel for his rage.

"Now, by God!" Wadman cried. He had recovered balance and had snatched up the bowl. As Adam turned, the ensign dashed its contents upon him. Blindly, the other leaped and struck against the table. It toppled and went over beneath him.

Adam heard, through the crash of the fall, Feltham's shrill yelp and then, while he struggled for breath and sight, feet pounding across the floor above and storming down the stair. As he wiped at his dripping face, a door opened and closed.

For an instant after he got to his feet, the room whirled. He shook his head and mopped again at his eyes. The wheeling faces grew stable. They pressed about him, harsh and gaping in the dim light. He peered around the taproom. The girl had vanished. His eyes, at the end of their search, rested upon Wadman. The ensign smiled as he set down the empty bowl. He ostentatiously dusted his hands and at the gesture a releasing mechanism clicked ever so faintly in Adam's skull.

"Now what in the seven circles of Tophet have we here?" a

voice bellowed and epauletted shoulders broke a pathway through the crowd. The babble broke into a yell, for Adam, stepping forward, had struck his open palm across Wadman's mouth.

An instant after the blow, Adam himself was smitten in the chest, thrust backward, and then yanked painfully erect. Too dazed to struggle, he blinked at the knobbed fist fastened upon his waistcoat, at the green and gilt sleeve from which it protruded, at Ethan Allen who towered above him and grasped with his other hand the snarling Wadman.

The ensign's face was creased and white. His breath hissed as he beat upon the restraining arm. His head snapped back, lolled, and jerked forward again as Allen shook him.

"Peace," the giant crooned, "peace and propriety in all things, my red gamecock."

Wadman, cowed by his captor's strength, gulped and stood still with Allen's fist still fast upon him. Its owner glared fiercely at his other prisoner.

"Now what," he demanded, "is the cause of this unseemly brawl? Gods of the Mountains! Is there not enough strife in the rest of the world that you must import it to this peace-loving hamlet?"

In the fiery blue eyes, Adam fancied he saw amusement stir. He said:

"This gentleman and I—disagreed."

"That I can credit. And what caused this unseemly disagreement and grievous wastage of good punch?"

"Politics," Adam replied at hazard. "A question of—Parliament."

Wadman eyed him with a flicker of respect and passed fingertips over his bruised mouth before he said, "I demand satisfaction."

"At your service," Adam answered promptly.

Allen had inflated his chest and now intoned.

" 'For forms of government let fools contest;
Whate'er is best administered is best.'

"Politics, forsooth? And the question appears to be still moot. So be it. Clear a space, boys, and we'll see it decided."

He nodded to the horse-faced man who whooped and, with

quick aid from others, righted the table, thrust it aside, and pulled back benches and chairs. As the scrape and clatter died, Wadman informed Allen, "His Majesty's officers are not bred to tavern brawls. This gentlemen"—he spoke the word delicately—"has promised satisfaction. Ensign Feltham will act for me. If Mr. Curler will name his second, we can adjust our difference on the morrow, with propriety and no assistance."

"I—" Adam began, but Allen's stormy voice blew his away:

"Now by the twenty-three eyeballs of the twelve apostles, sir, I declare you in error. This is not London; this is Bennington in The New Hampshire Grants. We look with reprehension, aye, even denunciation and repugnance, on bloodletting by bullet or sword."

"I can believe that. However—"

"However and howsomever and peradventure! We have our code, sir, founded by Nature and Nature's gods. The weapons we employ to reburnish our honor—which I avow is as bright as His Majesty's officers'—are Nature's own. This is Rome, sir, and the will of us Romans is that you comport yourselves Romanly."

He kept his gravity amid the responsive laughter. Men formed a ring. Wadman, still in Allen's grasp, was watching his fellow prisoner with careful eyes. It was Feltham who protested, "Gad, my good sir. My friend is no bruiser, to—"

"Neither, my good sir, is your friend an innholder, yet has he not served this young man overzealously with punch?"

"I protest—" Feltham began, but Wadman had finished his inspection and nodded.

"Be it so then," he agreed and, as Allen released him and his adversary, slipped out of his uniform coat. With Feltham's aid, he stripped swiftly to the waist and then waited, a confident muscular figure, while Adam, with the bungling assistance of the gleeful horse-faced man, got out of his coat, waistcoat, and shirt.

His hands were cold and clumsy and he listened with acid amusement to a spiteful inner voice that reminded him of his determination to pass peacefully and obscurely through The Grants. He nodded toward Allen, who still stood monumentally between him and Wadman.

"Lay on, then," the giant cried, "and a bowl of the Colonel Commandant's Particular to the victor." He stepped back into the human circle. Adam's volunteer second dealt him a stinging slap between the shoulder blades.

"Massacree the bastard," he counseled, cheerily.

Wadman waited, making small, precise movements with his fists and feet. The ensign's bruised lips were stretched in a half-smile. Men shouted counsel that Adam barely heard. He struck at that amused, obscurely zestful face.

Fire and then blackness filled his skull. Something pressed against his back and a blurred, distant sound grew into human shouting. He rolled over and got up, his body shrinking from the expected blow that did not come. Wadman waited, arms akimbo, while Adam shook the numbness from his brain.

The grin was wider now, and on the dark face Adam read purpose that Feltham's delighted smirk confirmed. Wadman was the stronger and more skillful. He would not be either merciful or brief. He would take pleasure in parading his ability before the men who had thrust this combat upon him and find greater pleasure in slowly, cruelly cutting down his adversary.

Rage lent Adam strength. He felt brief glee as his fist drove against the other's ribs. Then, breath burst from him and he reeled under the double impact of Wadman's counterblows. He struck at the smiling face that wove before him. . . .

On hands and knees, he saw the other check his rush and wait. Adam rose deliberately, heedless of the distorted faces and the counsel they screeched. This, he told himself gravely, could not go on. Already, he was battered, half beaten. His breath came painfully. The candle flames were blurred and rainbow-ringed.

His mind ran inconsequently. Wadman would hurt and humble him to the utmost—the proper British attitude toward presumptuous provincials. Would the Sherwood maid sorrow or laugh over this comic ending to Adam's chivalry?

He sidestepped as Wadman advanced, and hit him on the ear without immediate return. The ensign nodded grimly. He would exact payment, in his own good time. He was wholly confident now. This, Adam knew, was weakness, if he had enough remaining wit and strength to exploit it.

They circled. The plan that Adam's dazed brain presented was the best it could offer. He took a savage punch on the ribs. His body shook and begged leave to fall. He lunged forward instead, got his arms about Wadman, and clung.

There was salty stickiness in his mouth. Wadman's fists beat upon his back. Adam hid his face in the other's shoulder and clutched the slippery, twisting body. Slowly, beneath the ensign's hammering he sagged, bent his knees, slipped toward the floor, judging cannily the wrench and the heave as Wadman tried to shake himself free. A hand reached to tear his own locked hands away.

Adam let go and clamped a grip about the other's wrist. He took a dazzling punch on the head but his shoulder jammed into Wadman's armpit and pulled him off balance. He straightened his knees, felt the other's weight heavy upon his back, and turned with a swift, rolling shrug. His burden vanished.

A wild yell half obscured the crash of Wadman's fall. Adam, toppling and gasping, saw the body slide, roll over, and lie still. He heard the wolf call rise and staggered as his volunteer second beat him on the back.

Adam paid no heed to what the man was shouting. He blinked at those who crowded about him and wondered which might be the dark maid's brother.

The horse-faced man who now sat at Adam's right was Peleg Sunderland. Beyond him and raising the punchbowl was Robert Cochran, solid and red as a brick buttress, and past him was brown, angular Sam Herrick. On the other hand loomed the caparisoned bulk of Ethan Allen. The grave person directly across the slopping table was he whom Adam had striven to identify an hour— several hours—before: Justus Sherwood.

The plump, composed young man who at this instant rose and left the company was Jonas Fay, son of the landlord and a physician. The human ox with the honest eyes who had tangled in argument with Sunderland was Seth Warner. He seemed more sober than most of his associates, including, Adam thought with inner mirth, Adam Corlaer.

Yet Adam Corlaer had been able to name over accurately his principal companions. This, he informed himself gravely, indicated that he still was competent.

The glow within him had not completely driven pain from his battered body yet this had lessened greatly since, long, long before, Feltham, Dr. Jonas, Sherwood, and Sunderland had borne the still senseless Wadman upstairs and those who had tarried in the taproom had, by Allen's invitation, seated themselves at a long table to "toss the flowing bowl."

Adam, receiving it now, marveled that, though the drinking had been prodigious, the measure seemed to remain perpetually full. Possibly it was a pottery kinsman of the widow's cruse. The idea was infinitely humorous and he laughed heartily, reviving his merriment when it flagged by thought of what James Duane would say if he were to see his pupil tippling with the most notorious banditti of The Grants, two of whom now were outlaws.

Across the table, Sherwood rose. His pleasant speech checked Adam's mirth, "A good night to you, Mr. Corlaer, and another swift meeting. We ride north on the morrow."

He had made no intimate mention of his sister and Adam through delicacy had not referred to her. Now, as the man slung his cloak and bade farewell to the others, Adam felt sharp bereavement. He cried Sherwood's name but his voice was lost in the general clamor. Adam accepted the punchbowl from Allen and drank deeply. Liquor could not soothe this new dismay.

He had seen her, fought on her behalf, and now through his cursed reticence had lost her. He looked down the long table, half minded to rise and follow Sherwood. Sunderland and Warner still were arguing. Cochran, waving a finger before his own ruddy face, gravely conducted himself in song. Sam Herrick drowsed. Two men whose names Adam could not now recall slept at the board's far end, their faces cradled on their arms. Another rose and walked an invisible tight-rope to the door. Allen spoke, "Dr. Fay holds that your triumph was good fortune, Mr. Corlaer. I contend that it was malice prepense."

"Possibly you are both correct, sir," Adam returned, curbing a suddenly tricky tongue. "Joe Brant taught me that hold while I still was a stripling. The Mohawks delight in wrestling."

"Familiar both with savages and Oxford's halls!" the giant marveled. His drinking had served only to mellow him. "I envy your education, young sir. Providence has called me to defend an oppressed people but a philosopher was lost in me for lack of learning."

Dr. Fay, returning, caught Adam's eye and leaned across the table.

"Wadman and his friend sleep soundly, Mr. Corlaer. Your mind may be at ease."

"Now I warrant," Allen deplored in a melancholy rumbling, "that neither victor nor vanquished thanks me that he was restrained from that variety of murder men call a duel."

"Truly, I am your debtor," Adam acknowledged. "I never have fought a duel."

"Nor I, young sir. Strife is Nature's law; needless killing is the father of anarchy. It is my belief," the subdued giant pursued, "that the world turns to better things and that with Quebec's fall we have seen the end of war and its evils. Surely here, in this new country, we can breed a free people, unacquainted with slaughter."

Adam blinked, suspecting that he jested, but the rocky face was grave.

"Yet, Colonel, you wear regimentals."

"The habiliments of freedom, young sir. My gallant troops and I strive against York while she assails the rights of those who have possessed this land. We have shed little blood. We have killed no one. Such is my design."

His voice dropped lower and his blue eyes were intense as he leaned toward Adam.

"For, look you, Mr. Corlaer: A dead man is a lonely thing who cries for company. A man, harried and frightened, sows among others the seeds of his own fear. That, sir, is my philosophy and to it my Green Mountain Boys adhere."

He sat erect and shook himself so that his epaulettes flashed.

"Rob," he called, casting off his mood, "by the horns of Beelzebub, I vow you sing as Jed Dewey preaches—on two notes and both through the nose."

"Whoosh," Cochran rasped, pausing in his celebration of the prowess of "The Derby Ram" to wave a red-furred hand. "Divinity, harmony; what know ye of either?"

"Enough to be charmed by neither Jedediah nor you. Line out his hymns for him and spare us now."

23

"Ethan," Cochran said with great dignity to no one in particular, "is blind to beauty and deaf to religion—an unbeliever and blasphemer, God pity him."

"I'll not debate my beliefs with a drunken Scot, though they have the logic you and The Reverend lack."

"Ethan believes only in one god—Ethan," Warner announced. His heavy face was flushed and his tongue thick. Sunderland grinned and nudged Adam, while the giant in uniform glared at the giant in homespun.

"I believe," Allen answered at last, "in the law of Nature and the goodness of earth and the right of free men to win and to hold it, despite York's governors and His Gracious Majesty, aye, and Jehovah."

"Blasphemy, blasphemy," Sunderland bawled and again thrust his elbow into Adam's ribs.

"Yes," said Allen, lifting the bowl. "That is one name for it."

Chapter III

A SUNBEAM, striking Adam's eyelids, made him groan and roll over. He heard voices in the street and horsemen ride away. Each hoofbeat kicked up fresh anguish in his head. He knew where he was but he had no memory of when or how he had got to bed in this barren room. The sunlight had slid across the floor and out the window before he stirred again.

He sat upon the bed's edge and touched his throbbing skull with tender fingers. A seemly beginning for his journey through The Grants!

Adam observed that his outer clothing lay folded across the bench, the work he was wretchedly certain of some unidentified Samaritan. He leaned over with great care, retrieved his breeches, and had managed to get inside them before someone knocked on the door.

Dr. Fay, beaker in hand, regarded the sufferer with humorous gravity.

"I'm relieved, Mr. Corlaer, to find you still live."

"I've been wishing," Adam replied, forcing a smile, "that I did not."

He shrank from the draught the physician proferred.

"Drink it," said Jonas solemnly. "An antidote for the Colonel's Particular—and my most frequent prescription in these times.

"Drink it," he repeated.

Adam obeyed. He gasped and fixed tearfully accusing eyes upon Fay, yet almost at once felt an inner heat melt nausea and dull the hammering within his skull.

The doctor lounged in the doorway and talked easily while his patient dressed. It had been he who had brought Adam to bed,

25

and now they were the sole remaining members of last night's company. Even Wadman and Feltham had ridden away an hour earlier.

"Neither inquired for you," Fay reported with the wrinkle deepening about his clever eyes. "I had no need to confess that the victor now lay vanquished."

"The punch," Adam confessed with a shudder, "was devilish strong."

Fay permitted himself a small smile.

"Men are prone to underestimate the Colonel's Particular—and the Colonel."

He led the way down into the deserted taproom and, after recommending eggs and mulled cider for breakfast, tactfully left Adam in solitude to struggle with them. Food and drink slowly completed his revival. He leaned back and found that he was able to recall most of the night's preposterous events.

Tryon's proclamation still gleamed on the chamber's far wall. Yonder was the long table, freshly scrubbed, over which Ethan Allen had presided. That was a singular person with a peculiar wisdom that his trumpetings and his preposterous uniform belied.

All The Grants' folk, great and small, possessed bold irreverence and a rough, shocking freedom that Adam had not met elsewhere, either in England with its precise countryside and classes or in New York which was a more slovenly duplication of the homeland.

Perhaps the spaciousness of the wilderness got into men's blood, inspiring that breadth of mind which set Landlord Fay and his attendant son, Joseph, on a level with all their patrons; that permitted an insurgent chieftain's underlings to assume complete familiarity with him.

This equality Adam reflected, dreamily relaxed, must be a standard that wildernesses imposed, yet the girl who had walked, undismayed, into this very taproom had not been a barbarian.

His breath came more quickly as he looked toward the door by which she had entered, trying out of his memory to re-create her there, with the crimson hood about her face, the brightly smiling mouth, the eyes whose candor had startled and stirred him.

26

She had a warmth that he still almost could feel. It was strange that a woman—a child—whom he had seen for a moment's passage could stamp herself so deeply on his memory. She had come briefly and vanished and he had let her brother depart with his and her destination unrevealed.

Sherwood had said that he and his sister were riding north. Adam was to journey in the same direction. In a land so under-supplied with roads it was possible—it was probable—that he would overtake them. He rose and asked that his mare be saddled.

Sunlight was butter-yellow and the sky glazed blue. Allegra's hoofs rang clear on the frozen road. Though it was almost mid-day, the air on Adam's face was chill as the water from Stephen Fay's well, clearing the brain, cheering the spirit.

Bennington lay behind and the scored track of the North Road went alternately through gloom of great pine stands and the crazy patterns of light and shadow wrought by the sun through the bare branches of gigantic maples, oaks, and beeches.

Brush was thick beside the rutted way, but scant undergrowth endured within the forest. Adam looked through colonnades of tree trunks far along dusky aisles, opening and closing as he ambled past. The way shunned only grades that were too peril-ously steep for oxen and men ahorse. Now and again, after a girth-straining ascent, Adam saw on either hand, far and miraculously tall, the crests of mountains darkly clothed in fir or with thread-bare patches where leafless hardwoods stood.

Twice, he passed small gaps in the forest where trees sprawled among the stumps' pale discs and later marked in a larger clearing a half-built log hut. Winter had driven these pioneers back to the lower settlements until another spring.

Adam had begun to imagine himself and his mare the sole ani-mations in an otherwise deserted world when he met a lean and weathered traveler on an underfed roan. The stranger hailed him hungrily and, after the usual catechism, revealed himself a dealer in land shares who owned no politics but greatly deplored the strife in The Grants that had upset his market.

He offered to sell Adam for ten shillings rights to three hundred acres in the town of Neshobe, which, though still unsettled, was

27

a veritable Promised Land, reduced the price to five as Adam gathered up his rein, and cried plaintively as the mare moved away, "Two'n a half? Two?"

Long before the great trees stood aside, Adam heard, ranging far through the silence, the spasmodic wail of a sawmill. He came out at last into the unbroken sunlight that lay upon Shaftsbury's huddled dwellings. Log cabins and clapboarded cottages stood side by side and at the crossroads before him a smithy chimed and smoked.

He had difficulty in finding Munro's home. The smith of whom he first inquired peered, spat, and deliberately turned away, though Adam could feel the wary eyes following as he rode on. A second villager subjected the traveler to more than normal cross-questioning before he grudgingly granted directions.

Adam rode off with the sun in his face and the conviction that the settlement's massed scrutiny pursued him. The sense of still hostility that had plagued him on the preceding day returned. He was armored more heavily against it now. Somewhere before him a red-cloaked girl also journeyed through the wilderness. His thoughts were more on Sherwood's sister than on Munro when he dismounted before the man's small, red house.

"Health, sir," said John Munro and raised his tankard. He had driven off the dog that had circled, barking, about the stranger, had bidden an equally inhospitable young man to conduct Allegra to the barn, and finally had led Adam into a littered kitchen where plates from the last meal stood on one table and another bore heaped papers.

The strong cider prickled in Adam's throat. His host's regard was less agreeable. Grim gray eyes straddled a blunt nose that was slightly askew, and there was no warmth in the brown face. Munro wiped his stubborn mouth and set his wig straighter.

" 'Tis by grace of Mr. Duane's letter that I welcome ye, Mr. Corlaer. It is antidote for else I have heard about ye."

He blinked and Adam said stiffly, "I am sorry to learn that."

"The young," Munro pursued, "are by way of being reckless—as surely ye have been since ye entered The Grants."

He pursed his lips, shook his head, and readjusted his wig.

"Your journey, sir, has had a—shall we say, unpropitious beginning?"

He raised a stiff index finger and pursued.

"Ye recall, no doubt, two ensigns of His Majesty's foot, Messrs. Wadman and Feltham, the former sadly disfigured by bruises?"

"Very clearly."

"They dined with me, the noon, before they traveled on and mentioned ye with—shall we say, animosity? In these times, Mr. Corlaer, loyal men deem His Majesty's uniform well nigh as sacred as the cloth of the kirk. A matter of a tavern brawl, I believe."

"A brawl that was forced upon me, sir."

"Ah, weel! It may be so."

He lifted a second finger to join the other.

"Ye recall, no doubt, one Benjamin Buck. He rode to me half frozen last midnight and reported your presence in that nest of rebels, villains, and worse, Fay's tavern, from which Ethan Allen— God consign his sin-caked soul etairnally to the nethermost depths of hell!—forthwith drove him. And why did ye tarry there, Mr. Corlaer?"

"By a chance, sir," Adam said crisply, "that I deplore less than the mission that brought me here. I came to you at Mr. Duane's bidding. If it be distasteful to you to harbor me—"

"No, no, no!" Munro ran both palms over his wig in a dissenting gesture and his hitherto stern face was alarmed. "It is possible that I am overwrought. I am, sir, a greatly harried man. Sit ye by the fire while I fetch more cider."

He returned with the recharged tankards and twin clay pipes that he kindled with a coal from the ash-littered hearth.

"Ye'll be safe here, Mr. Corlaer," he resumed, rapidly puffing, "and, though this be bachelor's hall now, snug I trust. My wife and our bairns have been sent to Albany. This is no place for the helpless and the weak, sir, while Ethan Allen and his fiends run the woods."

Indignation overwhelmed his disapproval and he leveled a trembling pipestem at Adam.

"Ye heard the message sent me by Buck. Sir, I keep my office here as York justice of the peace at daily peril of my life. My offense is that I maintain the law in an otherwise lawless land. My reward"—his voice grew shriller—"is that my fences are over-thrown, my cattle turned into the corn, my haystacks burned. The more valiant hoot threats at me by day; the less, pin warnings on my door at night. Lately I found a coffin propped against it."

He seemed so desperately a creature brought to bay that Adam's sympathy was stirred. He ventured, "Then, since this is so, why—"

"Ay!" Munro broke in and resettled his wig. "My own wife has begged that I leave, and not a few settlers from York already have fled, thereby greatly encouraging the Mob. There still be some of us left in Shaftsbury, Mr. Corlaer, who have not bowed the knee to Baal. I shall persevere for"—he held up three fingers in succession—"my own sake, for the law's sake, for the sake of His Gracious Majesty."

The zealous gray eyes snapped. Munro cleared his throat and lowered one finger after the other, as he expounded.

"Firstly, for my own sake: I have cleared my land and built my house at no small cost, sir, bodily and feenancial. I have also ob-tained through the generosity of James Duane and William Kempe, for whom I am agent, shares in land patents that, when York prevails, will make my fortune. Shall I meekly permit the archdevil Allen and his imps to drive me forth to begin life again at my age?"

"I respect your resolution, sir," Adam said slowly.

"Secondly, Mr. Corlaer, I am a sworn officer of the law. The law is plain and I intend to uphold it. It is true that Benning Went-worth, the damned jobbing scoundrel, falsely proclaimed The Grants were Hampshire land and gulled the folk who settled under his fraudulent charters. If I buy a worthless right to land, may I, on discovering it, justly take your valid title? Let the folk Went-worth cheated seek restitution from New Hampshire, not steal New York's rightful territory."

He lowered the final finger—and pressed his wig into place, dropping his wrathful voice into a more reverent tone.

"Now, hark ye, Mr. Corlaer: By royal charter, York received this land. By the proclamation of King George, York's jurisdiction has been confirmed. By God, sir, the Mob raises rebellion not only against the law but the will of His Gracious Majesty. Ethan

Allen, who makes mock of God, dares also to oppose his King."

He brushed spilled ashes from his lap and set his pipe aside. Adam watched with unwilling admiration the sturdy, stubborn figure.

"God is not mocked," his host went on quietly, "nor His Majesty, nor John Munro. A sterner man now rules York province and already he has placed a price on the heads of the Mob's leaders. I pray I may aid in seeing that price promptly paid. Ye are journeying through The Grants at a propitious time, Mr. Corlaer. Ye shall see salvation—"

They heard in the twilight stillness a horse come galloping. It halted before the house in a clattering slide. The dog barked wildly and then yelped in pain. Munro, leaping up, had snatched down the musket from above the fireplace before he turned to peer through a window. He restored the weapon with a shame-faced smile and moved toward the door.

" 'Tis Billy Cockburn," he said over his shoulder, "Mr. Duane's chief surveyor. He was to meet ye here on the morrow."

The newcomer, pale, soiled, and bareheaded, plainly had ridden far and in haste. He clung for an instant to the doorjamb, coughed dryly, and said with a forced grin.

"I kicked your dog, Jack. It was comforting to strike at one hostility. My horse—"

His voice seemed to come from a great distance.

"I'll see to him," Munro promised quickly. "He's been hard-ridden. Did they—?"

"Aye. From daybreak until I outraced them, a half hour gone."

"Come in," Munro bade.

He himself went out, closing the door. Cockburn with great care crossed to the nearest chair and fell into it with a small groan. His leggings were torn and dust-stained and his deerskin shirt ripped. He rubbed his forehead with a grimed hand and squinted red-rimmed eyes at Adam.

"You'd be," the parched voice mumbled, "Mr. Corlaer of whom Mr. Duane wrote. I fear, sir—"

Munro returned, slamming the door. He took a jug from the shelf, filled a horn measure, and handed it to Cockburn.

"Rum," he said. "Ye look to need it."

31

"I did," Cockburn said a second later with hollow amusement. "Jack, I'm minded to go for a soldier. 'Tis a safer life than a surveyor's in The Grants and you are shot at more seldom."

Munro gave back the replenished measure.

"Eh, now?" he begged. "Tell us, lad," and Cockburn, resolutely holding fast to his lightness of manner complied, spacing his tale with sips from the horn.

He had completed in Rupert town the survey Duane had ordered and had seen his assistants turn back toward Albany before he had ridden on to Eliakim Weller's tavern in Manchester. He had been minded to tarry there and write up his notes before coming to Munro's to meet Mr. Corlaer on the morrow, but Eli had roused him at daybreak to whisper that Remember Baker and another had just ridden into town and the Mob was assembling.

Cockburn had heard the wolf howl rise while he still was saddling his horse. He had not returned to the tavern but had ridden around the barn and into the woods.

"It seemed—wiser, to leave all my gear and my notes," he said with a mirthless smile and then, self-possession leaving him, beat upon his chair arm.

"God damn them! Two full weeks labor come to nought!"

"Be grateful," Munro counseled grimly, "that no more was lost."

Cockburn drank and went on.

He had circled through the forest and had reached the road well south of the settlement. An instant after he had ridden from concealment, someone had fired at him. The ball had flown close to his horse's ears and the animal had bolted back into the forest.

"They hunted me, through the woods, out into the road, and back into the woods again with their damned wolf-yelling and thrice more fired on me."

He shook his head and managed a weak grin.

"I thought I had shaken them all when I got back into the road below Arlington but they must have found fresh mounts there for they came on, trying to run me down."

"How many?" Munro demanded, his face bitter, his fists clenched.

Cockburn shrugged.

"Several," he said vaguely. "Then two and at last, none. Thank

32

God for a good horse. I pray he bears me back as well to Albany on the morrow. I fear"—his bow toward Adam was only a feeble lurch—"I shall not be able to accompany you north, Mr. Corlaer."

His eyelids drooped.

"To bed, Billy," Munro ordered. "Ye're fair spent," and helped the sagging figure from the room.

When he returned he cleared soiled dishes from the table in silence. He told Adam at last, "We'll sup and get early to bed. It'll be wisest for ye to ride back with Billy, Mr. Corlaer."

"No. I shall go on."

"Are ye deaf? Did ye not hear what Billy told?"

"Not deaf," Adam answered, enduring the grim stare. "Nor yet a York surveyor, Mr. Munro. Why should not I, an unoffending stranger, pass in safety?"

"Mr. Duane has written ye down a stiff-necked youth. Man, ye as well might expect safety among Indians."

"I have lived with them in safety. This morning"—Adam kept concern from his face and voice—"a man and a maid rode north from Bennington tavern. If women may travel—"

"Aye; I ken. The Sherwoods nooned with Jehiel Hawley in Arlington. They are secure, Mr. Corlaer, because Justus Sherwood is of the Mob, though a stripe higher than his accomplices."

"I am still resolved," Adam said cheerfully, "to go north on the morrow."

Chapter IV

FROST was white on Munro's roof and had crisped the roadside grasses when Adam rode away from his grimly deploring host. The mare's hoofs rang through Shaftsbury with defiant cheer. It was too early and bitter for folk to be abroad but Adam felt faces watching him from every window. Allegra was eager and he was glad to give her rein. A gallop would warm him and dislodge the qualms roused by Cockburn's forebodings and Munro's despair. This early outset and the mare's willingness promised he might overtake the Sherwoods before the day's journey ended.

Despite the early hour, someone had preceded him over the road this morning—someone riding in haste. The knowledge troubled him and he went more slowly, bending forward to read of his predecessor and his purpose, but the hoofmarks were dim on the frozen earth and he had forgotten much lore the Mohawks had taught him.

Adam gave over and spurred his mare on, but the circumstance and Munro's warnings nagged. At last, he drew rein, opened the saddle holsters, and examined the primings of both pistols before he restored them and resumed his journey. He had no intention, he told himself, of submitting to Cockburn's ordeal.

Arlington sprawled at the foot of a mountain rampart as though its cabins and clapboarded cottages had rolled down the shadowy slope into the young sunlight. Adam was half minded to inquire here of the Sherwoods, but there plainly was only one, increasingly decrepit road they could have taken and he dreaded the delay the inevitable, everlasting questioning would cause.

He rode through the settlement, splashed across a stream whose rim-ice already had been shattered by earlier travelers, and

34

plunged again into the forest's clammy, penetrating chill. Allegra's smoking neck and shoulders made him belatedly aware how unwisely he had spent her, with most of a day's journey still ahead. He let her walk through gloom cast by great pines.

There was no wind, no sound in this dim place. Brown needles carpeting the road hushed the mare's hoofs. She and her rider drifted silently through a cold enchantment. Adam fancied that they floated along the floor of imperceptible vast water; that the pines were gigantic seaweeds, reaching from the depths toward a sky-blue surface. His mind and body were so engaged that the clap of the musket shot stunned him and Allegra's leap almost unseated him.

Adam dragged at the rein. The ball had slashed through overhead branches and a handful of severed needles drizzled down. They rattled loudly on his tricorn hat while he searched the forest ahead for movement or trace of smoke. He saw only the twilight spread beneath the pines and massed trunks where artillery might hide. Whoever had fired kept close ambush.

Fright that had stung his nostrils and salted his mouth vanished. Knowledge of its late presence sharpened his anger. It spurred his mind as violently as his rowels raked his mare's flanks.

At her forward bound came a second explosion. He saw the white puff from the priming pan and the blue gush of powder smoke. He caught his breath but the ball had flown wide. His frightened mount's hoofbeats were as quick as his own heart. The wind of their passage was icy on Adam's face. He laughed. There had been only two assailants and he had outwitted them by his charge, running through their ambush while both their guns were empty.

Trees whirled past as Allegra, with scant guidance, sped over the twisting, brown road. A half mile farther on, he drew her to a walk. Her body pulsed beneath his knees. Adam looked behind him. The brief visible arc of the curving trail was empty.

He settled in the saddle and reassembled a disordered mind. It had been sure and quick in the instant of peril. It moved less certainly now. The mare's breath was loud in silence heavy with foreboding. What Munro had predicted and Adam had disparaged actually was happening. Death might not threaten him, since neither shot had been aimed, but he plainly had been marked for that hunting and hounding that was the Mob's chief weapon. Why?

Clear conscience urged Adam to turn about, ride back, and face his enemies. The impulse died as he recalled the sundry indignities and worse that Munro had said York folk had suffered. Even if none of these were visited upon him, even if eventually he went free, he would have lost the present bright chance of overtaking the Sherwoods. He had got clear; he would go on.

He let the mare choose her own gait. His thoughts ran back along the road and found reason for the ambush. He had come to an insurgent land from New York that claimed it. By spending the night with the region's boldest Yorker, he had proclaimed his politics. Possibly, even probably, the ambush had been inspired or laid by the someone who had ridden hurriedly before him from Shaftsbury to Arlington. This was not empty wilderness; this was grimly hostile land and the silences of its forest were menacing.

The mare stumbled as she followed the steeply slanting way into a hollow through which an ice-bordered brook foamed. Adam let her drink briefly of the dark water and leaned foward as she scrambled up the farther slope. It was a long pull and she was wheezing when she reached the crest. When her rider paused to breathe her, a musket spoke downhill and dust spun from a tree hole. The mare tried to jump from under him. Adam's backward glance saw smoke roll out over the stream.

He heard the wolf yell rise and was angered by the sudden fear it quickened. The hunters purposed to follow until Adam surrendered or was run down. Clearly, they had fresher mounts than he. A twinge of panic urged him to turn off the road and into the woods. He withstood it. His pursuers knew the land and he did not. He would be wholly at their mercy in the forest, a blundering quarry to be harried and humbled as Cockburn had been.

The shame of his plight enraged him. He was no sheep to run before danger. As he urged his mare onward, he began to watch the ground before him with purposeful eyes and found at last what he sought—the mouldering body of a pine, fallen by the roadside—but did not draw rein. When at last he halted, he was beyond a bend in the road and invisible to oncomers.

Adam threw open the holsters and drew the pistols. Their

weight was comforting in his fists but he thrust them into his cloak pockets and, dismounting, tethered his mare. Then weapons in hand, he ran back the way he had come.

The road still was empty. Adam vaulted the prostrate pine bole and dropped behind it. He stifled as quickly as he might his own hard breathing and looked again to his pistols. They had been his father's: twin, finely fashioned arms of French make. Adam flinched at the loud sounds as he cocked them. The bark against which he crouched gave forth tiny crumbling noises in the long silence and his sweating face grew chill.

Only his eyes moved when, far away, he caught the clink of iron on stone, the mutter of voices. A man laughed and Adam heard the muffled sound of horses, trotting smartly.

He settled the pistols' butts firmly in his hands and rose with great care. For a long instant after he had stood erect behind his waist-high barricade, neither horseman saw him. The elder's fur cap was pushed back from his severe brown face and the fringes of his deerskin shirt shook to his horse's gait.

Adam recognized him and the dark youth who followed. They had left Fay's tavern together, musket in hand, two nights earlier. Their guns were borne across the saddle pommels now and the eyes of the pair were fixed upon the road. When they were almost abreast of him, Adam cried, "Stand!"

His anger fed on his enemies' alarm—the stiff surprise, the blank and gaping faces, the promptitude with which, under the pistols' muzzles, they jerked their horses to a halt. The dark youth, by accident or design, shifted his grip on his musket.

"No," Adam bade sharply and the other sat motionless.

"Wal—" the older man began in hollow jauntiness, but his voice stuck. He regarded the pistols with an odd mixture of dread and thought. Adam rested elbows on the trunk before him.

" 'Wal!' " he mimicked and then, more sharply, "Drop your firelocks. You, Baker; you, whatever your name is."

"Now bide a mite," Baker pleaded, while the boy uttered a choking sound. Adam's forefingers settled into the trigger guards.

"I fire when I've counted three," he promised cheerfully. "One —two—"

Baker leaned from the saddle and lowered his gun carefully, by the muzzle. His mate's weapon half slipped from his grasp and

37

clattered down. Adam's eyes did not leave his prisoners as he climbed over the fallen pine, stepped into the road, and kicked the muskets aside. He said firmly, "That will suffice. Now turn your nags about and ride back the way you came."

The boy's face was suffused and twitching but Baker's was screwed by what might have been intense reflection.

"Set store by that fusee," he offered at last in a tight voice. "Carried her to Ti in Fifty-nine."

"Turn your horses."

"Goddlemighty, young sir—whoever ye be—ye don't figger we aimed to harm ye."

"In some peculiar fashion, I got that impression," Adam answered, enjoying himself while he wondered whether the dark boy's face could grow more duskily red without a seizure. "I've twice bidden you to turn about."

Baker obeyed with such alacrity that his horse collided with his companion's. The anguish in the look he cast toward his musket roused compunction in Adam. He said to his captives' backs:

"I intend to tarry here a space. If you purpose to follow me— as I'm sure you do—I should not resume pursuit before noontide. As for your weapons, you will find them in the first brook that crosses the road. I shall cast them there."

Baker's backward glance was venomous but his voice was wheedling:

"Not in the water, young sir. On the bank."

"In the water. You can spend an industrious few hours drying them. My compliments to Mr. Allen and, when he next plans to waylay travelers, bid him send bandits less deficient in marksmanship and wits."

He stood in midroad and watched the pair ride from sight. Twice the younger man looked back but Baker, hunched on his mount, did not turn his head.

Anger, subsiding, left Adam weak. His knees were limber and his hands uncertain as he pocketed the pistols, picked up the muskets, and plodded back to his mare. He mounted with some difficulty and rode on. A mile farther, where a brook coursed through a ravine, he drew rein in midstream and tossed the guns into a pool below the shallows. He watched the current iron away the ripples, patted the mare's sweat-roughened shoulder, and chuckled. Munro was too wedded to law; one could deal best with savages savagely.

It was noon when he reached Manchester, a settlement more pinched and frostbitten than either Shaftsbury or Arlington. He now had twin reasons for haste but his mare was wearier than he and he sought refreshment for them both at Eliakim Weller's ungainly tavern, from whose new clapboards drops of gum still oozed.

Adam demanded at once from the bent and jaundiced landlord tidings of the Sherwoods and learned that they had spent the night here and had gone on that morning toward Pittsford. He parried counter-inquiries by professing with a mysterious air to be riding express with dispatches for Justus, whereupon the landlord stifled his curiosity and permitted Adam to dine in peace.

North of the settlement, the ailing road perished and only a dim path led through the forest from one blazed tree to the next. Adam paused scowling. Weller had urged him to stay the night. If the Sherwoods had not been ahead and Baker and his companion behind, the tired man on the tiring mare would have turned about now and followed the landlord's counsel.

Habitations would be rare in the wilderness ahead and Adam had only a clasp knife with which to make camp if night found him still unhoused. He possessed sufficient woodcraft to care for himself at need but Allegra would suffer.

Excitement's aftermath, fatigue, and the dull weight of the meal Weller had served bore down his spirit. He cursed the rashness that had hurried him into wild country with so little forethought that he lacked even an axe. He hesitated a long moment and then rode forward, obstinately adhering to his purpose and almost at once finding encouragement.

Horses had passed this way not many hours ago. Hoofs that had scored the frost-matted leaves must have borne the Sherwood maid. Adam touched the mare with a spur.

He found at once that haste would not serve. He was obliged to seek guidance from each successive blaze. Once, vaingloriously sure of the trail, he trotted past a gashed tree without pausing to mark down its successor and for a moment was lost. Thenceforth, he went more deliberately, fretting at the delay, unwillingly humbled by the stature and the silence of the forest.

He was not unacquainted with wilderness but he had seen no woodland so immense. The pines' great boles soared high and straight to support a distant roof of branches that repelled the sun. The canopy covered an entire country, and, like ocean, dwarfed the persons and spirits of men by its majesty and everlasting gloom.

Adam rode carefully from blaze to blaze. The marks led him uphill and down over frozen loam through a scentless, soundless desert. He passed lichened rock ledges, luminous in the twilight, and twice saw small open spaces where storm or landslide had overcast trees and the unhampered sun blazed on spindling saplings and the ghosts of brambles. He crossed brooks, each a little more ice-bound than the last. No other thing moved visibly in the winterlocked wilderness. Save for the sound of Allegra's hoofs and her loud breathing, he and she might have been specters, doomed to move forever through desolate grandeur.

He drew rein after hours of brief hastenings from one blazed tree to the next and looked about him. The twilight of the forest was thickening and it seemed the cold which midday had not wholly dispelled was closing in afresh.

A brook ran through the hollow before him. His eyes moved over the intervening ground as he wondered how far off darkness still lay and estimated what materials were at hand for a shelter. While he hesitated he heard, far ahead yet clear, a dog's sudden barking, quickly hushed.

Adam was startled by the immensity of his relief. It endured as he rode on toward the sound and even survived the squalid prospect that at last he discovered.

The blazed way led through girdled trees, black and stublimbed, toward brilliance. Sunlight still streamed over a clearing. A cabin in its center stood with swaybacked elm-bark roof pulled down about its ears like a disreputable hat. The building's brown walls were windowless and a deerskin curtain closed the doorway. Hemmed in by the forest, it squatted, dingy and forlorn, with cornstalks heaped beside a log barn. A plumping mill— a fire-hollowed stump with a long stone tethered to a bent sapling above it—stood before the cabin doorway. Smoke drooling from a chimney of wattled clay abolished Adam's hesitation.

Midway across the clearing, he remembered frontier custom, halted, and hailed the house.

Within, the dog barked and was hushed. The curtain was thrust aside and a man flung up his arm in a welcoming gesture. His grin, as Adam advanced, wrinkled his muzzle and almost closed his eyes.

"Adam Corlaer, sir. Bound to Panton from Bennington."

"Wal, b'God!" the other cried, slapping his thigh and then reaching up a grimed paw. "Welcome! George Scott, sir; first settler in Wallingford town. M'woman's t'other. Ain't this prime? 'Light, sir. I'll keer fer the horse. This is a joyful day fer Lois 'n' me."

He was brown, lean, and odorous as smoked venison. His unlimited delight warmed Adam.

"Enter," Scott bade, nodding to the doorway. "Set 'n' warm yesself with the folks. Leave the mare to me."

He talked to the animal as he led her toward the barn. For an instant after Adam had let the curtain fall behind him, he could see clearly only the hearth fire at the cabin's far end and the stir of figures between him and the blaze. He addressed the nearest shape.

"Mistress Scott? Adam Corlaer, your humble servant."

"Not Mistress Scott."

The voice took his breath. He turned sharply and drew aside the deerskins.

She wore the same red cloak, but now the hood was thrown back from her shining hair and her smile was warmer and more amused than he had remembered.

"Welcome, Mr. Corlaer. I am Felicity Sherwood, a wayfarer like yourself."

Her mouth was demure but there was laughter in her green eyes.

Chapter V

THE floor of the Scotts' dwelling was the hard-packed earth. Cold air that came in around the deerskin curtain warred vainly with a variety of smells.

Light, since darkness had fallen, was supplied by the fire and a twisted rag guttering in a pan of grease. Even such faint illumination still revealed the cabin's grime and poverty, wavering over the axe-hewn bedstead, bench, and table, the ladder reaching aloft to a chamber above the eaves, and the close-laid poles that served for its floor. The light dwelt fitfully on Felicity who sat with her brother across the rough table from Adam. While he covertly might watch her, he could ignore the cabin's lacks.

Sherwood's greeting had been so warm that Adam knew the man's sister had disclosed to him the cause of the strife at Fay's tavern. But Sherwood, Munro had said, was a leader of the Mob and Adam's anger still endured against the skulking, terrorizing crew. He had not mentioned the morning's encounter to the girl's brother; he would not. He had not overtaken Felicity to lose her again.

Lois Scott sat beside Adam in disapproving silence. Her guests' insistence that they all dine together had shocked their hostess. Properly, she knew, women should wait until their men had been fed. The innovation had ruined the stateliness she had planned.

The guests, it was true, used her three metal spoons while she and George plied wooden. They were supplied with her three pewter plates, withdrawn from the pail of sour milk in which she kept them bright, but the platters of whittled maple before her husband and herself marred the splendor she had hoped to achieve.

Lois's narrow face had the hue and gloss of well-tanned leather. The blue gingham that had been her wedding gown stressed her homeliness and her gloom. It was fitting that women should let menfolks do the talking, but disappointment as well as decorum kept her mute. Her excitement and ambition had wrought less than she had planned. Despite her guest's appetites she wondered whether they truly relished their vittles.

George had crushed their best Injun in the plumping mill for the mush. She wondered whether Sherwood was honest in his praise of the pork. Didn't he suspect that it was bearmeat, fat and salted? The maple sugar that flavored the baked pumpkin had been saved for some such great event. She doubted whether the quiet young man beside her appreciated it.

Her husband suffered no such qualms. He ate and talked prodigiously, scarcely letting the others get a word in edgeways. George wasn't drunk, though he had swigged his fill of the stinging, sassafras-flavored cider—or not on liquor, anyway. He might be a mite drunk over having company from below.

"B'God," he was proclaiming, "Wallingford's a-flourishin' tonight. Nary a soul here, a year come last spring. Now they's five."

Sherwood smiled at Adam and raised his cowhorn beaker.

"May it continue to increase!"

Scott slapped the table.

"It'll come. Won't be long when we mill our Injun that we'll hear neighbors doin' the same. That'll be a comfortin' to Lois— sounds through the woods of maybe two-three plumpin' mills goin' to once. Me, I like it quiet."

Adam was gravely astonished by his own contentment, by the kindness of fortune that had arranged that a loose shoe on Justus's horse should halt the Sherwoods exactly here. The girl's eyes met his inquiringly. He asked Scott in haste, "You came here only a year and a half ago?"

His host chuckled.

"B'God, that's when we both come. Ye see," he went on eagerly, " 'twas this way: Me 'n' Lois figgered on weddin', four year agone. I was hirin' out to Deacon Jackson, down to Cornwall, Connecticut province, 'n' seemed like they'd bury us 'fore we'd git to marry. I spoke to Deacon.

" 'No,' s'e, 'can't afford to pay ye no more. If ye're aimin' to set up on yer own, why'n't ye consider Wallingford town in **The Grants?'**

" 'Where's that?', s'I.

" 'Foller yer nose north 'n' then ask the way,' s'e. 'Ain't nobody there yet 's I've heered on. Go up, pick a lot, 'n' commence a betterment. I'll endorse ye. If some damn fool'll settle there, mebby the rights I hold'll 'mount to somethin'. Make a pitch, George, 'n' I'll give ye a cow.' "

The girl's neck was slender as a flower stem, though no plant bore so fair a blossom. Scott's gleeful voice ran on, "Two year I worked, fellin', burnin', buildin'—walk up from Connecticut, come spring; walk back, come winter. Last year, I says to Lois here, 'I got a house all ready 'n' the first tier laid for a barn. We'll wed 'n' go home. 'Wal, sir, Deacon was good's his word. Gimme Old Black, 'n' Lois's folks give us a bed. Lashed it to the cow 'n' set out."

"You walked," the girl cried, "all the way from Cornwall?"

Her hostess stirred and spoke briefly, "A cow ain't a ridin' critter."

Felicity caught Adam's eye. The intimacy of amusement shared tightened his throat. He felt that he was blushing like a lout and turned to Scott's wife.

"From Cornwall? I don't envy you, Mistress Scott."

"Neither," she said bleakly, "did I."

"But," George trumpeted, "we got here safe 'n' raised a crop. 'Tis good land, once it's cleared. Mite lonely, mebby, for Lois, but there was a surveyor bided with us not more'n six weeks gone and now you folks. Next summer we'll see settlers."

"A York surveyor?" Sherwood asked without expression.

"Wal, yes; seems so."

Sherwood started to reply, hesitated, and said in a plainly revised voice, "I hazard you've heard of the difficulty between The Grants and York?"

"Why, some, I guess. Don't consarn myself with politics overmuch. Live and let live." Scott beamed with pride at the quotation. "That's what I say."

"An admirable sentiment, sir—but if York declares this land is not yours?"

"Can't," Scott replied with tolerance. "We can prove 'tis. Walk

44

a piece toward any point ye mind 'n' then look round ye. Woods 'n' wild country, fit for nothin'. That's what 'twas right whar we're settin' now, when first I come. This here can't belong to anyone else. I made it, didn't I?"

"And," Sherwood persisted, without expression, "if anyone strove to wrest it from you, what then?"

Scott grinned confidently.

"What then? Hell's fire! What if anyone tried to run away with Lois here? They'd not prevail, sir, while I still had enough powder to drive a ball, or strength to swing an axe."

"Exactly," said Sherwood and smiled.

The talk slid away to less intense matters. While Scott spoke of bears and wolves, moose, deer, and Indians, his wife rose and bore off the empty dishes. Felicity aided her but Adam, half rising to follow, subsided under his hostess's glare. She would brook no more violation of propriety that evening.

Later when even Scott's speech lagged and his guests, seated before the fire, toppled with drowsiness, their host bore armsful of sweet hay into the loft. Adam and Sherwood, standing before the cabin, had their first opportunity for private speech.

The dark sky with its flashing stars seemed less lonely than the dark land below. The sound of voices in the cabin, the stir of stock in the barn, and a whiff of wood smoke borne on the polar air emphasized a vast emptiness. Sherwood ventured gravely, "I am indebted to you, Mr. Corlaer, for your succor of my sister."

"A privilege, sir, that I am not likely to underestimate."

"Nor one that I am likely to forget." He hesitated, weighing something that he did not utter. "This has been a fortunate meeting. I may make some small payment on the score by serving as your guide tomorrow, for the way is blind and settlements are few beyond here."

Again he paused and at last uttered the hitherto hidden thought:

"I am wondering why, Mr. Corlaer, you have attempted such a journey at this time of year."

The quiet voice warned Adam. He must move carefully henceforth, never forgetting that his pleasant companion was a member of the Mob, comrade to the men who had ambushed him that morning; always remembering that Sherwood was Felicity's brother.

45

"I wonder myself, Mr. Sherwood. A late bereavement, an idle curiosity to see The Grants for myself, and a business mission to Canada all were party to it."

"Canada, eh? Quebec?"

"No. To see my late father's agent in Montreal."

"We too are for Canada. My sister and a child in Panton look toward a winter's schooling in Quebec. Doubtless you purpose to take boat at Crown Point since beyond Panton there is only desolation."

"I fear, sir," Adam confessed with a laugh that he hoped was sufficiently fatuous, "that I have come without adequate plans. I had not expected such complete wilderness."

"Then," Sherwood pursued tolerantly, "perhaps I may prove of real service to you. We shall tarry in Panton only briefly while I inspect land I have purchased in nearby New Haven. Mindwell Royden will welcome you as my friend. Thereafter, we and her daughter can go on as a party to Canada."

"That," Adam told him with fervor, "will suit me extremely well."

He followed Sherwood up the ladder to the loft. It was warmer here and the hay was comforting to a worn body. Adam heard, as sleep immersed him, soft sounds below as Felicity and their hostess prepared for bed. He wondered dreamily what had become of Scott.

A rhythmic thudding woke him. The depression where Sherwood had lain was empty. Voices and a smell of cooking welled up from below. He paused to pluck hay fragments from his clothing before he went down the ladder to blink and bid an awkward good morning to Lois Scott and Felicity who were busy at the hearth. The girl's smile made him additionally aware of his frowzy state. He ruefully caressed an unshaven jaw as he pushed the deerskin curtain aside and went out into the morning's cold glare.

"Wal, b'God!" Scott hailed. "Begun to mistrust ye was dead."

He guffawed and returned to plying the tethered stone pestle of the plumping mill that was pounding corn into coarse meal. Sherwood looked up from the steaming wooden pail in which he was washing and smiled. He continued to be amused by Adam's attempt to shave entirely by touch, but only said, "I have been

46

belatedly protesting to our host who gave us his house last night and slept in the stable."

"Hell's fire," Scott protested, " 'twan't nothin', not to anyone used to a lean-to. Figgered ye'd sleep better two in a bed 'n' mebby if ye was comfortable"—his voice grew wistful—"ye'd tarry a mite longer. Won't be no one else through, I guess, till come spring."

"We must ride on," Sherwood replied. "The snow won't hold off forever."

Scott squinted at the cobalt sky.

"No sign, so far. Wish ye'd tarry a spell."

Two hours had passed by the noon mark above the cabin door before they overcame their hosts' final protest and mounted. George and Lois Scott watched them move across the clearing and waved. Then they turned toward the cabin to spend the next four months, with winter as their companion.

The wilderness swallowed the three riders yet Adam found the giant trees that dwarfed them, the great silence that mocked the ring of hoofs on frozen ground, no longer were oppressive. Continually before his eyes was the red-cloaked figure of Felicity, swaying to her horse's gait.

Beauty, he thought, spread from her and transformed the forest. The lately grisly shadows were filled with romance and the enviable dapples of sunlight which sometimes touched her were loveliness. Yesterday's travail and strife were paltry payment for this delight.

Sherwood dismounted to tighten his saddle girth. He told Adam:

"Joe Mead has a pitch in Rutland town. We'll noon there and then ride west toward Castleton. North of Rutland," he went on with slight bitterness, "there is not even a sure trail, thanks to York province that holds back settlement."

Adam ignored the challenge in his voice and said deliberately:

"I am so lately from England that I am ill informed, yet has not the King's decision upheld York?"

"By proclaiming Connecticut River the province's boundary," the other said quickly. "True. But Connecticut and the Bay Province now extend far west of the river."

"His Majesty also has proclaimed," Felicity supported her

brother, "that settlers in The Grants are to be left in peace until his further will becomes known."

"And York?" Adam prompted, hoping that her eager voice would press the argument. Sherwood cut in with an angry gesture:

"York defies the royal will. York evicts Grants settlers, reapportions land already surveyed. York now plans to include Clarendon town in the York patent of Durham, all this despite His Majesty's command."

He mistook Adam's silence for disapproval and pursued:

"I share in the strife against York, believe me, Mr. Corlaer, not because I lately purchased rights in the Hampshire town of New Haven but because, sir, your province disobeys the King, whose loyal subject I am. Ergo, I oppose York."

His voice was firm. Felicity looked at him fondly and, more to draw her eyes back to him than for other reason, Adam asked:

"But if King George declares New Hampshire titles invalid?"

"Submit," said Sherwood promptly, "as all good men must to the royal will, yet the King, God bless him, never will decide against plain men who are creating a new province for him. His Majesty is a just ruler and the land is ours."

He smiled with a faintly abashed air.

"Felicity often vows that I should have been a parson. I promise to preach to you no more, Mr. Corlaer."

They dined that noon at a cabin beside a beaver meadow in otherwise empty Rutland town and the eldest of Joseph Mead's ten children was hostess. She was a stringy girl, no more than fourteen, but her brothers and sisters helped her with the cooking and serving. Her father and mother, Makepeace Mead explained, had journeyed to a funeral in Manchester three days earlier. She did not expect them back for two days more.

Adam demurred as they left the shyly staring brood and mounted, but Sherwood only said, "They mature early in The Grants," and led them toward the westering sun and Castleton.

Here in the squalor and privation that attended a few men's grappling with the forest, Zadok Remington, a plump, ambitious person, was raising an oversize tavern that he predicted the tide of settlement would fill, once York's opposition abated. He, Sherwood, and two unsober pioneers became entangled in low-voiced argument, and Adam, ignored, went out into the twilight and

48

found Felicity on the doorstep, her face turned toward the sunset.

His confusion left him sufficient competence only to marvel that the wilderness should produce a woman, and she but a girl, who could violently stir his heart and impose on his mind and body such hapless awkwardness. He mumbled greeting. Felicity smiled at him and again watched the lemon sky above the jagged, black tops of the pines for a long instant before she turned and smiled again.

"You have come this long journey just to view The Grants? Does the prospect please you, Mr. Corlaer?"

"At the instant, extremely," he blurted. She pursed her bright mouth and ever so slightly wrinkled her nose at him.

"La, sir!" she mocked and then asked acutely. "You are for York, are you not?"

"Why do you say that?" he demanded and she answered quietly:

"Because I think you are."

"I am just returned from England—" he began but she caught him up with deftness beyond her years.

"And are on your way to Canada. There are easier routes thither from Albany."

"But none, I swear, so rewarding."

Her green eyes regarded him so searchingly that he felt his face heat. Anger that he should flush like a yokel before her made him redder and clumsier still.

"I can read you, sir, more clearly than you suspect."

He moistened dry lips and felt the evening's cold upon them before he ventured, "And are you affronted by what you read so clearly?"

"Should I be?" He could not tell, watching her vivid face, whether this were coquetry or childish candor.

"Never, if my prayers be of avail."

"I cannot match riddles with you," she told him calmly. "You have seen the world and I little save Connecticut and The Grants. Wait, sir, to confuse me until I have gained from Madame Dufresne's seminary in Quebec what my brother will take me thither to learn—music and French and the polite graces that country maids lack."

"You need none," he told her but she did not seem to hear and pursued:

"You will not know me a year hence, nor little Delight Royden who goes with me."

A strand of burnished hair had escaped from her hood and lay across her forehead. Adam knew with startling clarity how it would feel beneath his lips.

"A year from now," he said, "I hope to know you far better."

Again, her composure baffled him.

"Justus says that you are for Montreal."

"Yes, it is my hope that we may go down the lake together."

"Only as far as Montreal?"

"Is it your pleasure that I accompany you to Quebec?"

"I think it is," she answered, with a clear look that vanished as she puckered her mouth and wrinkled her nose again. "With so many of His Majesty's officers there, I may need your protection."

"I ask no better rôle," Adam said.

Chapter VI

THEY turned north again on the morrow, riding once more through forest. Sherwood led the way in a moody silence that was proof against his sister's gaiety. Adam, following her, wondered whether their brief encounter that still distracted him had wrought this blithe transformation in her.

The girl adorned the bleak journey with enthusiasm, provocative or ingenuous. Adam responded, marveling with her over pillars of ice crystals that had broken and raised the soil, admiring the brown shelves of fungus on a dead tree's bole, acclaiming her discovery of a moose's cloven hoofprints, fixed in the frozen earth. His laughter joined hers when his mare stumbled.

They halted at noon by the still unfrozen rapids of a stream and while they ate the journeycake and slabs of fried pork supplied by Remington, Sherwood spoke with sudden violence.

"I swear," he said to Adam as though it were obscurely his offense, "if this revolt against York were to be twisted into rebellion against the King, I should disavow it instanter, whatever the cost to me."

"Eh?" Adam answered vaguely. Felicity asked more practically:

"Who has said it will be?"

"No one," Sherwood admitted with a sour look, "but Remington's mind moves toward treason—or sidles dubiously in that direction. He and his tipsy friends confuse Tryon with George III."

"The first is the arm of the second," Adam offered dryly, pleased to find in the man he liked a shadow of his own distaste for this hostile people. Sherwood brushed crumbs from his knees with disproportionate vigor.

"That is not so. Tryon, and the governors before him, have been unfaithful servants of a just king, hungry for wealth and wheedled into theft by York's land gamblers—Duane, Kempe, and all their crew. God's curse on them!"

He atoned for his outburst by a shaky laugh.

"Perhaps I am unduly roused, yet it sickens me to hear men pollute a just cause with cant the Boston rabble spews. I tell you, sir, as I told Remington this morning: If The Grants oppose the King, I shall join hands with York and all loyal men everywhere. Treason is not among my vices."

"Isn't such concern over tavern babble at least a frailty, brother?" Felicity asked.

"Perhaps," Sherwood said.

It was midafternoon of the following day when they reached the Panton clearings and Adam felt relief that the rashly undertaken journey was over. Fatigue had been the minor, his failure to gain further private word with Felicity had been the major, cause of his resentment.

They had spent the previous night in Philip Stone's brave new house in Bridport. Their youthful host had welcomed the Sherwoods as old friends in a flat Bay Province voice and his wife immediately had snatched the girl away. Adam had supped glumly while the other men had talked without end of grants, rights, and the iniquities of York, and when it had become clear that Felicity would not return, he had gone early and angrily to bed.

His temper was not improved when the journey was resumed by the girl's tantalizing nearness and immunity. She was indifferent to the trials he had endured, the leagues he had ridden, the grim beds he had occupied, and the grimmer food he had eaten for her sake. Twice, Felicity turned and spoke to him. Adam hoped his brief responses would indicate her offense and inspire atonement, but after his second reply, she disconcertingly left him alone.

The woods had closed in on them again, but this no longer was unbroken forest. They followed a makeshift road and passed occasional clearings and half-built cabins. Once, through an opening, they glimpsed distant blue water and bluer mountains beyond. Sherwood, turning in the saddle, called back, "Champlain."

52

They crossed at a four corners a brush-choked way, wider than that they followed. Sherwood said the neglected route was the military road, cut through the wilderness from the Connecticut to Crown Point in the time of the last French war.

"And, thanks to the palsying hand of York that holds back settlement, used no longer," he said grimly.

Adam nodded without reply. He was surfeited with primal scenery, sick of the wilderness's cold arrogance. He wondered why folk should strive for its possession or why, if they craved it, they could not share it in peace. Here was more virgin territory than the land-greedy could subdue in a thousand years, yet the same James Duane whom Sherwood heartily had cursed had deemed a York title to property in Panton of value and had been willing to buy it.

Adam resolved bitterly to sell to Mr. Duane on his return, for a shilling and the privilege of saying what he thought of The Grants and its people—the lawless folk who had come hither: rebels, wastrels and ne'er-do-wells whom established communities could not stomach.

He jerked at the mare as she stumbled and swore beneath his breath. In the far distance a sawmill wailed and from nearby came the fitful pounding of hammers. Sunlight through the trees proclaimed another clearing. Adam followed his companions out into an open space, broader and more disciplined than any they lately had crossed.

Twin fields were fenced by the twisted black roots of overturned stumps and the lane between them led to log buildings and a frame house with a still unfinished ell. The sound of hammering swelled as the riders approached and ceased when Sherwood called.

Two figures came round the end of the ell. They were female, even to Adam's sun-dazzled eyes, though one had the breadth of a man and she who followed, a child's stature.

"Wal," the larger said, "good to see ye, Justus, 'n' ye, too, Felicity."

She bobbed a curtsey as Sherwood named Adam and subjected him to the unabashed scrutiny of her breed. There was strength in the square brown face with its honest eyes and mouth; in the rugged body clothed in the loose butternut dress; in the blunt, bare feet so firmly set on earth.

"Room for ye all," the woman announced at last. "Been pushed up a mite but it's most built now. Justus, ye might's well hear now's later: Been a-tradin' ashes with MacIntosh for timber, planks, 'n' clapboards. Traffickin' with the ungodly 'n' I know it, but we was set on gittin' the new house done 'fore snow flew. Would of, too, if Olin hadn't gone trapesin' off to Bennington. If ye can bear to bide with a sinner, light. My gal'll take your horses — Where's she gone to?"

Adam had seen the child slip into the house with the soft speed of a wild thing and a flash of bare feet. She reappeared now, demure and shod. Her gray eyes were overlarge, her delicate mouth quivered, and the small brown face below the sun-bleached hair strove vainly to match her mother's composure. She smiled shyly at the Sherwoods' greeting and gathered up the horses' reins. Adam's mare snorted and shied as the animals moved away and he stepped forward to grip her bridle.

"I'll take her," he said and followed the girl despite her mother's demurral.

There were new stalls in the log barn that had been until lately the Roydens' dwelling. Adam felt the grave eyes follow him as he ungirthed Allegra. While he rubbed her down, he said, to break the tight silence, "You are Delight Royden and you are going to go to—let me remember—Madame Dufresne's school in Quebec."

He was heartened to see the grave eyes light with a reflection of his grin.

"How did you know?" Her voice was sweet.

"I read the future," he assured her in a hollow voice and then doubted the wisdom of his levity. It was difficult to say whether she were a precocious Ten or an undeveloped Fourteen. Her brief regard made him uncomfortably aware of travel stains. She turned and with surprising strength whipped the saddles off the Sherwood horses.

"Let me help," he begged but she shook her head.

"Go in and rest yourself," she bade calmly. "Ma'd want that you should."

Adam heard, before he entered the house, Mindwell Royden's strong voice raised in dispute. Felicity had disappeared but the

54

woman, standing in a defiant posture on a kitchen floor already whitened by much scrubbing, included Adam by glance and gesture with Sherwood in her audience and pursued, "Man's work ain't woman's, Justus, but mebby I got some claim to be both. When we come down-lake with Olin after the tree dropped on Dan'l, he'd been buried a month 'n' the loghouse wa'n't more'n two-thirds done. Folks said we couldn't stay with Olin not growed yit 'n' Delight not too hearty but we did, beholden to none. Finished Dan'l's cabin 'n' planted a crop 'n', till that growed, lived on what we could git. When powder give out 'n' fish was scarce we et porcupines 'n' skunks, weeds 'n' lily bulbs, acorns, 'n' even turtles. When food got better, we worked harder. Ain't a seemlier place in the north; better 'n' ten acres plowland 'n' a new timber house."

Her eyes challenged Adam's and he nodded.

"Now wait—" Sherwood begged.

"You wait, till I'm done. Dan'l Royden bought this land 'n' the New Haven lot I'm sellin' you, Justus. Left me a clear Hampshire title. Colonel Reid, he still claims the hull of Panton under York patent, don't he?"

"I shouldn't borrow trouble," Sherwood counseled quietly but the woman's voice sawed on.

"Is it borryin' trouble that Colonel's goin' to try it again, come spring? Enlistin' settlers—Scotch rapscallions they be—now, so Donald MacIntosh says. When they come, what do we do? 'Colonel, here's the pitch Dan'l died a-makin' an' welcome. An' now, with your polite permission me 'n' mine'll go out into the woods 'n' starve to death.' Eh?"

She looked at Sherwood as though he were the usurping Reid. With soiled, hard hands on her hips and fervor flushing her square face, she seemed a creation of the wilderness itself.

"Mindwell," Sherwood told her, "if it comes to that, Olin'll know what to do."

"So I been told. Him and his Colonel Allen and The Green Mountain Boys! They ain't got back the sawmill at Otter falls, have they? Grants folks built it but Donald MacIntosh runs it now 'n' he's Reid's man. Justus, we've worked here, all of us. Real hard."

"Allen and his men can't do everything at once," Sherwood returned. "Don't distress yourself unduly, Mindwell. I'll talk to Olin when he returns and give him a letter to Allen."

The sense that someone watched him had grown in Adam and, now, impelled him to turn. The slight child who had gazed upon him from the doorway flushed beneath her tan, tried to smile, and vanished. The look he had caught for an instant in the grave, gray eyes touched him and lessened his chagrin. He had hoped to see Felicity standing there.

"Wal," Mindwell Royden was saying to Sherwood, "tain't no part of welcome to stand here lamentin'. I'll show ye where you 'n' Mr. Corlaer'll bed."

The family, to Adam's satisfaction, ignored custom that evening. Women and men supped together in the kitchen and Delight, moving like a shadow, served them. Adam was glad to be silent while Mindwell and Sherwood talked, for Felicity sat across the board.

Sherwood spoke of the boundary-marking he purposed to do next day on his New Haven property and of the tree-felling the Roydens' absent son had promised to undertake during the winter, while the other man thought that Felicity's eyebrows were like dark, spread wings. Mindwell deplored the scant wardrobe she had found time to fashion for Delight's Canadian sojourn and Adam marveled that the presence of one person could spread such fatigue-dispelling warmth. His hostess and Sherwood debated how soon, if the snow still held back, the party might set out for Crown Point and Canada while Adam wondered how flesh and blood could be immune to the spell wrought by the girl's loveliness.

Felicity ate with downcast face and said little, yet she was not unaware how closely he watched her, for her color grew bright and once when by accident she glanced up before he could look away, he saw mirth in her eyes and, ever so faintly, she wrinkled her nose at him. Not until the meal had ended did Adam discover that Delight, having served them, had eaten her own supper at his elbow.

While the women cleared away, Adam rose and, muttering something implausible about his mare, went out. He knew the hope that Felicity might follow was fantastic yet when after long delay he returned from the barn, sight of a dim figure in the dooryard brought his heart into his throat.

"You?" he managed to say and Delight's small, soft voice answered:

"Yes. It's me."

He asked, almost angrily, "What on earth are you doing out here, child?"

"Watching the stars," she said shyly. "I want to—remember how they look."

"Remember?"

"So that when I'm away, when I'm in Quebec, I can maybe look at them there and it'll be almost like being home again, won't it?"

She was a strange little thing—finer-textured than her burly mother or any of the harsh Grants' people he had encountered.

"Don't you want to go to Canada, Delight?"

"I guess so. Ma wants that I should go, anyway, and get more schooling. That's why she sold the New Haven piece to Mr. Sherwood. I guess I'll be homesick, though. I guess folks'll laugh at me, too."

"Laugh at you, Delight?" He found himself indignant at the thought. "Why should they?"

"My clothes," she said simply. "Ma 'n' I couldn't do as much as we figgered with the house to finish an' Olin away."

The calm acceptance woke more sympathy in Adam than open pathos could have quickened.

"Clothes," he told her with more vigor than verity, "aren't important, Delight. You would adorn whatever you wore."

She was silent for a moment. He wished that he might see what look the face that was only a pale uncertainty actually wore.

"Well," she said at last in a new voice, "well—thank you," and vanished.

She had joined the others in the kitchen when Adam re-entered. The women still were at work when Sherwood, set on an early start for New Haven, rose and went to bed. Adam followed him and woke at last to find the oiled-paper windowpanes bright yellow and his companion gone.

He was further abased by the charity with which his hostess condoned weariness to which she herself seemed immune.

"Justus," Mindwell said, setting before Adam a bowl of mush on which maple-sugar fragments were darkly melting, "held ye were clean spent and to leave ye lay."

"I had ridden," her guest said ruefully, "no further than he and I might have aided him today."

Mindwell, reading the question in his look, said that Felicity and Delight were inspecting the child's wardrobe.

" 'Twill do, I guess. Have to. 'Twas Dan'l's wish his children should git schoolin'. Olin never took to it overmuch. Mistrust Delight will, mebby."

An impulse opened Adam's mouth but caution closed it again. He was unfamiliar with these forest people, with their unstinted hospitality and untrammeled violences. It would be best to talk to Sherwood before advancing a proposal that echo of Delight's wistful voice had inspired.

He strolled about the dooryard in the bright, cold morning. The sun, blazing above a gray cloudbank in the east, cast little warmth and frost lay heavy on clapboards piled beside the still uncovered sheathing of the ell. Mindwell at his request supplied saw, hammer, and nails with reluctance that Adam hoped concealed approval and he set to work. He had barely warmed to his labor when Felicity appeared.

"Mercy!" she exclaimed with an extravagant astonishment. "He is a carpenter now! What abilities haven't you, Mr. Corlaer?"

She stood beyond the ell's frost-whitened shadow. The sun was fair upon her face and sparks were enmeshed in her hair.

"One," he told her, "always irks me in your presence. I lack fit words in which to praise you."

"I thought," she said with malice, "that you still slumbered."

"Perhaps I do, and only dream of you."

"I thought you would certainly dream of Delight. You have made a conquest, Mr. Corlaer."

"You mistake the reverence of the young for the aged."

"She has turned fourteen," said Felicity. "I have known maids of little more who were wed."

She laughed and he saw with alarm that she was about to leave.

"Stay," he begged desperately, "I—I am wondering whether you would grant me a favor."

Her pose of raillery faded as he explained in a low voice his

58

desire to requite the Roydens' hospitality, and set forth the plan that so lately had occurred to him.

"Will you be my agent in Quebec and buy for the child whatever is needful so that she will not be shamed among her schoolmates?"

"You are generous," Felicity said in a new voice that made him breathe quickly, "and kind."

The way she looked at him was worth more, Adam reflected, than all the gowns in Canada.

"I'm neither," he said a trifle hoarsely. "I am conscious of a debt and of an apprehensive little girl. I should like to appease both."

He picked up his lately discarded coat, drew currency from a wallet, and counted notes into her hand.

"Wait," she bade. "That will more than suffice. Delight will thank you, herself."

Adam shook his head.

"Delight is not to know until after we have parted at Montreal. As for her mother—"

He stopped abruptly, thinking that Mindwell approached. Felicity had turned and was looking intently into the sunlight.

"What is it?" he asked, at length.

"Strangers," she whispered. "Two of them."

Alarm prickled along Adam's spine as he strode forward. Horsemen rode toward them, tall in the morning light with long shadows running before. He already had recognized both when Felicity uttered a little cry and babbled, "It's Olin—Olin Royden. I was almost sure it was."

Adam in a frantic instant juggled several expedients and found dignity only in one. He folded his arms and waited, standing quite still. He saw with chill amusement surprise stiffen the first rider's grim face.

"B'God!" said Remember Baker and brought his musket to bear. Adam stared into the muzzle's black eye. Felicity's presence helped him to say, "I congratulate you gentlemen on recovering your weapons."

He heard the sound of the girl's indrawn breath. She looked from Baker to his glowering companion and cried, "Olin Royden! Have you lost your mind? This is—"

"No," he said with heavy relish, "I haven't. This fancy gentleman is a damned York spy."

Her light laugh sent color to his swarthy face.

"Mr. Corlaer is more of a gentleman than you will be, sir, if you strive till doomsday and Justus and I are in his debt."

"So be we," Baker said dryly, not lifting his eyes from his musket. Adam was only faintly heartened by the girl's defense. He felt, standing helpless and humbled, the numbing approach of greater, still unseen calamity.

Mindwell Royden's stalwart person half filled the doorway. Beside her, Delight looked from Adam to the newcomers with stricken eyes. Felicity's intervention had doubly angered Olin. He ignored her now.

"Ma, Captain Baker and I've trailed this Yorkite sneak clear from Arlington. He's gulled Justus and Felicity. He's—"

"He's done no such thing," Felicity cried, her face aflame. "Mr. Corlaer rendered me great service in Bennington. Justus esteems him highly and he is on the way to Canada with us."

"Olin," his mother bade, "s'pose you holler a mite less 'n' talk more sense."

The boy's unsteady face was crimson. He gulped and said hoarsely, "He rode from Bennington to Squire Munro's and bedded there. Next day, he waylaid us like—like an Abenaki."

The inquiry in Felicity's look roused Adam. He addressed the girl quietly for he still distrusted his voice.

"That is true in part. I did capture them. There were"—he glanced briefly at the horsemen—"only two of them, of course, and each had only one firelock. My excuse for taking them is that, for some reason beyond me, they had fired on me thrice."

He felt surer now and included the woman and the child in his speech.

"Captain Baker," he pursued, laying emphasis on the title, "besought me so pitifully to spare his musket that I left his and his friend's where they might recover them. An error I now deplore."

"You," said Baker violently, eyes sparkling beneath glowering brows, "are one of Reid's men, sent here to skulk and spy."

Mindwell asked intensely, "Be ye?"

"No," said Adam.

The wide gaze above the hand Delight had clapped over her mouth gave her the look of one who tried strangely to smother herself. Felicity said to Olin in a chill tone, "If you disbelieve me, pray ride to New Haven and inquire of Justus. Mr. Corlaer won't run away."

Adam's satisfaction in her defense was curdled by knowledge of his own helplessness. Baker said in a twanging voice over his still leveled musket, "Don't even know Reid, hey?"

"I do not."

"Or John Munro?" There was stealth in the query.

"I lately spent a night beneath his roof."

"Why?"

"Because," Adam retorted, feeling his way despite his growing anger, "a friend in Albany recommended him."

" 'Friend,' eh? Ye went thither to plot against The Grants."

"That is not so. I am a traveler recently returned from England and curious to see the country."

"No talk of York rights while ye was to Munro's, I warrant," Baker sneered.

"I recall most clearly"—Adam's temper was slipping—"that we talked of outlaws and treason."

Baker's leathery face twitched.

"This friend," he challenged in a nasty tone, "that sent ye—recall his name?"

"I do," Adam replied, off guard. "James Duane."

Baker's fists tightened on his firelock. He said to Olin: "Take him."

Chapter VII

THE swarthy youth dismounted with a wide grin. He hesitated as he approached Adam who stood rigid before Baker's musket. Olin looked up for guidance to his companion.

"Wal," the older man prompted acidly. "Proceed. Search him."

"No," Felicity cried.

Adam smiled at her.

"He need feel no apprehension. I am quite unarmed."

The taunt spurred Olin. He stepped behind the captive and, breathing hard, fumbled in Adam's breeches and waistcoat pockets, producing a penknife and a handful of coins that he held, without a word, toward Baker.

"Put 'em back. Yonder's his coat."

Mindwell Royden spoke. There was impatience with male foibles in her voice.

"Felicity's said only sensible thing so far, seems 's if. Justus Sherwood vouches for Mr. Corlaer 'n' Justus ain't an hour's ride away. Olin, you go after him. Rest of ye stop actin' desprit 'n' come in to the fire."

Baker nodded, lifted one hand from his gun and blew upon his fingers. Olin, who had reversed, one by one, the pockets of the coat now drew the wallet forth, and suddenly the prisoner saw the clear aspect of the danger whose shadow already had darkened his mind. Olin shuffled the currency and restored it; withdrew a document and unfolded it. For an instant it seemed to Adam that gloom within him spread outward through the world. He looked up, startled, to see the cloud from the east reach up to swallow the sun.

"More agreeable inside," Baker admitted. "Olin, you take—"

"By the Lord!" the boy said in an awed voice. He looked from Adam to Baker with glee, but it was Felicity whom he addressed at last.

"This gentleman," he said, drawing out his triumph, "whose parts and purity I may never hope to match, this 'gentleman' you defend—"

His voice broke under the weight of his tidings and the paper shook in his upraised hand.

"Mr. Corlaer," he began again, "comes innocently to tour The Grants and to see Panton town and in his purse we find rights in Panton under Reid's patent."

"Don't be an oaf," Felicity advised loftily.

Olin grinned and thrust the paper at her.

"You can read," he gloated. "Mr. Corlaer-who-travels-for-pleasure owns under York the land where you stand."

Slowly, the girl grew white; more slowly still, she turned from her tormentor to Adam. He looked away.

Felicity did not heed when Olin snatched the document from her and handed it to Baker.

"Ehyah," the man said at last in a dry voice. "York title to your prop'ty, Mistress Royden—for what it's wuth."

The girl went toward the woman who still stood solidly in the doorway from which Delight had vanished. Adam began, loudly and desperately, "I inherited this document from my late father—"

They were cheap words and he checked them. They did not seem to reach Felicity. As she passed into the dwelling Mindwell's big hand rested fleetingly on her shoulder. The woman turned and followed.

"No doubt," Baker said and Olin snickered.

The derision pierced Adam's apathy, rousing one emotion to which he could creditably cling. He lifted his head to look into Baker's leering face. He had settled too mildly an earlier score with this swaggering, ambushing woods-runner and the lout who was his jackal. Somehow, sometime, all items on the new account —those already set down and those still unentered—would be paid with interest. Hatred for a moment had made Adam immune to the encroaching cold. The wind clawed him with sharp fingers and he shivered.

"I do not," he said, defiantly, "tremble with fear."

63

"Give him his coat," Baker bade the boy.

"Coat! Strip him and seal him."

Olin for an instant withstood Baker's hard look, then cast the garment at Adam. He picked it up and crowded his numb body into it. Baker's fingers drummed on his musket's butt. His face, puckered by thought, spread at last into a grin.

"Mebbe John Munro or James Duane—the damned, bloodsucking macaroni—told ye of the justice we visit on Yorkers. Mebbe ye've heered of the beech seal."

Adam thought less of his jeering words than of the pleasure it would be to feel that corded neck between his hands.

"We whop bastards like you," Baker informed him with relish. "We whop 'em bareback with sprouts of the blue beech till they lament most grievous."

Adam slowly drew breath. Cold had stiffened his body, yet he might just possibly leap, strike the firelock's muzzle aside, and, locking his arms about that fringed deerskin frock, wrench its wearer out of the saddle.

But Olin was too close at hand. Olin, while his companion talked, had uttered small, unappeased sounds. He was watching Baker now like an expectant dog.

"Don't aim," the horseman said, twisting his face again, "to whop ye. Owe ye a mite. Didn't steal my firelock, in a manner of speakin'. Rid quite a ways into The Grants, Mr. Corlaer. Wal, ye can go back the way ye came."

Olin growled dissent.

"On foot," Baker added and lifting his voice, called, "Mis' Royden."

The woman reappeared. She stood with a face as still as her thick body.

"What gear of his'n's here?" Baker demanded, jerking his head. Mindwell did not even glance toward Adam. She answered, "Mare in barn; saddlebags 'n' cloak in yonder."

"Bring him his cloak," the man directed. "I'll set Mr. Corlaer on his way a piece."

Felicity, not Mindwell, brought the garment. She gave it to Adam without a word. Her face was white. He felt, as he slung the cloak about his shoulders, that he could not leave her unassured and said with a recklessness that warmed him, "Thank you. Will you remember my mission in Quebec? I shall see you there, or here."

He was heartened by the scowl that came to Olin's face and the coughing sound he uttered. Baker said grimly:

"Chances ye'll see anyone, anywheres, ain't real good."

"Ye'll never set foot in Panton again," Olin rasped.

Adam ignored them and told the girl, almost blithely.

"Here, if that pleases you, but only after I have seen this gentleman"—he nodded toward Baker—"where one of his talents belongs—in jail at Albany."

He found comfort and strength in the boast.

"Remember," he bade Felicity. "This is my pledge to you."

She did not answer but whirled and ran into the house. Adam bowed low to his captor.

"At your service," he said.

They faced each other an hour later in gloom cast by pines through which the wind went steadily. Baker said, with his musket poised, "Wouldn't try to turn back, Mr. Corlaer, was I you; wouldn't tarry, neither. Making to snow, seem 's if."

Adam looked up into the bitter, brown face with what he hoped was disdain. Fear of the darkening woods, dread of the life-less, unmapped leagues about him momentarily were little things, matched against shame and hatred. These seemed to have drained his body so that his cloak dragged heavily on his shoulders.

Inwardly, he cursed the man who was casting him out into the wilderness, who had revealed him to Felicity, and the woman, and the child who had made him welcome, as a fraud and a betrayer. They all must have seen Adam meekly plod away.

"Take pride in your woodcraft, eh?" his tormentor was saying. "Wal, ye got a chance to prove it. I've druv ye southward toward Munro's. 'Tain't more'n mebby a hundred miles thither—as the crow flies. When ye git out, tell Duane The Grants ain't healthy for his lackeys—if ye do git out."

He waited an instant for answer and seemed baffled by Adam's shrug and smile. Baker wheeled his horse. Wind, traveling through the pine tops with a sound of surf, hid the noise of his departure so that he vanished silently and swiftly as blown smoke. Adam stood and looked after him.

The forest had enormity that a horseman safely following a trail could ignore; the forest cherished eerie shadows and vast uncertainties which only a lone castaway could sense entire. It crouched in half-darkness to spring upon the strayed and helpless. It would bide its time, bewildering, then frightening, and at last robbing a man of his wits, before it would destroy him.

Arrogant trees, gray light, and the hoarse sound of the wind were becoming a dire entity. Adam drew a designedly slow breath, curbing panic that urged him to hasten onward. He must consider his plight and the most likely means of salvation before he moved. He must recall Mohawk ways and stratagems. Lichens on tree boles and the wind out of the east assured him he truly had traveled south. Then, somewhere to the right, lay the faint road he and the Sherwoods had followed to Panton.

It would be cold comfort to find that trail again, yet it would serve as guide, as a tenuous lifeline, if he could achieve it. He went forward with intentional deliberation. He must not hasten; he must shrewdly and carefully guide Adam Corlaer through the forest so that he might endure to find and requite Remember Baker and accomplish his pledge to Felicity. The chances, since he was foodless, fireless, and unarmed, were slight. He must diminish them no further by recklessness or panic.

A bramble plucked at his cloak and, releasing it, let an inner weight, that Adam earlier had detected but cannily had forborne to examine, strike against his thigh. He halted and delved in the garment's deep pocket.

He undid the package's cloth covering and stared at the chunk of journeycake and the hurriedly hacked slab of pork. His cloak now hung askew. Its other pocket yielded a flint and steel shaped like a miniature musket lock.

Adam forgot the wind's omen and the dusk that thickened at noonday. Here were food and the surety of fire. They thrust away the fell probabilities that lately had crowded about him. Here, too, was greater, more fortifying succor. His mind fed upon it avidly. He was certain who had secreted these treasures in the cloak before Felicity Sherwood had borne it out to him.

It could have been no one but she, herself. She of all that company was merciful. Despite the sorry and demeaning light upon

66

him, she had not turned away. Felicity had bestowed, not only material aid but new hope, new heart. Adam restored his treasures and went on almost gaily. With these tokens and his knife, he was armed against the rigors of the wilderness.

He moved forward through the gray half-light, with cushioning needles below and the pines' dark roof overhead while, imperceptibly, long-sleeping aptitudes revived. He found himself proving his course by frequent backward glances; assuming the loose-jointed trot whereby Indian runners thrust the miles behind them; pausing at intervals to sprawl relaxed for a few moments before resuming his journey; washing out his mouth and moistening his throat at each brook he crossed.

The forest no longer was a savage desolation. It had become, now that he was even so feebly provided, a benign and generous place. Each fallen tree was the foundation of shelter; every white birch promised an easily kindled fire.

The sense of competence uplifted him, yet did not rout or soothe his carking grudge against the man who had driven him thither. This clung, rooting more deeply as he shuffled onward. It was not by Baker's grace that Adam did not stand now upon extinction's doorstep. His cloak had been granted only so that he might not succumb too quickly.

Hatred, expanding, included Baker's riotous fellows, from the bawling, bedizened Colonel at Bennington to that hostile lout, Olin Royden. Adam detested all the raw, defiant crew, the unrefined, undisciplined, generally unwashed rascals who demanded a freedom that was treason's kinsman and fell like wolves upon dissenters. The Grants' rebels had abiding fortitude—he allowed them that—but no reverence for established order or decency. He wondered what combination of circumstances had induced Sherwood to stomach his associates.

The wind's voice had dwindled. Snow, small and hard as salt, sifted through the pines' dark roof. Adam traveled more slowly, weighing whether it might not be best to choose the next overhanging ledge or fallen tree as his tavern for the night, and without warning came out upon the road.

It was only a barren, less crooked aisle through the wilderness and the hissing snow fell more strongly here but his achievement warmed the castaway. He had accomplished the first of the un-numbered ordeals that eventually would bring him face to face with Baker and, later, Felicity.

The trail came out of gloom and led into further gloom. The frozen soil beneath Adam's quickened tread rang like iron.

He had gained as a boy the Indian's knack of remembering land through which he once had journeyed, yet the road seemed unfamiliar. He had ignored landmarks yesterday to watch a red-cloaked girl, yet he did recall there had been clearings and, now and then, empty, half-built cabins. One of these would afford better lodging than the snowy forest offered.

Adam plodded on while weariness that had been held off in the woodland by the need for vigilance pulled at him, since now the road guided him. Snow stung his face and glazed the way. The wind had died but the gray cold crept up his sleeves and down his bootlegs. He slipped, recovered, and stood motionless, forgetting his misery in a sudden, still dubious excitement, drawing short breaths like a questing hound.

The assurance his nostrils had proclaimed, though his mind doubted, came again—the faint but certain scent of woodsmoke.

Beyond a turn in the road, Adam came upon a small clearing. Smoke climbed aimlessly from a still unroofed cabin and he saw through the doorway a glitter of fire on the earthen floor. He called. A horse stamped within the log enclosure and a shrill voice answered. Adam went forward, not pausing to weigh his welcome.

He had the odd impression as he stepped across the threshold that he had intruded upon an intertribal council between a blanketed horse, tethered on one side of the fire, and a man who sat across it, in an angle of the walls with another blanket propped canopy-wise above him. He rubbed his knobbed knees and met Adam's regard with hollow, humble eyes.

"If," the stranger said, "you are proprietor here, I ask your pardon for my trespass. I am the Reverend Benjamin Hough, sir, a laborer in the Baptist faith, preaching the Gospel to those who need it sorely. Abijah has cast a shoe and, fearing to travel farther on a slippery road, I sought shelter here."

He might, Adam thought, have spent his life in the smoke, so dry and dingy was he. His sunken eyes peered out of sooty shadows and, below the cheekbones' ledges, the melancholy face fell inward to an intemperate mouth and a narrow, jutting jaw. His cropped hair was grizzled and his black clothing stained and patched. He seemed a proper evangel for this dismal region, gaunt, weathered, and wild.

"Mine is the trespass," Adam replied, warming numb hands above the fire. "I, like yourself, am traveling—toward New York."

"Afoot?" Something in the scrawny throat seemed ill adjusted and squeaked and rattled through every utterance. Eyes, white-ringed, stared at Adam's riding boots. Their owner said briefly, "Yes. By misfortune."

"Misfortune," the strident voice demanded, "wrought by man?"

"By Remember Baker of The Green Mountain Boys," Adam said grimly, eschewing fencing or pretense. "Call him a man."

Hough unlocked bony hands from about his knees, hitched himself over, and patted the empty space he had left on pine boughs spread beneath the makeshift canopy.

"God," he announced, "will punish Remember Baker and all Belial's seed. Sit you, sir. The fire is all I can share with you for I thought to reach Panton town ere nightfall."

"You shall sup with me, Reverend," Adam assured him.

While they ate bread and half-broiled meat together, reserving a portion for the morning, Hough learned of his companion's punishment and forthwith inveighed shrilly and comfortingly against Grants' folk who defied those set in authority over them and showed scarcely more reverence for the deity.

The minister, Adam learned, had built his own home in the York-patented town of Durham that Grants' adherents claimed as Clarendon, and had gathered about him a group of the law-abiding whom threats did not dismay. From there, he had traveled north to summon the ungodly to repentance with, Adam gathered, no conspicuous success.

"Even I, The Lord's servant, have been browbeaten and defamed, sir, yet He has given his angels charge over me. I shall be God's instrument in preparing a pit for the wrongdoer, aye, even that arch-blasphemer, Beelzebub Allen himself."

On the morrow, the rattling voice went on, Hough would retrace his steps, guiding Adam to Chimney Point on Champlain where John Strong had a house and a bateau laden with potashes ready to sail for Skenesborough at the lakehead.

"He will rejoice, sir, in your companionship and your aid. He is a hospitable man, though attainted, I fear, with heretical doctrine."

The snow had ceased. They fed the fire, shook flakes from the blanket-awning and with this and Adam's cloak as covering slept fitfully. They breakfasted on the remnant of the food and, leading the horse, plodded through the morning's white glare to turn west where the brush-grown Military Road crossed the trail. The forest at last gave way to second growth, half concealing black and crumbling chimneys.

There was satisfaction in Hough's strident voice.

"Thus, sir, God deals with idolaters. The papist French once raised a village here. 'And for the overspreading of abominations, He shall make it desolate.' "

On the stone foundation of an earlier dwelling, John Strong had built himself a square house. The lake wind cut at Adam's face as Chimney Point's sole settler and his stout wife welcomed him. Below the bluff on which the dwelling stood, lay white-capped narrow water. On the farther shore stood ruins of a French fort and behind it, silver-gray in the morning light, rose the greater stone stronghold Amherst had decreed at Crown Point. The garrison's flag was a tiny brilliance against the sad-hued hills.

"Ehyah," Strong replied to Adam's question. "Half company of the 26th. Comfortin' to have 'em, too. Injuns don't bother so much with soldiers near."

He was a hearty man, red-faced, with a calmly competent manner. He hailed the idea of carrying Adam uplake and, before they embarked, deftly reshod Hough's mount.

The north wind, pouring through the strait, caught the bateau's square brown sail and filled it. Strong, laboring at the tiller, brought the clumsy craft around and headed her south.

Water began a rhythmic crashing beneath the blunt bows. Wind that sung in the elemental rigging brought tears to Adam's eyes. He wiped them away and got a blurred view of the fort behind and the wider breadth of lake before them. On either hand mountains towered, close to the west shore, loftily blue beyond the forest on the east.

Adam watched The Grants' wilderness slide past and drop behind with a grim contentment. Hough had promised to seek out Felicity in Panton and tell her of the exile's safety. The boastful pledge Adam had made in anger was hardening into resolutions. He would go back as he had promised. The enmity of all the Bennington Mob would not restrain him. When summer came again, he would return to Panton and Felicity, but first—his mouth grew tight—he would pay in full his score against Remember Baker.

The bateau lurched along, overtaking the white-maned waves that earlier had passed it. Adam relieved Strong at the tiller while the man ate. As he resumed his post, Strong pointed ahead.

The lake shores slanted inward and, on either side of the water's blue and gold dazzle, hills rose. The western headland, slanting steeply from the lake, bore on its brow, sharply outlined against the sky, a crown of pale stone.

"Ticonderoga," Strong cried in Adam's ear. "We're makin' time."

Chapter VIII

JAMES DUANE rolled a sip of Madeira on his tongue, wiped his mouth carefully, and said with the air of one turning the pages of a mental ledger to an earlier entry, "You may recall, my dear boy, that I strongly counseled against the venture."

He viewed his wisdom with satisfaction and accepted the decanter from his host.

"On the other hand, if many here in Albany and in New York as well were to suffer your fate, it might dispel the danger to which most folk are still blind."

Adam did not answer at once. Duane drank again and considered the haggard face beyond the candle flames. Clearly, what the young man had endured had sobered and matured him.

"Danger?" Adam now asked. "In what degree?"

His guest's sleek certainty irritated him. The world was crammed with a variety of annoyances. Adam had known great bodily relief when the overland journey from Skenesborough to Albany had ended and his father's servants had welcomed him in the house that was now his own. It had been easy to rest and restore spent muscles. He was finding it harder to steady his mind.

The raw December fogs that cursed the town had crept into his spirit. In the still house that was filled with disquieting vestiges of his father, Adam half resolved to undertake again his thwarted journey to Montreal but relinquished that plan lest, having traveled so far, he should be tempted to go on to Quebec with his debt to Baker still unpaid.

Adam had planned a journey to New York but had abandoned this when Duane had appeared in Albany and had promised to dine at the Corlaer home. He viewed his host thoughtfully above joined fingertips, now, as he explained, "Danger, my dear boy, in many degrees. First and possibly the least important"—he blinked approval of his modesty—"I and my associates have larger investments in the so-called Grants than we can afford to lose. There is danger, too, for Munro and Hough and the rest of the law-abiding while the Bennington Mob holds sway. I fancy I need not emphasize that after what you have suffered. And finally—"

He hesitated, took snuff, and snapped the box lid with a resolute sound. His voice was low and beneath his smooth surface Adam for an instant fancied he saw urgency stir.

"There was a riot," Duane pursued with apparent irrelevance, "in Boston town last winter. Troops fired upon the Mob."

Again he paused. Adam prompted, "Yes. It caused a stir even in Oxford."

"Such things do, inevitably. I have never, my dear boy, inquired into your politics."

"Politics?"

"Exactly. I wonder how much your sojourn in England has altered you."

"The British attitude toward colonials has not made me love my own land less, if that is what you ask."

"That in part," Duane acknowledged and seemed to measure the dimensions of each word. "I think that the colonies in general reflect your sentiments. If His Majesty's government is to heed our grievances, they must be uttered with dignity and in unison—particularly in unison, Adam."

Again he took snuff and airily brushed his heavy nose with a wisp of cambric.

" 'Divide and fall,' my dear boy. That is where the danger lies. Riots in Boston, riots in The Grants; logic and legality abandoned for violence. New York cannot properly dispute British misrule while disorder in our province proclaims our inability to rule ourselves. The Grants trouble must be checked, sir, but how?"

"Possibly by negotiation?" Adam suggested at hazard, and for a second Duane's polished composure cracked.

"Negotiation! The scoundrels will have none of it. To every compromise York has offered, they cry: 'No. The land is ours!' How can you negotiate with such people?"

73

He emptied his glass and drew his rumpled composure about him.

"Certain friends reproach me for my association with Governor Tryon. I shall support, nay, encourage, him as long as he labors to suppress disorder. He strives to enforce British authority. I labor to strengthen York province."

Duane smiled at his own astuteness.

"The killings in Boston have wrought great evil. Slaughter obscures truth and thwarts justice. Eh?"

"I started, sir," Adam apologized, "because I heard a man in Bennington say the same thing."

"Then there is more wisdom than I suspected in Bennington. And who was this paragon?"

"He is called Ethan Allen."

Duane jerked as though he had been pricked and his composure blew away.

"Now damn him for an insolent, profligate rascal," he bawled. "It was he, I vow, who prepared the placard that has been scattered through Albany—a travesty of the governor's proclamation that outlawed him.

"It offers," the outraged man continued, words stumbling and jowls purple, "for the capture and delivery to Bennington of Messrs. Duane and Kempe, fifteen pounds reward for me and ten for the attorney general. I should be flattered," he pursued, struggling for control, "that I am quoted at the higher price."

"You are not esteemed in The Grants, sir," Adam said maliciously hoping to rouse him again. "I myself have heard you called 'a bloodsucking macaroni.' "

"And worse, I doubt not." Duane smoothed his flowered waistcoat. "It would be worth much to me and to York if we could lay one of these bandit leaders by the heels but, damme, sir, they are slippery rascals. If we could hold even one hostage, his accomplices might be less defiant."

"There is one," Adam said slowly, "that I should take great pleasure in haling to justice. Remember Baker."

Duane considered the fingertips he gently rubbed together. His voice was remote.

"If that be your ambition, it is possible I can further it. A man of your parts with your new knowledge of The Grants might be

74

of great aid to me. I cannot stay permanently here. I need someone who can confer with and direct my agents, meanwhile keeping me informed."

Adam asked slowly, "You wish me to serve you as a spy?"

"I am inviting you, my dear boy, to join with me in ridding this
province of internecine strife. I am offering you your best opportunity to requite this Baker for his villainy. I wish you to be my
deputy here."

This was something that might lead toward Felicity. Here was
employment that might further Adam's purpose.

"Tell me," he said at last, "what you want me to do."

The library in the Corlaer house no longer was a chamber
haunted by memories of Adam's father. It had become an office to
which so large an assortment of persons reported that Adam's respect for Duane's thoroughness mounted.

Peddlers, hunters, and men of less certain occupation brought
news from The Grants and received further commissions. Benjamin Buck was among the furtive crew and William Cockburn,
the surveyor. Hough and Munro sent frequent tidings by Bliss
Willoughby, a dry frontiersman whose voice was a parched and
cautious whisper. Adam fitted all the fragmentary tidings into a
pattern and wrote regularly to Duane.

Winter had imposed its truce upon The Grants and news was
heavier with portents than with actual violence. Though the snow
lay deep, there had been revelry at Bennington on New Year's
Day when Ethan Allen had reviewed his host, salutes had been
fired, oratory spent and innumerable toasts drunk, all to the confusion of York.

Thereafter, Allen retired to his home in Salisbury, Connecticut,
and in February Willoughby informed Adam that the Colonel's
cousin, Remember Baker, had gone to confer with him there,
leaving his wife and family in Arlington. His house, the messenger's whisper confided, was being watched. When the man returned, Munro would be ready to carry out Adam's orders.

The weeks crept torpidly past while Adam doubted if spring
ever would come and wrote letters to Felicity that pride impelled
him to destroy. He thought, too, of Delight and wondered
whether her new clothes became her and if she allayed home-

75

sickness by viewing the Canadian stars. It was shameful that folk as valiant as she and her mother and all the humble and undismayed who strove with the wilderness should be exploited by bullies and rabble-rousers.

March came in warm, with river ice rotting and bluebirds fluting in the maples. Willoughby appeared, splashed with mire and more than commonly hushed by the weight of his tidings. Baker had returned and the time was ripe.

"Watchin' him," the messenger whispered, "day 'n' night. Squire Munro says he's ready to take him soon's ye send word."

Adam thrust his chair from the desk and rose.

"I'm sending no word," he told Willoughby. "I am going with you."

Willoughby led him for two days through the forest, following a trail that circled wide about Bennington and brought them into Shaftsbury from the west. Emancipated water called through fog that filled the hollows and the sodden snow breathed dampness that chilled to the bone. Adam shivered all night in the lean-to his guide built, despite the fire at his feet.

It grew colder on the second afternoon. Snow was falling through the twilight when they rode out of the woods and over the freezing mud of a road to Munro's door. The man appeared at Willoughby's hail and stared at Adam.

"What brings ye here?" he asked sharply.

"The opportunity to meet Captain Remember Baker once more."

Munro nodded, thawing.

"Aye," he conceded, "I've heard how he served ye in Panton town."

He dropped his voice. His eyes shone.

"We'll have him, the morrow, sir. Like that," he grinned over his clenched fist. "Bliss, ye'll care for the horses."

There was excitement in his abrupt movements as he led Adam into the house. When cider had been drawn and they sat before the fire, speech burst from him.

"God, sir, the morrow will be a great day for me and a people long afflicted. 'He shall bind their kings in chains and their nobles in links of iron.'"

Munro slopped his drink as he bent toward Adam and, though they were alone, went on quickly in a half whisper.

Their plans had been completed with great stealth. Baker was unaware that they were watching him constantly. Now, horses and sled were ready to spirit the prisoner into York and four good men would aid in the capture.

"Surely," Adam objected, "it will not require six of us to take a single man."

"The loyal," Munro told him bitterly, "have been so long in terror that four are needed to supply the courage of one."

"But I alone, or you and I—"

Munro shook his head.

"Ye are here to pay a grudge, Mr. Corlaer, and small blame to ye, but I am a law officer intent on my duty. I shall take the posse I deem necessary. It will assemble here before daybreak, tomorrow, and shortly, please God, Baker will be lodged in the Albany jail."

Adam's body was stiff and cold as he groped downstairs next morning but his mind was strangely gay. The darkness, the hushed stirring within, and the stamp of horses without woke glee kin to the expectancy he had known at the outset of a hunt. He entered the kitchen and blinked at three strangers who loomed portentously in the wavering light of a tallow dip while they breakfasted on journeycake and cider. Their eyeballs shone and they checked their low speech. Munro named the trio hastily as he girded a sword over his heavy coat. He asked, "You are armed, Mr. Corlaer?"

The candle flame struck dull reflections from musket barrels and Adam made small effort to keep contempt from his voice.

"I see no need, with this array. Is it a posse or a firing squad?"

There was brief, nervous laughter. Someone growled, "My way, I'd riddle the bastard," and roused a mutter of assent.

Adam said quickly and severely, "He is to be taken alive and unhurt. This is Mr. Duane's order and"—stretching verity—"the governor's wish. Five men have no need of firelocks to capture one scoundrel."

He turned upon Munro, affronted by the shabby vindictiveness that threatened to spoil his revenge.

"I counsel you, sir, to leave the muskets here. York requires a hostage, not a cadaver."

Through the mumble of dissent, Munro spoke briskly, "All of ye leave 'em in the sled when we get there. Mind. If ye have no bludgeons of your own, choose from the woodshed."

He strode, sword clanking, toward the door. Snow had covered deeply the dooryard mud. Stars hung close in a dark-blue sky and the cold air made Adam cough. The posse with clatter and tittering clambered into the sled and the team moved off, spouting steam. Munro and his guest rode before them.

Echoes, thrown back by the dark houses of Shaftsbury, magnified the sound of their passage through the village. The pace quickened as they turned into the North Road. Munro's speech was jolted into fragments by his horse's hard trot.

"Willoughby is—watching the house. We—must hasten after he—is taken ere—the Mob is roused."

The paler streak through blackness that had been the road was growing more distinct now in the twilight that preceded dawn. Adam saw before them, dark against the snow, the waiting figure of a man. Munro spurred forward, outdistancing the toiling sled.

Willoughby's whisper came with difficulty through chattering teeth.

"Begun to wonder what was keepin' ye. He's still there but they've waked 'n' made a fire."

As the horsemen rode on, he swung aboard the sled. Munro after a space drew rein and advanced more slowly toward the forest's edge where tree trunks were bars before the daybreak. The violence of Adam's heart took his breath as he followed.

A wan star hung in the white east and a radiance that cast no shadow immersed the clearing and the cottage that squatted beside a window-high drift. From the chimney, smoke rose straight against the dawn. The stillness plucked at Adam's nerves. He flinched at each muffled sound as the sled's crew disembarked and, leaving the team at the forest's edge, stole forward. Each man, he made certain, was armed only with a club. They could, he told himself with satisfaction, at least obey orders.

He was shaking from excitement and cold. Munro climbed awkwardly from his horse and Adam, imitating, shrank at the snow's harsh response to each footstep. The mountains were sooty-black against a yellow sky.

"Quiet," Munro bade in a taut voice.

The others pressed forward behind him and Adam let them hasten. They must surround the house and, when each was at his station, Munro and he would advance and demand entrance.

His thought broke off. He stared stupidly. The dark huddle of men had not dispersed. At their leader's yelp, they had rushed the door. There was a banging and a splintering crash as it gave way. Above the thumping and whooping that raged within rose, clear and chilling, a woman's scream. Adam ran, slipping and floundering through the snow.

For an instant after he reached the threshold, he could see only dark confusion between him and the hearth fire. He heard brief outcries, gaspings, and the scrape of feet. A table went over and then, once more, splitting the worrying sounds, came a woman's cry.

He saw her now, among the lurching men, a thick wrestling figure in a torn nightgown. Hair streamed over her face. A hand crept down her arm and twisted an iron poker from her grasp. She screeched again. A child, huddled in the room's far corner, wailed.

"Remember Baker," Munro was bawling, face crimson, bared sword waving, "come forth and surrender! Come forth, you dog!"

Adam still stood in the doorway. The unscrupulous ferocity of long-cowed men dazed and sickened him.

"Beware!" someone yelled, and he looked up into Baker's face.

The man stood midway on the stair that slanted upward from beside the fireplace, naked but musket in hand. Willoughby pushed past Adam and ran from the house.

"Stand, all of ye!" Baker yelped and came a step further, raising his gun. Munro with a hissing sound slashed at him. The firelock fell and clattered down the stair. Baker reeled, and gaped at his drenched, red hand. He roared and leaped down, dodged back from the sweep of Munro's sword, twisted away from one who tried to grapple with him and jumped like a lynx for the stair again, to wheel and parry Munro's blow with the axe he had caught up. Drops flew as he swung it.

Those who had plunged after him stood still, all save Munro who bent and retrieved the musket.

"Surrender," he shouted, "in the name of—"

Baker grunted, wheeled, flashed up the stair, and vanished. They heard bare feet pound overhead. In the room's far corner, the woman and the little boy wept.

Revulsion to this savagery, anger that these blunderers had destroyed his purpose were ridding Adam's belly of nausea. The house shook. Munro cried:

"He's breaking through the roof!"

He wavered, musket in hand. They heard, above, a bursting sound and then, from outside, a howl of rage and woe. Munro, rushing toward the door, struck against Adam and knocked him aside. Before he had recovered, the others had stormed past. He ran after them.

Munro had paused at the corner of the house and with firelock half raised was dancing and shouting. Beyond him, the three remaining members of his posse were wallowing into the drift. Only the naked bust of the raving Baker showed above it. Around him were strewn fragments of the gable he had beaten out before he leaped. His fall had driven him deep into the snow. Each wrenching effort to free himself left fresh red stains.

"Surrender," Munro was squalling. "Surrender, ye treacherous dog!"

Rage and disgust unsettled Adam. The men who lurched toward Baker still held their clubs. Willoughby was running from the sled, musket in hand.

This was not legal arrest or even satisfactory reprisal. It was as vicious as a dog fight. Baker still writhed, fast embedded. Adam shouted at those who were floundering toward their quarry. One leaned far to strike at the helpless man. The club grazed Baker's skull and left a darkness on the sandy hair.

Willoughby was close now. Still running, he raised his gun. Adam kicked his feet from under him. The man fell and slid. The musket flew clear and Adam leaped upon it.

He wheeled on Munro with the weapon leveled. His thumb drew back the hammer as he bade:

"Drop your firelock and call off your pack!"

Munro laid down Baker's gun with slow, dazed movements. Adam stood above it and swung Willoughby's toward its owner and the men beyond him.

"Lay down your clubs and pull him out," he ordered and, when Willoughby uttered hissing objection, added, "I'll shoot whoever does not obey me."

He saw the lids droop over Baker's fierce eyes and his body sag forward toward the scarlet snow.

"Mr. Munro," Adam commanded, "get clothing for that man and bandages for his hand."

"Let him bleed—" one man shouted, then gulped and turned to help his fellows haul Baker's limp body from the drift.

The sun came over the mountain rim and Munro squinting, stammered:

"We cannot tarry. We have lingered too long."

"That," Adam told him, "is why I bid you haste. Do you wish to bear a dead man to Albany?"

Chapter IX

SOUTH of Shaftsbury, Munro who drove the sled with Baker's musket slanting between his knees, turned into a narrower, rougher track. They had gone only a little way when on the North Road a horseman drew his mount into a sliding halt, bent to inspect their trail, and then rode on, hell for leather, toward Bennington. Munro clucked to the team.

" 'T'will be hours before they can marshal pursuit and then we shall be too far for them to overtake us. We'll join the main road a few miles from the Hudson ferry."

He addressed Adam placatingly. He and his posse—the man who shared the driver's seat, the two perched at the tailboard, nursing their firelocks, and Willoughby who now rode Munro's horse—all had been humble since they had laid the bound captive in the sled body and had covered him with the blanket Adam had obtained from Baker's dazed and quailing wife.

They had striven to erase memory of their frenzy. Adam wished grimly, as they hurried along the uneven way, that they had succeeded. The satisfaction he had looked for when Baker was overthrown would not come and in its place stood shame and unwilling sympathy for the victim.

He let his horse fall back and, riding alongside the sled, watched the captive. There was dignity on the pallid, still face, despite the black tuft in the sandy hair where blood, started by the club's grazing blow, had frozen.

"You have your revenge, Mr. Corlaer," Adam told himself sourly. "I hope it pleases you."

If there had been fewer men against him or if he had not been surprised in bed, Baker might still be free. He was not the coward

Adam had deemed him. If he were typical of Allen's men, it was easy to understand why York did not prevail. The sled lurched. Adam wondered whether the hastily contrived bandage still held and cried for Munro to halt.

The cloth about the wounded hand was brown and stiff yet dry. Adam had had difficulty in stanching the flow. Baker looked at him now in silence. A thought stung Adam as he remounted. Soon or late, Felicity would learn of how he had triumphed over Remember Baker, with the aid of no more than five men. He shivered. The sun had not dispersed the cold. Even the tough pioneers on the tailboard looked pinched and wretched.

The team went down a steep pitch on its haunches and the sled followed with a thump to slide out of the byway onto the Albany road. Munro looked back and, meeting Adam's eye, nodded his gratification. The thoroughfare was white and empty behind them.

They moved more rapidly now, team and outriders smartly trotting. They would soon get across the ferry. On the far side of the Hudson, there would be no further need for haste. They then would find a doctor who could properly care for the prisoner's wound.

And, once Baker was jailed, Adam must write to Felicity immediately. She should hear of the affair before perversions reached her. He thought sourly that it would be difficult to present his case without discredit.

His stomach asked for food and a glance toward the sun told him it was past noon. They had come a long way and still there was no sign of pursuit. Each hour's passage lessened its likelihood. The wind ranged savagely along the road. Hot victuals and drink would re-armor them all against its attack. Munro stopped at a hilltop to breathe his team and the men slid off the sled to stamp and beat their hands together. Adam, dismounting stiffly, looked over a sideboard at the prisoner.

Baker's face was set in a quivering grimace and its lips were blue. Adam, thrusting a hand beneath the blanket, felt the body quake. He said to Munro, "This man must be got under a roof," and held up red-smeared fingers.

"We dare not—" Munro began, but Adam craftily headed him off.

83

"His wound must be stanched afresh. We have outdistanced pursuit, if truly they undertook any. Men and beasts will travel more swiftly having warmth within them."

The acclaim of chilled men silenced Munro's objections.

"Slake's Tavern," Willoughby wheezed, "ain't more'n a mile along."

They halted where Adam had nooned, months ago, on his way to Bennington. Baker obeyed, when his bonds were loosed, and he was bidden to alight, but he dragged his feet as he walked to the inn and dark drops on the snow marked his passage.

With Munro's aid and cloths supplied by the feverishly inquisitive landlord, Adam wrought a new bandage. Baker drank when they brought him a steaming bowl of flip. He seemed stunned.

The company was more cheerful when the journey was resumed. The men on the tailboard extolled the fleshly delights of Albany, and Munro, plying his whip, called to Adam, "We tarry no more till we reach the ferry."

Willoughby looked over his shoulder with a grin. Adam saw it vanish. He heard the man yell.

It came so swiftly that Adam's mind could not grasp it entire. He saw the road, long-empty behind them, black with hard-riding men. They screeched. Smoke spouted as the foremost fired over the lunging heads of their horses.

Baker's firelock bellowed close to Adam's ear. Munro clung to the smoking weapon and wavered an instant before he leaped and ran.

Then, the driverless team was bolting and in the otherwise empty sled the prisoner's bound body rolled and slued. Adam spurred, leaned far over, snatched at and finally caught a flying rein. Only later did he recall Willoughby lashing Munro's horse into flight and the rest of the crew following their leader's headlong retreat into the woods. The rein to which Adam clung tightened and whipped him from the saddle.

His fall burst breath from him. He knew that he hurtled over snow, first on his face and then less painfully on his back. He glimpsed in the white flurry a sled runner, plowing gigantically beside him. Then, just when his arms promised to be wrenched off, the strain upon them slackened and ceased. Still clutching the rein, Adam rolled over.

84

Hoofs were all about him, trampling, slipping. He drew himself into a ball and through the fading din in his ears heard nasal shouting. Hands caught his arms, his collar, hauling him up. A hard palm smote his mouth, another boxed his ears.

Adam's knees buckled but pride, and the men who held him, would not let him fall. He gaped at the horses that stood steaming with lowered heads; at savage faces that swam before him. Men bellowed threats and questions that he did not heed. He was roused by a concerned voice that cried his name, "Mr. Corlaer, in God's name, what finds you here?"

Adam squinted at Justus Sherwood and at last regained his voice.

"I believe," he said with difficulty, "it had to do with payment of a debt."

Adam lay in the Catamount Tavern chamber that once before had been his bedroom and now was his cell. He stared at the candle's still flame and wondered indifferently what his punishment would be. His captors were debating it in the taproom, and from the increasing tumult not overtemperately. Would drink, he asked himself numbly, make his judges more, or less, merciful? He was too bruised and spent to care.

Not even the thought of being hanged could rouse him. The wild men who had taken him had promised him that fate and had deplored loudly the absence of a rope, but they also had sworn to crop his ears, disembowel him, flay him alive, and flog him to death.

It had been Sherwood who had counseled postponement of the prisoner's case, had argued against pursuit of Munro and his fellow fugitives, and finally had prevailed upon the uproarious party to march back to Bennington.

Baker, with his arm in a sling headed the disorderly column. Adam rode, under guard and with his hands tied, at the rear of the sled to which his mount was tethered.

He recalled little of the return journey, so dazed had he been by his fall, but he did remember the rescuers' triumphal return to the settlement. People had swarmed out upon the Green to cheer the grinning horsemen, hoot at their prisoner, and, in the absence of more ignominious missiles, to cast snowballs at him. A few spectators had cried, "Hang him."

Adam doubted, and was vaguely surprised by his apathy, whether he actually would be hanged.

A roar surpassing earlier outbursts welled up from the taproom. Perhaps someone had proposed a specially ingenious penalty.

Acute dismay stirred Adam for the first time, a half hour later, when steps sounded in the upper hall. On fright's heels came pride. Whatever these half-savages had decreed for him, he would not beg for mercy. The door latch stirred. His misused body protested as he sat up on the bed's edge and looked into Sherwood's face with what he hoped was dignified calm.

"I regret the long delay," the intruder smiled, "but Ethan Allen has just returned from Salisbury and nothing would serve but that he hear the whole tale over again from its beginning. Do you prefer this chamber to our company below, Mr. Corlaer?"

"That depends," Adam answered with forced lightness, "what penalty joining the company entails."

"Oh, that!" Sherwood said carelessly. "Naturally there could be none. Baker has defended you, extolling your kindness. And willy-nilly you served our cause by insisting that Munro tarry at Slake's Tavern. Otherwise, though we already were assembled here to meet with Colonel Allen, we might not have overtaken you."

He was amused by the blank look on Adam's face.

"Surely you did not credit angry men's threats. We sow these lavishly in The Grants but they seldom sprout."

Adam passed his palm over his forehead in a dazed gesture.

"There is much that I wish to ask you, yet I find beginning difficult."

"Punch," Sherwood proposed, "might aid us both. By your leave, I shall order a bowl."

When he returned, the other man said slowly, "I should like you to understand how and why I first came to The Grants."

Sherwood listened gravely while the other spoke. Adam omitted nothing save the part Felicity had played in drawing him on to Panton and her act of grace when Baker had exiled him. This was too preciously his and hers to share with another. When he had ended, Sherwood said with satisfaction, "I thank you for your candor, sir. I am not commonly mistaken in my estimate of men."

Joseph Fay bore punch into the room, grinned at Adam, and asked in friendliness, "Wal, how's the mare?"

Sherwood, accepting the bowl, answered, "Still in Panton where I trust he shortly will claim her. Has Seth found Jonas?"

"Not yet, I guess, an' Cap'n is swearin' mad. Colonel's called for paper, ink and quill. He vows he's goin' to put what's happened into the newspapers."

He grinned again and left. Sherwood touched his lips to the bowl, before passing it to Adam.

"Your health, sir."

"And yours," the other replied and drank.

Liquor's soothing heat completed the reconstruction his confession had begun. Despite his abused muscles' protest at every movement, Adam felt clean and new. He asked as carelessly as he might, "Your sister is well?"

"She is. She and Delight are profiting by their sojourn in Quebec."

Sherwood laughed reminiscently.

"I found a pretty kettle of fish when I returned to the Roydens on the evening of your—departure. Delight was weeping and Felicity was in sore distress and both were proclaiming Olin and Remember monsters of iniquity. If The Reverend Hough had not brought his tidings, I think they would have gone in search of you themselves. I have your wallet and its contents with my gear. We are not thieves, whatever Yorkers deem us."

Reaction had filled Adam with fondness for this pleasant gentleman and all mankind.

"When men," he ventured, "are so greatly alike—York and Grants—why must they strive and brawl?"

"Eh?" Sherwood asked. "Well, possibly, Adam—with your permission, sir—because all men unfortunately are much alike."

At last, they bore the emptied bowl downstairs. Baker, seated with the horse-faced Sunderland and others whom Adam recognized as among his late assailants, looked up keenly. He grinned and slowly raised his uninjured hand, palm forward, in the Indian

sign of peace. Adam imitated the gesture while the company guffawed, as though a practical joke had had a pleasant ending.

They made place for the newcomer. It was hard to believe that
these friendly folk had been the raving men of a few hours ago.

"Mr. Corlaer," Baker began loudly, faltered and lamely abandoned his contemplated oratory, "I'm beholden to ye."

"And I to you, sir, from what Justus tells me."

Baker attempted a gesture with his bandaged hand and winced.

"Only made these numbskulls understand what ye done. Dead-
er'n haddock, else, by now, thanks to Munro 'n' his rascals."

"Shall we not all drink," Adam suggested, "to more fortunate
meetings henceforth?"

"A pleasure. By God," Baker pursued, screwing up his face,
"Man as good in the woods as you belongs with Grants folks."

Sunderland offered solemnly, "Remember has a passel of prime
lots in Arlington he'll sell ye cheap."

"B'God, I'll give him a hundred acres if he'll make a pitch
there."

Baker turned as Dr. Jonas Fay entered, followed by the hulking
Warner who called, "Here he is; ran him down at last."

The physician smiled at Adam and then assailed his patient:
"Ruffled and swaggered a little too much, eh, my cock o' the
woods? Now clear away," he bade the others fussily, "and let me
see."

A moment later he said quietly above the opened bandage, "I'll
have to take off part of that thumb, Remember. And no doubt,"
he went on, dodging the sympathy that almost had trapped him,
"you'll squeal like a stuck gilt."

"No doubt," Baker echoed staring at the red ruin of his hand.
"That sword-swingin' scoundrel could 'a' had the hull thumb 'n'
welcome, had he left my fusee. Closest shootin' arm in all the
Grants 'n' he's got her."

Fay opened his bag, chose a scalpel, and stropped it briskly on
his bootleg.

"Joe," he called, "a bowl of water here. No cause for alarm,"
he told his patient. "I shan't make you drink it."

He spilled instruments and some rolls of cloth on the table top
and, after threading a needle, thrust it into his lapel.

"Now," he bade briskly. "More light here and fewer spectators

—saving four strong men to hold this wretch when I commence."

He grinned down at Baker and added in a different tone:

"I'll hurt you as little as I may. Ready?"

"Ehyah."

Fay bent to his work. Adam looked away. Baker said, "Carried that firelock to Ti 'n' St. Frederic. Bided with her fifteen year."

"Steady now," Fay warned. "This won't be pleasant."

"Broke her stock in Sixty-eight," Baker went on, "but I made me a better of a clear piece of walnut with a real nice drop at the grip of her. As leave Munro'd taken my boy, Osri."

Adam saw the calm face go white and glaze with sweat. Warner was breathing like an ox beside him.

"We'll be through the worst of it in a minute," Fay said gently.

"Ethan," Baker announced loudly, "offered me three pound, Bay tender, for her once. Wish I'd agreed. She'd be in better company than she's keeping now."

Fay's red fingers plied the needle.

"Munro," his patient complained, "ain't got a feel for weapons. Look at the mess he made with his goddamn sword. And now he's got my fusee."

The physician was bandaging rapidly. Baker looked from the shining table toward Adam and his gray lips spread in a grin.

"Mr. Corlaer, I seem to recall ye mentioned a drink a while ago."

While the bowl went round, Adam was conscious of an occasional hollow noise, like a bull's distant bellow, issuing from elsewhere in the tavern. When Fay and Warner took Baker firmly between them and led him off to bed, the dismal lowing rose more distinctly in the silence. Sunderland chuckled.

"It is Ethan," he told Adam, "in labor—writing and moaning, moaning and writing. He isn't broken to the pen."

He beckoned furtively to Sherwood and on tiptoe led both men to a closed door at the taproom's far end, where he rapped and called, "Dr. Fay, Colonel. All tell me you are in great pain."

"Now by Satan's off ox," a voice trumpeted within, "this surpasses endurance—"

The door was pulled inward with a bang and Ethan Allen towered and glowered above them.

" 'Tis you, eh, ye woods-running lout. Well, by the Gods of the Mountains," he pursued looking with approval from Sherwood to Adam, "you have brought me in your zany way two men I most desire for counsel and correction."

The fierce blue eyes blinked satisfaction. Allen was stripped to shirt and breeches, as though composition were a physical struggle. There was ink on his fingers and a smudge on his jutting nose. Adam, looking past him, saw that the floor about the candle-lit table where he labored was littered with crumpled sheets of paper. Allen waved him and Sherwood into the room and thrust Sunderland violently out.

" 'Twould addle what brains ye possess to expose them to the converse of educated men. Sit ye, Justus, and you too, young sir. I would know how Oxford schooling judges this simple account by an unlettered person."

He swept together the pages strewn on the table. While he sorted them, Adam again felt that an energy mightier than the man's great bulk fumed within him. Allen thrust toward his visitor a batch of sheets covered with angular, awkward script and leaned back, breathing loudly through his nose as though already he scented acclaim. Adam, bending toward the table candles, read, "This wickid, innhuman, most Barbarious, innfamous crool, villianous, thievish Act was perpertrated and commited and carried into Ecsecution by one John Munro—"

"It may be," the author said with tolerance, "that spelling and periods lack polish but this I shall prevail on you and Justus to supply before I grant the narrative to The Connecticut Courant. Read on."

He wrote as he talked, Adam thought, explosively with massed charges of heterogeneous words.

"Well, sir?" Allen prompted when the reader had finished and had passed the script to Sherwood. The giant was so obviously certain of approval that Adam hesitated, feeling his way:

"A striking account, Colonel, but—"

"Eh? Out with it! But what?"

He would not wish, Adam thought, to face those fierily blue eyes with a greater offense on his conscience. As it was, he faltered, "Is it not a little overcolored? You write of wounded children; there was one small boy and he uninjured. Nor was Mrs.

Baker stabbed as you charge and even Baker himself was used less savagely than this proclaims."

"Now by the hubs of Gehenna," Allen cried, brushing away objections. "Compared to the fashion in which the York gazettes lie about us, this narrative, sir, is the pellucid, crystalline spring of truth itself. I have simply recited in a more polite form what Captain Baker himself has told me."

The indignation that brought color to his rocky face subsided a trifle and a glint of humor came into his eyes.

"Now possibly," he rumbled, "you take offense because mischance you were a member of Munro's skulking, scurvy, knavish, detestable, and altogether hellish crew. By the black wench who married Moses, sir, they miscall me a violent man, yet you outstrip me. Ravishment and profanation pursue you through The Grants like Peleg's hounds on a fox's trail."

"No," Adam returned, still unwilling to utter the intention that was forming within him. "I take no offense. I only doubted whether—"

"You must," Allen informed him emphatically, "fight fire with fire and lies with—well, possibly an overvehement presentation of verity."

He subsided and, while he grumbled and scowled, watched Sherwood narrowly.

"Justus," he exploded when the other had finished, "what say you?"

"Publish," Sherwood counseled. "It is time our grievances were made the public's property."

"Mr. Corlaer," Allen said, cocking a shrewd eye, "does not agree."

Adam summoned all his resolution and tact.

"I have," he began, "suffered considerably at the hands of Grants people who also have shown me mercy and kindness. I should be neutral if any man can be. I wonder whether your cause, sir, is best served by further brawling, bodily or on paper."

He withstood obstinately Allen's vociferous and Sherwood's calmer objections and felt his own face grow red.

"There are better ways," he lurched on, "of settling difficulties. Captain Baker did me injury. I dealt him a greater and he in turn served me more grievously still. Today it was my purpose to requite him and, had we succeeded, he would have been thrust into Albany jail, my enemy for life. Yet lately through a better understanding of each other, we have sat drinking together as companions."

"Now," said Allen with solemn vehemence, "by the Gods of the Mountains and all the wilderness, may Ethan Allen be plumped into the innermost brimstone depths of hell before he drinks or companions with Duane or Kempe or Butchering Billy Tryon."

Adam's intercession was compounded, he reflected wryly, of relief, sympathy, and punch, yet he persevered.

"I expect, sir, that their sentiments reflect your own. I still hold that violence breeds violence whether it be between Captain Baker and me or between Colonel Allen and the leaders of York. Might not," he went on craftily, "a philosopher win peace where a soldier fails?"

The fury that had been gathering in Allen subsided and his face assumed a more benign expression.

"Philosopher!" he repeated. "How, sir?"

Adam was encouraged to see that Sherwood was watching him with new interest.

"I ask you then, Colonel, as a philosopher, what is it chiefly that your people seek?"

Ethan Allen arched his great chest.

"Sir, we desire freedom and safe possession of our own. This people came up out of Egypt, alias Connecticut, to possess land that they lacked below. We hold that a man's property is his, as his wife is his and his children are his, and we further maintain that it must not be the will of a governor but the will of the governed whereby this people shall be ruled."

Sherwood was watching Allen as though he scented offense in the bluster.

"That, young sir," the giant pursued, relishing his words, "is the philosophy of our contention. The Philistines of York oppose us. I tell you"—he struck the table a mighty whack with his palm so that the candles jumped and toppled—"rather than see tyranny prevail, I would retire with my valiant Green Mountain Boys into the desolate fastnesses of these mountains and wage war with humanity at large."

The resounding period pleased him and his harsh face softened.

Sherwood asked, suspicion narrowing his eyes, "Do you mean by 'tyranny' the will of His Majesty?"

"It has been His Majesty's order," Allen retorted so quickly that Adam felt he had anticipated the question, "that the people of The Grants should be left in peace until the king's further will should be made known. I say that when York reaches to take from plain men the land they are aging themselves to subdue, that, Justus, is tyranny."

Sherwood blinked assent. Adam ventured:

"Would you make peace, if York confirmed all settlers' titles?"

Allen gulped and was silent an instant. Then he shook his head with a canny glitter in his eyes.

"Not peace until His Majesty decides. We may gain more from the royal proclamation than mere inclusion with York; perhaps recognition as a separate province."

"A truce," Sherwood advanced thoughtfully, "might bring an end to this rapine and turmoil."

"A truce," Adam amended, "leaving all disputes as they are now, forbidding further aggression by either party until the king's decision is proclaimed."

The colonel glared over his ink-smudged nose with the air of one brought to bay.

"Is not James Duane," he rumbled ominously at last, "your patron?"

"I have no patron, sir. He was my father's associate—and is as bitterly opposed to you as you to him."

"Hah!" Allen clenched his enormous fists. "I shall provide further fodder for that hatred. We will not sit in impotence on our backsides while Duane and Tryon issue more York patents. Young sir, you are more the wet-eared innocent than I suspected."

"Wait," Sherwood objected. "That is not what he proposed. We continue to occupy the land we now hold; York refrains from further aggression. Why should that not be to our advantage?"

"Because," Allen blared, "I have dealt too long with York and York's governors to trust either a single hair's width."

"But," said Adam, "if Tryon makes, then breaks, such a truce, he will stand condemned before the world. And you, Colonel," he pursued with inspiration, "could so proclaim him in another diatribe from your gifted pen."

Allen hesitated, eyes baffled, brows twitching. Sherwood said, "You summoned us here for a Council meeting, Ethan. Why not let the Council decide."

"I am," Adam said hastily, "neither emissary nor messenger, yet if the Council decides to welcome it, I think Governor Tryon might be induced to offer truce."

He looked from the thoughtful Sherwood to the still dubious giant and kept his face rigid against the inner surge of glee. Knowledge that Sherwood would praise his endeavor to Felicity was Adam's chief and unsettling satisfaction.

Chapter X

SHERWOOD on the morrow rode out from Bennington with his friend. The sun, aided by a soft wind, was filling the hollows with snow water and slicking the road with shallow mire.

"I saddled," Sherwood said, "because I was minded to speak with you away from blusterers whose cross-purposes bewilder the fair-minded. Ethan prevailed at the Council because Grants men now follow him blindly. We will not ask for a truce, Adam, but there are enough sound heads and loyal hearts to observe one if Tryon offers it."

His friend looked uncomfortable, facing the mission he rashly had undertaken.

"I have assumed authority that is not mine. After all, I speak only for myself."

"You could not ride on a better errand. There is a feeling in the air I do not like."

The puddles gleamed through the tender haze like fallen bits of sky.

"The day will be fine, I think," Adam said but Sherwood shook his head and pursed his mouth.

"I do not speak of the weather. I fear another storm. Throughout America, men ignore their duty and listen to those who speak infamously. If we can bring just peace to The Grants, it may be that the rebellious elsewhere will take thought."

He drew rein at a hilltop and held out his hand.

"I leave you here. You say you will come north when time serves? I bring Felicity and Delight back from Canada in May and shall begin a house in New Haven. You can be sure of your welcome."

"I should like," Adam stammered, "to recover my mare."

"An excellent reason for the journey," the other said solemnly. "God speed you."

It was late May before Adam rode again across the log bridge and up the hill toward Bennington. Twice he had entered the village fearfully. He looked forward now with abiding glee toward this journey's end. Something beyond satisfaction in his mission's success kept his heart thudding strongly beneath the letter he bore, written and sealed by Tryon's own hand, addressed to the Reverend Jedediah Dewey and proposing a truce.

That missive was no small warrant for pride, since so much of patience, tact, and persuasion had been required of Adam to obtain it. Duane, he reflected, letting his horse choose its own pace through the shining spring weather, had been more difficult to deal with than the governor himself.

Duane had been by turn icily polite, tautly suspicious, and explosively furious. He had heard that Adam had been about to be hanged and apparently regretted the execution's miscarriage. Munro had written his principal a dolorous letter describing the failure of the abduction and adding that he himself had been assailed in Shaftsbury by Seth Warner who had snatched Munro's firelock from him and, when he had objected, had clouted him over the head with a sword. When Adam had hazarded, grinning, that the musket probably was Remember Baker's, Duane had made a sudden, tormented gesture.

"How do I know whose musket it was?" he had bawled. "Five hundred muskets of a regular regiment should be marching into The Grants, this very day."

It had been hard to soothe the aggrieved man. It had been more difficult still to convince him of the wisdom of a truce.

"They'll never honor it," he had snorted. "The scoundrels will agree—and then betray their solemn pledge."

Adam had broken his opposition by using the stratagem he had employed against Ethan Allen, "Then, sir, York would stand justified and they convicted before the world."

With Duane as his sponsor, Adam's interview with Tryon, a solid, red man with angry gray eyes, had been briefer and calmer, though the governor, too, had raged against Allen, Warner, Baker, and Cochran.

"I'll not deal with them," he had sworn, "save by rope. Have these heathen no minister among them? Jedediah Dewey? Lord, what barbaric names flourish in that wilderness!"

There had been days of waiting before the letter to the parson had been forthcoming, but now and at last Adam was bearing it the final mile toward its destination. Bennington, set down among the tender greens of unfurling leaves, seemed uncommonly fair to his eager eyes.

The excitement that robbed him of half his breath and set his heart to shaking him was due only indirectly to his mission's near completion. It was what lay past it that greatly roused him.

Beyond Fay's tavern where he would lie that night, benign hills and the healing dusk of endless forest waited; swift brooks, a great, grave silence, and a road that ran north.

He delivered Tryon's letter before stopping at the inn. The minister, lantern-jawed and taciturn, broke the seal, read the message, and then dismissed Adam with no further comment than austere thanks.

A dozen horses were tethered to the tavern rack when he tied his own. He entered the hostelry with the feeling that he was committed at last to a long delayed quest. There was further cheer in the greeting he received.

Steven Fay came forward with a grin that almost hid his eyes in surrounding wrinkles. Joseph cried, "Hey!," clapped Adam on the shoulder, and, without bidding, went forth to tend his horse. Men about a table were so intent on sacks in which they stowed provisions that it was a long instant before one of them looked up and whooped.

"B'God," Remember Baker cried, advancing. "'Tis the accursed Yorker again! Adam, how be ye?"

"Well," the newcomer said through a tight throat. Sunderland and Warner came forward to pound his back and exchange unflattering comments on his appearance. Adam had not known such unfeigned warmth since his father's death.

The trio beamed upon him. Baker waved his mutilated hand.

"Good's new," he boasted. "Practic'ly. Got m' fusee back, too."

97

"Through the intervention of Mr. Warner," Adam supplied. "I heard of that even in New York town."

"Poultney freemen, they voted Seth a hundred acres for cloutin' Munro," Sunderland drawled. "If squire wa'n't so thick of skull, might of got a hull section for splittin' it."

"I think," Warner said, his blunt face reddening, "this calls for a bowl of punch."

He led Adam to the table where young men nodded shyly as he named them and went on lashing the food sacks into compact parcels.

"Where ye bound to?" Baker demanded. "Panton, eh? When?"

"As soon as may be," Adam replied. He purposely withheld mention of the governor's letter, having no wish to mar his welcome by dispute. The responsibility now was Dewey's and happily out of his own hands.

"Health," Warner said, touching the bowl with his lips and passing it to Adam. While the other drank, the big man muttered briefly to Baker who nodded and cleared his throat.

"Wal, we're ridin' north ourselves."

"To Panton?"

"Beyond. We've a mite of viewin' to do."

Adam looked at him helplessly. Baker grinned and interpreted with military formality, "Sir, a detail of Colonel Allen's regiment, Captains Baker and Warner commandin', is to scout the Onion River country to capture and punish that damn blackleg, Billy Cockburn, who is runnin' a York survey there. In haste to git to Panton?"

"I am," Adam said with warmth.

"Wal, then, if ye're put together stout enough, ride with us. No one'll git ye there faster."

Baker drank deeply as the circling bowl reached him and then explained: They would travel light and in haste and, with his own knowledge of the land to guide them, would ride cross country. It was Adam's instinct to accept. He longed for speed, and the prospect of fulfilling his pledge to Felicity in the friendly company of the man who had driven him from Panton had a pleasing drama, but he shook his head reluctantly.

Baker demanded whether his New York debauch completely had rotted him. Adam pointed out that his horse already had done

98

a day's traveling and could not be expected to keep pace with fresh animals. Baker grinned that he had an extra horse and professed the belief that Adam was hanging back because he was too high-stomached to subsist on pork and Injun while traveling daily from Can to Can't—from dawn to dusk.

Adam, a half hour later, mounted a Roman-nosed roan, wiry and small like all Grants horses, and rode out from Bennington with the detachment of Green Mountain Boys chosen to repel fresh York aggression.

His bizarre rôle did not trouble him greatly. The fact that this company would bring him sooner to Felicity pushed considerations of propriety into the back of his mind and, when they did intrude, he assured himself that he would have left the little column long before it reached the site of Cockburn's reported trespass. Duane had not mentioned that his surveyor was in The Grants. Surely, Duane would recall him now.

Adam found pleasanter occupation in admiring the skill with which the little column traversed the wilderness. Only small particles of sunlight penetrated the woods, now that trees were in leaf, and the horsemen moved like more substantial shadows over the deep loam, enduring in silence the persecution of the swarming flies, following Baker single file across hill and hollow and through successive brooks until, as twilight turned into night, they halted, built a fire, ate mush and pork, and rolled into their blankets.

Adam was stiff when he was roused at dawn to a breakfast identical to supper, and stiffer still when, fifteen hours later, he unsaddled to gulp a like repast. Secretly, he was satisfied to see that others were as spent as he. He was certain the dolorous look on Sunderland's long face did not conceal amusement and was pleased to hear Warner groan as he lay down.

Baker had not spared his followers. Adam's respect for Ethan Allen's men grew steadily. The dingy riders were alertly obedient and competent, quick to execute Warner's or Baker's soft-spoken orders, swift in making and breaking camp, tireless and uncomplaining.

Adam, on slumber's verge, watched sparks from the crumbling fire swarm up like bees and wished amusedly that Duane and

Tryon, for their own enlightenment, might have ridden on this foray with these "rioters." He doubted, considering his own abused body, whether either would have survived till now. He had been amused and reluctantly impressed by Allen, the posturing demagogue. Now he accorded new deference to the man who had raised and trained The Green Mountain Boys.

It was midafternoon of the journey's second day when they rode out of the forest gloom into the dazzling sunlight of a clearing. It was not until Warner had said soberly to Baker, "My congratulations, Captain," that Adam, squinting, discovered where they were.

"Bull's-eye, as usual," Sunderland muttered behind him and grinned.

Baker said in a dry voice:

"Been runnin' these woods quite a spell," and led them toward the Royden house that stood with its ell completed.

Excitement snatched Adam's breath and started a singing in his ears. His heart turned over as a girl appeared on the doorstep with a shielding hand above her eyes, but it was Delight, grown taller. The child ran into the house. As Baker threw up his hand to halt his little command, she reappeared and others came pouring from the dwelling—Mindwell Royden, Olin, Sherwood, and then Felicity.

She was, Adam told himself reverently, lovelier than he had thought. It was fitting that sunlight should surround her. She looked toward him. His stiff face returned her smile.

Then, as the first dazzling joy abated, he found himself reaching for an anticipated quality in this moment that, dismayingly, was not there. The scene that he had pictured so often was running askew.

Felicity had turned and was watching Sherwood who had stepped forward to speak with Baker and Warner. Olin after a grim glance at Adam, moved to join them. Only Delight's grave, friendly face was turned toward Adam now. He pressed his horse forward and heard Baker ask quickly, "How many of them?"

"A dozen," Sherwood replied, acknowledging Adam's presence by a brief smile and nod. "They say Colonel Reid is sending more."

Mindwell Royden said in a low voice, "Hold they've come to stay, this time; claim we'll move or be drove out."

Delight's hands laid tight hold upon each other. The gesture's quiet intensity lodged in Adam's mind. Olin hefted his firelock.

"Glad," he told Baker, "you've come."

"Hah! More'n they'll be, I mistrust."

Baker's eyes moved over Adam to the weary horses and sagging riders and then squinted at the sky. Sherwood was answering Warner's question.

"They came downlake in a bateau and landed this morning. I'd heard that Reid was planning to resettle. They're camped by the sawmill."

"They'll go back the way they came, I guess," Warner hazarded. Baker nodded approval and twisted about in the saddle to address his travel-worn followers, "Mite of viewing still ahead today, boys. Colonel Reid's tryin' to take over again. Leave all your gear but your firelocks. You ridin' with us?"

He addressed Sherwood. Olin already was running toward the barn. The other turned to follow, checked himself, and approached Adam.

"This is a sorry welcome," he said in haste, "but there's trouble. Reid, as you may know, claims Panton under a military patent and has moved in on us again. A persistent man. Tell me, Adam: Has a truce been established?"

He listened with a frown to the other's brief report and shrugged.

"Lacking sure knowledge, we must act. I pray this may be the last violence in The Grants."

All about them, dismounted men were unlashing blankets and food bags from their saddles. Before the door, Mindwell, Delight, and Felicity watched.

Sherwood sighed, patted his friend's thigh and turned away as Olin led two horses from the barn. Adam sat irresolute, uncertain—in the distortion of this long-sought reunion—what to do. The looming strife was not his concern, yet surely it would be shameful for him to desert Baker and Warner and their followers now.

Olin spoke to Felicity in a low voice. She smiled as he swung up into the saddle. Baker bade his followers, "Mount." Through the scuffle and the squeak of leather, Olin spoke again, more distinctly. He addressed Baker but his eyes were on Adam.

"Is this—gentleman to ride with us?"

There was humor in Baker's squinting regard.

"Ride or not," the leader said, "jest as he's a mind."

Adam looked from Olin's dark, hostile face to the girl's and felt compulsion snatch him up. It was impossible that he remain here while others went forth to protect Felicity and Mindwell and Delight. He gathered up his reins and said to Baker, "I have a mind to ride."

They passed from the clearing's brilliance into the twilight of the forest, with Baker at the company's head, Warner following, and the others moving behind them in single file. Qualms that had quickened in Adam immediately he had committed himself gradually were melting in excitement. He wondered, looking along the carefully advancing line of men on small, sure-footed horses, what Duane's comment would be were he at this instant to acquire second sight. The thought disturbed him but he told himself defiantly that he was now a free agent. Thereafter, he let the zest of the hunt possess him.

Deer moved no more stealthily. Once, Adam's mount clinked a shoe against a half-hidden ledge and he knew, by the faces instantly turned toward him, the gravity of his offense. The line slanted downhill and found more level ground. Water spoke close at hand and Adam caught glimpses of a river flowing between pale, flood-scoured boulders.

Below the immediate, light noise of the rapids, a deeper sound intruded and grew as they rode on.

"Otter falls," Sunderland turned to mutter. "Gittin' close."

His equine face was sad but his eyes sparkled. Only the wisdom of Adam's horse averted collision as the column suddenly halted. Baker rode back half its length and then spoke in a low voice that carried clearly.

"Orders. Heed 'em. Form line at the woods' edge 'n' jump 'em at the signal. Cap'n Warner, Sunderland, Sherwood, Royden, Clark, Whittaker, take care of the mill. Rest'll herd them that's outside. Quiet 'n' quick. See your firelocks ain't cocked. Shootin' " —with a brief grin—"is likely to make trouble."

He rode back. The column moved on. Ahead, Adam could see sunlight through the thinning trees and horsemen filing off to the right. He marked in the distance the shining water of a pond and, beyond it, an ungainly, weather-stained mill. Men moved about it. Smoke climbed across the bright west. The sound of the falls was mixed with the tumult in Adam's ears. His mouth was dry. The riders before and behind him halted, facing the forest edge. He turned his own horse.

The wolf howl rose, sad and clear in the stillness. The horsemen rode unevenly from the forest with the clash of scrub and the long roll of hoofs. The weary roan accompanied his lunging gallop with protesting grunts.

Low sunlight blinded Adam's eyes. When he saw clearly again, it was with a sense of anticlimax. Others, outdistancing him, were drawing rein before the mill. The rest were halting to form a half circle about a huddle of men and three ash-pale women. Baker, as Adam rode up, was saying harshly to the gaping faces, "Speak English, don't ye? Who's leader here?"

A red-haired man whose freckles stood out on his white, Caledonian face, gagged, gasped, and said at last with a Highland burr, "I am Colonel Reid's agent, if 'tis that ye mean. Mr. Colin Brodie, at"—he added unconvincingly—"yer sairvice."

Baker cocked a sandy eyebrow.

"The very man we come to see. We've a message to send to Colonel Reid by Mr. Colin Brodie, his agent. Ye'll bear it to him at once, sir, taking this rabble with ye."

Warner called from a window in the upper floor of the mill: "None within but one Donald MacIntosh."

"Bring him out," Baker ordered, "for Donald MacIntosh is about to leave us, too."

He turned again to Brodie whose little flock pressed close together as though contact might lessen the menace of the solemn horsemen.

"Mr. Colin Brodie, tell Colonel Reid this: Panton is Grants' property till hell has frosty mornings. Tell him further, damn his stubborn, stiff-necked Scottish soul, he's to send no more skulking, scurvy trespassers into this town. Understand, Mr. Colin Brodie?"

"Aye," the red-haired man said at last.

"And tell him this, too," Baker went on, patting his musket

butt with a most uninfectious grin, "that the next people he sends hither we'll welcome to the land in a fashion of our own. We'll divest them of thumbs and toes, crop their ears, roast them Injun fashion over slow fires, and add them to our soil in pieces no larger than that."

One women clapped her hands to her mouth. The others muttered quavering moans.

"It is plain," Baker condoned, "ye're furrin folk that Reid has gulled, so ye can go in peace to tell others what fate waits 'em here. Ye'll depart instanter, and"—as Sherwood and Warner emerged from the mill with a dusty captive between them—"this loon'll accompany ye."

"Sir," MacIntosh gulped, assuming an ill-fitting indignation, "ye can't evict me without cause. Olin Royden'll tell ye—"

"That ye've been a moderate man and a good sawyer. That's why we dismiss you without the beech seal on your back. This is a Grants-built mill. Ye're York, MacIntosh, and a tool of Reid. We're cleansing Panton town of all your like."

Adam watched the eviction from the mill platform. The burdened men were mute under the musket muzzles of Baker's followers who escorted them down to the sluggish river below the falls, but the women wailed in hair-stirring Highland cadences.

The bateau lurched as they swarmed aboard with headlong haste. Low sunlight dimpled in the wake and flashed from unevenly plied oars as the craft wallowed slowly downstream.

The women still keened. At Adam's shoulder, Sunderland spoke:

"Redded that up nice and tidy, eh? Ethan, I mistrust, woulda done it different, but no better."

Chapter XI

IN TORPOR, midway between sleep and waking, Adam heard a thrush's chiming. He was content to lie, still drenched by slumber, while the dawn breeze shook the maples and footsteps went softly past the window and the voice of the thrush called up the daylight.

His mind, reviving, told him where he lay. He was willing to linger for a space on the threshold of the brightness and the promise before him. At last he opened his eyes, closed them quickly against the room's brilliance, and, while his body roused, recalled dreamily his return last night from Otter falls—the dry satisfaction of Baker and his followers, Mindwell Royden's relief and restored friendliness, the enormous meal she had served them all.

Weariness and possibly the strength of Royden cider blurred his recollection, but he did remember the Boys' scramble for lodging in barn and stable and Sherwood's mirth when Adam had dozed off while tugging at a boot and had toppled from the bed's edge. There had been ample justification for his collapse. Sherwood had not ridden all the way from Bennington with Baker's raiders. Justus had risen but the silence indicated that these tough horsemen were still asleep.

Distant laughter, clearer and more reviving than the thrush's call, brought Adam completely awake. If Felicity already were about, then it was past time that he were out of bed. Yet he lay for one more luxurious moment, while anticipation ran through his body, to taste the complete flavor of this new day to be spent in her presence.

He had seen her only casually last night, as he had glimpsed Delight and Mindwell. Her slender hand had clasped his briefly. The vivid loveliness of her face had tied his tongue so that he had stumbled through response to her greeting. He had had no further chance to speak with her for the grave, lank horsemen had pressed about her and she had been greatly occupied in helping to feed them. Olin Royden, too, had followed at her heels like a vigilant dog. This morning, when Baker had led his followers away—

Suddenly, the enduring stillness took on a new significance. Adam sat up and blinked at the window where glass had replaced the original oiled paper. He swung himself from bed and overset a chair in his haste. Beyond the small panes, the dooryard lay, trampled and empty. He had slept through the detail's departure.

Adam cursed himself, as he gathered up his clothes, for a sluggard, content to lie inert while moments that he might have spent with Felicity sped. He hauled at his boots with defamatory mutterings and looked up at Sherwood who, entering silently, was closing the door behind him. His presence and the toil-soiled tow-cloth frock and leather breeches he wore leveled at Adam additional mute reproach.

"Captain Baker," Sherwood said in mild derision, "left you sundry affronting messages before he rode away. I come at Mindwell's request to find if there is any use keeping breakfast for you."

Adam's abused muscles objected as he stood. He retorted:

"Had you followed Captain Baker as long and as far as I, I doubt whether you would rise before supper time."

Sherwood laughed and sat down on the edge of the bed.

"Olin and I are about to ride over to my pitch in New Haven, but I wished greatly to speak with you privately first. You were too spent last night. Tell me more of the truce, Adam."

He listened intently to the narrative and, when it was ended, nodded approval.

"It is possible, my friend, that you have done The Grants a greater service than Allen and Baker and all their uproarious associates. I only wish," he added tentatively, "that you had tarried to determine how Tryon's offer was received."

"I was in haste," Adam stammered, "and Remember urged me to ride with him."

"Yes," the other acknowledged with a disquieting lack of expression, "I know."

He locked calloused hands about his knee and regarded the other with kindly eyes as he pursued, "I should be the last to decry your presence here. It is good to have a friend with whom one can talk without reserve. Loyalists, Adam, are becoming in this land increasingly lonely folk."

While the other weighed the impulse to explain his own imperfect allegiance, Sherwood shrugged off momentary gloom and spoke more briskly:

"If a truce is coming—and I pray that it may under the terms proposed—we have rid Panton of Reid's crew none too soon. I doubt, though, whether you were wise to share in that foray. It will scarcely recommend you as a negotiator henceforth."

"I have no desire to be one. I have made my effort."

Mirth pinched Sherwood's eyelids.

"I am learning not to be surprised at monstrous happenings in The Grants, yet I did marvel yesterday at the York owner of this very lot conniving in the eviction of Yorkers from Panton."

Adam grinned sheepishly.

"It seemed logical at the moment. I trust I have reassured the Roydens."

"You have only bewildered Olin, but Mindwell is much comforted. You will find yourself wecome here, particularly since" —amusement narrowed his eyes again—"Mindwell burned the deed Olin took from you. She believes that extinguishes your title. I have not enlightened her. These are a simple people, Adam."

"Good people, I think."

Sherwood nodded.

"I know no better, save for this mounting inclination among them for what they call 'liberty' and true men, 'treason.' "

He sighed. Again, Adam held his peace as his friend rose.

"My house grows," Sherwood said, "thanks to the aid of Olin. We shall wait for you if you care to ride over with us."

He heard Adam's specious excuses with the same disturbingly blank look and said with ponderous gravity, "By all means, rest today. Possibly you will have recruited yourself sufficiently to accompany us on the morrow."

With a hand on the doorlatch, he paused and added over his shoulder in an impersonal tone, "It is odd that Felicity who frequently goes with us seems to have a like need for rest."

The throbbing fullness in Adam's throat vanished when he

entered the kitchen and found Mindwell alone. The woman's greeting was brisk and brief, but he knew that the lavish breakfast she set before him was implicit apology for her late antagonism and possibly, Adam considered with secret amusement, a partial recompense for her destruction of his deed.

While he ate, he listened less to her succinct comments on the eviction of Reid's people than for sounds that would betray Felicity's presence, but the house was disconcertingly still. When he had finished breakfast, he postponed search for her and, instead, begged hot water from his hostess.

Adam had shaved and cleansed as well as he might his travel-stained clothing before he ventured with specious aimlessness out into the yard. It was empty.

He was angered yet amused by his wrath. He tried to read a favorable portent in Felicity's absence. Could it be that the same impulse that drove him to seek her had urged the girl to avoid immediate meeting?

He walked toward the stable with enforced deliberation, blind to splendor the sun spread over the intense green of young wheat and the small, spaced sword-blades of the corn.

Allegra whickered while he hesitated beside the stable's open door. As he went toward her, Delight's small voice spoke from the stall.

"Lord, child," he asked, startled, "what are you doing there?"

"Grooming her," Delight replied and added in haste, "I like to."

She looked at Adam across the mare's withers. Beneath the kerchief close bound about the pale hair, her face was shy, yet her gray eyes were steady. He considered her more carefully than he had in last night's confusion.

Delight was not only taller than when first Adam had ridden to Panton but he found new softness about the wistful mouth, a more delicate remolding to her cheekbones and straight, small nose. The enduring silence made him look in haste from her to the animal between them. Even in the gloom, the mare's coat shone.

"You have kept her well," Adam offered.

"I—like to," she repeated and bent abruptly to her work. Her shyness was infectious. He asked, with an awkward reaching for ease, "Did the stars help?"

The question sounded inane but Delight answered at once:

"A little." Schooling was wiping the nasal twang from her voice. "I was homesick for a spell—I mean, a while—but I liked it in Quebec, mostly."

"Do you wish to go again?"

"I guess so, if Felicity does, too, and I guess she will."

"And where," he asked as lightly as possible, "is Felicity?"

"She was writing in our chamber to the Skene girls. We are to visit them this summer."

"Oh?"

Her eyes met his. After a pause, Delight bent to her grooming again. Adam with a queer sense of thwarting walked from the barn. His wonder over a child's power to disturb him vanished as he saw Felicity come toward him. Her clear voice turned his knees to water and perversely parched his throat.

"Good morning," the girl cried, "Sir Slugabed."

The hand she offered had an ink-stained forefinger. He floundered in a welter of the unutterable and produced lamely:

"Sloth, this time, has great reward."

She smiled with a new self-possession.

"I thought that you had ridden to New Haven."

"No," he told her through a tight throat. "My mission ended when I saw you again. I promised you I should return. I was asking Delight where you were."

They walked slowly down the lane between the crooked roots of the stump fences. Adam ignored the pestering small flies. Felicity fanned them away daintily with her handkerchief and asked:

"Did Delight thank you for your gift?"

"Gift?" he repeated in honest bewilderment. "Oh! I had forgotten."

"Sheer pretense," the girl scoffed and wrinkled her nose.

"It is easy to forget everything else when I am with you. But the child was not to know who sent her the presents."

"I keep my promises, too," she said serenely. "I have not told her, yet I'm certain she knows."

The yoke of Felicity's short gown revealed the faint shadow

between her young breasts. Surely, she must hear the loud thudding of his heart; must feel the heat that enveloped him.

"She is an odd child," the girl offered at last. "Delight never may thank you, yet your gift has meant much to her. It will enable her to go with me to Skenesborough, this summer. She needs polite society. Are you acquainted with the Skenes?"

"I have passed through their manor."

He did not tell her that he had seen Major Skene's great stone house at the head of Champlain only from a distance on the day when, frowzy and soiled, he had landed from John Strong's bateau and, well-nigh penniless, had persuaded a teamster to carry him toward the Hudson.

"His daughters," said Felicity, brushing her nose with her handkerchief, "were at Madame Dufresne's. The Major's sloop is to come this summer for Delight and me. She will be additionally grateful to you then for your gift, though she may not say so. Pioneer folk are not lavish of speech."

"I myself," he blurted, "find at present that words are vain."

Her glance took his breath away. She laughed.

"In Quebec, I assure you, none are reluctant to turn a poor maid's head with flattery. La, Mr. Corlaer, I have learned much since last I saw you."

"I thought," Adam said, jealously stiffening him, "Madame Dufresne was more careful of her charges."

He could see that he amused her.

"My dear sir, Quebec is not Panton town. Captain Delaplace of the garrison is my brother's acquaintance and his wife has been kind to us. Delight and I were often at their quarters. This winter," she pursued, mischievously observing his rigid face, "I am to be presented to Governor Carleton at the New Year's ball. I am not the simple peasant you met last year."

The new deftness became her, yet it was disturbing to know that while she had reigned in his mind, other men had entered hers. Her light speech made his reply sound ponderous.

"I have never ceased to think of 'the simple peasant' who saved my life."

He managed to smile into the upturned face with its arched, inquiring eyebrows.

"Saved your life? I? How?"

"Did you not, just now, charge me with pretense? I have carried this with me ever since that shameful day."

He drew the flint and steel from his pocket and held it upon his palm.

"It has been my talisman. It never has left me since the moment I discovered it with the food you had secreted in my cloak. And, like Delight, I find gratitude hard to utter."

They had reached the lane's end and the forest loomed over them. Felicity turned, seemed about to speak, and looked from Adam to the mechanism he held. At last she asked in an odd voice, "It saved your life?"

"Insured it; gave me the courage to go on."

"How strange!" she said slowly.

He felt passion threaten to sweep him away. He knew Felicity, walking demurely beside him, waited for him to speak. Adam drew breath and laid a firmer hold upon propriety. When the moment came, it must be bright and unsullied by presumption. Before he declared himself, Sherwood must be consulted.

"Is it strange," he asked carefully, lest her expectant air lead him to say more, "that I have kept this by me? Is it strange that the life you saved is dedicated to your welfare? Will you remember me always as your grateful servant?"

They saw Delight issue from the stable, hesitate and then come toward them. Felicity's laugh was clear and blithe.

"Did you not lately proclaim yourself tongue-tied? La, Mr. Corlaer, the officers in Quebec might take lessons from you."

Delight, apparently overcome with shyness, had turned and was hastening toward the house. Felicity said in a graver voice, "Justus says that you have worked to bring peace to The Grants? Pray, tell me what you have done."

As they strolled to the dwelling, he told her, with the happy feeling that he laid gifts at her feet.

Olin and Sherwood returned early from New Haven that evening. In the presence of the silent young man, Adam was conscious of his dubious standing in the Royden household and, unbidden, went out to aid with the evening chores.

None of Olin's late enmity was visible now. His deep-set, brown eyes met Adam's calmly and his address was level and impersonal.

He had wrapped himself in the impassivity that normally hid his breed's most extreme feelings and it was not until milking was over that he briefly revealed them.

"Justus," he said, pulling out the words with obvious effort, "holds we were mistaken about you. Remember says so, too. Maybe they're right."

There was little warmth in the admission. Adam returned tritely, "Mistakes do happen."

"Ehyah."

Olin set down the milk pails and lingered.

"I am to wed Felicity Sherwood."

It was a statement, not a challenge. Adam asked when he recovered breath:

"You are betrothed?"

"No," Olin replied calmly, "but we will be, soon or late."

"A—praiseworthy ambition."

"Wanted you should know," the other replied, picked up the pails, and went away.

Sherwood, while he and Adam undressed that night, paused, cleared his throat, and asked abruptly, "Will you come to my pitch tomorrow with Olin and me?"

He endured his friend's stare with dry amusement.

"Otherwise, the work will progress slowly, since Olin vows he will not go again without you. I do not believe," he added, as Adam groped for a reply, "that it is a simple craving for your companionship that moves him."

Adam stammered, with the other's amused eyes still upon him:

"He warned me this evening—perhaps 'warn' is not the exact word—of his devotion to your sister."

"Yes, I know. If you'll come to my pitch with us each day, life will be simpler for us all."

Adam said, standing stiff and straight, "It is only honorable that I tell you what you may have surmised. Have I your permission to—?"

Sherwood's raised hand halted him.

"I beg you, Adam; not now."

He acknowledged the other's dismay with a harried smile.

"It is not entirely enviable to be Felicity's brother and guardian, too; responsible for her welfare. She is young, innocent, easily swayed. Wait till she has learned more of the world and her own mind."

He searched Adam's face for some hint of understanding.

"A year is a brief time. Will you wait that long before you speak to her? If you ask my permission now, I must give you the answer I have already returned to Olin, and I do not wish to say No to you, Adam."

His appealing eyes shamed the other who said gruffly:

"Would you prefer that I leave? Indeed, I should. I have no right to impose myself upon the Roydens."

"If you stay, it will vastly please Mindwell, who misjudged you, and it will be well for you to learn to know all these people better. As for me, I should be glad to have another pair of hands daily at New Haven."

Chapter XII

THE best part of a fly-ravaged acre on Sherwood's New Haven property had been cleared. Useless trees had been burned and stumps had been grubbed from a space about the house-to-be. The dry stonework of the cellar walls had been laid and the foundation stood ready for the sills. All this, the owner pointed out to Adam the following morning and indicated with quiet pride the two newly squared timbers that waited placing, the straight oak logs still to be shaped, and the pile of sawed lumber, drawn from the Otter Creek mill.

"Most of it," Sherwood said, "has been Olin's doing. So far, it is by right his house more than mine."

"Barring," Olin amended with a crinkling at his eyes' corners, "that Justus, when we traded, bought my labor along with the lot."

It was the first speech he had aimed directly at Adam since they had set out at daybreak from the Royden home, though some of his curt rigidity had vanished during the ride. He had grinned once or twice at his companions' talk and had pointed Sherwood's statements with dry comment. Now, the glaze of hostility had vanished from his eyes. He might be, Adam admitted, an engaging companion if there were no rivalry between them.

He wondered again, as he picketed and unsaddled his mare, at the extremities of pioneer nature. The decorous, innately friendly people of The Grants were chary of emotion as they were of other outlay. They hoarded their passions, but, when circumstance compelled expenditure, they were as profligately violent as any Mohawk.

Olin had stripped off his leather jerkin and had rolled back his sleeves. Now he picked up an adze, straddled a prostrate log, and squinted down its length before he swung. Bark crumbled and shavings curled away from the square blade. He worked with a loose-jointed ease that Adam recognized for skill. Sherwood again called attention to the already finished timbers.

"Four-square and hewn solely by eye. None in The Grants could do better."

Olin looked up and for the first time laughed.

"Teach either of you," he offered. "Easy enough, providing you'll begin, like me, at ten years old."

Adam, removing his coat, blocked future criticism by confession.

"I shall have to be taught far simpler things. You'll find I am a complete ignoramus."

Olin replied to the world at large.

"Man that Remember holds is good in the woods can't rightly say that about himself," and Adam, with a twinge of dismay, found himself almost liking his adversary.

Each day, as the westering sun bade them saddle to go home, they had brought the house another small step toward still far-off completion. Each morning, Adam, riding back to the clearing with Sherwood and Olin, resented less the toil he accomplished for the privilege of spending with the rest of the household a few hours in the company of Felicity. By Sherwood's design or by circumstance, he had no further opportunity to see the girl alone. He was too tired each evening to be more than faintly irked by the barrier between them.

It was satisfaction at supper and during the brief ensuing time before bed to watch and hear her. In the talk that prevailed, before the hearth fire crumbled and ashes were raked over it to preserve the embers till morning, Adam learned, piecemeal, more of Felicity's winter in Quebec—the friends she had made, the fetes the not too rigid rules of the school had permitted her to attend. He laid a miserly hold upon these small fragments of her life.

Twice, the girl yielded to her brother's persuasion and, bringing out the guitar she had brought from Canada, sang French songs to the silent company in a voice as soft and sweet as rain. She was gay and equally friendly with Olin and Adam and her fairness was not lessened by the presence of the solid, earthy Mindwell or the woman's shy, coltish daughter, who watched Felicity with adoration Adam dared not display. He might have been able to endure less patiently the impartiality his beloved accorded him and his rival if he had not seen sometimes in her glance a warmth that roused his heart.

Meanwhile, he was settling himself into the eternally toilsome life of a pioneer household where each element in the whole was dependent upon and responsible to all others. He no longer lay late but rose with Sherwood to aid in the morning chores and, on their nightly return from New Haven, helped in the daylight remaining with farm tasks that had been beyond women's strength or skill.

Sherwood spoke admiringly of his friend's increasing dexterity and Adam found himself looking upon his labor less as an ordeal than as romance since he was helping to create Felicity's own home. This made toil easier, yet it kept Olin and him from intimacy. No open conflict, no visible trace of friction marred their association but Adam knew heat still lurked beneath surface courtesy, as coals in the Royden fireplace held through the night beneath their white coverlid of ashes.

Mindwell, Felicity, and Delight accompanied the builders to New Haven on the festal day when the house frame was raised. Other Panton settlers came also to help manhandle the already mortised and tenoned wall timbers and to peg them into place. They labored for no other immediate pay than the food the Roydens had prepared and the rum, plentifully supplied by Sherwood, yet he, by frontier custom, was indebting himself to his neighbors for equivalent work in their own time of need.

The task was finished by late afternoon and Joe Pangborn, a stout, lively man, was moved by tradition and sundry visits to the rum keg, to mount the newly placed ridgepole and perilously dance its length. Adam realized, as Pangborn climbed down, that, standing with Felicity and Olin, he had joined them in laughter and applause as though no hidden strictures kept them apart.

The brief ease had evaporated before they reached the Royden clearing. Olin rode beside Felicity and Adam, following, wondered wretchedly what his low voice spoke that roused her laughter.

Sherwood left before daylight the next morning to help Zadok

Everest's ox team draw more lumber and Adam and Olin returned alone to the clearing. A gray sky that promised rain filled the forest with watery green twilight and the north wind was raw.

When they paused at noon to eat the cornbread and pork Mindwell had provided, gusts struck their sweating bodies and made them flinch. Olin lifted the rum keg and rocked it hopefully. Faint splashing sounds rewarded him and he grinned at Adam, picked up the iron kettle that held their drinking water, and set it down again to rummage in his clothing and curse.

"I had thought," he said ruefully, "that hot rum would fortify us, but we lack fire and I the means to make it."

"I have flint and steel," Adam told him.

"Prime!" the other exclaimed and proceeded to knock the bung from the keg.

When he approached, Adam had knelt and was blowing upon the pile of shavings he had collected. He heard Olin, standing above him, ask:

"How came you by that?"

He nodded toward the firemaking lock and trigger. Adam, looking up at the inquisitive face, found affront in the question. He picked up the device and stowed it away so hastily that Olin's brows twitched.

"Pa," he said, "made such a contraption for my mother. I have never seen its like. Let me look at yours."

His bidding was more command than plea. Adam felt a long-banked fire begin to stir and crackle. He got slowly to his feet.

"No. It is a keepsake and specially dear to me."

Olin scowled.

"You are a lout, so to answer a civil request."

Adam looked from the outstretched hand to the hostile face and with unscrupulous relief let go of his temper.

" 'Lout,' " he told the other precisely, "is the term a lout might use."

Olin's face was dark and swollen.

"Perhaps," he blurted, " 'thief' were better."

"Far better," said Adam cheerily, "since that leaves me only one course?"

"Indeed?" the other mocked. "And what may that course be, Mr. Turncoat Corlaer?"

"This," Adam replied, and slapped him across the mouth. Olin uttered a gleeful, grunting sound and leaped.

Adam had thought himself prepared, but he had misjudged the strength and quickness of the assault. He reeled as Olin's body struck his. Before he could recover, thick hungry arms were about him, heaving, wrenching.

Cannily, Adam let Olin thrash and tug. Rage had cleared his own mind. This was the moment of long-delayed requital. Olin's wrath made him clumsy. Adam, as they staggered back and forth with whimpers and quick gaspings, was alertly merciless.

He twisted one arm free and brought the heel of his palm up under the other's nose. Olin snorted, dodged, and for an instant slackened his grip. Adam, turning quickly, found the leverage he had sought. Compunction had shriveled in the heat of rage. All his strength was in the twist whereby he got his body beneath his enemy's, surged, heaved, and flung him.

Olin went down, headfirst among the strewn chips and Adam, staggering backward from the violence of his effort, caught his heel upon a log. In the instant of triumph, he felt himself falling. Fire blazed in his head and, vanishing, left blackness.

Something locked in Adam's skull was painfully trying to beat a way out. He lay with a glare in his eyes that was the sky. He sat up with a lurch and gasped as his head promised to burst.

Clearing vision informed him that Olin, on hands and knees, appeared to be closely inspecting the ground before him.

Memory, slowly reviving, impelled Adam at last to turn. He solemnly regarded the stump behind him. He must have cracked his tead on this obstacle when he had gone down. There was an egglike lump on his crown that was exquisitely painful.

Olin tried to stand, gasped, and, letting himself down hastily, turned a vacant face toward his late adversary. A scribble of blood ran down the dark young man's chin and a swelling over one eyebrow already was turning blue. He felt it gently and flinched. His feet stirred aimlessly among the chips and his eyelids narrowed. He cleared his throat and offered finally in a flat voice, "Well, don't see what that settled."

Adam's muscles slackened. He leaned back against the stump and, finding no residue of his late anger, gave a wan grin.

"I'm not quite certain now what it was supposed to decide."

The brown eyes that watched him were amused and unfeignedly friendly. Olin said, "I'd as soon you didn't remember. Sometime," he pursued sadly, "I could bear to have you show me how you did it, provided you're a mite more moderate and"—staring at the log over which Adam had fallen—"there's something handy for you to trip over again."

The two sat silent, surveying each other. Olin got to his feet with extreme caution and Adam, imitating him, sat down suddenly on the stump while the world went around. He saw at last that the other man stood beside him, kettle in hand.

"Try it," Olin bade.

Adam quaffed rum and water, coughed, and extended the kettle to the other.

"Health," said Olin, lifting it to his swollen mouth.

The draught revived and soothed them. When the vessel was empty, they regarded each other intently and then both were shaken by mirth.

"Been promising myself for half a year to whop you," Olin said at last and wiped his eyes.

"I had cherished the same intention myself."

"Ehyah."

Olin hesitated and then drew out confession with a jerk.

"Called you a thief. No warrant to. Knew all the time who put the sparker in your cloak."

"Eh?"

"Delight told me, after The Reverend brought tidings of your safety. I rated her soundly, too."

"Delight?" It was all that Adam possibly could say. Olin misunderstood his dazed look.

"Delight," he said, speaking slowly and loudly as though his companion still were stunned, "put it in your pocket, and food, too, because—well, why do girls do anything?"

"Oh."

"Queer critter, Delight," Olin pursued with brotherly tolerance.

"She is, indeed."

It was easiest to agree, while his mind groped and fumbled

among incredibilities. He looked with sudden suspicion at his companion but Olin's face was candid.

"If you're fit now," he ventured, "we'll best eat and get back to work. Else, Justus'll figure we spent the day clawing each other."

It was late afternoon when Sherwood and Everest arrived with their cartload of lumber.

"Took your time," Olin hailed. Adam saw his friend's eyes dwell on the bruised face but Sherwood made no comment while the clapboards were unloaded. When the task was finished, he offered, "The sloop lies in Basin Harbor to bear Felicity and Delight to Skenesborough on the morrow."

Adam, following his companions homeward, wondered with bitter humor how much of his confusion was due to the blow on his head, how much to Olin's tidings. His late enemy had had no apparent idea that his revelation had upset the world.

It had been Delight, the shy, silent child, not Felicity, who had moved to save Adam. The knowledge roused the secret, sour mirth that is the compensation of deceived males.

Felicity had accepted his gratitude, though properly it had belonged to another. Felicity had lied—

Justice made Adam retreat part way. Felicity had not actually said hers had been the rescuing hand, but she had not confessed it had been Delight's. She had been uncandid, unfair.

Olin's statement had brought a bright, unsubstantial fabric clattering down. More fragments fell as Adam rode through the darkening forest. He recalled the grim day when Baker had evicted him. For a half year now, he had clung to the belief that of all the then hostile household, Felicity alone had been his friend. The conviction had swayed and guided him, yet it had not been she; it had been Delight.

Why, among them all, had the child alone been merciful? It had been her home that had been threatened; it had been her people who had denounced him. Perhaps Felicity had prompted the generous act and Delight had done her bidding. Adam tried to cling to the belief.

"Eh?" Olin asked, looking back toward him. "What's the jest?"

"A thought that amused me," Adam told him, belatedly conscious that he had laughed aloud and bitterly.

He thought of Felicity's looming departure with new distress. She would leave in the morning with the puzzle unsolved. It was better she should go without reproach or accusation. Let her cherish the false belief that he still was her dupe. He tried to hold that resolution, yet as they rode into the Royden clearing, in his heart he knew he must strive to see her alone.

It was contrived more easily than he had dared to hope. Sherwood's announcement that the sloop was waiting immediately plunged the household into a frenzy of preparation during which Olin's bruised face went unnoticed. Supper was a distracted repast; Felicity and Mindwell talked continually of ways and means, while the men grinned and Delight sat drearily silent.

At the meal's end, Adam remembered he had failed to hay his mare and went out to the stable. He checked himself sharply as he emerged from the building's doorway. Felicity was hurrying toward him. At once, the accusations he had formed, the scathing words he had assembled, fled. He watched the slight figure approach through the dusk, with something like panic.

Felicity was breathless from haste but her voice was otherwise unmarred. She had come for her brother's saddlebags. They must be packed with possessions her portmanteau would not hold. Adam, still speechless, lifted the bags from a peg. The girl lingered, provoked by his silence. He was glad the thickening dusk hid her loveliness.

"We have had mutiny on our hands," Felicity said lightly. "Delight suddenly proclaimed that she would not go to Skenesborough. It has taken her mother, brother, and me to overwhelm her. She can be an irritating child."

Adam's mouth was treacherously dry and he spoke slowly:

"I owe her too much to think her so."

Felicity had half turned to go. She stood quite still for a long instant before she asked in a new voice:

"Owe her? What?"

"It was she and not you who moved to save me last winter."

He was prepared for vehement denial. Instead, after hesitation, she asked:

"Who told you?"

"Olin."

"And you are angry with me?"

"I don't know," he answered with a brief laugh. "I am confused. I do not understand why you—let me believe it."

She waited, motionless and dim, before him. The small rhythmic voices of insects shrilled across the clearing and at the forest's dark edge frogs drummed flatly. Felicity asked:

"Not understand? Not even suspect?"

"I said I was confused."

"So have I been," she admitted penitently. "It has troubled me ever since you thanked me. I am glad you have learned the truth. Yet it was little I stole from Delight. She is still a child and —and, it was sweet to have your gratitude—Adam."

"Felicity," he whispered, stepping forward, but she had whirled and was gone with a stifled sound that might have been a sob. He did not follow but stood, dazed, before the stable, while doubt and grievance washed away and a mounting joy replaced them. Felicity—Adam hesitated to accept so blindingly bright a belief— had all but confessed her love for him. The sky was thickly starred when he went back slowly toward the house.

The kitchen was empty but he heard a confusion of speech in the chamber where Delight and Felicity lodged. Sherwood called his name from their room.

"If you are wise," he said, as his friend entered, "you'll avoid women preparing for an excursion. Bed is the best place for us."

"Yes," said Adam, vaguely. "Of course."

Chapter XIII

OLIN, standing beside the led horse, gave a final, testing tug on the pack lashings. Sherwood bent and Felicity, placing her foot in his cupped hands, was lifted into the saddle. Adam, turning to aid Delight in like fashion, found her already mounted.

They rode off through mist that lay heavy in the clearing. From his post in the rear, Olin chuckled.

"Aimed to get going by daylight! Only an hour late with no more'n enough gear to take them to China."

Adam laughed. Felicity smiled over her shoulder and called:

"We still may reach Basin Harbor in time, if Justus does not lose his way."

Excitement had set her aglow. Delight, riding behind her, seemed by contrast additionally wan. Adam wondered why she had refused to go until the others had overcome her. She was a sensitive child for sturdy Mindwell Royden to have borne.

The fog was thinner in the forest and the pines' fragrance overcame its dank smell. Sherwood guided them surely across ground overlaid with brown needles and the squeak of leather was the chief sound of their passage. The dreamlike progress harmonized with Adam's mind that dealt with incredibilities.

It was hard to believe Felicity, irreverently mocking her brother's woodcraft, was the same softly appealing creature who last night had let Adam see her heart. The confessed frailty, proving her mortal, only had increased his devotion. Olin, impatiently yanking along Baker's horse, now serving as baggage animal, no longer was an implicit enemy, despite—or because of—the bruise upon his forehead. Olin, for all his confidence, had lost and Adam had won.

It was, he reflected, as though a play had ended and another had begun, with his companions cast in new roles. Delight, with her bobbing head and pale, straitly drawn hair, now had a more important and perplexing part.

Why had so mild a spirit opposed, however secretly, her family's judgment, to extend furtive succor to a condemned interloper—filching journeycake and hacking away the pork chunk when none was looking, hiding them and the flint and steel in Adam's cloak? Warmth compounded of gratitude and compassion laid hold upon him. He still was watching the child, and wondering, when blue water shone through the trees ahead and Sherwood's cry silenced his sister's disparagement.

"Basin Harbor and yonder the sloop still waits."

They rode out upon the pebbled beach of a quiet bay that gave upon the riverlike breadth of the lake and bluer mountains beyond. A sloop lay offshore, sheathed in cedar, with brasswork blinking in the sun.

Sherwood's hail was answered by a redcoated man who came from the craft's cabin. Two girls followed him to wave and call while Negroes drew on the line that tethered a rowboat.

Olin and Sherwood, supervised by Felicity, were unloading the packhorse's burden. Delight remained docilely upon her mount. She looked down and smiled faintly as Adam approached.

It was strange that such eloquent gray eyes should dwell in so mild and humble a face. Delight's faint air of desolation smote Adam. He said:

"I'm sorry you are going. Are you?"

Her mouth trembled.

"I'll enjoy it. Mother and Felicity say I will."

The warmth, that earlier he had felt for her, returned.

"Long ago," he told her, "you hid gifts for me in my cloak. You must not think me ungrateful, Delight, because I have not thanked you till now."

She shook her head with a small, uncertain smile.

"I didn't think you knew it was me. I thought you'd maybe guess it was Felicity."

The flush that crept into the thin face lent her faint, momentary loveliness.

"I learned only yesterday that it was you. Isn't there something you want very much, Delight?"

Her sudden, brilliant color startled him. The child shook her head.

"I guess," she faltered, "you've done more than enough for me." She swallowed loudly and added, "I never thanked you, either."

Adam turned as gravel rasped beneath the rowboat's bow. A Negro leaped ashore and drew it farther up the beach before the redcoated man alighted. He moved quickly and his boldly hewn face had a dark, polished hue wrought by long exposure to the weather and port. He bowed to the curtseying Felicity and offered his hand to Sherwood, who beckoned Adam.

"Major Skene, my friend, Mr. Corlaer of Albany."

"Sir, your most obedient. A friend of Mr. Sherwood is, with your permission, also my friend. I trust you will give me the pleasure of welcoming you soon at Skenesborough Manor."

Olin and the Negro were stowing the baggage aboard. Delight had slipped from her horse and stood watching them. Skene was muttering earnestly to Sherwood. Adam turned away and found Felicity beside him. Her smile for an instant excluded the rest of the world. She gave him her hand.

"Do you truly pardon me?"

"There was nothing to forgive."

"I shall miss you."

The look in her eyes took his breath. He said at last:

"I shall see you soon. Henceforth," he went on more boldly, "we shall not be so long apart."

He released her hand and felt no jealousy when she held it out to Olin.

Delight already was seated in the stern. Skene handed Felicity aboard, followed her. The Negro shoved off.

The boat moved swiftly over the bright water toward where the major's daughters waited at the sloop's quarter. Delight's face looking steadfastly back, dwindled into a pale dot. Adam remembered that he had not said goodbye to her.

They did not wait to see the craft sail but, each leading a horse, rode away. Olin guided them, not toward home, but cross-country to New Haven. They said little during the journey. Sherwood was the most silent of the three.

Something heavier than the depression of parting weighed upon him but he did not utter it until they had reached his clearing, had picketed the horses, and were eating their noontime meal. Then he offered in a controlled voice:

"Major Skene has word from Rhode Island that the rebels there have taken and burned His Majesty's schooner, Gaspée."

Adam, seeing how indignation had starched his friend's face, held his peace, but Olin slapped his knee.

"Burned her, eh?" he exulted. "By God!"

Sherwood grew red but picked his words precisely. "You seem to find destruction of the king's property an estimable act."

Olin was momentarily balked by the chill speech. He rallied: "While the king holds provincials a lesser race than Englishmen, what less can freemen do?"

"In other words," Sherwood asked, his temper momentarily slipping from him, "you approve of treason?"

Adam watched Olin's dark twitching face and sympathized with his struggle for self-control. He, himself, intervened with more haste than discretion: "In other words, Olin and I hold loyalty to America and Americans above loyalty to a king who understands neither."

He saw Olin's grateful look. Sherwood rose quickly as though better to endure his indignation.

"So," he said quietly, "the plague has smitten you, too? I had hoped that one so lately returned from England—"

"Would esteem George III above all else?" Adam supplied when the other hesitated. "British treatment of provincials is not likely to increase their love for the kingdom or the king, Justus. And you will find many men there, too, who esteem George III as little as Olin and I."

Sherwood said with violence, "You and Olin raise hands against God Himself when you lift them against my sovereign who is God's anointed."

"Oh, fiddle-dee-dee!" Adam retorted, driven out of patience. "You do not believe that ancient nonsense!"

Olin grinned and Sherwood, marking it, grew paler still and spoke now in a dull, stubborn voice. "True men believe in God and the king and hold it their privilege to serve them."

"Justus," Olin soothed, rising, "Adam and I haven't been

schooner-burning. Why reproach us? Let be and get on with the sheathing."

Sherwood set teeth upon a trembling lip and Adam, watching, felt a pang of pity.

"Olin's right," he said. "There's work to be done—and this isn't Rhode Island."

"No," Sherwood admitted dully, "no, that is true," but his anger flared once more before it subsided.

"I ask you to remember this: All of my line have been loyal men. No rebel has ever allied himself with us. None"—he looked hard from one man to the other—"with my permission ever will."

He picked up a hammer and strode away. They worked until toward sunset without further dispute, and Sherwood joined in their talk as they rode toward Panton, but Adam saw distress still puckered his eyelids and drew his brows together. He went directly to the house when they dismounted, leaving the others to lead the animals to the stable.

Olin, as they entered the building, stared at a horse already quartered there and grunted.

"Oh, God!" he said. "Now we shall have further ranting from a worse source."

Adam, considering the fleabitten creature, felt a stir of recognition.

"Abijah!" he said. "The parson's horse!"

"It is," Olin replied with no enthusiasm. "Benjy is here to threaten us heathen with hellfire again if we do not acknowledge that God is a Yorker. Cloth or no cloth, if I were Ethan—"

The Reverend Mr. Hough rose like a ruler unfolding from the kitchen settle he had shared with Sherwood and looked from Olin to Adam with shadowed, sunken eyes.

"I had scarce expected," the rattling voice proclaimed, "when last we met, Mr. Corlaer, to find you here in—"

"The house of the ungodly," Olin supplied.

"I trust not, young sir, and so pray early and late. Well, well, this is parcel with the mighty things wrought in The Grants by Him whose mercy endureth forever."

He rolled his eyes violently as though in a seizure and lingered so long over utterance of his tidings that Sherwood announced with warmth in his lately remote voice:

"The Reverend has brought great news. Truce has been established between The Grants and York, to endure until the king, himself, decides the quarrel."

He smiled on the others, his recent indignation forgotten. There was so much of pride and admiration in the look he gave Adam that he felt his own face grow red.

Hough reseated himself and rubbed sharp, black-clothed knees with still bonier hands. He snuffed the odor of the supper Mindwell was preparing as though it were the incense of reconciliation. The firelight dealt strangely with the tired eyes, the hollow cheeks, while he laid hold upon Sherwood's statement as though it were a text. His grating speech dropped rapidly into a pulpit singsong.

He had been in that latter day Gomorrah, Bennington, when the delegates chosen by The Grants, Stephen and Jonas Fay, had returned from their conference with Tryon. They and the governor had agreed that neither party would make more settlements, that no man would be disturbed in his holding of Grants land, until the King had decided the dispute. Hough had witnessed the jubilation, had heard the terms of the truce read to the multitude by Jonas Fay.

"God, sirs, chooses strange instruments for the performance of His will, yet I presume not to judge. Through the magnanimity of York, peace has come to The Grants, at least for a season."

"If," said Olin who has listened with a dubious frown, "it be a real truce, then our generosity is at least as great as York's."

"That, young sir," Hough said with large tolerance, "is one view, to be sure. I only sorrow that the strife has ended without a halter looped about the iniquitous neck of Ethan Allen."

"I still have," said Sherwood hastily, sensing from Olin's look the imminence of explosion, "a few drops of rum among my stores. If someone will bring hot water and a bowl, I shall strive to create a proper drink in which to celebrate this happy day."

The minister's nostrils spread and the whites of his eyes shone.

"The Apostle, himself," said he, smacking thin lips, "recommendeth wine for the stomach's sake and by straining a point—"

Olin, when supper was over, went promptly to bed. Sherwood

and Adam, a little later, seized a pause in the parson's Jeremiad on frontier iniquity to bid him good night. In their own chamber, Sherwood beamed and clapped his friend warmly on the shoulder.

"I could not have believed this noon that I should sleep tonight with so light a heart. Whether or not," he went on wistfully, "you truly are the insurgent you proclaim yourself, you have done great things for peace."

His sincerity was so moving that Adam said huskily, "You do me scant justice. I detest rebellion only a little less than I do tyranny."

Sherwood frowned at the word but evaded argument. He stood by the window, looked out upon the murmurous summer night, and said without turning. "You have had schooling I lack, yet I believe mankind moves forward so slowly because it forever accuses governments of frailties that are, in truth, the sum of all men's defects. Must we tear the house down, Adam, because a leak has come in the roof?"

He looked at the other with a smile and a shrug.

"It seems I have caught the preaching habit from Hough. Good night, my friend."

They were midway to the barn, next morning, and Olin was grumbling over the vast appetite of his guest for homily and hominy when he broke off suddenly to stand, alert and breathing warily through a half-open mouth.

"Hark!" he bade as Sherwood started to speak, and turned in the direction of the now-perceptible sound. Adam caught a distant murmur that grew into a clash of voices and a mutter of hoofs. Olin, standing with eyes puckered against the young sun's light, grunted.

"By God, 'tis Remember and his scout, and not"—squinting more intently—"returning empty-handed."

The blur of movement at the clearing's edge became a file of mounted men. Sunlight could not enliven the dust-colored company. Adam saw now that the horses were crowbait-thin and their riders gaunt. Most desolate of the trail-weary band was a bareheaded man who sat with bound arms on a led horse.

"Cockburn!" Olin said in glee. "They've caught the old fox at last."

He lifted his voice in the wailing wolf howl. Baker's grin split his bearded face. He raised an arm in salute and, kicking his horse into a shuffling trot, reined in beside Sherwood.

"Wal," he proclaimed jerking his head toward the prisoner, "we got him."

"Yes," Sherwood said briefly, "I see."

"And a pretty chase he led us, too."

Baker climbed decrepitly from the saddle, bestowed an affectionate cuff upon Olin, and crowed, "Still here, eh Adam? How be ye, boy?"

Behind him, the little column had halted and men were dismounting. In the haggard, bearded company, Adam saw Sunderland, with a sprout of reddish whiskers and the weary giant, Warner. Only Cockburn remained ahorse. There was a bruise on his dirty face. Baker was saying, "Aimed to git here last night, but 'twas too fur an' dark. Mebby Mindwell could bait us. Fare's been a mite thin."

"Certain," Olin answered and hastened toward the house. Sherwood asked, nodding at the inert captive, "What are you doing with him?"

"Got orders to bring him in," Baker replied with relish. "Been warned 'n' chased often enough. Now he'll stand before a judgment seat."

"Might be," Sunderland offered, "that when Ethan's had him sealed, he'll willingly bide in York hereafter."

Adam stared at the prisoner. Cockburn blinked but no expression stirred the slack, soiled face. Sherwood was saying gravely, "That would violate the truce, gentlemen."

"Truce? What truce?" Baker demanded.

"Bid your men unsaddle while you come to the house with me. Bring your prisoner, too."

Mindwell and Olin, whom she had drafted in this crisis, were too active in the kitchen for conference there. Five men crowded into Sherwood's and Adam's small chamber that the bulk of Warner alone seemed to fill. Baker and he perched upon the unmade bed; Sunderland and Adam stood. Sherwood, before he had gone in search of Hough, had led Cockburn to the room's single chair. He sat now, mutely rubbing his unbound arms and flexing his fingers.

The least flicker of interest stirred the captive's face as Sherwood came back with the minister and bade him retell his tidings. Baker, who had glared at Hough when he had entered, scowled increasingly as the scarecrow figure announced the truce and then rattled on through Biblical parallels. Warner at last interrupted heavily:

"What knowledge have we that all this is not a Yorker trick?"

Hough stiffened with indignation and his eyes rolled white.

"I, sir, am a minister of the Gospel. I—"

"Ye, sir," Baker retorted with a blaze of enmity, "are also a pimp of Butcherin' Billy's. One day, if ye persevere, we'll broil ye on a cord or two of yer Gospels."

Hough cast his eyes upward, invoking retributive fire.

"God," he intoned, "is not mocked. Take that to heart, Remember Baker—you and that arch-blasphemer, Ethan Allen, blind leaders of the blind."

"Not wholly blind to what ye preach and practice in that Clarendon rats' nest, as, truce or no truce, ye'll learn, ye Yorker liar," Baker said.

Hough's hollow face grew dark. He stalked to the door and, before he vanished, threw a bleakly savage look at the company.

"Wallow then in evil if ye will," the strange voice clacked. "I wash my hands of ye."

Baker, his eyes angrily slitted, rose as though to follow.

"Let him wash his own hands," he wheezed, "when I've haled him before a judgment seat, parson though he be. The—"

He lunged toward the door but Sherwood stayed him. "No," he bade.

Baker and Sunderland listened with ebbing suspicion while Justus told quickly of Adam's part in the negotiation with Tryon. Warner, when the speaker had ended, nodded approval.

"Wal," Sunderland demanded dryly, "what now?"

"There is only one course." Sherwood nodded to the prisoner. "Free him."

"Free him!" Baker squalled. "After we wore our breeches' seats off huntin' him up and down Onion River? If there be a truce, he has broken it. I recognize no truce that lets a York surveyor run lines through The Grants."

Cockburn stirred and looked toward Adam who begged,

"Wait!" and then pursued uncomfortably under Baker's and Sunderland's hostile and Warner's grave regard:

"Cockburn has broken the truce, it is true; yet unwittingly. If you knew naught of it, how could he?"

He was heartened by Warner's nod and hurried on.

"I am more your ally than I am the governor's. I say to you that if you wish for peace in The Grants, release your prisoner and let him go home, unharmed."

"He is right," Warner's heavy voice announced and Sherwood added his assent. Baker's stubbled face screwed up with an intensity of thought and relaxed at last into a grin.

"As ye will then, but we'll do it our own way. Let him ride, free 'n' clear, to Bennington with us. If we find then that there is, in truth, a truce, we'll send him home, unmolested."

He turned to Cockburn and spoke loudly, "Hear, Billy? Ye're free—in a manner of speakin'."

Cockburn blinked, rubbed his face with swollen hands, and nodded. Exhaustion had so drained him that he seemed half asleep.

"Be better," Sunderland promised, "like the rest of us, when there's something solider'n wind in his belly."

Sherwood, on hands and knees, groped beneath the bed and rose with a jug.

"You look," he told the newcomers, "as though you all needed something, this gentleman most of all."

He held the jug to the spent man's lips. Cockburn's throat worked. He drew away at last, wheezed, and muttered gratitude. The others in turn drank long and expertly, each supporting the vessel on an angled arm. Baker sighed, wiped his mouth on his palm, and leaned back, considering Adam with watery, contentious eyes. He passed the jug to Sunderland and said with an air of bland amazement:

"Wal, wal! So the Fays and Corlaer here girded up their loins, in a manner of speakin', and brought peace to The Grants! Wal-wal."

"I had little to do with it," Adam disclaimed, incautiously. Baker took the jug back from his companion, drank again, and stared in elaborate admiration.

"Modesty," he marveled, "becomes him. Adam Corlaer's a man of parts, Peleg. Makes a truce with one hand 'n' routs poor Colonel Reid's tenants from Otter Falls with t'other."

Sunderland's last pull on the jug had brought brilliance to his eyes and a deploring look to his long, whiskered face.

"Violent man, Adam," he informed Baker. "Minded me to the falls of a drunk Abenaki. Led us on, didn't he, Remember?"

"Ehyah. Flogged the men."

"Abused the women, too."

"Not forgettin' the infants in arms." Baker elaborated. "Wal, Tryon has strange tastes in peace-makin'. Always held so."

He leered at the flustered Adam, and he and Sunderland were shaken by silent laughter. Olin, appearing in the doorway, summoned them to eat. Warner slipped a big arm about Cockburn and helped him rise. Baker and his accomplice followed, still loudly deploring Adam's ferocity. Sherwood, smiling at their horseplay, turned to its target and grew grave.

"Surely," he said, "you are not offended. It is their habit to defame those whom they truly like."

"I was thinking," Adam returned, "that I had best ride south with them."

"You have a reason for going?"

"None, save that I have no better for staying, and the warmest welcome in time must cool."

Sherwood placed a hand on his friend's shoulder and shook it lightly.

"No one considers you either idle or a guest. There is work here in plenty for us all. Stay, Adam, if it pleases you. It will greatly please Olin and Mindwell and me. Stay, at least, until after Felicity's and Delight's return and I go with them to Quebec."

The little column rode off that afternoon with the liberated Cockburn. Baker bore a letter from Adam, promising that it would be forwarded to his household in Albany. Next day, the three men returned to the New Haven clearing.

Adam wondered, as weeks slipped by and evenings grew long and cool and Sherwood's house moved toward completion, why he tarried so contentedly in this wilderness. He awaited Felicity's return, yet with more patience than he once had deemed possible.

Something beyond the sedative of daylong labor bemused him, something beside the satisfaction he found in the waxing trust of Mindwell and her son and Sherwood's steady friendship.

The silence of the forest that once had oppressed him; the quick, unbridled brooks; the clean winds blowing, all were part of the odd serenity. So, also, were the folk among whom he moved—the Roydens and their few neighbors, the earnest, willing and hopeful people.

In rare moments of idleness Adam's mind played pleasantly with a plan to buy a tract here on the frontier's rim. Felicity and he could be tranquilly happy in this rough Arcady, in this empty land that gave to the questing its own spacious liberty.

Sherwood's house had been clapboarded and the chimney was almost finished when Everest brought a letter that had been put ashore from Skene's trading galley. The major wrote that his daughters had persuaded Felicity and Delight to accompany them directly from Skenesborough to Quebec and named the day when Sherwood must join them at Basin Harbor. He enclosed a note from Felicity listing the items her brother should not fail to bring.

There was no mention of Adam in the message. He tried to lay the omission to maiden delicacy yet it irked him. Felicity was still little more than a child. It was only natural that a creature so lately aware of her beauty's power should turn eagerly from the frontier's monotony to the Canadian capital's gaiety. So Adam told himself, yet sourly questioned the validity of his own excuses.

He withstood Sherwood's invitation to go with him to Basin Harbor and thence downlake on the Skene sloop by pleading that his Albany properties needed attention. A plan for repayment of his debt to Delight was fortifying his purpose. Since Felicity had sent him no message, Adam resolved sullenly, he would go home with no word for her.

She had known him only in The Grants where he already had tarried too long. He would set his affairs in order and then journey to Montreal and Quebec as befitted his station. He would show the girl and her brother that he was something more considerable than a houseless vagrant. If Felicity esteemed fashion's graces, her lover would prove to her that he was enabled by birth and fortune to hold his own with the youth of Canada.

On the morning that Sherwood rode toward Basin Harbor, Adam set his mare on the long way to Albany.

Chapter XIV

MAPLES were shining in the dusk, as though the red leaves had their own inner glow, when Adam dismounted before his house. The tardy welcome of his surprised servants did not lift his spirits. The dwelling's airs, the faint smell of dust and dampness in his bedroom, oppressed him. His housekeeper, superintending the hasty building of a hearth fire, informed him that Duane had lately been in Albany and had been disturbed by Adam's continued absence. The implicit reproach in her manner stressed the strangeness of the homecoming.

He dined with no other company than the ghost reinvoked by his father's late possessions. A melancholy restlessness oppressed him. He identified it, at last and with mild consternation, as homesickness. It was preposterous that it should seize him, here in his own house. He wondered as he sipped Madeira whether he had come back to the place of his birth, to discover that another country and its people now were first in his mind.

The wine served only to increase his depression. He considered the shining mahogany, plate, and glass before him and drearily thought he would exchange them all for a seat at the pine table in the Royden kitchen with Olin, Sherwood, Mindwell, Delight, and Felicity.

While he emptied the decanter, Adam wondered why he had come home. None had need of him here and he, himself, no clear purpose in returning. Duane, he knew, wanted to cross-examine him on conditions in The Grants and the state of the truce. Adam shied from thought of further cooperation with Duane.

The housekeeper, when he had risen from the table, led her employer through the dwelling. He listened absently to her prattle of repairs that should be undertaken, replacements that must be made. He would sell the place, he told himself intemperately, and all save its most intimate furnishings. He would desert stolid, smug Albany.

"Eh, sir?" the housekeeper asked.

"Nothing," Adam replied and dismissed her, to consider the implications of his sudden resolution.

It was possible that Felicity, on whom his future hung; Felicity, with her hunger for gaiety; Felicity, who already had been enraptured by her small venture into the world, might esteem, above any wilderness home he could build her, the luxury of this Albany house.

He winced, pressing again upon a soreness that had troubled him ever since he had ridden from Panton. Felicity's half-admitted fondness for him naturally was less than his devotion to her. She still was young, as her brother had said and had placed a holiday at Skenesborough above Adam's companionship. She had accompanied the Major's daughters to Canada without tossing her suitor even a word of farewell.

His mind plodded again over the worn course while he undressed: If Felicity had left him inconsequently, he could not justly reproach her. He himself had let Delight go with the full measure of his gratitude still unspoken. He thought with a recurrent twinge of penitence of the child's pale face looking toward him over the stern of the rowboat at Basin Harbor.

Tomorrow, he would discharge his debt. He had made the plan on the journey back to Albany and reconsidered it with approval as he thrust himself into bed and felt the warmed sheets soothe his weariness. His gift would speak his gratitude to Delight and Olin and Mindwell, too. It would be, if the truce failed, insurance for them all.

He woke at dawn, thinking Olin had called him, and for an instant could not be certain where he was. Knowledge that he lay in his own home brought no satisfaction. He rose and looked out upon the rutted street, the yellow brick gables of the opposite houses, and the smoke of breakfast fires that soiled the daybreak while he thought of a clean, bright silence and of hills, tall and black against the sunrise. He could almost smell dew and the pines' sharp scent.

Albany's registrar of deeds said, as he handed Adam the newly prepared paper, "A profitable transfer for you, I trust, Mr. Corlaer?"

"I think so," the other answered, pocketing the document.

The official sighed and regarded him mournfully over steel-bound spectacles.

"We receive, alas, sorry tidings from The Grants, sir. It would appear the truce in which some placed great hope falls away again into anarchy. A sad time, sir, when every scoundrel presumes to make his own laws."

"Yes," Adam agreed. The truce, he thought drearily as he left the room, was destined to fail as all such efforts must when men place their own material interests above peace. Tryon had furiously denounced Baker's eviction of Reid's tenants from Otter Falls, and Allen had written him a defiant letter in reply. Thereafter, though the peaceful in The Grants still clung blindly to the hope of compromise, Tryon resumed the issuing of patents to land in that region and Allen's men picked up their bloodless warfare against recalcitrant Yorkers where briefly they had suspended it.

There was too much of obstinacy and suspicion in New York and The Grants, Adam reflected, for any truce between the willful factions to endure. In the corridor, he brushed against a hurrying man but heeded the contact no further until on the street he heard quick feet behind him and a voice half whispering in his ear:

"Mr. Corlaer!"

Adam turned.

"Buck; Benjamin Buck, sir, and as ever at your service."

The bared head was sleek in the sunlight and Buck's smile was obsequious yet his shallow black eyes glittered.

"I did not recognize you," Adam said distantly, wondering how to get rid of him. The brevity did not dismay his companion who bowed again so deeply that the other could see the greasy ribbon about the clubbed hair.

"Back from The Grants, eh, Mr. Corlaer?"

Beneath the fawning manner, Adam sensed a furtive attempt to drive something still hidden into the open.

137

"I am."

"I thought so, sir," Buck ventured with a gratified writhing. "I did, indeed. And Colonel Allen came with you, eh, sir?"

"Allen?" Adam exclaimed in honest perplexity. "I have not laid eyes on him since last spring. It is unlikely he would venture to Albany with me, or anyone."

His candor dashed Buck, but he rallied.

"And yet, sir, I could swear I glimpsed Colonel Allen riding along the river road not an hour ago. I followed on foot but he outdistanced me."

"I advise you to be more careful in your swearing. Allen would not come to Albany unless the truce has canceled the reward for his capture."

Buck leered at him with eyes as wily as a rat's. His voice sank.

"The reward still stands, Mr. Corlaer. I was seeking the sheriff when I encountered you. You may recall the way the Colonel used me in Fay's tavern. Twenty pounds' reward, sir, is not too great a fee for that insult."

He looked up expectantly and licked his lips.

"No doubt," Adam said.

He disengaged himself and walked away, revolted by Buck's mercenary vindictiveness. Ethan Allen would never risk his safety in a town whose officials as well as its traders in Grants' titles had due reason to wish him in prison. He would keep close and safe among his own people. Adam was thinking half-enviously of him as he climbed his porch steps.

"Now may God strike me blind as Saul of Tarsus," a brassy voice proclaimed when the door opened, "if it be not the prodigal himself!"

Adam stared at the enormous figure in travel-stained brown broadcloth that was lifting itself from the drawing-room sofa.

"In the name of God," he asked at last, "why are you here?"

Ethan Allen grasped the hand his involuntary host extended and tried to hide his glee under nonchalance.

"The matter of a wager," he replied largely. "Rob Cochran pledged five pounds that I dared not ride to Albany and there post Tryon's new placard proscribing us."

"And?" Adam prompted, to end the dramatic pause.

138

"This," Allen went on, pride shattering his pose of indifference, "I have just accomplished, unaided, unscathed."

Adam reached for a chair with the slow movements of the dazed. His guest reseated himself cautiously on the creaking sofa.

"I then bethought me that it might be prudential to ascertain whether you were here or still safe in The Grants. Your servitor has informed me that you returned last night."

If it were possible for a man to beam upon himself, Ethan Allen accomplished it, so intense was his delight in his Robin Hood exploit.

"The five pounds you have won," Adam said slowly, "is scarce worth the danger."

"Danger!" A vast hand waved the idea away. "Not from your tallow-headed Albany folk. At the Pinetree Tavern where I affixed the placard, they believed me a minion of Tryon himself."

"There is a tallow-headed person named Benjamin Buck."

"There is, indeed. Munro's skulking hireling."

"He knows you are in Albany," Adam said quietly, "and is now seeking another tallow-head, Sheriff Ten Eyck, to bring about your capture. Where did you leave your horse?"

Allen's lately triumphant eyes grew narrow.

"Tethered on the street beyond this. I am too old a woods-beast to proclaim my burrow."

"If you will accept my counsel," Adam offered, reaching for a call bell, "we will drink a stirrup cup together and you then will ride from Albany before Ten Eyck and his posse come down upon you. It is not unlikely Buck will lead them here."

"If you will accept my counsel, sir," Allen retorted with secret relish, "you will ride with me."

Adam paused with the still-silent bell in hand. Allen dangled an immense boot across the other knee, in a pose of ease.

"I have been to Westchester County in York province," he said airily, "with Captain Cochran to confer with one Edward Burling concerning a Hampshire grant he holds in the Onion River country. From Burling's hand, I had a placard newly published by Tryon and offering fresh rewards for the chief villains in The Grants—myself, Seth, Remember, and one more miscreant, a scurvy, turncoat rascal who, so His Excellency holds, has visited barbarism, savagery, rapine, and mammocking upon Colonel Reid's pure and peaceful settlers at Otter Falls."

There was mirth in the blue eyes and the stony face twitched. Allen added, after another pause, "This miscreant is known as Adam Corlaer."

Adam carefully set down the bell. He looked at his companion, suspecting jest, but the other shook his head at the unuttered question.

"That, sir, is why I came hither after posting your and our iniquity at the tavern. I believe I bore the first of the new placards to Albany, but others will follow and all the town soon must know you have been proscribed."

"Proscribed," Adam repeated stupidly. Indignation curdled into alarm and gave him understanding. Baker's and Sunderland's half-drunken mockery in the Roydens' dwelling had been borne as fact by Cockburn to York province and at last had reached Tryon's ears. Allen was warning, "Take not too great a pride in your elevation. We ancient evildoers now are listed at fifty pounds each and you at only twenty-five, yet you have shown no small progress for one who a few months ago was the accursed Munro's accomplice."

Mockery fell away from him. He said quietly, "If you have a horse at hand, Adam, you had best saddle and ride to The Grants with me."

Adam looked about the stately room that suddenly seemed a trap. Allen misunderstood his movement.

"A pleasurable and enviable mansion, sir, but choice furnishings and the ornamentations of luxury will little avail you if you are clapped into Tryon's jail. I sympathize with your reluctance to forswear them but—"

Adam rose quickly. The dreary aimlessness had fallen away. Fate, while he had moped and girded, had prepared the road for him. He considered it now with relief.

"You might be surprised," he told his companion, "if you knew with what ease I can forswear them."

"We shall," Allen blared, "make a proper Grants man of you yet. No," he pursued, reading Adam's hesitation, "if Ten Eyck and Buck seek me, we have no time for stirrup cups. Stealth and

speed must be our watchwords, man. It were best if we did not
ride from town together. I shall wait you at the ferry."

A quarter hour later, Adam stole downstairs, crossed the yard
unperceived, and entered the stable. He saddled Allegra, led her
out by a back way, and, with the zest of an erring small boy, rode
decorously to the edge of town and then lifted the mare into a
gallop.

From a distance, Allen saw him and raised an arm in greeting.

"You made good time," he chuckled as they led their horses
aboard the flatboat ferry. "If I had the deftness with the pen that
I would were mine, I should write a ballad on our exploit."

The trees along the road to Bennington flared like torches
and the late sunlight was warm on the riders' shoulders. Adam
drew in the spiced air and from a rise looked with emotion that
surprised him toward the far, red hills.

"It is," he said huskily, "a fair country."

Allen, whose great body dwarfed his sturdy horse, turned
brilliant eyes on his companion and said solemnly, "The Lord God
Jehovah provided a less likely land for his chosen. Truly, I believe
Providence withheld The Grants until it had found a people
worthy to possess them."

Breath whistled through the big nose. Adam ventured, hoping to plague him, "And a new Moses to guide them?"

Allen nodded.

"I have considered that often," he answered simply, "and no
longer can doubt it is so."

They rode for a time in silence through the bedizened, silent
wilderness. Allen offered at length, with an odd commingling of
pomp and distress, "I have laid hold of late on a weapon mightier than the jawbone that Samson wielded. Sir, to one skilled
in its use, no thing can equal the pen, for it bites deeper than any
sword and outranges all ordnance, great or small. The Grants, till
I seized the quill, had no champion able to confute the claims of
the gentry of York. Thunder of Jehovah, Adam! I already have
stabbed Tryon shrewdly with my letters. I have written him concerning his fraudulent truce and, had I the schooling I have lacked,
I would engage to overcome him and his damned province with a
handful of pens and a gill of ink."

The triumph faded from his voice and he pursued, wistfully, "Yet I find it more labor to write a fair page than to fell and limb an oak. I need a midwife's services to ease the travail and when the child is born to cleanse and clothe it before the world shall see it."

He looked narrowly at his companion who held his peace, not quite certain where the eloquence was leading.

"Someone," the giant pursued, almost beseechingly, "to order my writing, copying it in such fashion that the purblind printer of The Connecticut Courant may read it without error and the meaching pettifoggery of York—aye, and some of the same breed in The Grants—may find no cause for mirth over its spelling and the like."

He seemed a vast and anxious child as he gulped and then asked, "Have you an immediate purpose, once we reach Bennington?"

"I have been thinking that I should journey on into Canada, to see my late father's agent in Montreal."

"Does time press so that you could not aid me in the compilation of a letter The Council has urged me to write to Tryon, ere we declare the truce a failure and dead?"

Adam hesitated.

"One letter only," Allen urged. "Two fair copies, one for The Courant, one for Butchering Billy. Thereafter, I will accompany you to Skenesborough and see you get immediate and easy passage down the lake. I am not without influence in that quarter, sir."

"I shall be most willing to serve you, then," Adam answered.

Allen whooped and slapped his thigh so mightily that both horses shied.

Chapter XV

SKENESBOROUGH'S proprietor was absent when Allen and Adam rode down the last of the dwindling hills to the manor where a sawmill screamed and smoke from a forge drifted over the roofs of cottages. The two passed fenced fields where horses still grazed and came to the great stone house that, flanked by slaves' quarters, looked out augustly over Champlain's mud-stained headwaters.

From the liveried black butler who welcomed Allen as a familiar guest, they learned that Skene had gone downlake to Ticonderoga whither, if they wished, they might follow him. His trading galley even then was loading with lumber. The craft's destination was St. Johns, with a pause at Otter Falls for a deck cargo of potash.

They dined alone in a chamber so vast that it might have awed a lesser man than Adam's companion who ate and drank gustily, ruined the butler's decorum with ribald jest, and firmly arranged his own and Adam's plans. They would take passage on the galley to Ticonderoga, leaving their horses here. Adam, if his resolution held, could continue on to Canada.

"I myself shall return hither with the Major. We have," Allen added with an air of mystery, "much of importance to discuss."

He offered no further explanation until the galley was moving down the riverlike reaches of the upper lake, past the low, painted hills and the marshes' still fires. Four Negroes crooned as they swung the heavy sweeps. A fifth handled the tiller and trimmed the single square sail that the mild south wind fluttered. The passengers looked back at the retiring pier and shipyard and the small, compact village below the manor house that its proprietor might have lifted entire from Kent to set down in the midst of wilderness. Allen informed his companion in an unwontedly low voice:

"The Major, sir, is a man of parts whom I am proud to call friend and associate. Our purpose," he pursued, still more huskily, "in which many in The Grants have joined, is to induce Britain to establish the land to east and west of Champlain as a separate royal province, with Major Skene as governor, and I not the least of his officials."

From his stately pose it was plain that already he imagined himself appointed. Adam asked, "Will York agree to this? Will she not protest?"

"Like a pig in a bear trap," Allen replied cheerfully and with obvious relish in the prospect. "We are weathered by now to York's protests. She has uttered nothing else since the first pioneer commenced a betterment in The Grants."

The galley's blunt mast complained as the freshening wind thrust against the sail. The sun had not yet gone below the western ridges when the stream dilated before them and they bore toward a low hill capped by gray stone and red-tiled roofs. They anchored off a point where cordwood was piled.

A corduroy road led uphill through woods and cutover land. Adam and Allen, stumbling along the uneven way, overtook and passed a working party from the garrison, dourly plodding behind an oxcart laden with firewood. The men seemed more spent and glum than a day's work warranted. Their sullen response to his greeting made Allen sniff and mumble to himself.

The sun still was visible when they reached the fort but, far below, where the outlet of Lake George flowed sluggishly through swamp to join Champlain, the western hills extended shadows that turned the broader, united waters from blue to the hue of steel. Beyond the lake, no farther than a cannonball might carry, glowed the forest of The Grants, rolling toward distant mountains. Adam grew aware that Allen was muttering again and turned toward his companion who, staring at the prospect before them, said still half to himself:

"A hundred brave men, creeping unseen to where we stand, could rush in and seize this fort."

"Granting," Adam amended, "there were no defenders on the ramparts."

144

"Pooh! Defenders cannot see at night. The advance should be made then."

"To what purpose?" Adam was puzzled by the giant's intensity. Allen waved his arm widely.

" 'Purpose,' forsooth! Who holds Ticonderoga holds the lakes, man."

"Such an exploit," Adam suggested dryly, "would do little to advance The Grants' cause, or discommode York."

"True, but if—"

He let the sentence hang.

"If what?"

The query drew Allen from his rapt mood. He turned amused eyes on his companion.

"Nothing," he answered with faint mockery. "Simply, 'if.' "

They entered the stronghold unchallenged and moved toward the moldering, red-roofed barracks and storehouses that formed a hollow rectangle about the parade. Neglect hung like an illness over the area. The ground had been washed and gullied by rain. The nearest building was swaybacked and a rank of tiles had fallen from the roof of its neighbor. Allen looked from a brass eighteen-pounder, askew on its rotting carriage, to the slovenly detail a sergeant marched past them.

"Were I Britain's king," he said loftily, "I would take better care of my property."

A great door of iron-studded oak with a smaller wicket gate set into its expanse was open wide. A sentry in a soiled uniform woke from apathy and brought his musket to port with a rattle as the two men approached but relaxed again and waved them on as Allen spoke Skene's name. Their footsteps roused clattering echoes as they passed through a wide, low-arched tunnel and came out upon the bare parade ground.

A soldier directed them to the officers' quarters at the quadrangle's west end. They climbed a stair that slanted up the outside building wall to a landing before a second-story door. It opened as Allen raised a fist to beat upon it and Skene came out.

The Major welcomed the newcomers with as much hearty surprise as though this were his own dwelling and led them into a chamber where a stout captain in a yellow-faced uniform sat glowering at a paper-laden desk, and a doleful subordinate, standing before it, evidently considered the intruders a welcome diversion.

These, Skene's introductions revealed, were Lieutenant Arthur Aspinwall, in immediate command of the post, and his superior, Captain William Anstruther, who had come from headquarters at Crown Point to inspect the garrison and was less than pleased with what he had found. His indignation boiled over when he had greeted Adam and Allen.

"On my word," he blurted, slapping the returns before him, "let this neglect continue a few more years and we shall have here not a post but a ruin. You need not look so doleful, Aspinwall. It is falling apart no more rapidly than the Crown Point fortifications. Take comfort from that, if you may."

He groaned and blinked at the strangers.

"However," he went on more cheerfully, "since we are blessed with guests, let us postpone further lamentation. You are most welcome, gentlemen, and, if the storeroom be not as lacking in rum as in other necessities, we shall strive to make your sojourn pleasant."

Anstruther smiled but his grievance overwhelmed him again.

"I know not for what iniquity, moral or military, I have been set down in this wilderness to maintain two forts by prayer and the efforts of a single understrength company, but I am expiating my sin in full. Major Skene, if you will guide our two guests to the chamber next yours, we shall lodge them there, providing the roof does not fall in."

The dreariness of the room to which Skene led them did not depress Adam's spirits. He thought, surveying its flaking walls and splintered floor, how accustomed he had become in the last year to lodgings more barren than these. He was, he remembered with a spasm of elation, launched at last on his long-delayed journey to Canada, to Montreal—and Quebec. Major Skene, to whom Allen had been speaking in a low voice, met Adam's eyes now with a bow and a pleasant smile.

"It is my continuing regret, Mr. Corlaer, that I have not yet welcomed you to Skenesborough. It is small amends for my absence to ensure you passage to St. Johns."

"I am most grateful, sir," Adam said, bowing in turn.

Skene's smile grew reflective.

"It seems our fate to meet only in odd places—Basin Harbor and now here. I trust our next encounter will be where I may offer you proper hospitality."

"I trust, sir," Adam returned with a pose of indifference, "that you left your daughters and their friends in good health at Quebec."

"In excellent. I have lately returned from there. My girls and Delight Royden are content with school but Felicity, the baggage, seems intent on setting all the young men of Quebec by the ears."

He chuckled and shook his head in admiration.

"Gad, sir, not every maid of her age can boast that one swain has called out another for her sake!"

"Indeed?" Adam kept his face still and his voice cool, though something inside him had leaped frantically. Skene selected Allen as a more appreciative audience.

"A duel, and she still little more than a child! Sherwood was much perturbed at the noise the affair made. I told him Quebec was the proper place to thaw Connecticut frost out of his and his sister's bones. If Wadman chose to run Legendre through the shoulder for her sake, that was not Felicity's fault."

Wadman! The name smote Adam. While he sought to recover his pretense of unconcern, Allen slapped his thigh and trumpeted, "Wadman? A black-a-vised ensign in the Twenty-sixth?"

"The same," Skene nodded. "You are acquainted?"

"Slightly," the other replied with an outburst of laughter. "Mr. Corlaer knows him more intimately."

"Eh?" Skene queried, frowning. His face thawed as he viewed Adam's confusion.

"So the wind sets in that quarter? Rivals? Then, Mr. Corlaer, I counsel you not to tarry in Montreal but to press on to Quebec and enter the lists."

They sat at table that night for what seemed to Adam an endless time after supper had been cleared away and drank more punch than he desired. Liquor only increased his perturbation, at one instant enraging him against Wadman: the next, driving him to denounce Felicity as a trifling flirt and curse her brother for allowing her undue freedom. Sherwood had stood between

Felicity and Adam, Felicity and Olin Royden. Colonials must keep their distance but licentious young bucks in the service of Sherwood's beloved monarch might brawl for his sister's favor!

Adam dared not ask Skene for further information, lest the chaos within him be plain to all, and the Major, having seen how raillery had irked the young man, refrained from mentioning the Sherwoods again.

Adam's head was humming when he went to bed and throbbing when he awoke. Allen still snored lustily but Skene had arisen and, after a brief breakfast, led the way down to the shore in the red light of a sullen dawn.

The hillside was pale with frost. Mist that hung along the lakeshore crept coldly into Adam's flesh. He was trembling when Skene, having given the galley captain his final instructions, bade the passenger farewell.

The hills beyond Ticonderoga threw back the bang of the sunrise gun as Adam was rowed to the galley. He saw a crimson wisp creep up the flagstaff of a toy fort. The Negroes chanted as they hove in the anchor. They sang more briskly, straining at the sweeps.

Adam wrapped himself closely in his cloak yet continued to shake. It was as though the dank air was filling the hollows of his bones. The sun, emerging, glared at him briefly without warmth, then hid itself again in a mass of curdled cloud. An east wind woke and pierced him. He huddled in the lee of the sail and was too wretched in body for anger or jealousy.

The water was leaden under the gray sky and the colored hills slowly slid past. Adam felt with a touch of panic that illness was upon him. He must endure it, not in his own home, not in Bennington, not even at Ticonderoga, but here on the lake, ever further removed from friend or succor. He saw that the helmsman was looking at him and tried to smile.

If he sat on the hatch, the throbbing ache in his back and legs might ease. If he lay with his cloak close about him, he might escape a little from the searching wind. It was whipping up waves. The galley had begun to roll.

After a space, Adam felt a hand upon his shoulder and looked up into a black, anxious face.

"All right," he said thickly. A blanket was drawn over him. He

148

mumbled thanks. A small core of heat began to burn in his belly, spreading and driving away his chill. This, he thought, was fever and he did not greatly care. His untethered mind wheeled and swooped, now to Canada where he and Wadman were about to duel with monstrous swords while Sherwood and Felicity cheered his adversary and Delight, wringing her hands, begged them to refrain; now to some less certain land where Buck and Allen pulled at him and clamored nonsense in unison. He slid at last into slumber too deep for dreams.

It seemed he had known for a long while that the galley's plunging had ceased, though the sweeps had continued to creak and splash. It had taken a dull shock and men's loud voices to rouse him. There was a weight in his head that rolled violently about as Adam sat up.

The roaring that assailed his ears was not internal. He blinked at water, crystal and white, falling over a cliff above him to churn a pool in which the galley lay. There were yellow trees on the stream's far side. On this, stood a pier to which the Negroes were mooring their craft and, along it, men trundled barrels. The noise increased Adam's headache.

A figure paused at the pier's end to look down at him and wave, but the man was a flat shadow against the glaring sky and what he called was indistinguishable. A Negro shouted in reply and Adam watched without interest as the man swung down to the deck, spoke briefly with the helmsman, and then came toward him.

"Adam," the intruder said and, more loudly, "Adam Corlaer. Lord, don't you know me?"

Adam squinted and licked dry lips with a dry tongue.

"You," he returned with what dignity a parched whisper would permit, "are—are Olin Royden."

He lay back again on the hatch and did not even try to understand the talk that went on above him. He submitted indifferently to hands that raised him. It was well, he thought with dim satisfaction, that they did not ask him to walk.

He lay, wrapped in blankets, on the floor of a vehicle whose ponderous jolting befuddled him. It was a long while before he discovered that Olin sat beside him.

149

"Quiet," his friend's voice bade close to his ear as he tried to sit up. "We'll be home soon."

"Home," Adam repeated faintly.

He clung to the comforting word and slipped calmly down a long declivity into blackness.

Everest's ox team halted at last before the Roydens' house. Olin told Mindwell, "Brought you someone to nurse, Ma. Found him on Skene's galley at Otter Falls."

"Why," Mindwell breathed, leaning in over the cart tail, " 'tis Adam!"

She climbed in with startling agility and knelt to lay a hard hand on the senseless man's forehead.

"Lake fever," she told her son. "Bear him in carefully."

Chapter XVI

OLIN and Everest undressed Adam and got him to bed in the chamber he had shared with Sherwood, while Mindwell in the kitchen hung a pot over the fire and drew from the cupboard munitions she had stored for such a crisis. She muttered, as she sorted them, certain spells old women had taught her. She felt they did no harm and might be of benefit, but she placed her prime reliance on her packages of dried leaves, roots, and bark. Choosing from these, she prepared for battle.

While the water heated, she returned to the room where her patient lay, observed the flushed cheekbones, the restless movments, the shallow breathing, and issued orders to her respectful son. The ill man's lungs were affected, wherefore the windows must at all times be kept closed against the deadly outer air. He was fevered and must not drink any liquids save those of her preparation and, most particularly, no cold water.

Mindwell bade Olin bring additional quilts from the dresser and spread them over the heated body to induce sweat. She had regional fame as a doctor. Adam, in the days that followed, required all her skill.

The woman fought the fever by drenching her patient with repeated draughts of red-willow bark and boneset tea. She purged him with infusions of rhubarb root and, when he still did not respond, attacked his liver with a concoction of burdock root and wild-cherry bark, boiled in cider.

There were days when it seemed that all her resources would not be enough; when the ill man thrashed in delirium and the woman by his bed watched with dread for his hands to pluck at the bedclothes, sure sign that her ministrations had failed. She did not tell Olin, who was distracted by the numberless tasks that must be accomplished before the snows came, how often in his bab-blings Adam spoke Felicity's name.

One night, Mindwell, having sent her weary son to bed, entered the sick chamber to find her patient's lips blue and his breathing fainter. She did not rouse her son. This was her responsibility and she would face it alone. Hour by hour, she heated flaxseed poul-tices and applied them, steaming, to the patient's chest. By dawn, Adam's flesh was parboiled but his breathing was stronger. The woman broke off her vigil and turned to the performance of her own day's work. At noon, entering the chamber still another time, she thought she saw a glistening on the bearded face and, placing a palm upon Adam's forehead, found it cool and damp.

Hosannahs swelled in Mindwell's heart but all she said aloud was, "Wal!" She went to the kitchen to prepare, not an additional draught, but venison broth.

Adam, waking next morning, knew that a long, dark journey had ended. He saw through the window leafless trees and looked with wonder at his clawlike hands.

"How," he whispered when Mindwell appeared, "did I—get here?"

"That'll wait," she told him crisply. "Drink this."

He was willing to lie sousing himself again and again in slum-ber, while the lately scattered intricacy that was he reassembled itself. With each meal Mindwell brought, he felt a new, small in-crement of competence return. The woman and her son shied from mention of their sacrifices as though these had been inde-cencies, and Adam, observing their distress when he tried to thank them, learned to hold his peace.

Silence did not lessen his new affection for them both. One day he begged Olin to bring him his coat and, assured that the deed he had drawn still rested within it, felt more at ease.

It had snowed by the time Adam could sit up and thrice more before he was out of bed and tottering about the house. When he spoke of leaving, the Roydens pointed out vigorously that travel through winterbound wilderness was beyond many hale men and made him understand, by manner more than speech, how much they counted on his companionship in the arctic months ahead.

Adam was surprised to find that he was willing to stay. His

mind and convalescent body were languid and shrank from enterprise. Here, in snow-imposed tranquillity, he might in time find answers to questions that still were too heavy for him to weigh.

The days crept past, a few memorable for the visit of a snowshoed neighbor or a violent storm, most of them as indistinguishable from each other as the waterdrops that compose a stream. Adam had ample time to think.

In the long, slow hours when Mindwell was occupied and Olin was abroad, Adam fumbled with many problems and solved none. He wondered what the fate of his Albany property had been, now that he had been proscribed. He debated what his course should be when spring had ended his serene imprisonment here and asked himself where, in this time of strained allegiances, his own loyalty should lie.

None of these ponderings was more than mildly disturbing. There were too many uncertainties for any to seem supremely urgent. It was easier to dismiss the accidents, coincidences, and incautious personal impulses that had lodged him here as a pattern wrought by fate and to leave the future in her hands.

The drifts crept up to swamp the fences and climb the windowsills. Thought of Felicity alone had urgency. The serenity of this timeless sojourn could not dull the sharp anxiety with which Adam's mind dwelt on her. He bitterly matched his own devotion against her gay inconsequence. Jealousy cut him as he imagined the frivolity through which she moved, pursued, so Skene had said, by the youth of Quebec and already the cause of one duel. The girl was not to blame. It was her indulgent brother's fault. Adam came, by wretched brooding, to denounce, almost to dislike, Justus.

The Roydens had continued to look for Sherwood's return until in November they had received word that business would keep him all winter in Quebec. Adam spoke of him, when they sat by the kitchen hearth on a day of whirling snow and squealing wind. Olin shrugged.

"Truth is, Justus finds Canady company more agreeable than us. He's a king's man."

"Aren't we all king's men?" Adam asked idly.

"So far—mebby, but I figure I'm Olin Royden's man, first, Grants' man, second, and His Majesty's loyal subject no better than third. Willing to leave it there, if George is. Justus puts it t'other way round. He's first for the king."

"Lord!" said Adam, stretching his feet toward the fire. "Were men ever before so disturbed in their beliefs and loyalties?"

"Wars 'n' rumors o' wars 'n' men's hearts failing 'em for fear," Mindwell supplied in the special voice she used for Scripture.

"Know well enough where I stand," her son said. "So does Justus."

"I'll find them both in Canada, come spring," Adam promised, "and bring them back where they belong."

He thought he understood Olin's quick glance. They had spoken rarely of Felicity. Adam proposed, lamely, "Come with me, when I go."

"Ehyah," Olin grunted in scorn. "Nothing for a man to do here when winter's spent."

"I shan't leave," Adam said quickly, "until your crop is planted."

"Paid for your keep 'n' more," Mindwell protested, "since ye got hale again."

"There are some things you can't repay."

Olin said in haste, "Heard a crow yesterday. Must be gettin' into March."

"Keerless of me," his mother acknowledged. "Failed to keep the day-tally while Adam was sick. Never have got it straight, since."

"I've caused you much distress," Adam said.

Mindwell twisted uneasily in her chair. "Wouldn't s'prise me none if we had an early spring."

That night, while Adam undressed, he looked up and saw Olin in the doorway. The intruder cleared his throat.

"Just wanted to tell you. No call to put off your journey when the lake's clear. Just—"

The obviously rehearsed speech ended in a gulping sound. Adam asked, smiling, "You wish to get rid of me?"

Olin shook his head with violence.

"Hard to say it," he said unnecessarily and with a wretched smile. "Only—wal, Ma's come to set great store by you."

He stuck again.

"And I in you all," Adam returned, trying to ease him. "Your sister succored me, long ago; your mother lately saved my life."

Olin shook his head again.

"Neither here nor there. Soon or late, Felicity'll wed me, Adam."

His certainty was affronting. His voice, running on, scattered Adam's instinctive anger. "Warned you—sort of—last year. Rivals, I guess, you and me. Ma, she opposes me, too. Don't want it. Justus put me off; you, too, eh?"

His dark face was flushed; his air candidly miserable. Adam nodded, bewildered.

"She'll wed me when the time comes," Olin staggered on with odd hangdog confidence. "Know it; always have. Only—"

He gulped again and met Adam's stare with a sickly smirk.

"Win her, if you can. You won't; but try, an' welcome. Only—"

He crept back lamely to his earlier protestation: "Come to set great store by you."

Adam realized suddenly that affection, not jealousy, inspired the disheveled utterances. Olin, in his fantastic surety, was trying to guarantee a friendship. Adam said, touched and secretly amused, "Be easy, I understand."

"Miracle if you do," the other gasped with a crooked grin and fled from sentiment's baneful presence, leaving Adam to wonder uneasily whether some pledge from Felicity had inspired Olin's strange faith in himself.

Snows gave way to spasms of rain borne by damp south winds. Drifts grew sodden and, where the sun dwelt longest, wet, black earth shouldered out of the thinning cover. Water spoke with myriad voices and mud grew abysmal. As it dried, innumerable needs of the awakening farm reached out avidly to clutch both men.

Day after day, the land's demands compelled them. They rose stiffly at dawn and sat down, soiled and drugged with fatigue, to supper in the late twilight. Week by week, Adam postponed his departure; until the spring plowing was finished; until the corn was in; until stumps had been grubbed and the waste timber burned and another half acre had been wrested from the wilderness.

Shadblow and cherry were frothing on hillsides when Olin, who had ridden to Chimney Point to get seeds Strong had promised to bring downlake, returned in triumph. Sherwood drove a borrowed team and within the cart Felicity and Delight rode, knee-deep in baggage.

Adam stood, impassive as Mindwell, while Sherwood leaped down and, wringing his hand, babbled of smallpox in Quebec that had closed the school betimes; of his good luck in finding Olin at the lakeside when an army bateau had set them ashore and the better fortune that had let him meet Adam here.

Olin swung Delight from the cart and the girl rushed to embrace her disconcerted mother. He held up his hands to help Felicity alight. The brilliance of her face, the whirl of petticoats as she leaped down, her gay laughter dazed Adam.

She was, for all the sobriety of her dark-green cloak and gown, a splash of scarlet across a sad-hued world. Felicity, still laughing, kissed Mindwell deftly on either cheek and, turning, held out her hand to Adam. He bowed above it, suddenly and wretchedly conscious of the stained leather shirt Olin had lent him, of the sagging linsey-woolsey breeches Mindwell had made, of the loamed and broken shoes.

"My faith," Felicity cried with mirth like chiming bells, "you have become a proper pioneer, indeed, sir."

The months of separation had polished her, rubbing immature softness from her face and giving each feature new delicacy, filling her eyes with radiance. Her dainty poise made Adam feel additionally clumsy. He knew how desperately men might strive for her and, recalling the tale of the duel, grew clumsier still. He was not certain what he had said, but Felicity cried merrily to them all, "I call you to witness how fickle a gallant is Mr. Corlaer. I find him tarrying here with Mrs. Royden though he promised to attend us last winter in Quebec, didn't he, Dee?"

Delight turned from her mother and Adam had the lonely feeling that she, too, was half a stranger now. In his confusion, he could not be certain wherein lay the change. It was not only that she was taller and slender now instead of sharply thin. Delight smiled at him. He had never marked before how amusement crinkled her eye corners.

"He made no pledge to me," she answered and Adam wondered whether the reply was wholly artless. Felicity's dark eyes met his. He felt their provocation ripple through him. Before she could

156

speak again, Mindwell said briefly, "Been busier'n he figured on," and led the way into the house.

They supped that night in gaiety that flowed from Felicity. Her laughter brightened, her clear voice adorned the smoke-stained kitchen.

While her brother watched with pride, she chattered of school routine that Sherwood's presence had enabled her to evade, of the fetes they had attended, of Captain Delaplace and his wife who specially had befriended them, of the gallantry of Quebec's young men and the garrison officers, refining what otherwise might have been boasting by mirth and delicate mockery.

Olin listened in unconcealed rapture, but Adam wondered, and straightway was ashamed of his suspicion, whether the blithe recital were not designed to quicken ardor in her suitors.

Once, when Felicity provoked laughter, Adam turned to share it with Delight and for an instant thought the way she smiled at her companion's jest made her seem the older.

"Isn't that true, Dee?" Felicity cried and the girl replied with her new serenity:

"You forget I was not there. Mrs. Delaplace bade me, but I had tasks in school."

"Your sister," Felicity informed Olin in bright despair, "can be a most tiresome person. Mrs. Delaplace was quite mad about her, but she would hide herself away in books. She is too provoking. George dubbed her 'The Country Mouse.'"

Adam checked the sharp impulse to ask whether George's other name were Wadman. Sherwood, when they at last were alone in the room they were to share, also irked him by the satisfaction with which he confided his own activities in Quebec.

"His Excellency," Justus said, galling Adam afresh by the reverence in which he clothed the title, "gave me employment near his person. I am not at liberty to disclose its nature even to you, my friend, but I think I performed it with some credit. General Carleton is a wise and liberal man. I was much in the company of him and his staff."

"Most gratifying, I'll be bound," Adam said deliberately. Sherwood raised his eyebrows and considered his companion more carefully.

"Your illness," he said, obviously changing the talk's direction, "has done you no harm, surely. You look fit for any task."

Adam ignored the tact and asked bluntly, "Was Wadman, perchance, among the sanctified on 'His Excellency's' staff?"

"George?" Sherwood gave further offense by use of the Christian name. "No, he is a lieutenant now in the Twenty-sixth. He spoke of you," he pursued in haste, marking Adam's scowl, "with rueful respect. He harbors no grudge, I assure you. We found him a polite and gracious gentleman."

"Whose manifold virtues," Adam offered acidly, "included dragging your sister's name into another brawl."

"You heard of the duel?" Sherwood asked equably. "From whom?"

"From Major Skene," Adam returned, curbing the impulse to tell his friend he would have been better employed in guarding Felicity than in truckling to His Excellency.

"A regrettable affair," Sherwood said, speaking so lightly that Adam felt he considered it nothing of the kind. "But young men in His Majesty's service are hot-blooded and particular of their honor. Moving among them, I could not but esteem their code."

"The good people of Boston"—Adam spoke dryly to hide his irritation—"might not agree."

"If in time they do not, theirs will be the fault. I tell you, Adam, His Majesty with great forbearance is striving to appease his provinces. With governors like General Carleton as merciful instruments of the royal will, further disorder will be unwarranted and wicked. You cannot see facts clearly, my friend. You have been too long in The Grants."

"Then," Adam said with controlled bitterness, "I am likely to remain blind, since one of His Majesty's merciful instruments has placed a price on my head."

Sherwood stared in silence a long instant. "What do you mean?"

He listened with waxing distress while Adam told him. When he had ended, Sherwood said, "This can and must be expunged. If I can serve you, you have but to command me. It is accident alone that has brought about your plight. This is not your country, your people, or your quarrel."

"I was thinking," Adam explained at last, meeting his friend's regard, "how wholly wrong you were. What other country have I now?"

In the long silence he could hear his ears thin ringing. Sherwood drew a resigned breath.

"We should have a better time and place to talk. I still cannot believe you ever will stoop to treason, whatever wrong has been done you."

"No wrong would make me a Grants man," Adam replied slowly. "It would be the good I have found here."

Chapter XVII

SLEEP evaded Adam. He listened to Sherwood's calm breathing while his own mind leaped irresponsibly from Felicity's heart-rousing fairness to the flaw that had reappeared in his friendship with her brother; from thought of the long-unpaid debt he still owed Delight to wonder over his own future.

He heard the dry yapping of a fox and the sound of dew, shaken from the trees by the night breeze, falling loudly on the roof. He would, he resolved, declare himself to Felicity at the first opportunity, yet his decision faltered when he considered the dubious material gifts he now could offer her. If his New York property had been confiscated, the fragment of his fortune still held by his father's agent, James Morrison, in Montreal was all that remained. For a brief space Adam's way was plain. He must make the long-postponed journey into Canada.

He turned over once again and at last fell asleep to wake with a start in full daylight and find Sherwood gone. He dressed in haste and stole penitently to the kitchen where Mindwell and Justus, seated, regarded him with amusement. The man explained pleasantly, as Adam bolted breakfast, that Olin had been persuaded to declare this a holiday, and all, save Mindwell, were to ride to New Haven and see how the Sherwood house had survived the winter.

Olin and Felicity, Sherwood added, were harnessing the borrowed team to the cart and Delight had just gone out to aid them. He resumed with Mindwell his discussion of a new report that the persistent Reid would attempt to reestablish settlers in Panton this summer and Adam left the kitchen.

The low sunlight smote his eyes so that it was not until she was close at hand that he recognized who came hurrying toward him from the stable. There was unwonted color on Delight's face and her breathing was quick.

"Indians?" Adam asked her in elaborate alarm. "Yorkers?"

She granted him an uncertain smile.

"Neither. I—forgot something."

Yet for all her professed haste she seemed willing enough to linger. As the silence grew, he suggested, "Perhaps I had best go aid the hostlers," but she shook her head.

"There is no need," she insisted. "They are almost ready," and before he could speak again, asked, "Are you to bide with us all summer?" adding belatedly, "I hope so."

"That surely would sway me," he told her and at once regretted the flattery, seeing her face grow scarlet. She looked quickly away.

"I mean," Delight said in a hurried voice, "we should be glad to have another man here with Olin. Mr. Sherwood has heard in Canada that Colonel Reid will try to seize our land again."

Her tidings smote his memory. He begged, "Will you wait here an instant?" and, when she nodded, left to return with the document he had brought from Albany.

Before the stable, Olin and Felicity were hitching the team to the cart. Adam said quickly to Delight, "This is a guerdon of the debt I owe you. Put it in a safe place where you can find it quickly at need."

He pursued, in a hollow voice, to dispel the bewilderment in her eyes, "It is a charm, prepared in the dark of the moon with the most dreadful incantations, to preserve the Roydens and bring confusion to all Yorkers. Protect and cherish it. Do not even read it yourself, lest you break the spell. Promise?"

There was amusement on her face as she nodded. He had not seen until now how sweetly her mouth was molded.

"But if," he went on, "Reid or other miscreant lays claim to Royden land, then have recourse to this magic. Give him the paper and bid him heed it. It will smite him helpless, I warrant you. Will you remember, Delight?"

The cart rattled as Olin drove toward them. Delight hesitated, nodded, and slipped into the house with clasped hands holding the document against her bosom.

"Do hasten, Dee!" Felicity called. Compared with the child's moonlight pallor, she was, Adam thought, fashioned of the sun's own brilliance.

They left at last, jolting out of the clearing's heat and onto the half-erased way through the forest to New Haven. Sherwood drove the cart, Felicity and Delight sat on its hay-cushioned floor, while Adam's legs dangled from its tail. Olin, mounted, rode before them to clear the trail of branches winter's storms had cast across it.

The cart lurched and groaned. Sunlight, striking boldly through young beech and maple leaves, flashed across Delight's bare head and kindled in Felicity's hair a dusky fire. Adam trusted himself to look at her only briefly. It was enough for the moment that they were drenched together in the warmth and the piercing scents of spring. Thrushes chanted in the aromatic shadows and, overhead, warblers flashed like sparks through translucent foliage.

Presently, Felicity's voice rose above the coarse sounds of their passage, caroling with birdlike ease an old voyageurs' song:

"A la claire fontaine, m'en allant promener,
J'ai trouvé l'eau si belle, que je m'y suis baigné—"

Adam found his eyes were damp. He dared not turn about to praise her when the wistful song had ended.

Sherwood drove them into the still heat and glare of the New Haven clearing and Delight cried out to see how thickly it was spangled with violets. Adam looked with parental pride at the sturdy dwelling, standing blindfolded and patient, its once shining clapboards already dulled by weather.

He slid from the cart and helped its passengers down. Felicity's hand, lingering in his the barest unnecessary space, seemed to close about his heart. He watched her and Delight unpack the food Mindwell had provided and wondered if it were possible that his beloved, laughing so artlessly with her friend, could be unaware of the yearning that possessed him.

At length, he followed the other men toward the house. Its door stood open now and Olin was sweeping litter from the step. The dwelling's harsh chill halted Adam on the threshold. Lingering there, he heard Sherwood's feet strike echoes from the empty rooms as he returned from his inspection.

"Snug and tight, upstairs and down," he said with satisfaction. "We builded well. 'Tis a house in which we can take pride."

"More than you'll take in your crop this year," Olin offered dryly, "if you don't get it in real soon."

Sherwood paused and said at last, in a voice so precise that Adam knew he had rehearsed his announcement, "There'll be no planting till next spring. I have a mission in Boston that will prevent my settling here at once. Felicity," he added, his face relaxing in a faint smile, "has persuaded me to take her with me, wishing no doubt to compare Quebec's gallants with those of Boston town."

A sudden emptiness kept Adam from speaking.

"Oh!" Olin said, blankly, and then, recovering, "Wal, found a place on the brook where you could set a wing dam simply enough. Want I should show you?"

"After we have dined," Sherwood replied more easily. "It appears that the table is set."

The meal had been arranged on the top of a still-ungrubbed stump in the shade cast by a maple tree. Felicity waved and called gaily, *"Diner est servi, mesdames, m'sieurs."*

They sat about the makeshift table, with the bouquet of violets Delight had gathered in its center, and for a space appetite and the day's heavy warmth abolished rigidities and doubts. It was, Adam reflected, as though time had slipped and this noon had deserted the preceding year, coming back to restore old certainties.

He wished the enchantment were complete and he might forget Sherwood's new remoteness and the disquiet his projected journey to Boston had roused. Justus was his old, gravely pleasant self while he jested with Olin. It was Felicity and Delight who proclaimed time's passage. She whom he always had thought of as a child was, he realized with a twinge of dismay, childish no longer.

Adam lay in the shade and watched Delight smile demurely at Olin's and Sherwood's talk and join in pretended small quarrels with Felicity. He could not tell, remembering her shy awkwardness, whether he welcomed her new grace. He had not noticed, until she turned her head to speak with her brother, the clear purity of her profile.

She was a foil for her companion. Her pale delicacy heightened Felicity's vivid beauty. It was deep, abiding joy merely to lie here propped on an elbow and watch Sherwood's sister; to gratify, lavishly and unreproved, one of the five senses that continually cried for her. No one observed him, unless it were she herself.

Adam lay back with a sigh and continued to watch from beneath a shielding forearm. The brilliant face, the glowing hair, were lovelier still in the cool presence of the girl who sat beside her. No passion, he thought with reverence, could be so intense as his without fulfillment.

The time must come when, despite her brother's loyalties, despite prejudices and oppositions and thwartings, Adam would claim her. He found his mouth was dry and his heart pounding.

He listened to the easy voices, the fly-pestered horses stamping in the shade. He looked away from Felicity and saw above the treetops at the clearing's edge a mushroom of ivory cloud, thrust up into the bleached sky.

"I don't think," Delight's voice proclaimed, "I have ever seen violets so thick. I shall pick a nosegay for mother."

Olin rose and stretched. "Lord, but it's hot! Thunder weather. Justus, shall we seek the site for your dam?"

Adam did not stir. He had the awed feeling that fate was dropping events into place to form a purposeful pattern. He heard Olin and Sherwood depart and the girls' light speech die away. When at last he sat up from his pretended slumber, they all had gone.

The remnants of the meal lay on the stump, neatly folded in a cloth. Squinting against the glare, he saw Delight midway across the clearing, bending, moving, and bending again among the violets. Leaden shadows were gathering in the hollows of the swollen cloud-mass. Felicity had vanished. Slowly, with a travesty of unconcern, Adam strolled toward the house.

The door stood open but the inner chill lingered and was sharp upon his sweating face. He halted beyond the threshold to listen as carefully as he might through the thick tumult of his heart. For a dismaying instant there was silence. Then he heard a stir overhead and little shoes tap-tapping across the floor. He had moved to the foot of the stair when Felicity appeared at its head.

Slim ankles for a second's dazzling revelation made him conscious of all the sweet wonder of the body encased in the dusty-brown gown. He could not speak for an instant. At last, he said, "I was wondering where you were."

Her face was a brilliance against the gloom. Her voice was gay with unconcern, or understanding.

"It is cooler here. I have been trying to decide which chamber is to be mine. Justus bade me choose."

He stood, looking up at her. Felicity hesitated and then came slowly down the stair. As though a force beyond himself swayed him, Adam advanced to meet her. She did not shrink, but paused and, when he was close, asked in a small, clear voice, "Shall I show you?" and held out her hand. Still without speaking, he reached and caught it.

It was strange that he should have known how supple and slight her waist would be beneath his palms, how his body would be exalted by the pressure of her breasts, how fragrant her hair would be beneath his cheek.

Felicity lifted a pale face and he, seeing the smile that parted her lips, laid his own upon them. . . .

At length, she drew her head away. Low laughter bubbled in her throat.

"Is it true, then?" she whispered.

"What?" he asked blankly.

"What you have just told me, with your lips and your arms and your eyes."

"Increasingly, it has been so," he murmured, "since I saw you, coming like the spring into Fay's taproom."

She pressed small hands against his chest and with soft laughter held him away. She suddenly grew grave.

"Adam," she faltered. "Have you spoken to Justus?"

"Long ago," he assured her with a faint stirring of guilt.

"Almost a year ago, wasn't it?" she said slowly. "Much has changed since then."

"The year has made you more lovely."

Felicity smiled.

"I was thinking of you, Adam."

"And of nothing else, hereafter?"

"Adam, listen, I beg you. Justus finds you embittered, reckless, rebellious."

He was silent a moment, baffled by her charge.

"No," he told her. "Rebellious? No—not yet. Tryon has offered reward for me, Felicity."

"I know. Justus told me. Adam, what are we to do?"

He tried to drive the worry from her eyes.

"Love each other, more every day, in a thousand new ways."

Felicity hesitated.

"Must you shame me? We are plain folk, Adam, and I have small dowry to bring you."

"No man ever held so great a wealth."

She laid her hand upon his mouth and said beseechingly, "Don't confuse me, don't look at me so when I am trying to think."

"This is no time to waste in thinking?"

"Oh, my dear," she told him tensely. "Try to understand me. Adam, I cannot wed against my brother's wish."

"No," he said in a soberer voice. "I should never ask that."

"And you must not," she caught him up quickly, "speak to Justus now. You must wait."

"Must I? Till when?"

"Till—you shame me again, Adam—you can offer his sister what he deems her due. Don't frown. I must think, if you will not."

Reason had no place in this moment. It was chilling their rapture, dulling its radiance. Adam spoke more bitterly than he had intended, "You mean I must cleanse my name of the stain Tryon has cast on it? Better men than I have been more darkly smirched. You mean I must make my fortune snug and tight before I may wed you?"

"I mean," she told him steadily, "that is what Justus will wish, and he must approve before I wed."

They stood, looking across the strangeness that had risen between them. Felicity's clasped hands moved upon each other. At length, she faltered, "Do you find the price too high? Would you wish less for your own sister?"

A giant ponderously cleared his throat. They did not heed the boding sound or the brief gust that thrust warm air into the dwelling.

"What do you wish me to do?"

The half-sullen question startled her. She caught his hands and held them tightly.

"You must answer that, not I. How much do you care? Adam, how can we plan if you—? Adam, my sweet—"

Her body suddenly grew rigid. Her wide eyes looked past him down the stair. He heard her breath catch and asked quickly, "What is it?"

Felicity, still peering beyond him, answered in a low voice.

"I thought I heard—someone stir below. Adam, we have stayed here too long."

She clung to his hand until they reached the lower hall, then walked before him out into the heavy warmth of the afternoon.

The cloud-mass, magnified, had swallowed the sun. Grass and the trees beyond the clearing shone unearthly green in the precocious dusk. Thunder rumbled again. Adam looked for a long instant at the looming storm before he said, "I know you are right. I should have ordered my life. I should have spoken again to Justus, before I wooed you."

"But I am glad it happened to us," she cried. "Do you hear me, sir? Glad and proud. Only—"

She stopped abruptly on what he knew was the verge of further persuasion. Her compunction made Adam grope toward equal generosity. Dreams, so long-cherished that they had become half reality, new beliefs, loyalties lately formed, were small sacrifices to the splendor that enwrapped them both. He said, groping for words, "It shall be as you wish, my own dear love. I promise you. How, I am not yet sure."

He rubbed his forehead with the heel of a hand.

"I find it," he complained smiling ruefully, "difficult to think," and stirred with his toe the wilting violets that lay on the doorstep.

"How could either of us," she asked in a soft voice, "think clearly now? Oh, my dear," she pursued, with a tender smile that roused fresh turmoil, "I know. I know, too, that together we must find a way. Your place is not here, Adam, in this wilderness. You belong to a better world."

"I belong," he told her, professing his faith to exorcise a lurking dismay, "with you wherever, forever, Felicity, my love."

Fire pulsed in the lowering cloud and thunder rolled across the sky. The girl gave a small cry of alarm. A drop fell and broke darkly on the doorstep and a soft roaring swelled in the forest. They saw, through the thickening twilight, Olin and Justus run into the clearing and race toward the house before pursuing grayness.

A cool, wet wind outstripped them. Flame leaped crookedly across the sky and thunder cracked and boomed. Trees began a frantic thrashing and a loose shutter on the house banged.

Olin reached the dwelling and looked over his shoulder with a breathless grin as Sherwood plunged up the steps. A gust of rain raked them while they pressed into the house and closed the door. Olin panted, "First thunderstorm of the summer and making amends for the delay."

"A close escape," Sherwood gasped.

The downpour trampled on the roof, and the empty house magnified its tumult. Faint light that passed the streaming windows scarcely lessened the gloom in which they huddled. The cannonading thunder swelled, faded, and rose again. Lightning, subsiding, left thicker darkness.

"Trust," Olin offered in a lull, "the horses stand. If they break free, Felicity and Delight'll have a long walk home, without we carry 'em."

He squinted at another flare and asked in a new voice, "Where is Delight?"

They stared at each other's dim faces.

"I thought—" Adam began but could go no further.

"Delight," Sherwood called loudly. The word, echoing through the house, was abolished by a crash and the rain's renewed outburst.

Chapter XVIII

DELIGHT had run until her strength had failed. Shame lest she be seen, lest someone hail her and, direst possibility of all—ask what ailed her, had driven her. She had run as though by supreme effort she might shake off her woe and, somehow, recover what she had lost.

The slight figure flashed across the rare pools of sunlight, flickered through shade like a dryad invisibly pursued. Delight ran on until her legs grew limp and each breath scored her throat. She stumbled and went down headlong on the pine needles' deep, rough carpet, to lie quaking and know, as the paroxysm eased, that she had not outstripped her misery.

It was true that here beneath the great, dark trees lay silence and seclusion. She cowered in the shadow like a wounded deer, desolately safe. A deer would have turned to the woods for refuge as instinctively as she.

The breathlessness and the faint nausea were passing. The grief that had caused them would endure, she was sure, for the rest of her life. For that matter, most of her life, she thought, already had ended.

It wasn't, she reflected humbly, that she ever had hoped for very much. It was just that never again would there be anything worth hoping for, anything to make her careful about her dress and manners, anything to build daring and beautiful stories around before she went to sleep, to inspire her to do well at school.

There was no real use in going back to school, now that she knew that Felicity and Mr. Corlaer loved each other.

She wasn't angry with Felicity or jealous of her. Delight had always looked with awe and pride upon her friend's ability to enchant men. She didn't feel unfriendly toward Felicity; just empty and lost, the way she had long ago when they had told her her father was dead. She was going to miss Mr. Corlaer more, she guessed, though she was sure this was wicked. He had made living gay for her.

Mr. Corlaer was stirring to see and kinder and more generous to Delight than other folks ever troubled themselves to be. She liked the way he stood and walked and the way he wore his hair. She prized his voice and the eyes that looked merry, even when his face was solemn, and his neat, nice ways. There really was nothing about Mr. Corlaer that she didn't like.

He had belonged to no one until now, and Delight had had a right to think of him as she pleased. It had done no harm and it had helped her. Now he was Felicity's.

In a little while, Delight would get used to it. It was soothing to lie here, face down, with the healing shadows over her and the scent of pine needles in her nose. She had been wise to hide until she got her mind tidied up again. It would have been dreadful if anyone had seen her, all fallen apart.

Delight had been thinking of Mr. Corlaer while she had been picking violets for her mother. She had taken the nosegay to the house because she had thought it would keep better in the coolness. From the doorway, she had heard Felicity and Mr. Corlaer talking on the stairway and what they had said had stunned her so that she for a minute had been unable to stir though her eyes, adjusting to the inner gloom had seen them, quite clearly, together. Her first thought, she remembered now, had been the wish that she were decently dead.

The fortitude that was a pioneer people's substitute for philosophy was coming to her aid. In a little while, she would go back the way she had come before anyone missed her and never, never would she by word or deed reveal her unwilling eavesdropping. She quailed at the thought of what anyone who had seen her peering into the house would have presumed.

Delight looked up and was alarmed to see how dark it had grown. While she stared through the pines that loomed enormous in the dusk, thunder uttered a long, low growl.

The girl scrambled to her feet. Thought of enduring a storm alone in the wilderness terrified her. She had taken a dozen quick steps before uncertainty made her halt. The brown carpet, the lichened ledges, the monumental trunks looked different in the half light. Perhaps, uneasiness tittered, this was not the way she had come.

Thunder, pealing again, increased her doubt. She heard, far away, the great sound of advancing wind. Delight looked quickly about her, altered her course, and walked resolutely forward. Presently, with the hounding voice of the blast drawing near, she ran.

The wind rolled above her through the pines with the sound of surf and after it came rain, climbing down the interlacing boughs to drench her. Lightning glared on the falling drops and flashed across the wet ground, filling the world with fire, leaving it, as thunder exploded, in deeper gloom.

Delight's wet skirt tripped her and she fell, scrambled up, and ran on, a frantic, unconsidered mote in the tumult. She could not hear her own scream as a fiery spear stabbed the forest. The shock of the clap half-stunned her.

Overhead and unperceived, the storm moved on. The wind slackened, thunder subsided into distant rumbling, though water still drizzled from the overladen branches. The spreading quiet halted Delight. She should never, she told herself tardily, have run. It would have been better, looking dully at her soiled and draggled dress, if she had stayed where she had been until the downpour had ended.

Mist was spawning among the darkly gleaming tree trunks. Delight pushed fear back and searched the dripping forest. She got no enlightenment from the visible fragments of sky, little more from the wilderness itself. Once she called, but her voice was so small an intrusion on the silence that it frightened her.

She must not run again. She must go carefully, certainly north and west toward the clearing. She saw, while her throat tightened, how the mist was thickening. She must not think of Olin or Felicity or Mr. Corlaer. She must forget for the moment tales about those the wilderness had taken and never returned, but watch her course, ignoring small brief sounds that could be wolf or panther, bear or Indian.

The silence of her passage over the soaked earth was nerve-taxing. Each moment the fog drove away more light. The clearing could not be far.

Her wet clothing dragged upon her waist and shoulders. The gray-blue mist had grown so heavy that she stood on the bank of a slow stream before she was aware of its presence. Relief dazed her. All the region's watercourses led to the lake. This must be the very brook that crossed the Sherwood pitch. She need only follow—

For an instant, she could not believe her sight. Foam on the murky water, that must flow lakeward, was moving in what was, to her, the wrong direction.

The girl's knees gave way and dropped her at the stream's edge. She felt the forest's cold animosity press in upon her and knew that, unless a miracle had happened and water ran uphill, she was utterly lost.

The drenched searchers returned at last to Sherwood's house.

"Sign of her?" Olin repeated in a voice rasped by shouting. "What sign could there be? The rain would have washed away an ox team's tracks."

"When did you last see—?" Adam began, but Sherwood interrupted him.

"We have been over that already. Haste is the necessity now. One of us must stay here, in case she returns. Olin must ride ahead and bring back firelocks. Shots may guide her where our voices fail. Adam or I will drive as swiftly as may be to Panton and rouse the neighbors."

"I'll stay," Adam said. Sherwood nodded.

"Hurry," he urged, and strode swiftly toward the tethered horses. The others followed. Sherwood bade Olin as they fumbled with the slimy harness.

"Bring rum, too, if you can manage."

Olin jerked his head. Adam, seeing his stiff face, tasted dread, unfamiliar to him, that had sickened his friends—the settler's abiding fear of the wilderness, waiting, balefully patient about the clearings to destroy the unwary.

Felicity touched his arm. Her eyes were enormous. She said in a low voice, "Could it have been she I heard while—we were on the stair?"

He did not pause to weigh the sense of guilt her question woke.

"I think it was," she murmured. "If so, she cannot have strayed far."

"No," he said and bent again to his work, revived by the secret they shared. Sherwood glanced at the sky. Below the gray cloud, the west was kindling.

"Ride hard," he said, quietly, "or it will be sunset when you return."

Olin pulled himself into the saddle and whirled his horse around. Mud flew back from the galloping hoofs. Sherwood lifted Felicity into the cart and, climbing in, seized the reins. The girl raised an arm in silent farewell as they rocked across the clearing.

The forest took the cart and dulled its rattling. The sounds faded, returned faintly, and then died. Adam moved slowly toward the house. Once, he paused to call but the silence swallowed the thin sound from his abused throat.

It was, he assured himself, only anxiety that made the stillness so taut and breathless, yet he could understand why his Mohawk friends had peopled the wilderness with the spirits of evil. He could believe the forest watched him now with mocking, hooded eyes.

Thrushes in the shadows beyond the clearing began to call, their voices cleansed and sweetened by the rain. Thus they had rung their chimes only a few hours ago when he and his companions had ridden hither. He remembered the lilt of Felicity's plaintive song and the sunlight flaring, dying, and blazing again on Delight's pale hair. He recalled how her shy smile had crinkled the corners of her eyes. She was lost and wrapped in terror, somewhere in the dark, dripping wilderness. One instant, she had been plucking violets for her mother; the next, the forest had snatched her.

Had she sought more flowers in the woods and wandered too far? He tried to think how long he and Felicity had been together in the house, but passion had blurred time's passage. It should have been too brief a space for Delight to lose herself, yet he and Sherwood and Olin had searched, vainly shouting, all along the clearing's edge. The downpour seemed to have erased her as completely as it had abolished her tracks.

No beast could have attacked her, no far-roaming Indian could have captured her. Her friends would have heard her cry. He recalled the storm's tumult and new alarm twisted him. If he could see where Delight had left the clearing, he would have made a long forward step toward finding her. There were not enough men in Panton town to search the forest thoroughly in all directions.

Adam paused before the house and, looking down, saw a plucked violet the rain had trampled into the matted grass. He stared at it, stunned by its testimony, and, reviving, searched further and found two more.

Excitement filled his throat. Felicity had been right in her hazard. Delight had lingered where he stood now only a few moments before he and the girl had come from the house. He called with hoarse urgency that hushed for an instant the thrushes' voices. He did not shout again but circled the dwelling with his eyes fixed on the ground.

Midway between the house and the clearing's edge, Adam caught his breath, bent and picked up the broken and battered remnant of Delight's nosegay.

She had cast it here impelled by some urgency, fright perhaps. Fright of what? Adam shied from the question. He summoned the neglected skill his Indian friends had taught him. The best of Mohawk trailers could have found no trace of Delight on the rain-beaten earth.

He ranged back and forth and, at length, close to the forest's first tall trees, found reward. A single thread of fabric still dangled wetly from the blackberry thorn that had jerked it free. This, then, was the way she had come.

Again he called, "Delight!" and roused only a distant, jeering echo. While he hesitated, a breeze touched his neck and set the leaves to talking. The sun, unmasked by the passing cloud, cast Adam's shadow into the woods. He drew a deep breath and followed it forward. By circling wide through the wilderness, he might possibly cut across the girl's fresh trail.

A breeze began to sing through the pines and Delight, looking up, saw the fog shred and drift away. A narrow bar of sunlight slanted down through the branches to turn a handbreadth of wet earth golden. The girl watched it glow and fade. She was too spent now to feel acute fear. The weight of her weariness almost kept her from rising and compelled her to walk with caution, lest she should fall again.

Delight followed the sluggish brook but, when it spread into a swamp that filled a hollow, she scanned the hummocked expanse with dreary relief, knowing how far beyond her strength it was to cross or skirt it.

She let herself collapse beside a boulder and leaned back against its moss-covered face, thinking wistfully of her home and her mother, of Olin and Mr. Corlaer doing the chores together and the pleasant smell of pork frying for supper. But they wouldn't, she thought, pulling herself back to reality, be readying for supper tonight. Surely, by now, they had missed and were searching for her.

All she could hear was the stream's thick gurgle and the endless passage of the wind. Still listening, she must have dropped briefly to sleep for she suddenly saw the sunlight in the treetops had turned a richer yellow and heard somewhere, aloft and invisible, a robin singing his twilight song. Night soon would be here with its darkness and its stealthy sounds and nameless terrors.

Delight had wickedly wished that she were dead. A night spent alone in the forest, even if Indians, bears, panthers, or less clearly imagined horrors didn't slay her, would, she was sure, frighten her to death before it passed.

She wept quietly for those dear and lost to her: for her mother and brother, for Felicity and Mr. Corlaer. Her despair was so complete that when she looked up and through her tears saw Adam come toward her, bent forward, scanning the ground, she believed him an illusion born of longing.

Not until he looked up, cried, "Delight!" and ran, was she certain it was truly, surely, he—and the immensity of her relief whipped away the last of her self-control.

She knew only that he held her and would not let her fall again; that, ignoring her soiled and sodden state, he allowed her to cling to him, a precious stability in a dwindling nightmare. She could not check her sobbing, though its violence tore her.

"Delight, dear child," he was saying in her ear. "Don't, I beg you. It's all right, it's all right now."

She wished the warm voice would continue, that his arms might sustain her for the rest of her life.

He supported her, still gasping and shivering, with one arm, and wiped her face with his own kerchief before he lowered her to her seat beside the boulder to stand, looking down at her with smiling concern.

"I'm glad," he said simply, "that I've found you. You've given us a monstrous fright."

"Not as much," she whispered with a pitiful striving for poise, "as I gave myself."

He did not ask her what had taken her into the forest but she said, for fear of the possible question, "I was looking for flowers and ventured too far. And then, the storm scared me."

It sounded unconvincing but he accepted it without comment while he looked carefully about him.

"Do you think," he asked, "that you can walk?"

Delight drew her feet under her and asked, "How far?"

He frowned, then grinned at her. "That's the trouble. I don't know. I'm a little lost myself."

He went on rapidly, lest he rouse her fright, "You see, I was swinging a circle through the woods, Indian-fashion, when I cut across your trail. It ran so crookedly, and I had to heed it so carefully, that now I'm not sure where it has led me."

He paused a moment, smiling down at her with assurance. "We could strike directly west, but we might miss the clearing entirely. It will be better to backtrack my trail, since that must lead us out at last."

She had never seen anything so splendid as he, standing over her with a half smile still on his face. She looked away, afraid that he might read her eyes, and, when she dared to lift them again, he was staring upward.

"We had best start if you are able. There is not much daylight left."

Adam led the way, watching the trail with care. Twice he looked back and each time, seeing her pallor and her breathlessness, halted for a space. The second, as he held out a hand to raise her, he asked lightly, "Would it frighten you to spend tonight in the woods?"

"With you?" She feared to say more and shook her head.

176

"We may have to," he pursued. "We've still a long way to travel. We'll have a fire," he went on hastily, mistaking her look for alarm, and drew the trigger-and-hammer mechanism from his jerkin pocket.

"I am never without it. We still have at least an hour of daylight, if you are not too weary."

Her valor smote him. Dazed though she was by weariness, she smiled. Adam wondered whether her pretenses were so transparent to all who knew her. And yet, he thought as he helped her up, she had the baffling obscurities of all womankind. Her tale of how she had come to be lost was a concealment. She had said she had entered the woods to seek more flowers. Then why had she cast her violets away at the forest's edge? The only answer he could supply woke a sense of guilt. He quelled it by pinning his attention to the trail. After a little, he said, "There is a brook beyond the rise. We'll make camp—"

The distant report snapped his speech short. Adam threw back his head and yelled through cupped hands so violently that he coughed.

"Olin," he wheezed exultingly. "Trailing me. You'll sleep in your own bed tonight, dear child."

He found on the haggard face so scant a reflection of his glee that he said quickly in self-reproach, "You're more spent than you think. Let me carry you."

Delight withstood temptation.

"No," she insisted. "I can walk."

He drew her elbow within the angle of his own.

"Let me bear part of you, at least," he begged as they moved forward again. The pressure of his hand made her dizzy.

This was something, she thought light-headedly, to remember all of her days. This was something to tell when she was old. She had been hopelessly lost, but Mr. Corlaer had sought and found her. That made her, in a fashion she could not explain yet knew for verity, Adam Corlaer's possession.

Not, she corrected herself hastily, that he had need or wish for her. He would never know—particularly, he must never know after what she had seen and heard that afternoon—yet her life henceforth would be his. It was a warming thought.

Adam, glancing anxiously down at her, marveled at the transformation relief had wrought. The lately drawn face now wore a calm, almost dedicated look. Delight, he thought, must have been far more terrified than he had suspected.

The musket exploded again, so close at hand now that the girl flinched. Adam shouted and peering through the forest where dusk's veil was drawing, grasped his companion's arm more tightly. Two men, with firelocks trailing, came over the ridge ahead and trotted down toward them. The foremost shook his gun aloft and howled like a wolf.

"Baker," Adam cried. "Remember Baker. What on earth—?"

Olin ran past his companion and reached them first. He panted in anger and relief, "Lord, Dee, what a fright you gave us! Roused the whole settlement and—"

He choked, rubbed sweat from his eyes, and glared at his sister as though her safety were an affront. Baker leaned on his musket and pushed back his fur cap to inspect the bedraggled girl before he offered, "Don't look 'sif she done it a-purpose."

His canny eyes puckered as he turned.

"Adam, how be ye?"

"Fit. How came you here?"

"Downlake," Baker replied unsatisfactorily, "with Stub Allen. Stopped to visit to Strong's. Come over to see whar they'd buried ye, found Olin steamin', 'n' rode back double with him. Olin, we'd best pull foot for Sherwood's pitch. Else we'll have the woods full of folks huntin' her 'n' gittin' lost more complete."

He grinned at Delight. Adam said protectingly, "She's worn out, Remember. We'd best make a litter."

The girl shook her head. Baker drawled, "Made a wide circle, Mohawk-fashion, didn't ye? Guide ye straight cross-country 'n' git ye thar 'fore dark."

Chapter XIX

SUNLIGHT still clung to the tops of the tallest trees when Baker led them into the clearing, where Olin's weary horse was tethered and armed men were climbing out of the cart with its lathered team.

The thwarted rescuers yelped and ran to press about Delight, babbling questions until Olin, at Sherwood's muttered bidding, mounted and reined in close to the dazed girl. Baker and Adam swung her up behind him and they rode away, with Delight's arms clasped about her brother's waist. The wan smile she cast back at Adam dwelt in his mind.

Delight, Mindwell Royden told them, her weathered face calm, her bare feet planted squarely as though she challenged a greater upheaval to overset her, was abed, with Felicity tending her. Supper was ready and she'd cooked up plenty for them all. Felicity did not reappear until after the guests had eaten immensely, had acknowledged the Roydens' brief thanks with greater brevity, had picked up their muskets and gone.

"She's asleep," the girl reported when she entered the kitchen. "She has taken no harm, I think, thanks to you."

She included the four men, but her eyes, touching Adam's, dwelt there longest. When she had eaten, and Baker, Sherwood, Olin, and Mindwell, still seated at the uncleared table, were tangled in debate over Reid's intentions, Felicity rose and returned to Delight. The glance she gave Adam in passing sent a prickling down his spine. He waited until he heard the front door softly open and close, then rose as idly as he might and went out.

She was not, as she seemed for an instant when he saw her, a shadow among deeper shadows but warm and exalting in his arms. Her long kiss set the stars to whirling.

"No," she gasped softly when she had drawn away. "Not again —now."

She gave the low, contented laugh already dear to him, and for an instant pressed her hands against her face.

"We must take care, Adam. We must drive no one else into the forest."

"What do you mean?" he asked, thinking with pity of Olin and his groundless certainty.

"Adam, I am sure Delight saw us on the stair—and ran away."

"But why?"

Felicity's mirth was brief and brittle. "Because, my dear man, the child fancies herself in love with you."

"Delight? What nonsense!"

"Nonsense? Is that flattering to me?"

She drew closer. Adam ignored for a moment the prompting of her upturned face. Delight, the grave, quaint child, in love with him? The idea was comic. Yet it was pathetic, too, and, in an undefined way, disturbing.

"It can't be," he said aloud, but his profession did not dispel unwilling belief.

Delight's rapt attention when he talked to her, the odd gravity in her eyes, the passion with which she had clung to him when he had found her, the smile she had cast back when she had ridden off with Olin—these and other memories were linking themselves into unity. Poor child, he thought; poor, pitiful, endearing child. Felicity breathed softly in his ear: "Kiss me."

She laid small hands on his arms at last, thrusting him away so that she could search his face. She asked, "Have you been thinking?"

"Of you," he answered, rocked by the need of her, "in what scant time has been granted me."

"I sought no compliment, sir. Adam, what are we to do? You must not stay here?"

"While you stay," he insisted but she shook her head.

"Someone, everyone would know."

"Let them."

Her hands tightened on his arms.

180

"Let them know? Tell Justus that a Grants outlaw, who may be penniless as well, seeks to wed me? Cannot you imagine what my brother would say? I have been thinking, Adam, if you have not."

It was right, he told himself, stoutly repelling dismay, that she should look forward prudently. He envied her ability to summon and dismiss passion at will. He asked, "You wish me to leave you?"

"We go soon to Boston, ourselves. I wish you to return to me, no longer an outcast, lurking here, but your old self, as first I saw you and"—dropping her voice—"loved you."

"You still do?" he asked, not wholly in jest.

"Idiot," she told him and raised her mouth to his.

Still holding her close, he said thoughtfully, "Baker left young Allen and a boat at Chimney Point. They are bound for St. Johns, and James Morrison, my father's agent, dwells in Montreal. I should have visited him long ago."

"Then go now, dolt," she bade, shaking him. "Was there ever such a sluggard? Go, for my sake and your own and even for little Delight's. It was better for her not to see you daily. Go and find how grave is your plight and then come to Justus for aid. He is not without influence, Adam. Go, my lover, with my blessing."

After a while, she pulled herself firmly away.

"No," she whispered, when he would have followed her to the house. "Tarry here a space and then go in by the kitchen door. Lord, sir, are you deft only in woodcraft?"

Baker, next morning, climbed into the cart and took the reins. Adam wrung Olin's and Sherwood's hands and bowed correctly over Felicity's.

"Tell Delight farewell for me," he said to Mindwell. "Bid her recover at once and stay out of the woods till I return."

He hesitated an instant, looking down upon the woman's square brown face, and, seeing a softness in the steady eyes, on impulse placed his hands upon the thick shoulders and, bending, kissed her cheek.

"Goodbye—mother," Adam muttered and swung his baggage and himself in over the tailboard.

Remember clucked to the horses. Mindwell stood silent, looking after Adam with a calloused palm pressed against her face.

"More folks like her in The Grants," Baker offered over his

shoulder, "be a deal of trouble for a spell, 'n' then mebby none at all."

John Strong and his buxom wife made them welcome. Ethan Allen's youngest brother, a solid youth with dark, liquid eyes, a hawk nose, and a prim slot of a mouth between chubby cheeks, gave Adam a quick, mild handshake and thwarted Strong's hospitable intentions by pointing out the favorable set of the wind and the need for haste.

His precocious authority prevailed and he led them, Adam a little ruffled by his insistence, down to the boat, urged them aboard, and thrust off. Baker set the mast and trimmed the sail. Froth spun from the craft's prow as it swung past the gray fort on the farther shore and pointed for the wideness of the lower lake. From the center seat that he shared with Adam, Baker called to Ira Allen, sitting squat and vigilant as a woodchuck at the tiller, "Learn anythin' more?"

The steersman shrugged. "Little enough. Strong says Tryon wants to evict all Grants men and give them wasteland in return. Generous, ain't he? Truce is dead and stinking, but the parcel of Aunt Abbies who oppose Ethan set 'round the corpse and mourn while the Yorkers move in. What was it Ethan called 'em, last Council meeting?"

"Forgit," Baker deplored. "Had 'pukin' 'n' pettifoggin' 'n' Pharisee' in it. Real resoundin'."

He turned and spoke defamingly to Adam of the cautious elders who, still adhering to the truce, opposed the use of violence to repel York encroachments, lest resistance prejudice His Majesty's awaited decision of the dispute.

"Ain't made up his mind, yit," he snorted. "Aims to be king, why don't he work at it? Else, by God, we'll mebby git a better. Eh, Stub?"

Young Allen shook his head and his eyes were thoughtful.

"Don't pay," he said deliberately, "to be hasty—sometimes. Ethan's taken to cursing the king, like Boston folks. Wal, Bay Province has grievances against George, wouldn't be surprised. We ain't—not that I've heard of."

"Grievances!" Baker squalled. "Don't Tryon want now to

turn Grants folks off their farms 'n' give 'em to Yorkers, lettin' us have in trade land nobody wants? Don't—"

"That's Tryon," Allen told him crisply. "Not George. Tickle Tryon breathless to have The Grants defy the king. Got a handful with York, ain't we? Takin' on the British, too, might be a bit too much. Bargain with George if we can, I say. With all his troubles, he might be open to a dicker."

He shifted the tiller and blinked serenely at his companions. For an instant, despite his youthful air, he seemed the eldest of the three.

"Let's go careful," he counseled the grumbling Baker. "Need to, if we're to hold that."

He nodded toward The Grants shore that slid by with a wave-washed wall of gray rocks between the water and the forest. The mast creaked under the full sail's straining. The boat pitched sedately and mountains west of the lake's blue and gold slowly crept into new groupings.

His companions' untempered speech was bitter tonic for Adam. It had been easy to forget in the uneventful rhythm of frontier days that elsewhere strife went on; that irreverent, audacious men like these still were holding fast to their farms and infant towns. He felt as though Baker and the young Allen had roused him from sleep, yielded momentarily to the contagion of their insurgence, and then firmly thrust it aside.

Felicity, he thought sadly and instantly was ashamed of his regret, out of her love had shown him the way that would lead to possession of her. If it were not for Felicity, his aimless life might be pledged to the folk who resisted all authority but their own, who groped toward an end still too vague for any man— Adam, or the mature young Allen with his poet's eyes, or Baker, jesting of his king's dismissal—to see entire.

Adam wondered what had brought his companions to Champlain. Clearly, they were on an errand for that Whole of which each Grants' man was part. He found himself envying them and asked their purpose with incautious bluntness. Ira Allen raised supercilious eyebrows, but Baker replied promptly.

They were bound at Ethan's behest to St. Johns, there to learn if possible whether the forts' garrisons were to be reinforced this summer.

"We've heered," Ira said, abandoning caution, "that Reid will ask military aid to secure his settlement in Panton. If the army takes a hand—"

He shrugged. Adam turned to Baker. "Didn't Justus know?"

Remember called, through the south wind's freshening blast, "Justus Sherwood was to Roydens, Stub. Talkin' compromise 'n' headin' for Boston town."

The squat young man flattened his mouth and moved it thoughtfully across his teeth before he asked, "Where's he git the money?"

Baker leered. "Found a gold mine, mebby."

"Mebby. Guy Carleton Mine, milled pieces in every shovelful."

"Mebby," Baker echoed and spat overside. "Real anxious to find out what you and me was up to. Didn't."

"Spyin', you figger?" Ira asked gently.

"Wouldn't amaze me."

The acid voices stung Adam into defense.

"I question that. Justus has built a house in The Grants, he rode against Reid's people last year, and, before that, to rescue you, Remember."

"Ehyah, from you 'n' Munro," Baker acknowledged with a grin that turned his eyes to slits. "Justus spent last winter in Quebec with the quality—him and his sister."

Adam felt his face grow hot. Ira said in a thoughtful voice, "A year does more to folks now than it used to, seems 'sif."

They camped in a primrose sunset on a beach halved by a river's wide mouth. The stream, Baker told Adam, was the Onion and drained rich land.

"When we've done our chores to St. Johns, 'n' if there ain't no real call for haste, Stub 'n' me figger on skulking up river a ways. Good country, ripe for settlin'. We'll look her over. Always providin'," he added anxiously, "Stub don't give out."

"Fears," the composed young man informed Adam, "I'll wear him down. Knows I can outwalk him, outrun him—"

"Kin outtalk me 'n' outeat me," Baker conceded.

"And outstarve him," Allen pursued calmly, still ignoring his traducer. "Dugout tipped him and me into the Otter. Traveled fifty mile on less'n a pound raw salt pork."

184

"He et the whole of it," Baker pursued dreamily. "Eat anything. Et so many suckers one spring, bones 'n' all, they worked
through his hide 'n' we couldn't git his shirt off him till fall."

Ira grinned and addressed him directly, "Wal, we'll look over
the land you're so choice of. If half you claim is true, I'll survey,
sell, and settle it."

"Tryon won't let ye."

"Won't he? Possession's nine points of the law. I forget what the
tenth is," Ira pursued thoughtfully, "but it ain't of no real con-
sequence."

Adam lay after the others were asleep in hollows they had
scooped in the dry sand and watched the campfire waste to ash.
The course that he and Felicity had plotted, the night before,
was more tangled and difficult than he had thought.

It was easy to dismiss his companions' suspicion of Sherwood
as slander, in which all Grants people were adept. It was less agreeable to imagine what Baker's and Allen's estimate of Adam, himself, would be, were they to learn that he purposed to make his
own peace with Tryon.

The price the governor had set upon Adam had been his prime
recommendation in The Grants. It had warranted and distinguished him, opened the doors and minds of settlers, included him
in a casual fraternity from which, when his present intention was
fulfilled, he would be barred. Nevertheless, he had set his foot on
his course and would not, could not, turn back now.

Did a lover's dreams, Adam wondered while frogs thudded and
the fire whispered as it fell apart, always run far beyond love's
reality? Felicity until yesterday had been an imaginary beloved,
reflecting his own desires, believing as he believed, echoing his
wishes and his plans. She had been, in his untrammeled fancy, as
indifferent as he to wealth. This dream creature was not the flesh-
and-blood Felicity.

She was fairer, more intoxicating, than his fancy had made
her. His breath came faster, recalling her softly eloquent hands,
the promise of her ardent body. She was fair beyond imagining
but she was not his own reflection. She was an individual with a
will and intentions of her own. Thought of Olin's confident rivalry popped into his mind and troubled him.

The frog's rub-a-dubbing, the lisp of water along the beach, lulled him. At last he slept, to dream that, armed and armored, he rode wildly over an endless waste to save Felicity from peril and found at his quest's end, not his beloved, but Delight, wandering draggled and weeping, in a forest.

The south wind still blew on the morrow and all day bore them downlake, through the glitter of its greatest breadth where remote mountains hung cloudlike, and into the quieter water of the channel that snaked between clustering islands. Swallows flashed, gulls yelped about the rock-rimmed masses of feathery green, and the wind-crisped inlets and lagoons were a braver color than the sky.

Toward midmorning a canoe—Iroquois, Baker said, since it was sheathed in elm bark—went by at a distance, its brown crew digging briskly with their paddles, and toward noon another Indian appeared on an islet's point and by signs begged to be taken aboard. Baker mumbled and half reached for his musket but paid him no further heed.

They saw no other men until toward sunset they met a bateau, heavily laden, butting the waves and urged along by eight splashing sweeps. A redcoated man in the stern waved as they passed. Allen and Baker, peering carefully at the clumsy craft, debated whether this were part of the rumored reinforcement of the lake forts' garrisons, while Adam felt that tingling wariness he had come to accept as part of the Grants' atmosphere.

They passed William Gilliland's garrison house, standing white and lonely on its point, and camped on lowland beside Champlain's outlet.

Next morning the mild current bore them down the willow-bordered Richelieu and brought them before noon to St. John's, drowsing on the stream's west bank.

The moldering ramparts of the old French fort, the single idle soldier in the group that saw them land, the empty wharves, belied the rumored military activity. They drew their boat ashore alongside the pier where an armed sloop was moored.

"H. M. S. Enterprise" was the faded legend on her stern but her crew seemed to consist of a single watchman, smoking disconsolately astride one of her brass six-pounders.

At the tavern, whither his companions led him, Adam learned

that a freight wagon was leaving and would bear him to La Prairie, across the St. Lawrence from Montreal. Baker, when his friend departed, followed him to the taproom door.

"Mite dismayed," Remember said, swaying ever so slightly, "t'see ye go without anythin' happenin'. Mostly when ye 'n' me meet, hell pops. Wal, take keer of y'self, Adam. Want I should hold ye a share in Stub's Onion River prop'ty?"

He waved as the other climbed up beside the red-sashed habitant driver and Adam, returning the salute, felt desolation. If he accomplished his entire mission, however honorably, it was unlikely that Remember Baker ever again would hail him so warmly.

Chapter XX

THE spring's multicolored leaves had been disciplined into uniform green and corn stood mid-shin high on the meek little French farmsteads when Adam, worn by delay and pulled by conflicting impulses, returned to St. Johns. He sought and could find no immediate prospect of transportation up the lake. This was a capstone set upon the monumental thwarting he had endured. He wondered drearily as he put up at the inn where he had left Baker and young Allen why he ever had undertaken so ill-starred a venture.

Time had run through his fingers like a clenched handful of dry sand from the hour when he had reached Montreal to learn at Morrison's counting house that its owner was absent and would not be back in less than a week. Adam waited for him at a tavern and wandered aimlessly and fretting through the town where old French houses jostled newer British buildings, and swaggering voyageurs, scornful redcoats from the garrison, and an occasional Indian followed by a burdened woman, enlivened the traffic of the crooked streets.

He haunted the riverfront to see the singing crews bring down from the West long canoes, deep-laden with the baled furs of last winter's catch. At night, in his chamber, he wrote letters to Felicity that he had no opportunity to send. It seemed a month before Morrison returned and then Adam's ordeal was just beginning.

The dry, freckled Scot welcomed him like one from the grave, proclaimed that a recent letter from Duane had hazarded that Adam was indeed dead, marveled at his resemblance to his father, and at length read from a folio an account of his own stewardship.

Morrison held for Adam, according to yesterday's balance, five hundred and thirteen pounds, nine shillings, threepence-halfpenny, all prudently invested.

"I am not one, Mr. Corlaer, to bury my principal's talents in a napkin. It will require time to liquidate your holdings profitably."

He tickled his nose with the quill feather and regarded Adam as though he were an asset before the buzzing Gallic voice ventured, "In view of the seetuation in which we find the rest of your inheritance, we canna but exercise extreme caution with this fragment, eh sir?" and prodded by Adam's questions told the tale grimly.

His principal's York property, real and personal, Morrison revealed, fortifying himself with excerpts from Duane's latest letter, had not yet been confiscated but had been sequestered, pending its owner's appearance before the provincial court on charges of rioting and inciting to riot.

"Aye," Morrison concluded, watching the disconsolate young man from beneath thick, sandy brows, "resistance to authority is rife in the world and lads will be lads and Tryon will be—Tryon. To recover his countenance and your fortune, you must do penance, young sir."

"I intend to." The meek profession had a bitter taste. "How long before I can realize on my holdings here?"

" 'Twill take a wee bit time," Morrison repeated.

Weeks, each longer than the last, went by. There were moments when Adam, driven frantic by delay, swore windily that he would abandon the enterprise and leave. Such brief rebellions were quelled by knowledge that departure from Montreal only would hasten the more ignominious ordeal he must suffer in Albany.

He had written to Duane, expressing penitence, imploring his aid, and for a moment after the letter was finished had been minded to destroy it. The abject appeal revolted him but he gave it nevertheless to Morrison for forwarding.

The damp heat of the advancing summer wilted the town. Adam thought wistfully of the endless shade of The Grants, its cold springs, its clear streams. He knew downright homesickness for the Roydens. Though it was uncertain when he should see them again, he bought woolen cloth for Mindwell, a silver chain and locket for Delight, and then, lest it should seem that he had neglected her, spent most of his remaining cash on an opal ring for Felicity. The fire in the stone's heart seemed a symbol of her own spirit. He dedicated his distress and loneliness to her but did not find this made the trial notably easier.

On the day of final accounting, which Adam had begun to believe never would arrive, he swept up the paper and coin Morrison had counted out with care, scribbled his signature on a receipt, and was about to blurt thanks and farewell when he was checked by the canny look in his agent's eyes. Adam suffered the silent appraisal until at last the other cleared his throat.

"The delay has been longer than I thought, Mr. Corlaer, but ye have not suffered thereby, feenancially. I trust, sir, yer impatience will not bear ye into further difficulty."

"It is quite likely it will," Adam replied with an unhappy grin, "since I now am for Albany."

Morrison looked relieved.

"That is wise, sir. I am glad ye are not to entangle yourself again in The Grants. Wild folk, sir, that a gentleman will do well to avoid."

"I have not found them so," Adam answered, startled by his own vehemence.

Morrison held up a bony hand.

"Do not mistake me, Mr. Corlaer. Freedom is not a word to which I am indeeferent. It is my hope that Canada may join the lower provinces in upholding our liberties against the Hanoverian usurper and toward that end I correspond with Boston's notables but, sir, The Grants indulge in riot and uproar seemingly for their own sake."

"You can scarce expect it to be otherwise," Adam retorted and felt his face grow hot, "when York province, while inveighing against oppression, oppresses us—I mean, The Grants' people."

Morrison gave a relinquishing gesture.

"Ah weel! I trust that is not the gospel you will preach in Albany."

"I hope not, myself," Adam confessed.

"And it may be," Morrison pursued tolerantly, "that The Grants have seen the error of their ways. Colonel Reid's settlers have reoccupied Panton town, this time without resistance."

"Reid?" Adam echoed and, with more difficulty, "Panton?"

"Aye," Morrison confirmed. "I have rented him lately a house in Montreal. He intends to tarry here till his colony is well established. But I know you are in haste, young sir. A fortunate journey to you."

He rose. Adam shook his head.

"No," he said with forced lightness. "You are not rid of me yet. I must wait on Colonel Reid before I go."

There was no end, he told himself angrily, as he followed Morrison's directions, to the maze that involved him. On the threshold of emancipation, he was deliberately tangling himself in matters no longer his concern; if, indeed, they ever had been. So he muttered, yet knew that the safety of the Roydens was of more importance than his own future.

Olin was his friend, Mindwell and Delight had succored him. He had assured the girl that the document whose validity now had become dubious would protect her and hers. He must see Reid. One could not break faith with a child, particularly one so trustful as Delight.

Traffic with the Colonel would not be pleasant but it would be more abhorrent still to leave Montreal without facing him. Once this had been accomplished, Adam promised himself savagely, he and The Grants would go their separate ways.

Colonel Reid, when he entered the room where Adam waited, proved to be a solid man with an unsmiling mouth above a stubborn chin and eyes more supercilious than even years of military command would warrant.

"Mr. Adam Corlaer," he said with no warmth. "Your name, sir, is not unfamiliar to me."

"No," Adam admitted meekly. "I feared that would be so."

"Mr. Duane," Reid went on, not heeding the interruption, "spoke of you when Mrs. Reid and I were last in Albany. And Governor Tryon also has mentioned you—indeed, cited you publicly."

His voice rasped over the last words and color came into his blue, close-shaven cheeks.

"I am aware, sir," Adam groped, "that I cannot be welcome here."

"You cannot be, indeed," Reid assured him. "If this were York, my gillies should hold you till the sheriff's arrival."

"Sir," said Adam, swallowing indignation resolutely, "though my notoriety is due to a mistake—"

"A mistake," the Colonel confirmed unpleasantly. "Yours, sir, not mine."

"I am not likely," Adam plodded on, "to cross your path again.

I am on my way to Albany now, to surrender to the authorities there."

"Eh? Oh." Reid blinked and patronage replaced hostility in his speech. "A praiseworthy purpose, if a belated. I am glad you at last have seen the light, sir. You owned a share in Panton at one time yourself, I believe."

"Which I conveyed last year to folk already settled there, warm friends to whom I am much indebted."

"Aye?"

"The purpose of my intrusion"—Adam gulped the nauseous dose—"is to beg you to instruct your people in Panton that the Roydens are to be left in peace on their property since they hold it now under both Hampshire and York."

Reid shook his head with cold relish.

"Mr. Corlaer, I made it my business when lately in Albany to inquire concerning this share of yours. Its conveyance, I was assured, was invalid, since the transfer was made after you already had been outlawed. Are you aware that all your property has been sequestered?"

Adam nodded, not trusting himself to speak. His desolate bearing brought a glint of satisfaction to his adversary's cold eyes.

"Sir, I was young once meself and hotheaded, but hark ye: The land called 'Panton' by Grants' rabble is mine by military patent from His Gracious Majesty. I mean to have it and hold it."

"I am not appealing to you, Colonel, on my own behalf."

"I am aware of that and you are not beseeching a vindictive man. Trespassers will be accorded ample time to remove themselves and their chattels, they behaving as becometh, but, sir"—Reid's face turned coppery and the blare of command crept into his voice—"many of my present settlers are from my old regiment. They will resist if attacked and Governor Carleton has promised that the garrison at Crown Point will aid them, at need.

"Let The Grants' banditti try to oust me at their peril. If they succeed"—he waved the preposterous fancy away—"I shall admit defeat."

Adam picked up his hat.

"I am wasting your time, sir, to no purpose."

"Ye are, indeed," said Reid.

The roiled mind Adam bore to St. Johns was not cleared by discovery that Skene's trading sloop had stood upriver, bound for the head of Champlain, only an hour before his own arrival. He chewed savagely on this and associated grievances while he paced his meager tavern bedroom. If he had not paused for his futile interview with Reid, he now would be launched on a further stage of his mission.

Still tramping back and forth, he told himself that he had been too long in the forthright Grants to stomach easily the wheedling meekness his interview with Reid had entailed, the greater abasement he would have to suffer in Albany. Ethan Allen, or Baker, or even Olin, Adam knew, would have had none of it. There was something comparatively decent in open rebellion. Grants' folk fought for their purposes; they did not crawl and truckle.

Adam, swearing softly, wished that he had Ethan's brimstone powers of imagery in which to denounce his own enterprise. It had been cursed from the moment he had reached Montreal. Now ill fortune had imposed still another delay here at St. Johns so that he might savor the full flavor of his misery.

It seemed, in his desperate mood, as though he must move feebly from mishap to mishap the rest of his days, never attaining his quest, never again seeing Felicity who had thrust him—for their own best interests, to be sure—into this predicament. He tried to sustain his spirit by pinning his thoughts to her but found that the Roydens kept intruding.

He could see Mindwell standing, wet-eyed and expressionless, with one hand against her cheek. He remembered Olin had added still more cleared land to the property from which they now were to be driven. He flinched, recalling Delight's grave air of faith when he had presented her with the deed. She would no longer think that she loved him when she learned how empty his assurances had proved.

He groaned and swung his arms in a dispelling gesture. He would endure no further haunting by the Roydens. He had done his final utmost for them through his humiliating appeal to Reid. He was cutting himself off from The Grants. That chapter of his life had ended when Reid's door had closed after him. Another, more exalting would begin when he had done penance in Albany.

He halted to stare through the small-paned window at a crumbling angle of the distant fort, with its overgrown glacis. The further, smooth flow of the Richelieu was pale in the fading light. Adam heard the thump of the sunset gun and drums' harsh calling. His bedroom, so overcrammed with doubts, was becoming a prison. He snatched up his hat. He would find means to traverse the lake, if he had to buy a boat and row it himself.

His room stood near the head of a long stair. His wrathful intention had so blinded him that he was halfway down before he saw a plump, climbing figure in a flowered gown. He flattened himself against the wall to let the woman by. China-blue eyes touched his and fled in immoderate haste. A blond head, on which a chip hat found scant foothold, inclined. A laden reticule bumped Adam's knees as its bearer passed with a murmur of gratitude and a trail of scent. He had taken a few downward steps when behind him rose a faint cry and a thudding, clattering sound.

A lemon bounded past and on downstairs, then another and a third, accompanied erratically by a ball of yarn transfixed by knitting needles. A perfume vial rolled from tread to tread with an enameled box, as Adam turned to face the onrush. Plump insteps that overlapped small slippers were level with his eyes and the unlatched maw of the now empty reticule gaped at him. On every stair between him and the woman lay disgorged items—jars, parcels, and articles of clothing, several of them evidently intimate, since their owner stooped and snatched them up with a gasp.

"Oh, gracious God! Oh, *quel dommage!*" her high voice cried as Adam began to regather the jettisoned cargo. "Beauty in distress!"

"And I, bending at beauty's feet," Adam supplied.

"La, sir! Not only a gallant but a wit! How can I ever thank you?"

She uttered pigeonlike sounds as he handed back her properties. Her manner, Adam thought, observing the contours of the powdered face, was as inappropriately youthful as her hat and raiment.

"And how can I ever thank fortune that Billy-boy was not present? I should never have heard an end to it. He warned me this already was too heavily laden but, Lord!, when one ventures into the wilderness one must go supplied with comforts, don't you think? Yes, that is everything, I'm quite sure, save one lemon. Ah, there it is, the rascal, hiding beneath the chair."

They had pursued the runaway articles to the foot of the stair and now stood, flushed and laughing. The woman adjusted her hat with ineffectual pats of her hands and faltered: "If you have the least wee-wee curiosity whom you have rescued, I am Mrs. Captain Delaplace, bound—with her husband, of course—on a visit to the lake forts."

Adam bowed and named himself. She was quicker at identification than he for she gave a small cry, clapped her palms together, and marveled: "Mr. Adam Corlaer? Oh, no, no; not really you! Not the friend of Mr. Sherwood who is our dear friend and whose sister is our dear, dear, dear friend!"

The miracle seemed for an instant more than she could endure but the opening of the tavern door restored her and, turning, she called, "Billy-boy. Come quick-quick. You'll never imagine whom wifie has found."

Captain Delaplace was a thin, grave warrior, worn and slightly faded like his uniform, but his smile was pleasant, his handclasp warm, and his voice, when it prevailed over his wife's amendments and interpretations, agreeable. He pronounced it a privilege to encounter in the flesh one whom Justus and Felicity so often had mentioned. They were fond of the Sherwoods and their little protégée, Delight Royden.

"An elf, a shy little frontier fay; don't you find her so, Mr. Corlaer?", Mrs. Delaplace cooed and explained with gestures that she and her husband were devoting his leave to a survey of Crown Point where in another year she direly feared they would be stationed. If the fort proved as dreadful as she feared, she almost certainly would urge Billy-boy to sell his commission. Otherwise, she knew she would die of loneliness.

Delaplace consulted his watch with stealthy anxiety and Adam asked permission to withdraw. He still must search, he explained, for some craft to bear him uplake.

"You are going up Champlain!" The woman was transfixed by the coincidence. "Billy-boy!"

She rolled prompting eyes at her husband who, reviving, exclaimed, "Why, of course! Mr. Corlaer, an army barge is to convey Mrs. D. and me to Crown Point on the morrow. We should be honored, sir, by your company."

"I accept most willingly and gratefully," Adam replied, marveling at the aspect a relenting fortune assumed.

Chapter XXI

THE barge's six oars lifted her out of the Richelieu's current and into the lake. The craft that had crawled upstream on even keel heeled under the thrust of the west wind and commenced a mild rolling. Millicent Delaplace's vivacity slackened. The gay voice that had adorned scenery, persons, and incidents with lavish superlatives fell into a dismal murmur. Her husband found a lemon in her reticule, halved it in haste, and handed it to her. She raised her complexion mask and sucked it with wan eagerness.

The channel widened. Waves slapped the barge's flank. Mrs. Delaplace dropped the lemon halves and moaned to her lord. Supported by him, she tottered below to the tiny cabin. The sergeant commanding the barge's crew winked at Adam. He shouted to the oarsmen as the Captain reappeared.

"Mrs. D.," he confided with a sympathy Adam suspected covered a certain relief, "is prone to *mal de mer*, poor, devoted lady. It will be better for her to lie still while the wind endures."

The islands' small forests slid by on the left, each on its pedestal of foam-washed rock. Here, where the channel widened, the waves were white-crested. The barge lurched and crashed through uneasy water. It rounded a long cape that the sergeant said was Cumberland Head and the no longer hampered wind leaped upon it.

At the tiller, the sergeant yelled. Sweeps blundered and splashed; the craft wallowed as it came about and sought the lake's west shore. Adam, standing with Delaplace in the leaping, plunging bow, felt the blast gather up and bear away the remnant of yesterday's gloom.

Full-sailed clouds made passage. Their purple shadows coursed

196

the tall blunt mountains ahead. Between these and the blue ranges, standing back from the further shore, peacock-colored miles of water blazed. The vehement beauty lifted Adam. Delaplace touched his arm, pointed and cried through the wind's clamor, "Yonder are The Grants?"

Adam nodded. The panting oarsmen were pulling the barge into calmer water.

"It seems to be fair country," the Captain offered.

"I have seen none like it."

"But peopled by a stiff-necked, greedy folk. Surely," Delaplace pursued, staring toward the rolling rampart beyond the lake, "there is land a plenty there for all the children of men."

"Colonel Reid might not agree with you," Adam replied with a dull sense of returning anxiety.

"Reid? Oh, yes. I hear we are supporting his new venture," Delaplace said vaguely and, marking that the barge now ran easily, close to shore, added, "I must go and see how Mrs. D. fares."

It seemed as though the Captain bore away Adam's brief peace of mind. The cleansing joy in beauty failed. Delaplace's scorn of The Grants' people, the distant sight of their actual land revived discomfort he had hoped was safely dead. His eyes followed the contours of the distant ranges surging away to the south.

Somewhere below the farthest dim slope lay the Royden property. A man had died in its clearing. His woman and their children had maintained his valor and his hope. The home they still were building was a monument to Daniel Royden, husband and father, yet still more to the ambition all Grants' folk shared —to gain through travail land of their own, to possess, through no lesser labor, themselves. It was a simple ideal, yet not ignoble. Its maintenance was a finer enterprise than Colonel Reid pursued, with his tenants to bear its brunt and regulars at his back.

The memory of Mindwell Royden, the plain stalwart woman, as she had stood, watching Adam's departure, came unbidden into his mind.

The barge moved smoothly now along a mounting wall of lake-side bluffs, and Delaplace was helping his wife up on deck. Adam went toward them in almost fugitive haste. If he were put ashore in Panton, he could find out for himself how Reid's new invasion was progressing and how the Roydens fared.

Before Mrs. Delaplace had completed a clinical account of her late seizure, Adam's impulse languished and, dying, left behind it scorn of himself as a trimming and wavering lover, willing to abandon his quest at the first distraction.

"Poor, little, trustful me," Mrs. Delaplace was sighing, "to believe those who vowed Champlain was a calm, untroubled water! And Georgie-porgie was foremost among them, the bold, bad boy."

"Lieutenant Wadman, of my company," the Captain interpreted to Adam.

"And a dear, dear lad," his wife pursued, clasping her hands, "even if he did deceive me. Quite my favorite—among the younger officers, of course," she pursued with an arch glance at her husband and appended in haste, as though she feared Adam might misunderstand her confession: "Georgie-porgie is quite mad about Felicity."

"All the subalterns are—and some of their elders," Delaplace confirmed. His wife rolled her eyes at Adam.

"I marvel, Mr. Corlaer, that you should be immune, or perhaps your affections are already engaged."

"Completely."

"How sweet! And what a fortunate maid is she! As fortunate as Georgie-porgie, I'm sure. The dear boy, next year, comes into a large inheritance."

"Young Wadman," Delaplace intruded loudly, "is the only lad the little vixen can't lead about by the nose. Fought a duel over her. Gad, she is a baggage! Were she mine, I'd wish her well wed."

"But, Billy-boy," his wife shrilled gaily, "they will be as soon as Georgie—"

"Millicent!"

His wife pressed plump fingers against her lips.

"But, lover," she went on after an instant's display of contrition, "I only voiced what—"

"We were told in confidence, my dear," her husband reminded her firmly. "We must not divulge a friend's secret."

"Not even to Mr. Corlaer, Billy-boy? Not even to Mr. Corlaer of whom Felicity and Justus have spoken so highly? I know he would hold his tongue, wouldn't you, Mr. Corlaer?"

"Millicent, my sweet," the Captain bade sharply, "hold your

own. Lord, sir," he addressed Adam in haste, "I wonder the law is not woman's special province since she always can find a loophole in any covenant."

It was hard for Adam to reflect Delaplace's rueful grin. The Captain regarded his wife with fond despair.

"If," he said solemnly, "you have drawn conclusions from what Mrs. D. has uttered, I ask your word as a gentleman that you will divulge them to no one."

Adam cleared his throat with an effort.

"I pledge myself, sir," he replied.

They anchored at sunset in a cove overshadowed by dark hills. The sergeant and his men built a fire on shore and spread tarpaulins for shelter. The Delaplaces, remaining on board, shared food from a hamper with Adam who, when at last the Captain and his wife had gone below, wrapped a borrowed blanket about him and lay in the craft's bow. He had craved the loneliness of this moment while he had smirked at the woman's aimless chatter and had vaguely answered her husband's questions. He was sure now that, with justice, they considered him a dull young man.

Sparks whirled up from the beach toward the steady stars. The mutter of speech came across water that lapped the barge's flanks. The anchor line squeaked faintly. The low sounds did not quiet Adam. His mind, dangling from a tether of surmise, swung to and fro. Lying still and tense, he tried to scoff at the Delaplaces' half-told tale.

The secret, which the woman had respected not at all and the Captain only after his fashion, must have been confided by Wadman. Adam wished, clenching his hands, that he had broken his rival's neck long ago in Fay's tavern. It must have been boasting which the Delaplaces had mistaken for verity. Wadman, with his damned army insolence, doubtless had bragged to them that he would wed Felicity.

It could be nothing more. Adam must hold to this belief. He could not press his companions for further revelation. It would demean both Felicity and himself. He tried to re-create the splendor of moments when they had seemed a single entity. Possessing such memories, how could he doubt her?

The anchor line creaked. There was silence on shore and the fire was dwindling. Peering overside, Adam saw that mist, clinging close to the water, had obscured the reflections of the stars. He lay back again. His alarm had been shameful. Felicity was his, as he was hers. Her plea that he recover his place in that world where, until lately, he had dwelt, was a maid's natural wish for the man she was to wed. Felicity's love of excitement, her hunger for gaiety were part of her charm. She had indulged them in Quebec. She had led all the young men by the nose. All, save Wadman, Delaplace had said.

Adam rolled over with a hushed groan. Felicity would have told him of Wadman if they had had more opportunity for intimacy. He should not have hurried away so quickly to see how great a fortune he still might lay before her.

He could hear, welling from below, a muffled snoring. He felt the rising mist come over the gunwale and cool his face.

Baker had believed Sherwood was in British pay. No disgrace lay in such employment. A man with Justus's sense of loyalty would deem it an honor to serve his king. Perhaps his Boston mission had been completed now and he and Felicity had returned to the house in New Haven.

Adam winced under the sharp necessity to see them both again. He could not confront the girl with the Delaplaces' gossip—he had pledged himself to mention that to no one—but he needed desperately to hold her in his arms, renewing his faith.

In the blackness beyond the dying fire, a barred owl shouted. Often that doglike baying had come from the forest to the Royden clearing. It woke a homesickness for vanished certainties, for the sure, unvoiced friendship of plain people. Sudden resolution cleared Adam's mind.

He would go back. He would break his journey to Albany. If the Sherwoods had not returned, the Roydens might need such dubious counsel as he could bring. From Crown Point, he would cross the narrow water and return briefly to Panton. Whatever Adam found there would be less dire than further wretched hazard.

It was late afternoon when he rode the horse he had borrowed from John Strong into the Royden clearing. The silence doubled the anxiety Strong's grim report had wakened. Reid's men not only were established at Otter Falls; they were building a village and had warned all settlers to leave the region.

"And what are The Grants folk doing?" Adam had asked. Strong had shrugged.

"Waitin' for help. Don't come. Olin took out for Bennington, seems like weeks ago. Ain't heered of him since."

"And the Sherwoods?"

"Ain't heered of them, neither."

The stillness in the clearing could be desolation. In Olin's absence, his mother and his sister might have been driven away.

Adam had ridden out of the forest's long shadow before, with relief like the sudden end of pain, he saw Mindwell come to the doorstep and look toward him, shielding her eyes against the sun's glare. He kicked his horse forward.

The woman reached back into the house, brought forth a musket, lifted it slowly. Adam dragged at his rein.

"That's an odd welcome," he called.

Mindwell lowered the weapon and, still grasping it in one hand, laid hold upon the doorjamb. Her face was sallow and twitching.

"Wal," she said. "Glad 'tis you, Adam. Sun in my eyes; thought 'twas Hutchinson back again."

"Hutchinson?"

"Ehyah," Mindwell nodded briefly. "Leader of Reid's folks to the falls."

She set the musket down with care. Her hands caught and tightened upon each other. The steady voice went on, "Warned us to leave. Else, he says, he 'n' his'n'll drive out Delight 'n' me."

A stir behind her drew Adam's gaze. Delight had come to the doorway, small hands laid upon her throat. She smiled wanly and tried to speak but tears were suddenly in her eyes and the lately pale face shone scarlet. She whirled about and vanished.

Mindwell raised the musket and uncocked it. Adam coughed to break the tightness in his throat. He asked at last, "What has happened?"

The horse, held by a slack rein, grazed with tearing sounds that spaced Mindwell's speech.

Bateaux had come, by night and unobserved, up the lower creek to the foot of Otter Falls and had landed James Hutchinson, many men, and some women and children. They were orderly but determined, had occupied the mill, and had disembarked most of their gear before The Grants' settlers had discovered them.

Olin, Everest, and others had ridden to the Falls where Hutchinson had cast their warning back at them. The land was Reid's. His people purposed to occupy it, entire. All trespassers on the Colonel's property must leave. Olin had come home, dismayed and dubious, and, at Mindwell's urging, had ridden toward Bennington the next morning.

"That left Delight 'n' me alone for quite a spell," the even voice pursued. "Then Hutchinson came. Told us we'd have to go—final notice, he said—'n' if we didn't, his folks 'ud drive us."

Mindwell blinked. The fingers of her clasped hands were sharply red and white. After a pause, she went on with no perceptible emotion.

"Ain't goin', Adam."

"Of course, you're not," he answered gruffly but she strove against his assurance as though it had been denial.

"Buried Dan'l on the betterment he'd commenced. Figgered to lay beside him, soon or late. Been our home—his'n 'n' mine 'n' ours. We made it. Won't leave it, livin' or dead."

She drew breath, pressed her lips together. The face that momentarily had been shaken was still again.

Some of the fainter-hearted Grants' settlers, Mindwell went on, already were packing to leave. Hutchinson had too many men for the threatened handful to oppose. Those who were unready to obey him waited day by day for Olin, returning with aid. No word had come from or of him. Vigor crept into the woman's voice.

"Whar's Ethan Allen? Whar's him 'n' his boys?"

Knowledge of his own helplessness piled fuel on Adam's anger. Mindwell's shrug was apology for the outburst.

"Ain't findin' fault with ye. Done all ye could a'ready. Delight showed Hutchinson that paper ye give her. Said 'twas no good, but wouldn't give it back."

"No?" Adam asked. Harsh lines pulled down his face; his eyes were bright. The horse's head jerked as the reins were gathered.

"I'm going to talk to Mr. Hutchinson," Adam said, tight-jawed. "I'm going to get that deed tonight, or—"

"No," Mindwell told him flatly, "ye ain't neither. Hard onto sunset 'n' ye'd git lost in the dark, like as not. Bed 'n' bait your horse 'n' bide with us. It'll pleasure Delight 'n' me to have a man in the house."

"I'll go tomorrow, then," Adam promised, started to lead his horse toward the stable, then paused and asked, "You have heard naught of the Sherwoods?"

Mindwell hesitated, swallowed, and at last replied:

"Not since they left for Boston town."

Adam unsaddled and rubbed his horse with undue gentleness, lest his simmering rage break loose against the unoffending. Uncertainty that had assailed him during his ride from Chimney Point had been swept from his mind. He thought of the weeks he had cooled his heels in Montreal, of his meekness in his interview with Reid. Instead of fawning before the pompous Scot, he should have—

He could not find an alternative and swore viciously as he sought hay and grain. The stable already was investing itself with the mute eloquence possessed by the belongings of the vanished.

This had been the Roydens' first dwelling. Daniel, himself, had felled, cut, and notched logs for its walls. His wife and children had lived here while they had advanced the dead man's dream. They had raised a better house. They had enlarged the little opening in the wilderness that had become stump-fenced fields, now deep in wheat and corn.

Adam surveyed them bitterly as he returned from the stable with his saddlebags over his arm. It would be like death for Mindwell to be parted from her farm. He would see Hutchinson and compel him to return the deed. Knowledge of how little else he possibly could accomplish sharpened his anger.

Delight opened the kitchen door and stood there, waiting. She had changed her dress and her tormented look had vanished.

"I'm glad you have come back, Adam," she said serenely. Never before had she addressed him by his Christian name.

"I should never have gone away," he told her and wondered, having spoken, what he actually had meant.

Chapter XXII

LONG before he reached the open land that lay about Otter Falls, Adam, following the river down through the forest, could hear the pulsing whine of the sawmill and, as the woods thinned before him, the brisk patter of hammer blows. He urged his horse out through brush and paused to squint in untempered sunlight at the gleaming new timbers of the town Reid's men were raising beyond the weather-beaten mill.

Cottages were mushrooming up on the left of the older building. Some were only framed; others already had been roofed and sheathed. About them and upon them, with clamor of voices, rattle of hammers, panting of saws, swarmed so many workers that Adam caught his breath. The invasion, this time, was in force.

He rode forward, turned when he discovered that he was invading a field where corn and barley flourished, passed in the distance mowers who halted their hay cutting to look after him, and at last breasted the slope that led into the settlement. Men, kilted or breeched, dropped their work to stare. The hostile scrutiny made him nervous. His voice, when he asked a red-headed lout where he might find Hutchinson, was so sharp that the man flinched, scowled, and made no other reply than to jerk his thumb toward the mill. Adam felt surly eyes follow him. A woman with a nursing infant looked at him narrowly and spat. He wondered whether she had been among those whom Baker had cast out the year before.

Adam's temper was not improved when, in the turbulent mill, a worker pointed out a long, bald man seated behind a table with a wig and papers before him. For a full minute after the intruder had asked, "Mr. James Hutchinson?," the other paid him no heed but continued to scribble with a quill, mumbling and pursing his mouth. At last he turned, looked Adam up and down with insolence, and said:

"Aye?"

Black eyebrows climbed higher on the hairless skull as Adam crisply repeated his own name and, in wrath, swung his sole weapon.

"I have come, sir, to receive property belonging to the Roydens of this town and taken by you—a deed executed in Albany."

Hutchinson blinked, studied his visitor with greenish eyes, and sucked in his cheeks while he sat and adjusted his wig.

"Ye're a bold young mon," the harsh, Highland voice proclaimed at last. "Why should I not, Mr. Adam Corlaer, lay ye by the heels and send ye to Albany where, as ye must know, they earnestly want ye?"

Knowledge of how easily he could accomplish this kept Adam silent while Hutchinson's cheeks relaxed and his mouth spread in a derisive grin.

"As for the deed ye demand, it has no value. I have been so instructed by my principal, Colonel John Reid, himself."

Adam thrust away thought of the joy it would be to jerk the gaunt, smirking figure from the chair and stuff the scratch wig down the corded throat. He said with desperate inspiration, "I was informed of the deed's invalidity in Montreal by Colonel Reid himself."

He saw Hutchinson's ink-stained hands clench. Their owner contemplated them thoughtfully before he looked up again. Uneasiness, Adam knew, lay behind his calculating air.

"Ye ken the Colonel?"

"I have just said so."

"Colonel John Reid. A small, fair man, eh?"

"He is large, black, and unfortunate in his servants."

In the long pause, Adam strove to restrain any expression but chill disdain. Hutchinson grunted at last, pawed through the papers on the table, and uncordially surrendered one. His uneasy eyes tapped and pried. He was unwilling, Adam saw, to risk offending a person who might have won his employer's favor. Further attack might avert Hutchinson's intention to cross examine his visitor.

"I say 'unfortunate' since Colonel Reid also told me that he had given special command to leave The Grants' settlers in possession of their personal property."

"Aye," Hutchinson admitted, "so he bade me, but—"

"But, nevertheless, you took this deed by force. Since you now have returned it, let me counsel you, sir: You will not drive the Roydens from their land until you have killed her who owns it and if she dies, defending her property, and I have an ounce of influence in The Grants, I'll see you hanged for it, Mr. James Hutchinson."

The man's face turned dusky. His fists clenched and then, while Adam waited tensely for further hostile movement, slowly opened again. Hutchinson shook his head.

"My orders come from Colonel Reid, not from ye. I'm sending an express downlake this day, asking when I shall oust these stiff-necked interlopers. On my own responsibility, young mon, I'll match threats wi' ye: Whatever the Colonel's orders I shall execute them as faithfully as though I still were sergeant and he commander of the Forty-second. Aye, all the wild, woods-runnin' loons in The Grants will not wean me from me duty. Bring 'em, Mr. Corlaer, and welcome. There'll be redcoats at need to deal wi' ye and yer scum. Gie ye gude day."

The dismissal was like a slap across the face. Long after the forest had hidden the settlement, Adam still could hear the sounds of building, like jeering voices belittling him further.

Anger, deep and enduring, laid hold upon him and alarm came with it. The village at the Falls menaced not only Panton's settlers but all the people in the clearings and the little towns, north, east, and west from Bennington. The houses rising by the mill, the pompous man who had decreed them, the monarch by whose whim the invasion had been authorized, endangered the patient folk who fought the wilderness with axe, spade, and plow.

More than this, Reid's men and the law that justified them imperiled the dream The Grants' settlers, still half blindly, followed. Suddenly, in the shadow of its destruction, that vision was brave and bright to Adam.

His horse stumbled. He spoke to him gently and rode on with greater care. A new intention was ordering his mind and he watched the trail vigilantly. His purpose was too urgent for him to delay it by losing his way.

Ethan Allen, long ago, had voiced belief in the goodness of Grants' earth and the right of free men to win and hold it. Had the giant seen the heights and the perils in that profession? Was he aware that if Reid and his tenants prevailed, an older rigid rule would be reimposed upon those who were groping toward liberty and equality?

A man might creditably dedicate himself to such a cause. The anger that possessed Adam shrank and dwarfed the lately distracting problems, turned his mind away from Felicity, the Delaplaces' gossip, his own broken enterprise. These were matters to be dealt with in a less pressing time. Something like destiny had turned him from the road to Albany.

He did not ride to the Royden stable but tethered his horse to a dooryard tree and strode quickly into the house. Mindwell turned from the hearth to look at him through puckered eyelids. Delight had started from her chair when he had entered and one hand was creeping up to the delicate throat that, he saw, was looped by the silver chain of his gift. He tossed the deed onto the table and then, since the dramatic gesture seemed cheap, atoned by saying:

"Henderson holds it is worthless and I am afraid he is right."

Mindwell stood, solidly. Adam asked her, "Have you word for Olin? I am riding to Bennington."

"Bennington?"

The woman studied him with such care that he said impatiently, "To find what holds back Allen; to find why he does not send aid."

Delight turned luminous eyes upon him. Her mother said gravely, "Adam, this ain't your trouble."

He gave an excited laugh.

"I am just beginning to learn how much my trouble it truly is."

Mindwell and her daughter stood in the doorway and watched Adam leave. Something in Delight's expression recalled her look when she had ridden behind her brother from the Sherwood clearing.

"Wal," John Strong drawled, when Adam paused at Chimney Point to explain his mission and beg further loan of the horse, "was I you 'n' in haste, I'd take his teammate, too. Ride one, lead t'other, 'n' shift saddle frequent. Cover a lot of ground that way, if ye can hold yeself together."

He led the way quickly to the stable.

Now that he was committed, now that uncertainty had ended, elation gripped Adam and urged him on. His purpose grew as each mile fell behind him.

He rode toward Bennington, not primarily to succor threatened friends or to drive interlopers from Otter Falls. He followed the faint roads and the dimmer trails that led past infrequent clearings from one raw town to another for sake of the thing dingy men and smoke-stained women purblindly were building.

None of them could have told him plainly the dream's scope and substance. It was too vaguely outlined still for men to see it clearly, but it had dignity and stature of which the humble were aware. Adam rode with little mercy for his horses or himself.

He slept, one of the two nights of his journey, deep in wilderness. On the other, he lay in a settler's cabin. He tarried briefly in each village he entered to announce his tidings. Always, he was stirred by lean faces, grown suddenly grim, by eyes that turned instinctively toward the firelocks above the hearths.

"Rouse The Green Mountain Boys," was the burden of Adam's summons. "Tell them what happens in Panton. Bid them stand ready."

Toward noon of the third day, he rode, saddle-sore and aching, up the last hill toward his goal. His horses were almost as spent as he; his body begged for rest but he had set horns to blowing on the farms, had seen messengers mount and gallop. Whatever apathy possessed Bennington's people, the folk along the North Road were arming.

Yet Adam's satisfaction was dashed by the tranquillity of the little town. None of the excitement that had sustained him was visible on the sun-drenched Bennington Green or among the small houses that sat decorously beside it. The gaunt bulk of Fay's tavern drowsed in the noontide. It comforted Adam to see that the stuffed catamount still kept its station, still snarled toward New York.

He dismounted stiffly before the inn, tethered his horses, and, looking up, saw Olin smiling at him from the doorway. There was offense in his air of ease that his joyous query compounded.

"What on earth are you doing here?"

"I came," Adam replied bleakly, "from Panton to ask that of you."

His friend's smile vanished.

"Trouble?"

"Didn't you know?"

Olin grew red. He followed Adam into the tavern without further word, stood aside while Stephen Fay welcomed the newcomer, and then, unbidden, trailed after the landlord and his guest to an upstairs room. When Fay had left, Olin closed the door and, leaning against it, asked quietly:

"What has happened?"

His friend's late cheer made Adam perversely withhold his tidings.

"I have ridden," he replied, "a considerable distance to ask you that."

He wondered whether it were guilt that turned the other's face dusky red. Olin persisted, "Ma and Delight; nothing's happened to them?"

"When I left"—a new wariness prescribed Adam's reply—"they were much concerned about you."

He took savage satisfaction in seeing how his reticence galled Olin. The dark young man scowled and spoke with heat.

He was quite as concerned as Adam but Grants' leaders—Parson Dewey, Stephen Fay, and others—who had heard his tale of Reid's trespass, had urged moderation and had bidden him wait. They still were trying to salvage the truce and establish a peace. If a lasting agreement could be reached at the Council's meeting tomorrow night—

"If!" Adam interrupted. "Do all of them—Allen, Baker, and the rest—coo so softly of peace?"

Olin gulped over the sneer, and went on carefully:

Allen only that day had returned from the Onion River country which he had been exploring with Ira and Remember. All were fearful that he might, out of sheer hotheadedness, denounce and wreck the negotiations.

"You may think me indifferent or laggard if you will," the quivering voice ran on, "but Justus himself assures me that I can best protect our pitch by making no charges against Reid until the peace is established."

His mention of Sherwood, whom Baker and Ira Allen had

thought a spy, plucked at Adam's nerves and quickened hitherto aimless suspicion.

"Justus is here? At the tavern?"

"No," Olin answered sullenly. "He lodges with Jonas Fassett when he is not in Albany. It is he who is doing most for the composition of our troubles with York."

"And Felicity?"

"Here also."

Adam said at last with deliberate scorn, "For so confident a suitor, you take great pains to secure your interests."

Olin caught his breath with a sharp sound. He hesitated and then turned toward the door.

"I had best go," he said in a strained voice. "I have no wish to quarrel with you. See Justus before you condemn me entirely."

"That I shall do," Adam promised offensively. "I should like to know how far his struggle for 'composition' has weaned him of sympathy for his neighbors."

The door closed behind Olin. The gentle sound abashed, then angered Adam. As he trudged wearily across the Green toward the Fassett house, he rancorously defended his own suspicions. Sherwood was a Tory, and Ira and Remember undoubtedly were right in their belief that he was an agent of Quebec's governor. A man so enraptured by his sovereign that he admired dissolute officers in the king's service and would submit to the soiling of his own sister's name by the scandal of a duel was not likely to let the welfare of the Roydens and their neighbors bend his damned, fatuous loyalty. He would wear out his knees to serve the royal governors, Carleton or Tryon.

Adam swore with irascibility born of weariness that he would seek no aid from Sherwood. He would not even reveal the plight of the Panton folk to him. He would find assistance for them elsewhere, even if that entailed intruding on the Council meeting, tomorrow evening, and pleading their cause himself. So he resolved as he rapped upon the Fassett door. It opened and he gaped at Felicity.

In her flowered gown, she was fairer than a June day. Her joy, following close on amazement, unsettled him.

"Adam!" she cried. "Oh, Adam!"

Her hands caught and clung to his.

"My dear, what is it? Are you ill?"

"Tired," he said, alarmed to find how swiftly his grievances melted in her presence. "Trail-weary, that is all."

"Come in," she begged, still holding his hands. She did not release them until she had led him into the darkened parlor. The Fassetts, she explained over her shoulder as she opened the shutters, had ridden to Pownal.

"Where is Justus?"

"Lord, hear the man!" she cried merrily. "He is on his way back from Albany. Have you come to see him and not me?"

She held out her arms.

After a little, Felicity drew away and looked into her lover's face as though their contact had given her insight.

"Something is wrong," she told him softly.

"Many things. Colonel Reid's folk are in Panton again."

"Oh, that!" She dismissed it with a confident toss of her head. "It will be composed, never fear. Justus has been working in Albany toward that end. I wonder you did not meet him there."

"Felicity," Adam said heavily, "I have not been to Albany."

She stepped back and studied him.

"I thought," the girl said with a brittle laugh, "you had come to ask Justus—for me."

"I did not know you were here. I came seeking help for Mindwell and Delight."

Her face was suddenly bright; her words, crisp. "If their peril is so great, was it valiant of you to leave them?"

Her hand flew belatedly to her mouth.

"I should not have said that," she whispered. "Why must we, who have so much to give, forever hurt each other?"

He wondered why such things must leap upon him—this, and the half-quarrel with Olin and his doubt of Sherwood—when weariness had drugged his mind.

"I don't know," he said dully. "I am too tired to be sure of anything."

Felicity took his hands again and gently drew him down beside her on the Fassetts' angular settee.

"Will you tell me what troubles you, Adam? Will you let me understand?"

He knew the respite it would be to share his distress with her yet caution delayed him. He searched the sea-green eyes that were soft with sympathy.

"Will you keep what I tell you our solemn secret—yours and mine?"

She laid a soothing, perfumed hand against his cheek.

"Need you ask?"

"Hiding it even from your brother, if I think after I have talked with him that he should not know?"

"Haven't we long had secrets that he still does not share, my dear?"

His arm was about her shoulders; his face was against her hair, as he spread it all before her—Reid's invasion, Hutchinson's threats, the Roydens' plight, his dispute with Olin. Felicity, when he had ended, lifted her head and kissed him.

"Poor boy," she murmured. "Poor, poor Adam. Must you always look at the darkest side, beloved? There will be a compromise and peace. Justus is sure of it."

"Justus hasn't talked to Colonel Reid, or been at Otter Falls to see how James Hutchinson and his men are blasting the truce."

Her fingers played in his hair.

"Will you talk with Justus?"

"As soon as may be. Until then, you'll not even say that you have seen me?"

"My dearest, I've already promised you."

Felicity stirred and drew Adam's head down to stroke his hair. His face lay upon the thrilling softness of her breast. She whispered, "Do you bring me only the tale of others' woes? Have you nothing that is yours and mine?"

"I have," he told her slowly, "considerably less to bring you than we planned. I have been to Montreal. I shall not go truckling and whining for pardon to Tryon."

Her hand was still. After a little, she asked, "What are you trying to tell me?"

He sat straight, the better to rouse his torpid mind, and endured her searching eyes.

"I don't quite know," he forced himself to say, "how I can make you understand. I have learned in the last months that, while this strife goes on, I am of and for The Grants."

"So is Justus, my dear. He—"

Adam shook his head stubbornly.

"He believes and serves authority."

"Oh, Adam!" Felicity spoke as though he were a loved and stubborn child. "Must you always be so difficult? Have you no compromises?"

"I should have still less of value to bring you, if I followed your brother and his fellow appeasers instead of my own heart."

"You will not change, even for me?"

Her eyes reproached him. He asked bluntly, "Submit to Tryon, or we do not wed: Is that what you mean?"

Felicity smiled and spread her hands in a helpless gesture.

"Would you have your own sister wed a penniless outlaw? Don't scowl, my dear. Isn't that what you are?"

"I did not scowl," he answered heavily, "at what you named me. That is true enough."

"But it need not be true," she cried in exasperation, stamping a little foot and holding his hands the tighter. "Adam, Justus is your friend. He is older and wiser than you. Can you say that you are wholly right and he, wholly wrong?"

"I don't know," he said after hesitation. "At the moment, quite truly I don't know."

"Justus will return soon. Wait for him with me, Adam. Oh my dear, why must you be so wrong-headed and willful?"

His weary body was her ally, whispering that nothing he could yield would pay for the joy and ease of laying his head against her breast.

"I think," Adam said slowly, "that I had best go."

After an instant, she whispered, "Adieu then, poor, tired lad. Kiss me, once more."

Her mouth beneath his was soft and yielding as a flower's petals. He released her and went toward the door. He heard her softly speak his name but did not turn. He remembered as he moved away, that the opal ring still lay in his pocket, unbestowed. Each bone in his body had its own soreness as he plodded across the Green toward the tavern. He tiptoed up the stair and fell upon his bed.

Chapter XXIII

FROM far away and rushing nearer, Adam heard the hoofs of a monster come storming through blackness and woke at last to find the room golden with late sunlight and a thunderous pounding proceeding against the door. He rolled from the bed and drew back the bolt.

In Baker's gnarled, brown face, the eyelids were puckered with amusement.

"Figgered ye was sick, beddin' down by daylight, but after I'd stove in m' knuckles, mistrusted ye'd perished."

"I have come a long way," Adam said, striving to match his dryness, "with not too much rest."

"Whar from? When ye start? Wal, ye didn't waste time, did ye? Ain't puny as ye look, b'God."

He stood, solid as a spruce stump in his wear-blackened buckskins, while Adam blurted his mission. When he had ended, Baker's slit eyes wore the absent look of a drowsing cat.

"Don't seem 's if 'twas the best time for Ethan 'n' me to go land-huntin', eh?"

He swallowed with a frown some unuttered thought.

"Minds me why I roused ye. Stub Allen's gone on to Salisbury but Ethan's here. Him 'n' Peleg 'n' Warner 'n' me politely invite ye to sup with us."

Baker, lounging at the door while Adam made ready, leaned out to look either way along the hall, cleared his throat twice and then said in a low voice, "Things has got outa hand, seems like. Dry-rotted nincompoops think they can out-dicker Tryon. They're watchin' Ethan like a lynx on a deer run, fearful he'll kick up 'n' spill the pig pail. Damned, meddlesome trimmers have unstarched everything. Got even the best folks bemused with

214

their talk of peace. Olin Royden: Justus 'n' his sister've worked on him till he's unsure whether A ain't Zed. Have done with yer prinking, Adam, for God's sweet sake! Ye ain't suppin' to White-hall."

He led the way downstairs and through the taproom. Men at the tables looked up as they passed and Adam knew by a prickling on the nape of his neck that curious eyes were following them toward a further chamber into which Baker, stepping aside, thrust him.

The company rose with a scraping of chairs and noisy greeting. The giant who still managed to appear martial in a leather shirt and homespun breeches, the hulking Warner, and the grinning Sunderland wrung the newcomer's hand and beat him on the back.

The unbridled welcome, the bold grinning faces loosed tension in Adam. He returned the rowdy hails with vast relief. These loud men would not trim or quibble or meekly submit. There was a lump in his throat as he seated himself at the table that a great ham, an enormous dish of succotash, and an uncut loaf shared with a bowl, surrounded by sundry jugs and flasks.

Over this assembly Ethan Allen presided. He glowed like a crag at sunrise as he grinned at Adam.

"Now broil me," he proclaimed, "till Judgment Day on the bluest brimstone of hell if we all are not well met! Behold, our house already was swept and garnished and now we have taken to ourselves another devil worse than the first. Thus is Scripture ful-filled."

He sipped the brew before him, shuddered, and poured fu-riously from this and the other jug.

"Adam, by the horns of Moses, I have heard little of you since we parted at Ti, and none of that good. Where have you hid?"

"I have been in Montreal and came here by way of Panton town."

Baker scowled but the other faces were unmoved. None save he, it was plain, had heard the news Adam had brought to Ben-nington. He cleared his throat that excitement had parched, and cast a cautious look over his shoulder. The door into the taproom stood wide.

"Let be," Sunderland drawled, staying him as he rose to close it. "It is harder to eavesdrop at an open portal."

Allen was sampling again the contents of the bowl. He gasped, coughed, and added a modicum of water to the mixture.

"The good peasants of Bennington," he grumbled, "think I am not woods critter enough to know when I am followed. Remember and I have been peered at, pried at, and continually trailed since we entered Bennington this morning. By the twenty-three eyeballs of the twelve apostles, I shall not endure it longer."

"Folks are afraid," Warner informed him solemnly, "you'll fly off the handle and spile the peace."

"Angels, archangels, principalities, and all celestial powers!" Allen cried, and his eyes were points of blue fire. "Spoil the peace, is it? I will have you to know that none loves peace as dearly from the river to the ends of the earth. Let it be a proper peace, and I mean to determine that it be so at the Council meeting tomorrow"—he smote the table with his palm so that the dishes leaped—"and I will gladly sheathe my sword and toy for the rest of my days with philosophy's gentle charms."

He contemplated the prospect for an instant, then chuckled explosively.

"Nevertheless," he informed Adam with a grin that bared strong teeth, "future generations will proclaim that the peace, if peace there be, in actuality was brought about by Ethan Allen. I veritably believe, Adam, 'twas the letter I wrote Tryon—with some help from you—that showed him his error, even as Paul was smitten with understanding on the way to Damascus. By God, our missive was a thunderbolt, if ever one was launched."

Baker raised prompting eyebrows at Adam but before he could speak, Allen grasped the great bowl and swung it aloft.

"I give you a toast," he blared, "that should be the rule for peace: Liberty and Property—free land and freemen to hold it, by God."

He gulped loudly and thrust the bowl at Adam, who also drank and, surrendering the vessel to Baker, turned to address Allen who had fallen to sawing pink and white slabs from the ham.

"I have come here from Panton," he began, and paused seeing all eyes had turned, not toward him, but the door. Justus Sher-

216

wood stood there. He was smiling calmly but Adam felt, even as his friend stepped forward and clasped his hand, that worry lay beneath the smooth composure.

"Olin told me," Sherwood said, "that you had arrived and hazarded that I might find you here. Gentlemen," he addressed the others, "your servant."

He withstood the invitations to join them, calling attention to his dusty boots and clothes with a wry smile.

"I have but now returned from Albany," Sherwood pursued and again scanned Adam's face, "and came here in haste lest our friend in his natural concern alarm you unduly."

"Alarm?" Allen's voice clanged the word. The other went on easily.

He had understood that Adam had been concerned by the presence of a few of Reid's men in Panton. Olin had been disturbed, too, when he had come to Bennington, but Sherwood, thanks to the frequent conferences he had been holding with Albany authorities, had been able to reassure him. The intruders, if one might call them so, though they were there under a military grant authorized by His Majesty, were a handful of inoffensive persons who had taken no occupied land and wished only to live on good terms with their neighbors.

Adam sat straighter. He opened his mouth, then winced and closed it for Baker had kicked him smartly on the shin.

"In truth," Sherwood was saying earnestly, "what happens in Panton will prove whether we favor a composure of our difficulties or no; whether we will submit to a just peace."

"Mebby," Sunderland drawled, his long face somnolent, "ye'll tell us yer idee of a 'just peace.' "

"Gladly. An end to violence, a general amnesty, the possible formation of a new county here with all men equal under the law. These and other concessions," Sherwood pursued with his engaging smile, "are outlined in a letter I have brought from no less a person than Governor Tryon himself and delivered to Parson Dewey. He will read it at the Council meeting tomorrow night. Meanwhile"—severity crept into his voice—"I warn you all against the undertaking of any action whatever."

Warner's heavy voice ended the brief silence.

"On my word, we have been considering none."

"I am glad of that," Sherwood said, relaxing and laying a friendly hand on Adam's shoulder. "I feared this gentleman was infected, as Olin had been, by the Royden women's alarm."

He looked down with a smile that Adam, with Baker's foot pressed firmly upon his instep, managed to return.

"They were greatly exercised," he admitted carefully, "and they did rouse my concern.

"Women will exaggerate," Sherwood shrugged. "There can be no peace without a yielding by both sides and even a hint of rioting"—his smile vanished and he looked squarely at Allen—"at this stage of the negotiations would be condemned by the best men everywhere."

Ethan acknowledged the warning with a nod. The expression on his crimson face made Adam think that Baker had kicked him, too. Sherwood's hand pressed Adam's shoulder.

"Olin sups with us tonight and I came to bid you to join us, but since you already are agreeably committed, we'll meet on the morrow. Gentlemen, your most obedient."

He bowed and withdrew. The silence in which they heard his boots clack across the taproom floor was ended by Baker.

"Mebby," he said to the ceiling, "he ain't turned his coat 'n' mebby I be an Abenaki squaw."

"Keep your voice down," Warner bade huskily. "What makes you think so?"

" 'Tain't what I think," Baker replied. "It's what Adam here knows. He has a tale I want you folks should hear."

"Justus Sherwood is either," Adam said, forcing out the words reluctantly, "prodigiously misinformed or a monstrous liar."

"Now, by all the gods of the wild—" Allen began furiously but Sunderland's dry speech hushed him.

"If ye must beller, Ethan, bid all the folks come in so they can hear everything easier. Go on, Adam."

He seemed to drowse while Adam spoke. A frown grew deeper above Warner's honest eyes. Baker watched Allen, whose face as the report progressed was afflicted by twitchings and quiverings, as though a pent force struggled beneath its surface.

"By—" he exploded as Adam's tale ended and quenched his voice with a long, gurgling draught.

"Wal?" Baker prompted bleakly, ending the silence. Warner stirred in his chair.

"Then there are more of Reid's people than Sherwood—believes?" He chose the last word delicately.

"Many more."

Allen breathed with the sound of a hard plied saw. Sunderland asked sleepily, "Sartin troops'll interfere?"

"I have been so assured thrice—by Reid himself, by Reid's factor, and by a captain of regulars with whom I journeyed up the lake."

Again, silence fell. Warner offered at last, "Considerable job to take on the British army."

"We can try," Baker said mildly.

Allen snorted, then said in a muted voice, "We shall try, by the holy great toe of the Pope, if they were all the legions of Belial and Beelzebub. Reid's minions will summon assistance if attacked, eh? 'Tis a simple problem, gentlemen. We must hit so suddenly and so hard that they'll have no time to get aid."

"The peace party'll holler," Sunderland warned.

Allen's hard mouth spread in a smile.

"The peace party or Reid's people won't know what has happened till after it has come to pass. We'll strike without warning and abolish utterly. But to do this, hark ye, we must keep absolute secrecy and preserve innocence's own aspect. Seth and I must linger here till after the Council meeting tomorrow night, lest our absence rouse suspicion. Meanwhile—"

He looked about the table and the air of a vast, scheming child fell away from him. When he spoke again, bluster was gone from his voice. It cracked like a whip.

"Captain Baker."

"Sir," Remember said, stiffening.

"Get up into the north. Order out not less than one hundred men, well mounted, these to assemble at Castleton no later than the ninth."

Baker nodded with a fierce grin. Warner said, like one who thinks aloud, "A hundred men. Will they be enough?"

Allen favored him with a glare.

"It will suffice. What could Gideon and Jehovah accomplish that Ethan Allen cannot?"

The meal had ended and the bowl was beginning its rounds when Baker slipped away. It was still circulating an hour later when Adam left the company, pleading weariness that was, in truth, reluctance to risk again devastation wrought by the Colonel Commandant's Particular. He felt the need, also, to arrange in solitude a mind that drink and the day's events had roiled.

Yet satisfaction in his mission's outcome accompanied him up the stair. He had roused the rescuers for whom Panton's settlers had looked long and vainly. He considered, too, in admiration, how Ethan Allen's peculiar mind had dealt with the crisis, driving directly at the problem's heart.

Adam chuckled as he walked along the upper hall. He had accomplished more in a few hours than Olin in twice as many days. There was a light in his room. He thrust the door inward sharply.

"I want to talk with you," said Olin, rising from his chair. "I've been waiting quite a spell."

"Oh," said Adam and closed the door behind him. The wariness that squeezed his midriff was not warranted by his visitor's mild voice and manner. Olin's speech circled cautiously about his purpose.

"Justus said that you were supping with Ethan. It worried him lest some new sort of hell was brewing."

"He has no cause for concern," Adam lied blandly, wondering whether Olin had been sent by Sherwood and waiting for his friend to press the inquiry, but Olin only hesitated, frowned, and with an effort pulled further speech from himself.

"I came because—well, because I value your esteem. You hold I have been wrong to tarry here, eh?"

Adam shrugged, unwillingly moved by the appeal on the swarthy face.

"How can I tell whether you have done rightly or wrongly? Yet I am surprised that when your mother and sister—"

He must not go too far. If he stressed Panton's plight and his companion reported it to Sherwood, it might alarm him and imperil Allen's stroke. The care with which he was obliged to tiptoe through suspicions and intricate cross-purposes revolted Adam. Olin, misinterpreting his look, was saying almost humbly:

"I have done what Justus believed to be best and it seemed that way to me, too, Adam. Ma's always been overscared we might lose our land. Justus says there is no danger. I figured if peace was coming it would be best to wait and bear the news home with me."

He looked hopefully at his friend for some trace of sympathy and approval. Adam, touched by the uncommon meekness of a cocksure man, grinned suddenly into the troubled face, sat down on the bed, and offered, "Shall we speak in confidence, agreeing that what either says will go no further?"

The other nodded violently.

"Good. Then, Olin, do you wholly trust Justus Sherwood?"

Olin gaped in astonishment so complete that it shook Adam's suspicion.

"Trust Justus? Far's I'd trust myself; further, maybe."

"You're sure?"

"Certain-sure. Never's done a mean thing in all the years we've known him."

"He is a Tory."

"Yes. That's so, but it don't mean—what are you aiming at, for God's sake?"

Adam compelled himself to say, "I am wondering whether he might be a turncoat, a spy. Lately I have heard him called both."

Olin shook his head with decision.

"Lord, Adam! In The Grants they call anyone whatever they can lay tongue to. Don't take talk to heart."

How much of his defense, Adam wondered unhappily, was sound; how much the product of Sherwood's possible duplicity; how much more due to Felicity? Jealousy stabbed at him and he thrust it away. He would not discuss the girl with anyone, least of all with a rival whom he had defeated.

Adam sighed, grinned crookedly at his companion, and spread his hands in a helpless gesture.

"Please God, you're right, for he has been my friend as well as yours. I do find it strange that he pays court to Albany and forgets his neighbors in Panton."

That, Olin explained zealously, was because of Sherwood's eagerness to compose The Grants' troubles. He had said openly that he strove for peace no less for his king's sake than for his neighbors' and had told Olin that it would be his great pride if he were to aid in abolishing strife from one precinct of His Majesty's turbulent dominions.

"And he does not neglect the Panton people, Adam. This evening, he sent a letter to Reid's tenants apprising them that peace was near and warning them not to molest Grants' settlers."

"Sent it by whom?"

"The Reverend Hough," Olin chuckled. "Brimstone Benjy must be in Shaftsbury by now, if Abijah has not fallen apart."

"You read the letter?" Adam asked idly.

"No. Justus told me he had sent it and I saw the Reverend depart."

They talked thereafter with less restraint of tomorrow's Council meeting and what it might bring forth. Sherwood, Olin revealed, planned to return to New Haven in due course but he himself intended to ride northward immediately the decision was known. Adam, with an increasing sense of perfidy, reassured his friend concerning Mindwell and Delight. It seemed an interminable time before the comforted Olin rose yawning and left.

Adam, when he got to bed, found he had cast off with his clothing all wish for sleep. He lay wide-eyed, while the tavern's noises faded and a lopsided moon came to peer in at his window. He had drunk just enough of Allen's punch to spur his mind. It ran, quick and irresponsible, from problem to problem and dealt finally with none.

Felicity moved distractingly through his thoughts. Now she was glowing and tender; now tarnished by doubt which, even while he weighed it, shamed him. Had she permitted Wadman to woo her? Had it been her deliberate coquetry that had filled Olin's spirit with a pitiful confidence?

It was shabby and vulgar to lie here, juggling suspicions of his beloved and her brother. Ira Allen had charged that Sherwood was in Britain's pay. Might he not have been subsidized to use his influence, and Felicity's as well, to attain Britain's ends?

If this could be, Adam told himself with harsh satisfaction, Sherwood's purpose would come to nothing. If he condoned some infamous plan to sacrifice Panton's settlers, Baker already was riding; Allen, Warner, Sunderland, and Adam himself would follow to thwart him.

222

His mind stumbled over a surmise and paused, alarmed, to consider it. Hough was bearing a message from Sherwood to Reid's people in Panton. Justus had told Olin it urged moderation. Justus might have lied.

Suppose Sherwood had learned of Allen's projected raid; suppose the letter carried by the cadaverous parson, rankest of Yorkers, bade Reid's people warn the Crown Point garrison of the impending blow? Olin had not seen the dispatch. It might be part of a plot devised in Albany to smash The Grants' troublesome militia. Hough might be bearing word to Hutchinson to set the trap.

Adam tried to drive the thought away but it harried him like a vicious dog. For an instant he was impelled to rise and launch immediate pursuit of Hough. Someone still loyal to The Grants' cause must read Sherwood's letter.

Common sense halted him. He could not go pelting off at midnight to find the minister when he did not even know where in Shaftsbury Hough would lodge. Adam remembered the venerable steed that bore the parson, and lay back, relieved. He would wait till morning. Then, if the need still seemed urgent, it would be easy to overtake Hough.

With one quandary resolved, the less immediate lost their power. Adam slept and woke to see the morning star burning in the pale east. Slumber, he found, had not diminished his suspicion. He rose, dressed and went softly out through the cool dawn to the barn.

Chapter XXIV

No ONE appeared to help Adam saddle one of Strong's horses and fix the lead rope to the other. No one hailed him as hoofs rang loudly in the silence. He was grateful. The venture, by daylight, had acquired a sorry flavor. It would have taken small persuasion to have restrained him.

The sun was a handbreadth high when he rode down into Shaftsbury. People gaped from doorsteps and windows, and a man before the tavern met his inquiry with heavy-lidded, hostile reticence that collapsed when the questioner named himself. Outlawry, Adam reflected wryly, enduring the suddenly released flood of speech, was a touchstone in The Grants.

The parson had arrived after dark, had bedded at Squire Munro's, and had not yet ridden on. The speaker also volunteered a long list of ingenious torments that Munro and his guest should suffer if right-thinking folks had their way.

At the crossroads, Adam turned toward Munro's house and was so occupied with framing a tale to justify his appearance there that he did not mark the approaching rider until the man was close. He went past at a gallop. The dust of his passage was sifting back into the road before Adam remembered him and wondered uneasily whither Benjamin Buck rode in such haste. He shelved the thought when, a few minutes later, he saw Abijah bear Hough toward him.

The minister's response to Adam's greeting was forbearing. His raiment was rustier, his eyes more widely ringed with white, his voice even more grating than when they last had met. He accepted with no apparent suspicion Adam's story of a suddenly necessary journey to Panton and Sherwood's request that he relieve the minister of the letter and bear it himself.

"Sir," Hough's voice rattled, "you should have stayed, not me but him who passed you. Since Mr. Sherwood said the message was urgent and embodied the will of His Excellency, God bless him, I gave it at Squire Munro's suggestion to one of his servants who is carrying it forward with more speed than I could manage, Abijah being an excellent thing for safety but lacking in ambition."

"Well," Adam shrugged with simulated unconcern, "I have done my best. And now, sir, I wish you good morning, since I am in haste myself."

Yet it was not until he had turned north at the crossroads, and had drawn out of Hough's sight, that he spurred his horse. Scruples were gone; suspicion had solidified. Munro's hand in the forwarding of Sherwood's letter, Buck's consequent hurry, confirmed the belief that the message was designed not to admonish but alarm Reid's tenants.

Adam curbed his elation and let his pace slacken, though the tracks freshly stamped into the dust before him proclaimed that Buck still galloped. Horsemen did not race the strength out of their animals at a journey's outset. If Buck persisted, the pursuit would be brief. Adam would welcome its end. Already his own mount's jolting, plowhorse gait was reawakening yesterday's soreness.

He was relieved when Buck's trail showed that he, too, had slackened speed, since this indicated the man was unaware he was followed and was likely to ride more and more deliberately as the day advanced. It was a long way to Panton, Adam reminded himself cheerfully, and soon or late he would overhaul his quarry.

Holding to this preachment, he followed the vague road over brown hillocks through the forest while, beyond the lofty roof of interlocking branches, the morning unfolded. It plunged bright lances into the lower dusk and loosed upon the dank air warm, spiced odors.

The rapture of the hunt grew, closing Adam's mind and eyes to all but Buck's trail. There, for a space, he had walked his horse; yonder, he had briefly dismounted; here beside a brook's green edge, where Adam paused to let his animals drink, the man had tarried to water his own beast.

Buck, Arlington's blacksmith told Adam, had preceded him through the village by only a quarter hour yet it was not until the hunter rode up the hill into Manchester that he caught the first, distant sight of the man, a tiny figure that climbed upon a toy horse and galloped away from puppets who transformed themselves, as Adam approached, into armed men. They halted him.

Among the rawboned persons with sprigs of evergreen in their hats, Adam recognized one to whom he had passed the alarm when he had ridden to Bennington.

"Wal," the man told him with a crooked grin. "Come, like ye said 'twould, hey?"

The group, he explained, were a company of Green Mountain Boys, assembling by Captain Baker's order to ride on to Castleton and by their own responsibility halting and examining all travelers into the north. They had let Buck proceed since he was riding express for Justus Sherwood.

"You would have saved me a deal of soreness if you had held him a moment longer," Adam thought but he uttered no reproach.

The afternoon stretched before him and his horses and his own fasting body needed refreshment. He turned toward the tavern. His chances of overtaking Buck would not be lessened if he rested an hour.

He transferred his saddle to the led horse before he rode from Manchester, wishing as the unyielding trot tormented him again, that he had Baker's sure knowledge of The Grants. Then, by cutting cross country, he might head Buck off and end the ordeal. He forgot his discomfort in the tale the tracks resumed.

Buck must have seen Adam ride into Manchester, possibly had recognized him, certainly had realized that he was pursued. He had not checked his pace when the road had turned again into the forest but had galloped farther than an unalarmed traveler would have urged a tired horse and, after letting him walk a brief space, had urged him on again. Adam smiled grimly. No unfed man and animal could long maintain that speed.

A half hour later he saw with satisfaction how briefly Buck's mount could be lifted into a gallop. Steaming manure proclaimed that a scant interval lay between pursuer and pursued. Twice, Adam fancied he caught, through the crowding trees before him, the distant thud of hoofs but when he drew rein he could hear only his horses' syncopated breathing. He went on, a shade more slowly, while he dealt with a question that, in the fascination of the chase, he had not hitherto considered.

What should he do when, presently, he overtook Buck? The man's haste spoke of panic. Even so cringing a person, if terrified, might resist. In any event, since already he was alarmed; since he was Munro's man and knew Adam for an outlaw, Buck would be unlikely to surrender Sherwood's letter meekly. He might be armed and his pursuer had only a belt hatchet and sheath knife with which to overcome him.

Adam suddenly found derision in the woodland's silence, as though the wilderness were enjoying his plight. He cursed himself for the rashness in which he had rushed off from Bennington, telling none of his intention, taking no adequate weapon. If Buck were overtaken, guile could be the pursuer's only resort and his quarry was himself a guileful man.

Adam was so preoccupied with his difficulty that it was a shock when his mind accepted as last what his eyes had been announcing patiently: Buck's tracks had vanished.

The pursuer stared long and without belief at the barren road before him. He wheeled and rode slowly back the way he had come. At length he drew rein, bent to stare, then chuckled as understanding came. For an instant he almost had believed Buck's horse had taken wing.

Adam was irked that so bald a subterfuge should even briefly have baffled him. Where a low, broad outcropping of rock crossed the trail, Buck had turned his mount out upon it, had ridden its length—torn lichens and a faint powdering of crushed stone betrayed his course—and, when the ledge sank back into the soil, had gone on into the forest.

Amusement at the transparent trick dwindled. Adam considered the roof of branches. Leaves were translucent green and gold in the late sunlight. In hardly more than an hour, dusk would be gathering here; in two, the forest floor would be steeped in the darkness of a cave.

Adam, scowling, accorded Buck's strategy tardy respect. It might be only the frantic expedient of the hunted. It might be evidence that the man knew the land too well to need the road's guidance. Or the fugitive might even purpose to circle back and get into the trail again behind his pursuer. Whatever the intention, Adam realized and gathered up his rein, he must break off the chase or follow Buck.

The hoofprints were deeper and clearer on the soft mold but Adam found that, without the road's guidance, he could not follow them so swiftly. The spongy earth absorbed the noise of his passage so that he and his animals seemed to drift rather than move by volition. The silence twitched at his nerves. He assured himself impatiently that he was intruding on no greater danger than he already had faced. If Buck had planned ambush, there had been ample opportunity before now to lay it.

Nevertheless, the tracker found himself advancing more slowly through the haphazard colonnades. Knowledge that his quarry might be stretching the distance between them could not overthrow caution. The scathing voice that earlier had reproached Adam for reckless enlistment in a wild-goose chase was reviving. He was bothered by the feeling that Buck no longer fled but led him on, perhaps even paused at times to observe maliciously his slow progress.

Yet he found in the fugitive's tracks no sign of such halts. Buck moved forward, occasionally at a trot, more frequently at a walk, and the hoofprints were growing harder to read. It was not due, Adam saw with a start, to harder soil. The sun had gone from the forest's lofty canopy and the trunks that massed before him were swathing themselves in dusk.

A little way ahead, water's small voice broke the silence. Adam reached the fern-plumed bank of the rivulet and bent, squinting. Buck's trail crossed the dark flow and climbed the further slope.

The horses drank long and at last lifted dripping muzzles to stare about them, prick-eared. Adam climbed decrepitly from the saddle.

"I've had enough and so have you," he told them. "There are worse places to bed and, unless he has owl's eyes, he can't travel farther tonight."

He picketed his animals and, while darkness thickened,

228

mounded dry needles, bark, and twigs for the beginning of a fire but, with Delight's gift already in hand, hesitated to ignite the tindery heap.

Ahead where the forest's outlines melted into uniform blackness, Benjamin Buck also must have paused. A campfire, though Adam knew it could not be seen far through the thronging trees, might proclaim to the hunted man that he still was followed, might even bring him stealing back to end the chase by a shot from just beyond the firelight's rim.

Adam stood, weighing the flint and steel in his hand, while anger that he knew might more justly be directed against himself centered upon Buck. He quailed as a breeze went softly through the foliage above him, swore, and put away the lighter. Since he feared the fugitive might turn upon him, he would stalk Buck himself.

He had faith that his sense of direction would not fail him, even in this flat blackness. If he could not find where Buck camped, he had only to face about and return to the brook. Yet the chances of discovering anything in the dark void seemed preposterously slight.

While he fretted, at once eager and reluctant, Adam stiffened and sniffed. Air, moving torpidly through the night, had brought an eloquent scent, the diluted, far-borne odor of woodsmoke. He drew off his boots, made sure that knife and hatchet hung at hand and groped his way up the brook's far bank.

He found, almost at once, a nightmare quality in his progress. He moved, a few inches at a time, unable to see whence he came, whither he went or how far he had advanced. His pace was so slow it was hard to tell whether he was going uphill or down. The darkness was a fabric whose texture muffled him. His eyes, outraged by their failure, launched into aberration, creating looming monstrosities, blacker than the gloom, that his outstretched and fumbling hands assured him were not there, filling the void with delusive sparks and glowings. Behind him, the voice of the brook, his surety and guide, seemed as it grew fainter to implore him to return.

Adam's fingers, outthrust like antennae, scraped upon the boles of unseen trees and were his only guide. His unshod feet by stealthy scufflings determined his next step. His straining ears atoned for his blindness by magnifying each sound, building up his breathing into tumult, making each cautious footfall a ponderous crashing.

The air current failed and the scent of smoke expired. Adam's intention perished with it. No one less demented than he would take such a venture. He would relinquish it and obey the brook's summons. While he hesitated, the smell revived and enticed him onward, each movement a planned enterprise, each small advance a delicately contrived accomplishment.

He believed when at last he saw a small glinting through a chink in the treetrunks' screen that his eyes again were tricking him, yet the tiny brilliance endured and, as he crept forward, resolved itself into flame and soaring sparks. He heard mild crackling, the heavy stir of a horse, and sank on all fours. Thus he advanced, cringing at each slight sound.

He could see firelight shaking over a prostrate tree whose trunk Buck's saddle bestrode. He could see, after further agonized approach, the tethered horse and, beyond the small spouting of flame, Buck himself, propped against the fallen tree with his head inclined toward the fire.

With immense care, Adam drew his feet under him. His movements were slow and soundless even to his own ears yet something roused his quarry. Buck lifted his head. He seemed to look across the fire squarely at his stalker. Buck sharply withdrew his hand from his cloak's folds. It held a long dark pistol. The sound of its cocking was succinct.

"I am armed," Buck said hoarsely. "I shall defend myself."

The swarthy face shone as though it had been lacquered. The eyes, reflecting the fire, were uneasy sparks. Though the man, in some occult fashion, had sensed the danger, he still was uncertain where it lay. Utter silence, Adam told himself, might reassure him.

But Buck, with his pistol poised, was scrambling to his feet. He glared about the precinct from which his fire held back the night, took a quick step forward, squinted into the darkness and strode again, directly toward his squatting, still unseen enemy.

Buck paused to peer and then advanced another abrupt stride. In two more he would stumble over the ambushed man.

Adam's hatchet was heavy in his hand. He flung it, not at

Buck, but in a lobbing arc toward the prostrate tree. It struck the rotting wood with a thud and a brief clatter. Buck spun about at the sound. Adam snatched out his knife and leaped.

His arms caught Buck's legs. They gave. There was a yelp, an explosion as the two men fell. Snorting and thrashing rose as the frightened horse strained at his tether while beside the fire his overthrown owner half rose and fell again.

Buck's body was beneath Adam's now, but terror had made it as devious as a stranded eel. It twisted, jerked, uttered small moans. The hand still gripping the discharged pistol flailed wildly. It dealt Adam a glancing blow, blinding him with brief fire before he could catch the weapon and twist it free. Buck's wail pinched out as Adam got astride the plump body. He saw the dark eyes in the creased face dilate as they caught the knifeblade's glitter. Buck gave one convulsive heave that almost overthrew the other and then lay quivering with the steel against his throat.

"Quiet, you dolt," Adam gasped and added, ignoring the present and immediate past, "I don't mean to harm you."

He rolled free, rose, and stood above his victim, a weapon in either hand. Buck lay still, breathing in shrill bursts.

"Sit up," Adam bade and the other obeyed quickly, dread still glazing his eyes.

"And before you rise, surrender the message you bear to Panton."

Buck's hand moved toward his bosom and stayed.

"Immediately."

The knife flashed. Buck gasped and held out a sealed white oblong. Adam, bending to the fire, identified Sherwood's hand and thrust the letter inside his shirt.

"I have saved you a weary journey, Mr. Buck," he said and grinned.

Still stupefied by violence, Buck pulled at his rumpled clothing with ineffectual hands. Adam strode to the fallen tree, rummaged in his victim's saddlebags, and extracted an embroidered bullet pouch and a small metal powder flask.

"I am taking these and your barker, lest you have any idea of reprisal. You are to stay here until full daylight and then, on no account, to follow me. It can be disastrous to be followed, as you must be aware."

231

"I—" Buck said explosively, his round, dark face twitching. "Yes?"

The other shrugged in shabby defiance.

"Then," said Adam, "a very good night to you, Mr. Buck."

It was dawn and a straight, gray smoke rose from the campfire's ashes into the universal grayness. The unfed horses stamped and stared reproachfully. Their rider's mind slowly roused his reluctant body. The clammy silence held. The fog might have been the threshold of Creation. Out in the dimness where the thinning mist was reforming a ghostly forest, Buck still must be cowering or else had stolen away during the night. If he were moving now, the dank air would have brought the sound.

Wincing and tottering, Adam rose. Faint crackling accompanied his effort and, erect at last, he drew Sherwood's letter from his shirt. Already, it was creased, grimed, and its superscription faintly blurred.

"To Colo. Reid's Factor at the Falls of Otter," Justus had written. "By the Hand of the Reverend Mr. Hough."

It was an unhandsome trophy for so much effort.

Adam found small relish in reviewing his success. He counted its cost:

Item: Whatever good will Buck had borne him. Item: Sherwood's friendship. Item: Felicity's trust. At this price, he had acted the highwayman and had confirmed the label of outlaw Tryon had affixed to him. It was a mad world in which a man loyal to his friends ruined himself while Justus could wear the halo of official esteem though he wrote to Hutchinson, bidding him—

Adam's diatribe halted so abruptly that he grunted. What had been Sherwood's bidding?

He took out the letter again, turned it over. Compunction stirred but he thrust it aside. He must compound felony. He must know the extent of Sherwood's perfidy.

Adam plucked at the red wax seal on the folded sheet but a canny thought checked him. He thrust his knife into the campfire's ashes, in a moment withdrew it and applied its edge to the blob of wax. The hot metal freed the seal, intact. He unfolded the page with trembling fingers and read:

"Sir: Word has reached me this Day that you purpose to proceed with Violence against present Settlers in Panton Town. I am in Communion with His Excellency, the Royal Governor of New York, leading Gentlemen of that Province and advise you in the strongest Terms to do Nothing enemical pending further Word from Government there being now good Hope the unhappy Difficulties with The Grants may be composed. I assure you it would be His Excellency's Wish that you make no Divigations from this Counsel. I am, Sir, your urgent & most obt. Servant, Justus Sherwood."

Adam laughed. The dry mirth was brief but the instant before he moved was long.

The burden of Sherwood's letter, so contrary to all his now ignominious suspicions, momentarily had stunned him. Then into the blankness had crept smarting appreciation of his own preposterous antics. He had stalked, assaulted, stolen—and his prize was nothing more dangerous or treasonable than a message he himself might have written, had he been Sherwood.

Scorn of his own twittery apprehensions, shame at his misjudgment of his friend, were jostled aside by another starker thought.

"Word has reached me this Day—" Justus had written. Adam had borne that word and had confided it to Felicity.

Again he laughed, still more unpleasantly. By the warmth of her sympathy and her body's soft persuasion, Felicity had drawn the whole tale from him and straightway had broken her pledge of secrecy and had babbled it to her brother.

Dismay and anger were curbed by corrosive amusement. Adam had been thoroughly duped. The girl's quick betrayal and its implications were too vast for him to consider entire while squatting on his heels, here in the misted forest. He stirred with the feeling that he was just awaking. A crooked smile was stamped on his face as he chose his immediate course. Clearly, it was now his duty to bear the stolen letter to its destination. That, too, was part of the sardonic comedy into which he had thrust himself.

He resealed the message with the aid of his heated knifeblade, saddled one horse, and, leading the other, rode back through the watery dawn toward the road to Panton. There, after a moment's hesitation, he shook his head and turned north.

He had gone only a brief way when brush clashed before him and a horseman pushed from the forest into the trail. Adam opened his mouth to hail but found no words. There were matters beyond explanation or apology. He drew aside in silence to let his victim pass.

There was earth on Buck's clothing and on his flabby face. There was black hate in the eyes that for an instant met Adam's. Buck rode on south without a word or backward look. His despoiler watched him out of sight and then spoke to the horses.

"We had best," he told them gravely, "get this letter to Panton sooner than he could have delivered it."

Chapter XXV

MINDWELL ROYDEN said in a level voice: "Pangbornes has had final warning; so's Everests. Readyin' to go."

She swallowed with a curt, dry sound.

"I ain't."

On her stool by the fireplace, Delight, with the dust of late hoeing still on her slim brown legs and arms, pressed a hand to her mouth and looked at her mother as though she might absorb fortitude from her.

The woman had stood beside the kitchen table that was no more firmly set than she while Adam had told of his journey and its outcome. She had shaken her head when he had urged her to sit, as though it would have been weakness to meet adversity otherwise than squarely erect.

"I ain't," she repeated now.

"Nothing," Adam assured her, "can happen today."

Mindwell nodded.

"Ehyah: Tell myself that, each sunset time."

"And tomorrow," he pursued, "I'll bear Justus's letter to Otter Falls."

"Justus!" she said in a quietly blighting voice and for an instant gripped the table's edge so hard that the knuckles of her big hand glistened.

"Where's Ethan Allen?" she asked and the question twanged like a plucked wire. "What ails him 'n' his Boys? Need them now; not letters."

Adam shrugged. He was pledged to secrecy and unwilling, too, to quicken undue hope.

Mindwell released the table and placed her hands on the broad shelves of her hips. She atoned for her outburst with a matter-of-fact briskness.

"Wal, we're beholden to ye, Adam. Done what ye could. More'n—"

She checked herself. Adam knew by the small clicking noise that she swallowed her son's name.

"There's times," Mindwell offered, "when things all come apart. Wal, endured 'em before."

"It's a mending time now," Adam told her, drawing lavishly on his confidence. "Justus is sure peace is on the way. I shall see Hutchinson tomorrow. Hold fast a little longer. And now," he added, pulling himself up from the chair with an effort, "I'd best see to the nag I didn't leave at Strong's."

Delight had risen more quickly than he. She said in a low, eager voice, "I'll tend to him," and was at the door before he could protest. Mindwell's headshake silenced Adam.

"Let her," she bade. "Ye look wore down."

"I'm tired, that's all."

The girl had vanished. Adam obeyed Mindwell's gesture and sat again. The woman lowered her solid body into another chair and looked at him. Awkwardness grew in the silence. Mindwell cleared her throat. She asked in a steady voice:

"What about Olin?"

"I've told you."

Again she shook her head. He eyes were troubled.

"No, ye ain't. What about him 'n' Felicity?"

"What about them?" His face grew stiff.

Mindwell, drawing a long slow breath, pressed resolutely on, "Got him, ain't she?"

The question was strained, as though she deliberately were hurting herself, but he found no enlightenment in the still, brown face. He said, "I don't know what you mean. I explained why he had not come back."

"No, ye ain't," she said with bovine persistence. "Ye told me what he told ye. An' ye came back; he didn't. Holdin' him ain't she? Wal"—with resignation—"folks is as God made 'em, mostly."

"You're not fair to Olin."

"Ain't, eh?" He was too occupied with his own difficult thoughts to mark the new edge to her voice or the darker hue of

236

the wooden face. "Ain't blind either, Adam. Seen 'em together while they was here. Watched her bait him with Canady airs 'n' graces 'fore Justus took her to Boston."

Adam tried to break in upon the dull roll of speech but she took the words away from him.

"Good for girls to be sperrited. Good for Olin to be led round by the nose. Boasts no female can, but she has, seems. Improve his gait, mebby. Say so myself if I wa'n't his mother 'n' hadn't known Felicity's mother. Like, they are, as peas in a pod. Mad for men, both of 'em."

There was no animus in her judgment, only resignation as though she deplored something as irremedial as the weather. She baffled Adam, who, with his own late betrayal in mind, could offer no reassurance. Mindwell laid a hard palm briefly upon his arm. The affection he saw in the direct eyes smote him. The woman went on with meekness that was dignity's kinsman, while her blunt fingers nervously pleated the soiled and patched fabric of her gown:

"Girls together to Salem, Felicity Kent 'n' me. She wed early 'n' I—didn't. John Sherwood was a good man to her—too good, folks thought. Real ghostly, recallin' her, to see her daughter now."

Her eyelids puckered. The voice plodded:

"Moved to Hartford, Sherwoods did, when Justus was a little boy. All kinds of tales why they left. After Dan'l 'n' me was wed, John Sherwood come back with Justus 'n' the girl baby his wife had died a-bearin'. Justus was still in his 'teens when his father died, some said of a broken heart."

She paused and though her face was still, the clicking sound came from her throat.

"Don't want," Mindwell said, "that Olin should be served the way John Sherwood was. Felicity ain't molded to be a plain man's wife, Adam."

He stirred, wishing he might honestly cry out:

"Felicity doesn't love Olin, Mindwell. Felicity loves me, and there's an end to it."

He found himself desolately unsure. He could only say, "Olin must be on his way home now. You worry yourself needlessly."

She shook her head. The steady voice cut him.

237

"Ain't needless to sorry over my son 'n' over our pitch. Them 'n' Delight is all of Dan'l that's left to me, Adam. Him 'n' me, we fitted together real seemly 'n' close, like—like a lake to its shore."

"You're to lose none of them, I promise you," he answered through a swollen throat.

The kitchen door opened. Mindwell sat straighter and brushed at the lines she had creased into her gown.

"Wal," she said loudly, "mistrust I ain't talked so free to no one since Dan'l died. Delight 'n' me'll fix supper now 'n' let ye git to bed."

Adam strode through the sunrise to the stable next morning to find his horse fed and groomed, and Delight straining at the saddle girth.

"There was no need of that," he exclaimed and thrust her almost roughly aside. She made no protest but stood watching him and, as he prepared to mount, asked quietly:

"You will come back?"

Slight and shabby, she endured his stare.

"Come back," he repeated. "Of course, I shall. What on earth —?"

She shook her head.

"Mother still believes they are going to take our land."

Sympathy quickened for the wistful child. He told her, cheerfully, "You are not to lose your land. Will you remember that, Delight?"

She answered in a low voice with her head held high, "I will remember," and added simply, "I'd truly try to do anything you wished."

She did not falter and he, looking at her, had the sudden illusion that her clumsy dress, her sunburned face and toilworn hands were lit by a tranquil, pale radiance. Delight said in a voice surer than her usual utterance, "We owe you a deal. All the while, we owe you more."

"You owe me nothing." He was puzzled by her rapt poise. "Friends don't keep accounts against each other, my dear child. And you—and your mother and your brother—" he included hastily, "are dear to me. Never forget that."

"I have never forgotten anything you ever told me."

238

She offered it like a profession of faith and her clear eyes were unwavering. Because her air of dedication disturbed him, Adam shied away from gravity.

"Shall I bring back with me the wicked Mr. Hutchinson's humble submission or his caitiff body across my saddlebow?"

He had not seen before how a dimple lent demureness to her smile. Adam looked back when he reached the clearing's edge. Delight still stood in the stable door, watching him.

The man who won her, he thought despondently, would have a calmer wooing than his own, with none of the doubts and pains that seemed to spring up for his bitter harvesting wherever Felicity's little, high arched feet had trod. He wondered how she thought of him now. The tale of the assault and theft he had committed upon Buck must have reached her ears.

The sawmill's throbbing voice came to him through the forest's silence and, a little later, the brisk, defiant drumming of hammers.

Whatever their sins, Adam reflected, trotting from the woods' edge toward the settlement, Reid's tenants were an industrious crew. Many of the houses were occupied now. The hay was stacked in portly brown cones upon the shorn meadow and the corn and barley were flourishing. Men past whom he rode through the growing village accorded him only sidewise glances but Hutchinson appeared surprisingly pleased to see him.

Reid's agent stood on the closed hatchway of the mill observing men who levered at a boulder in a half-dug cellar hole.

"Mr. Corlaer," he cried. "Ye're just the mon I was thinking of, no less."

The wig was in place. His eyes were bright, his thin mouth smiled, and his gaunt body was enlivened by some secret glee.

"I was wonderin' where ye had taken yerself, and then—hoot! —here ye are. Ye have come for me hangin', mayhap? Eh, Mr. Corlaer?"

"I have come," Adam replied, flushing at memory of the angry threat, "from Bennington with a letter for you."

"Aye, Bennington? The rebel rats' nest?"

Hutchinson accepted the letter but held it unopened while he rasped, "Colin, gin ye an' Jamie canna howk yon wee bit pebble, I'll come doon an' aid ye."

The diggers, purple and grunting, heaved out the boulder and thrust it away from the excavation's lip.

"Ye see," Hutchinson proclaimed, "what a mon can do when he tries. Weel-weel, so someone has writ me a letter an' ye 've been gude enough to bring it, eh, Mr. Corlaer?"

He unfolded Sherwood's message and read with his thin mouth silently forming each word. The men in the cellar hole rested their arms on its edge and panted.

"Weel-weel," Hutchinson said and snapped a contemptuous fingernail against the page, "explicit instructions, verra polite, from Mr. Justus Shairwood, whoever he may be."

"He is among other things," said Adam, irked by the jeer, "a friend of Colonel Reid."

"Now, is he?" Hutchinson inquired, his eyes half closed. "Each time ye come, Mr. Corlaer, ye bring the Colonel a new friend. First 'twas yersel'; the noo, 'tis Mr. Shairwood."

"I never," Adam said, with the unpleasant feeling that he was being baited, "boasted of friendship with Colonel Reid. I said I knew him."

"Aye," Hutchinson beamed, "and well he kens ye, too, for I had an express from him only the morn, mentionin' ye; a most speceefic express, Mr. Corlaer, that would enable me to answer Mr. Shairwood forthwith, could I but reach him."

He sucked in his cheeks and his eyes strayed from Adam, to the exhumed boulder, to the men still resting in the pit.

"Ye hinna viewed our navy, have ye, sir? Come with me. It might interest ye."

He left the bulkhead and led Adam along the mill wall. The ledge that the building crowned dropped vertically and far to black, foam-splotched water. A herd of bateaux nuzzled the shore and close to the cliff stood the jetty where the stricken Adam had been carried ashore. A slender craft with a single mast was moored at its end. The sweating wheel at the dam-ward side of the mill groaned and unreeled a ribbon of froth across the basin.

"Aye," said Hutchinson, "we came this time weel prepared, Mr. Corlaer. Yon"—he tossed a pebble down upon the tethered boat—"is the Colonel's own shallop that this day brought his orders to me. A sweet sailer, sir. We shall use her to rouse the Crown Point garrison in case of need."

Again, Adam had the uneasy sense of feline play, of an ominous tapping by claw-sheathed paws. He met it directly.

"I trust, sir, in executing Colonel Reid's orders you will give consideration to Mr. Sherwood's advices."

"Now trust as ye may, Mr. Corlaer," his companion exulted, "I shall do naught of the sort. This is the Colonel's land, sir, and from it he has bidden me oust every trespasser, forthwith. Those that do not leave today, we evict on the morrow."

He grinned acidly.

"This, despite the letter of Mr. Shairwood; this, despite the hangin' ye promised me, Mr. Corlaer. I see ye have come again wi'out yer posse."

He squinted, enjoying the other's dismay. Adam said, curbing his temper, "It might be well, sir, to consider what amounts to counsel from the Governor of New York himself—"

"Oho! So the deil is quoting Scripture?" Hutchinson cried. "It was in my mind that ye and other rapscallions held Panton to be in truth not York but Grants' land. In the absence of certainty, Mr. Corlaer, I shall obey me principal's orders and to hell with York and The Grants and ye, yersel', sir."

"If you think—" Adam began, but the other raised a delaying hand.

"I do indeed think, sir, of one special bidding in Colonel Reid's recent letter. It reads: 'Should this young Corlaer interfere with the execution of my orders, in any way, you are empowered to arrest him and convey him to the nearest York authority.' And 'tis my judgment that ye are so interfering now, me bold callant."

"Indeed? And you intend—?"

"To arrest ye forthwith," Hutchinson shouted and dealt him a violent shove. "Jamie, Colin! Take him!"

Adam, staggering backward on his heels, trod upon emptiness. He toppled and, as he came down into the cellar hole, its occupants dived upon him. The impact burst the last particle of breath from him, left him no strength to oppose the weight of his captors' sweating bodies. While he still gasped for air, he felt himself grasped roughly and hauled to his feet.

Chapter XXVI

IF HE had not been supported, Adam would have fallen again, since legs and will had failed him. He had a blurred impression of figures against a glaring sky. These became, as his lungs refilled and his sight cleared, jeering men, gaping women and children, and, looming tall and dark above them all, James Hutchinson.

"So, Mr. Corlaer," he said, "the haughty sperrit goeth before a fall, eh, sir? Colin, Jamie, help the gentleman oot."

They chuckled and heaved him up toward outstretched hands that caught and clung, thrusting Adam here and there, pushing and jerking him back until his head swam and the gloating faces grew vague again.

"Enough," Hutchinson shrilled at last. "Let be, lads. We mustna be discourteous to our visitor. No-no. Hold him, ye loons, but a wee bit gently."

Adam rocked, with a man clasping either wrist, and blinked up at the bony face with its look of false concern.

"Weel, weel, Mr. Corlaer, I warned ye. Dinna deny it. And noo—" He burlesqued elaborate thought.

"We'll no delay ye long," he finally offered. "Pursuant to the Colonel's orders, we'll send ye where ye'll be more welcome. Meanwhile, where will we keep ye safe?"

He drew in his cheeks and pursed his mouth. Adam breathed less painfully now. Heat was driving the clammy sickness from his belly. He thought, inconsequently, standing pinioned and abased, of his vainglorious promise to Delight. He moved his arms a little and, as his captors tightened their hold, let them dangle lifeless. With hangdog aspect he endured Hutchinson's cackling.

"Doon the hatch!" the man exclaimed and smirked at the grinning crowd. " 'Tis dark and cool to ease a hothead, while Donald and Andy make ready the shallop. And for safety's sake, pairhaps, we'll roll yon boulder upon the door."

The gabble of approval obscured the high singing in Adam's ears. Hutchinson bent and lifted the hatchway's slanted portal.

"In here," he said with the travesty of a bow, "if ye'll be so gude, Mr. Adam Corlaer."

Adam's captors thrust him. He kicked the feet from under one and as the man pitched forward tore his own right hand free. He drove his fist against the face that gaped beside his left shoulder. The man yelped and let go. Adam ran.

Those who bellowed and lumbered in pursuit cut off the way to freedom. He dodged Hutchinson's snatching hands and found himself cornered. The pressure of the mill's wall was across his shoulders and Buck's pistol was in his fist.

There was harsh satisfaction in the sudden silence, in the abrupt halt of men who had plunged after him, in the way those nearest the weapon's muzzle flinched and tried to draw back. Hutchinson, beside the open hatch, cleared his throat.

"Ye're being a verra seelly young mon, Mr. Corlaer," he reproved.

"Doubtless," Adam said. "Stand back."

Reid's agent looked at the pistol with a sorrowful air.

"Ye might hurt someone wi' that thing, laddie."

"That is my purpose, believe me. Someone; preferably you."

Whatever the outcome, he was cleaner for this. He could see no safety beyond the present moment but that did not cool him. Wrath, hard and bright, kept him indifferent to what must happen later. He would have done his utmost by then to fulfill the pledge he had made to Mindwell and Delight.

A man in a red knitted cap bent his knees and advanced one foot stealthily.

"No," said Adam and halted him. Hutchinson was watching with an air of pious disapproval.

"Ye'll do yersel' a favor," he offered, "to hae done wi' this play actin'."

Adam ignored him. His eyes, passing over the taut semicircle before him, dwelt for an instant on the cornfield, the haycocks shimmering in the midday warmth and the dark forest wall beyond. The sun caught and dwelt upon a brilliance there. There was blurred movement at the woods' edge.

Excitement parched his mouth and tingled in his nose. He scowled again at the hesitant crowd, lest his hope betray him.

"Young men will be feckless," Hutchinson was saying. "If ye'll gie over that pistol, Mr. Corlaer, I'll overlook yer bad manners."

Adam's eyes slipped from the rigorous face and into the distance again. Horsemen had come from the forest. The sun glittered on their leader's uniform.

"Ye may shoot one of us," Hutchinson pursued. "I dinna deny that, but if ye do, 'twill be ye that hangs, I promise ye."

A dozen horsemen in uneven line were coming across the hayfield. Nausea stirred in Adam. There were a dozen of them and here were four times that number. Was this the sum of Ethan Allen's bragging?

Hutchinson was waiting with his mouth pursed, his cheeks indrawn. Lest he turn and see the forlorn advance, Adam croaked, "And if I do surrender?"

"Gie me that pistol wi' no more nonsense and we'll convey ye uplake to York and milder punishment than ye'll receive if ye resist further."

The riders were halfway across the field. Pretense fell away from Adam and he stared openly. There were a dozen, spurring forward, and another dozen, and through the corn a score more galloped. More, unnumbered swept in from beyond the haystacks.

He saw the flash as their leader drew sword. He heard the wolf yell slash, keen and wild, across the silence. They bore down on the settlement from three sides, dingy men lashing their horses and shaking their muskets.

Close at hand, a woman's scream ran like a burning fuse to set off an explosion of voices. Men darted from the group before Adam, hesitated, and dodged back again. The crowd broke apart, regathered, wavering, wailing. Below the human outcry a murmur was born that became the windy roar of many hoofs.

"Stand still," Adam called to the dazed Hutchinson. "Stand quite still."

Two men broke from the cowering group as, in an instant,

244

the street filled with howling riders. They drove past, bodies slanted back against their reins. Out of a dustwhirl beyond the mill, where horses neighed and plunged, men came running toward Reid's stunned tenants, to herd them into a tighter huddle with blows of musket butts and barrels. The invaders bawled ghastly threats, apparently wavering on the threshold of massacre.

The road smoked up like a comet's tail behind the brilliance that was Ethan Allen. His steed, reined in upon his haunches, slid far and halted. The great voice trumpeted, "Captain Warner, get those horses out of the road. Thunder of God, man, turn them into the corn."

"I told you to stand still," Adam reminded Hutchinson. The man's wig was awry, his face slick with sweat. More raiders seemed to sprout from earth to hedge in the cowed men and women with flourished firelocks and yowled imprecations. Allen's sword clanked against his boots as he strode forward.

"Clear every house," he roared. "Make prisoners of all, old and young. By Father, Son, and Holy Ghost, he who resists shall be dealt with slowly in the Iroquois fashion. Captain Baker! Where's Baker? Tell him to report to me."

In the dust-filled air, the bedizened figure blazed. It waved its arms; it bawled abuse at the captives, commands to their guards, and seemingly by lungpower alone got a semblance of order. Men came through the mirk, frog-marching additional prisoners, and thrust them into the stumbling, closely guarded column.

"You two," Allen bellowed, marking the pair who stood stiffly beside the bulkhead, "fall in with the others or by the toenails of Jehovah—"

He broke off, gulped, and stood for an instant squinting.

"Adam Corlaer! Now fry me in Gehenna's hottest grease! Where have you been? With whom did you ride?"

He beamed and staggered the other by a fond pat on the shoulder.

"With no one," Adam gasped. "I have been a prisoner of James Hutchinson, Colonel Reid's agent."

He nodded toward his sweating companion.

"And Mr. Hutchinson," Allen supplied, noting the pistol, "had a bear by the tail, eh? Lad, I love you like a brother."

245

He stepped forward to tower above Adam's captive and address him in a hushed roar.

"You will join your fellow trespassers, sir. You will inform them that at the first sign of enmity, I will slaughter them all, from the babe at the breast to the eldest, though Otter Creek run red. I am a ruthless man, sir, to whom the blood of his enemies hath a sweet savor."

He caught Hutchinson by the coat's breast and lifted him from the ground.

"And if you should survive, if I do not follow my inclination and, pinning your entrails to a tree, beat you around it with a firebrand until your bowels are unwound, you will bear this message to your damned Colonel Reid: Tell him that this is Grants' land and what mercy I show his dupes, I shall not display again. Tell him to send to Panton henceforth only those who yearn for unmarked graves in a charred soil, for so we will serve malefactors henceforth."

He relaxed his hold, letting his victim jar down on his heels. Hutchinson pulled at his rumpled coat.

"Sir," he protested, though a quaver marred the valor of his speech, "under the law—"

"Law," Allen bellowed. "We have our own law, my law, mob law, Grants' law. And by it you are deserving of hellfire. I shall abolish this settlement utterly. I shall make of it the abomination of desolation."

The man flinched beneath the blast and looked wretchedly about him. A hundred horses were grazing in the corn. Smoke went up from the haystacks and flames, pale in the sunlight, climbed over them. Baker, his musket slanted rakishly, his fur cap tilted, came padding toward Allen. Hutchinson's face twitched.

"Sir," he cried in anguish. "This is rapine, no less. Ye have no warrant—"

Baker gripped his shoulder and spun him about. Hutchinson blinked at the maimed hand that shook beneath his nose.

"Warrant?" Baker squalled. "Here is my warrant, God damn yer guts and liver. Sunderland, Leftenant Sunderland, take this blitherer away."

His eyes widened and he smote his thigh.

"Adam! B'God, like always; you 'n' me 'n' trouble!"

246

He checked himself, stood straighter and saluted.

"Colonel Allen," he rasped, "all Reid's folks are in custody, seems's if."

Allen looked at Adam with earnest inquiry.

"You saw none escape? Crown Point must not get word while there is anything left here worth a rescue."

Sunderland with repeated prods of his firelock's muzzle was urging Hutchinson toward the huddle of prisoners. Baker slouched along the mill's wall toward the cliff's edge.

"Two men," Adam said slowly, "bolted when you rode in. It—"

Baker yelped and waved. He, Allen and Adam, standing at the edge of the rock's sheer fall, looked down upon the beached bateaux and the shallop moored at the jetty's end. One fugitive had boarded the craft, the other was busy with her lines. Baker slowly lifted his musket and settled his cheek contentedly against its stock. Allen struck the weapon down.

"No," he roared, "you have your orders, sir."

The fierce blue eyes clashed with the defiant brown. Baker shrugged and uncocked his firelock. Anxiety squeezed speech from Adam.

"They'll rouse the garrison. It's a swift boat."

Allen glared about him with so wild a look that Adam, for an instant, believed he would hurl himself down upon the craft that rocked far below. The man on the jetty finished casting off and leaped aboard the shallop. The uniformed giant no longer was at Adam's side. He stood above the boulder two men earlier had levered from its bed.

"Captain Baker," Allen blared, "take a detail down and arrest those two."

He bent, clapped great hands upon the rock, caught breath, and raised it smoothly. Adam, staring without belief, saw the burdened man trudge toward him. Veins were branched welts on Allen's temples. His gilt epaulettes quivered as he balanced himself on the cliff's lip, raised his missile higher, and thrust it from him with a coughing sound.

Below, a yell was cut off by a great, curt crash. Spray, subsiding, revealed the shallop, swamped and settling among the bobbing fragments of what had been her bow. Twin sleek dots were the heads of her late crew who swam toward shore.

Allen grinned into Adam's awestruck face.

"There's more than one way," said he, "to skin a cat."

He strode off, brazen spurs flashing. Before the mill, he paused beside Warner who with his sword was hacking a length of green cloth into strips.

"Boys figured," he said nodding toward the dusty, grinning men before him, "they could use this stuff for cockades. Right color. Houses all cleared, Colonel, of anything larger than mice."

"Burn them," Allen bade.

Smoke, rank, hot, and spark-infested, rolled over the prisoners until their guards marched them further into the meadow. They moved, Adam thought, like sheep, close-huddled, jostling. A woman looked back at the burning village and keened softly but her companions seemed stunned by the fury, the clamor, and the bloodless violence.

Adam's wonder grew as he considered what had been wrought in so brief a time. The garish, blustering chieftain of an unsoldierly host had been unbelievably deft or fantastically fortunate. Allen's uniform glittered before the mill. He blared directions to men who, with confiscated tools, tore the structure apart. The thud of sledges, the groan of pried timbers rose above the gusty crackling of the fire.

Windows of the cottages were spouting flame. A roof fell in with a great upswirling of sparks. A sooty-faced rider drove more horses past to join those who fed steadily among the corn and barley. Adam called, still only half believing:

"Olin! Olin Royden!"

The man stared, wheeled, and galloped toward him.

"Adam!" he cried and slipped from the saddle. "God's name! What are you doing here?"

"Or you," Adam returned. "I thought—"

He checked himself but Olin's face darkened.

"I rode here from Bennington," he said stiffly, "with Warner's men to refute his suspicions—and your own."

His resentment fell away and, clapping hands upon Adam's shoulders, he shook him joyously.

"Mother? Delight? You've seen them?"

"Safe," Adam assured him, "and when they learn of that"—he nodded toward the destruction—"with nothing more to fear."

Olin's eyes followed his.

"Well," he said grimly, "one way of closing off the debate about peace. Best way, maybe, though Justus isn't likely to agree."

He babbled replies to Adam's questions, intoxicated by excitement and the closing of the rift between them.

The council meeting from which Sherwood had expected so much had been wrecked by Ethan Allen. Tryon's proposals had been vague but there had been hope of continuing negotiations until Allen had risen.

"Stood up in his regimentals," Olin reported with a crooked grin, "and hollered. Went through Justus's arguments like a bull through peabrush and, pretty quick, he'd got most of us hollerin', too. We prevailed. Louder than the peaceful, anyway."

When the meeting had collapsed, Olin had found himself standing near Warner who had accused him bluntly of having gone over to York.

"Told him he lied and rode here to prove it. Feel a deal better now, most ways, but—"

He looked from Reid's tenants to their blazing village and shrugged.

"Yes," Adam admitted. "I know."

Allen galloped into the field, drew rein beside the prisoners, and shouted:

"Leftenant Sunderland, get these people down to their bateaux. They are to depart instanter. And harken, all of ye"—the voice clanged brazenly—"I solemnly promise that each shall suffer death, most hideous, ensanguined, and lingering, should he ever return. This is the pledge of Ethan Allen, by God!"

The captives trailed miserably away. Allen saw Adam and thrust his horse toward him. The rocky face shone; pride seemed to have added to his stature.

"A word with you," he trumpeted. The grin that half closed his eyes endured while he looked from the plodding column to the flame and smoke and the disintegrating mill.

"By the bulls of Bashan," he exulted, "the stiff-necked and fish-headed Colonel Reid will have difficulty in securing more loons

249

to settle at Otter Falls. 'Twill be Grants' land, uncontested, here-after, despite Tryon and the army and His Majesty, himself."

"The redcoats," Allen pursued, rising in his stirrups to tower more tremendously, "may come now to take what remains, and welcome. If they delay a week, a blockhouse shall rise here, like Phoenix of old from the ashes, that no force without cannon will overcome. Our land; Grants' land! Eh, boy?"

He dealt Olin a buffet that made him cough and then redden with delight. The Colonel turned to Adam again and asked with an odd air of concern,

"And what are your intentions, eh?"

"Colonel," Adam blurted. "I want to go home."

"Home?" Allen repeated, lifting his eyebrows.

"To the Roydens, sir." He wondered at the slip. "Women are alone there, and fearful."

"And after that?" the giant persisted. Adam shrugged.

"I beg to go with him, Colonel," Olin said earnestly.

"Furloughs for both of you," Allen bellowed. "Adam, stay at Roydens' till I see you again. I have a task for you, sir."

He waved a dismissing arm and galloped away.

The west was scarlet when Adam and Olin reached the Royden clearing. Delight, issuing from the barn with her light body slanted against the weight of the milk pail, set her burden down, stared, and ran like a deer toward the house.

Mindwell was waiting in the dooryard when they dismounted. Her daughter stood beside her, with shining eyes. The woman was obdurately calm but Adam saw her face light as she saw her son.

"Wal, Olin," she said, and added after a pause, "Glad ye're back. Most time."

"Mite delayed on the way," Olin told her gravely.

His mother looked from him to Adam and compressed urgency into a single syllable.

"Wal?"

"You've nothing to fear now," he told her and sensed, without actually meeting, the intensity of Delight's look.

"Hutchinson and his people are no longer at Otter Falls. Ethan Allen is there with a hundred men."

250

Delight uttered a small, stricken sound and fled into the house. Mindwell searched Adam's face. He saw a tear spill and run down a leathery cheek.

"Wal," she said at last and looked about the clearing, "that's real good news."

Chapter XXVII

OLIN, returning from Chimney Point, where he had gone with Strong's long-borrowed horse, found Adam hoeing corn and stood a long moment watching him before he said, "The Sherwoods are in New Haven."

Adam leaned on his hoe.

"Yes?" he asked at last.

Justus and Felicity, Olin reported with a worried scowl, had stayed at Strong's two nights earlier. Led horses had borne their baggage and more was coming down the lake. The Sherwoods had gone on next morning to their hitherto unoccupied house. Olin paused and then voiced Adam's own uneasiness, "Never stopped to visit, or let us know they were here."

His friend knocked loam from the hoe blade.

"Justus is angry. No doubt, in his place, I should be, too."

Olin's tidings had been like an attack from ambush. Adam had been clinging to immunity that, suddenly, was there no longer. He had managed by daylight-long labor to keep troublesome thoughts at bay. In time, he had known, he must confront Felicity, who had beguiled him. Meanwhile, when the knowledge had pressed upon him, work with spade or axe, hoe or scythe had served to abate it. He had evaded the problem that Mindwell's confidence had made still more difficult and now, without warning, this had been thrust at him.

"Justus," Olin was saying dolefully, "has been a good friend to us."

"And to me," Adam acknowledged.

He thought with sharp guilt how wretchedly he had used that friendship. His robbery of Buck, the suspicion that had prompted it, seemed ever more shameful. It had been easy to postpone an accounting with himself while the Sherwoods still were far away, but they were in New Haven now. The knowledge of their nearness was like a sponge that, passing over idle scribblings on a slate, left only the bare necessity to go to Felicity. It dismayed him to find how completely that need swayed him.

"Justus," he told Olin, "has more cause to be angry with me than with you. Seek him out at New Haven and ask why he avoids you."

Olin yanked a weed loose and stripped leaves from its stem with an irresolute scowl.

"No," he said defiantly, "let him come to us. I have done nothing I am ashamed of and there's enough to occupy us here, if we are to make a crop 'fore frost."

At supper, Adam felt Delight was watching him but he tried in vain to trap her eyes.

Days passed, while the neglected farm was redisciplined. Sunderland, riding south with a detail to bring powder and ball from the Bennington store, nooned with the Roydens. He reported that Allen's force was disbanding in the absence of any sign of reprisal. A dozen men were to garrison the almost completed blockhouse against further aggression by Reid which, Sunderland believed, would not come.

"No one," he drawled, "will pour money down a rathole forever, special a Scot. Sherwood was to the Falls yest'dy. Seemed reconciled, or forbearin'. Ain't sure which. Anyway, he's back on his pitch."

"Ain't been anigh us," Mindwell sniffed.

Adam, that evening when supper was over, went restlessly about the dooryard, heedless under irresolution's nagging of his weary body's protests. Day by day, he had suffered the knowledge of Felicity's nearness, had resolved to seek her on the morrow and then had embraced a new farm chore as excuse for delay.

He was reluctant to face the quarrel Sherwood's continued disregard of the Roydens made ever more probable. Knowledge that his friend's indignation was just made the prospect of meeting him no easier. It would not be a happy task, Adam thought sourly as he wandered aimlessly about, to defend himself against the anger of one whom he had suspected of treachery and whose messenger he had hunted down and robbed. Yet, until he had made his difficult peace with Justus, he could not bring about an accounting with Felicity. She was always, he reflected unhappily, a faithful echo of her brother.

Sherwood had visited Otter Falls. He had talked without animus to the men who had cast down his hopeful plans. Yet he still kept away from the Roydens'. His rancor against Adam must be deep indeed.

Delight, at the kitchen doorstep called, "Oh, are you there?" hesitated and then, uninvited, came out, closing the door behind her.

Adam was puzzled, yet relieved. The child had a soothing quality that eased crises, whether she was helping her mother with a balky kitchen fire, aiding in the search for an axe that the overheated Olin insisted had been stolen, or outracing on flashing bare feet a runaway calf and cajoling it into return. She startled rather than comforted Adam now, for she asked:

"When are you going over to the Sherwoods?"

For an instant he could only stare down at the slender figure and the dim, uplifted face.

"Are you a witch?" he inquired finally. "I was asking myself that very thing."

"I thought you were." She paused and then went on, "You should go, Adam. Truly you should."

He sought to contrive some jest that would break her precocious gravity but, as though she had heard the question he had not spoken, Delight asked, "What you have done to help us has set Mr. Sherwood against you, hasn't it? It isn't right that you should suffer for our sakes. I've almost been minded to seek out Mr. Sherwood and tell him so. Please go, Adam. It's unfair that we should be secure and you unhappy."

"What makes you think I am?" he evaded and she answered quietly:

"Because you love Felicity."

Delight conquered hesitation. Her clear young voice went on, "I've known it since—for a long while. I've told no one else. I never, never would. How can you and she help but be unhappy while Mr. Sherwood is angry?

"I would be unhappy," Delight said gravely, "if Olin were

angry with the man who wooed me. Will you ride to New Haven tomorrow, Adam?"

He was silent a moment, wishing the darkness would let him clearly see her face, thrusting back the desire to confide in her, the one person in the world, the tale of Felicity's perfidy.

"Yes," he told her. "You're quite right. I'll go in the morning."

"I'm glad," said Delight, turned and was gone.

Memories that were strung like beads on the dim, twisted strand of the road to New Haven gave Adam the eerie feeling that he journeyed back through time. Here, Sherwood had stopped to breathe the horses on that morning in spring when they all had ridden together to the new house. Yonder still lay the windfall he and Olin had moved from the way. On this very slope Felicity had raised her voyageur song.

The venture over which he had hesitated so long had been disconcertingly easy to launch. He had had no opportunity, after he had told Olin of his intention, to supply his own carefully ordered excuses.

"Someone ought to see him and smooth him down," Olin had agreed heartily. "Don't like a neighbor to bear a grudge. Take the horse and welcome. I'll go instead, if you want," he offered, but looked relieved when the other shook his head.

It was odd, Adam thought now, that he, against whom Sherwood had the greater cause for grievance, should be the peace emissary. It was strange that Olin had made no effort himself to seek out Felicity. It was not Adam's own stoutheartedness that had set him on his errand. That had been Delight's doing. There was a clear quality in Delight. The mission she had urged proved that she had rid herself of her childish infatuation, if Felicity had been right and it, indeed, ever had existed. Adam was glad that one of his swarming problems had settled itself.

He rode at last into the Sherwood clearing. It lay so empty that he thought with craven relief its owner must be absent, and only belatedly saw smoke rise from the dwelling's chimney.

Midway between the forest's edge and the house, Adam remembered frontier custom, and halted. Weeds grew tall about the flat stump where they all had dined together. He felt a pang of homesickness for that simple, easy time. He cleared his throat and called. Echoes ran away with his hail and he had begun to believe the house was unoccupied when Felicity stepped from its door.

His heart paused and then raced. The sleeves of the girl's green dress were rolled back and she dried her hands on a cloth as she looked toward him. After an instant, she raised her half-bare arm and cried his name.

He dismounted clumsily under her regard. The silence endured.

"Felicity?" he said and, seeing her hesitate, as though recalling his guilt, or her own, felt heaviness within him. The girl flung down the cloth at last and held her hands toward him in a gesture almost defiant. He bent and touched them with his lips.

"I thought," said Felicity softly, "that you were never coming."

Adam searched her face so intently that her mouth at last was troubled with an unwilling smile and then she suddenly was shaken by laughter.

"Adam," she faltered, "you look like a little boy who expects a whipping. And I should be the last to say that you do not deserve it."

"I have come," he said awkwardly, "to try to make amends to Justus."

"Oh, Adam," she reproached, "will you never come for my sake? Justus has gone to Chimney Point to see whether the rest of our chattels have come. We are living like savages now. Can you endure finding no one at home but me? Or, failing to see Justus, will you desert me again?"

A force greater than he was drawing her toward him, was abolishing her faint resistance and his own.

"I am less angry with you than I should be," she said in a breathless voice. "Oh, Adam!"

No memory could cherish entire, no expectation could wholly re-create, the warmth and the beauty and the rapture of her body. He released her at last, fearing whither the bright compulsion might lead him.

"Adam," Felicity said faintly again. "My wild, foolish dear."

The blanched and lovely face, the wide eyes at once urged and stayed him. The girl freed one hand and rubbed her forehead with a dazed gesture.

256

"It must," she whispered in sad uncertainty, "mean less to you than to me."

"That is not true," he told her hoarsely. "You know that."

She shook her head. Her voice was clearer.

"Am I brazen, am I light," she asked with faint bitterness, "dragging you ever lower?"

"You are—" he began.

"I know what you will say, I know it by heart, but how can I believe it, Adam?"

"How can you ask, when—"

"When despite my pleas, in the face of my urging, you go rashly on, lowering yourself still further?"

"Oh!" he said and then asked gravely, "Felicity, can we talk together? Can we strive to understand each other?"

Her smile was barren.

"Adam, have we not tried? We talk—I hope and you pull the hope down."

"I try to understand you," he told her with a faint edge to his words. "Will you not—?"

Again, she broke in upon him.

"Have you thought of what is left to you now of all that was yours when first I knew you? And of what you have further endangered since we met in Bennington? Are you dedicated to your own ruin, for no better reason than to defy those who love you?"

"Do you think that has been my intention?" he asked her. "Do you truly believe that?"

His gravity disturbed her. When she spoke again, reproach had left her voice. Only sadness remained.

"Tell me if it is not true that you have dissembled, assaulted, stolen since last I saw you; yes, and rioted, too? Justus has learned that you were in the mob at Otter Falls."

Felicity gave a little despairing shrug.

"That is a strange way to show your love for me, Adam."

Her eyes were steady and accusing. They roused in him anger he tried to curb.

"Do you think it is perversity that has driven me to all these sins, Felicity?"

She shook her head.

257

"I sometimes wonder—and can you blame me, Adam?—how high a value you place on me."

The prim reproach stung him.

"Do the men you know best appraise you in pounds, shillings, and pence?"

"Meaning," she asked after a brief silence, "that I am scheming and prudential? Why don't you say so?"

"You already have deplored my lost fortune."

"And how can I help wishing that you still had what you have thrown away for no better reason than to deride me?"

"That is your belief?"

Her small hands were clenched. Under his stare, her mouth trembled and her eyes filled with tears.

"Why," she whispered, "do you make me say such things? Why must we hurt each other?"

For an instant, he resisted the soft compulsion of her hands. Her body's pressure burned away reluctance and he held her as though he might forget in passion the thwarting and the discord.

Felicity freed herself at length and, observing his dazed desiring face, gave a confident little laugh.

"Bless us! Must all men deem a maid is fashioned of hickory wythes?"

She ran smoothing palms down over her dress. Adam asked, "Do all men?" and when she only stared, repeated, "Do they?"

She winced, rallied, and wrinkled her nose at him with forced gaiety.

"I am not wed to you, sir, or even betrothed—yet, that you may demand an accounting of me."

Her eyes were uneasy. Under their regard, Adam felt the bursting release of his latest grievance upon the jealousy that, seeping from many sources, long had been dammed within him.

"Nor do you truly love me," he told her. "Isn't that what you have been trying to say?"

"Oh, Adam," the girl exclaimed in elaborate, half-amused reproach, "you can ask that, after—"

She moved her hands over her rumpled gown.

"You still will not answer me. I told you in Bennington that I would not go cringing to Tryon for the sake of my father's estate."

"Yes, and did I not beg you then to talk to Justus?"

He felt his body gather itself as though it launched an actual blow.

"Why should I have talked to Justus when you straightway broke your word to me and told him all I had confided to you?"

He saw her flinch and struck again.

"Quebec and its fine, honorable folk have changed you, Felicity."

Her face was dangerously bright.

"It is not I who have changed. This wilderness and its fine and honorable bandits have debased you. Justus only today said—"

"I don't care what Justus said. I have used him ill and I came here to confess it and ask his pardon, yet I do esteem the bandits at whom you sneer more than the men who now enrapture you and Justus, place-holders like Tryon and Carleton or popinjays in His Majesty's service like, at a venture"—he threw the name at her—"Leftenant George Wadman."

Felicity's face turned white, then scarlet.

"Who if he were here," she bit off the words, "would demand satisfaction for that slur."

"Would he?" Adam asked with a short laugh. "Again?"

Later, he knew, would come pain, regret, demeaning self-reproach. He plied his voice like a lash.

"I have heard much of your champion, Georgie-porgie, and his duels on your behalf."

"To your other accomplishments," she asked, her eyes coldly bright, "you have added playing spy?"

"There was no need to spy, I assure you. I came uplake with Captain Delaplace and his lady."

He saw the girl start and went on without compunction.

"A talkative couple, the Delaplaces, and indiscreet as well. I can't congratulate you on your friends."

"I prefer them vastly to outlaws who thrust themselves upon me. I should be happier never to have known you."

"That can be remedied," Adam said heavily. "It was a mistake to come. I shall not repeat it."

It was strange, he thought as he rode slowly back toward Panton, that the world could be overturned and yet appear unchanged. The way led up and down, unaltered, beneath the high, dark roof of leaves. Adam's own aspect, he supposed, bore as little trace of catastrophe.

Anger, still smoldering, kept tardily offering him blighting retorts that, in the flood of his resentment, he had not had the wit to utter. His plight had its scalding humor. He had made a pilgrimage to appease Justus Sherwood. He had succeeded only in snapping the frayed ties that had bound him to Felicity. It had been, at least, a thorough accomplishment. Adam's laugh was like a bark. He dug into his pocket, drew out the long-borne ring in its cubical box, and flung it far into the forest.

Regret, he thought, letting his horse take its own pace, would come, in time, to bedevil him. His mind held nothing softer now than impenitent satisfaction. The break must have come, soon or late. Felicity and her brother followed one orbit; Adam another. He was committed to The Grants' cause and its uplifting, still half-unuttered promise. The Sherwoods' was an older, more rigid loyalty, that, in Felicity at least, justified betrayal of a lover.

It was inevitable that intimacy should strain and snap, whatever the girl's frailties or virtues. It was well that the fracture had been so quick and whole, though it left him to look on emptiness.

For almost two years, Adam reflected, his life had been tinctured and swayed by Felicity Sherwood. Already, he was savoring the foretaste of the aimlessness that was certain now to afflict him. The map of his future, blurred and vague though it had been, was destroyed. He had neither the impulse nor the resource to plan another.

His immediate welfare was secure. The yield from his father's Canadian holdings would maintain him for a space, but how or where, he could not tell. Certainly, he told himself viciously, he would see to it that his and the Sherwoods' paths crossed no more. His horse snorted. Adam saw Justus riding toward him.

For an instant, Sherwood looked as startled as he. He was thinner, more worn. The two drew rein with their mounts' noses almost touching and the older man said with a half smile:

"Well, Adam!"

"Well, Justus!"

"I have been to the Roydens in the hope of finding you."

"And I to New Haven for the same reason."

Adam's mouth was dry. Speech lagged and, as though he

dreaded what silence might bring forth, Sherwood asked, "You found Felicity there?"

"Yes." Lest the other press him further, Adam stumbled on in haste. "I went to admit to you my—my misbehavior and to ask your pardon. I would blame you not at all," he added, "if you withheld it. I have used you very badly, Justus."

Sherwood looked at him with sad amusement, more difficult to bear than anger, and loosened his feet from the stirrups to let his legs hang free.

"What did you do with the letter?" he asked at length.

"Bore it"—Adam's face grew hot—"to Reid's agent at Otter Falls, who was about to evict the Roydens and made me prisoner when I protested."

"Oh, God!" Sherwood said in quiet despair. "I was assured that Reid's people were peaceful."

"They were not."

"Nor were Allen's men. Violence piles on violence, Adam, and I am heartsick."

He shrugged and gave a small laugh.

"Even you suspected me. That might gall me more if I had not become weathered to doubt and deception this summer. If I had as many eyes as—Argus, was it not?—I should still be hood-winked and groping, thanks to the vindictive folk in this unhappy country."

"I am truly ashamed that I misjudged you," Adam offered clumsily.

"You were not alone. Because I fear what otherwise will come, I have worked all summer for a peace through compromise. Compromise imposes giving as well as taking, wherefore men like Tryon resist it and men like Ethan Allen will have none of it. He believes peace may be obtained by taking all, yielding nothing."

"As does Colonel Reid."

Sherwood nodded.

"In large part," he agreed. "He is grasping and ruthless but under the law the land belongs to him."

"York law; bad law."

The other's mildness cheapened Adam's vehemence.

"Even bad law," said Sherwood, "is better than none. Obedience to those set in authority over us is only a lesser duty than fealty to God."

"You yourself decry Tryon's obstinacy. I think law should come from the will of all who must endure it, not from authority."

Again, the mournful friendliness in Sherwood's eyes abashed him.

"The Boston disease, Adam. Spread by Adams and Otis and the other rabble rousers. Men strive through the centuries to build. Then madness seizes them and they rage to pull the building down."

"That something better may rise in its place."

"Is there truly such a hope? We have grown apart, my friend. 'Something better,' framed by the hands of Ethan Allen and his accomplices, who have gobbled up Hampshire titles and riot lest they be made worthless?"

"I find," said Adam stiffly, "that I condone even rioting when it protects people like the Roydens; when it leads men toward freedom."

Sherwood gently beat a fist upon his other palm.

"So I believed, until I saw where violence was leading. You stand where I stood, Adam, two years past. I pray you may learn more quickly than I that what you uphold imperils all Americans have won in a hundred years."

His face did not change when the other shook his head.

"Well," Sherwood went on with resolute cheer. "I feared I should preach to small avail. I've been scarcely more successful in my efforts toward peace, so we've returned to our pitch, Felicity and I. At least, if the worst befall, we are close to loyal Canada. Visit us often. Let us strive to convert you."

Adam replied with difficulty: "Felicity and I have quarreled, Justus," and then wondered whether it were relief that for an instant changed the other's face.

"Oh!" Sherwood said blankly, and after silence, "I am sorry, though not wholly surprised. She is young and hot-tempered, Adam. Let us keep from quarreling, you and I, for as long as we may."

He thrust his feet back into the stirrups and gathered up the rein. As his horse went by, Sherwood leaned from the saddle and laid his hand on Adam's shoulder. The hard, brief pressure was like a wordless farewell.

Chapter XXVIII

THERE was dreary comfort in the knowledge that he had nothing left to lose. Adam could see, looking back, how blindly yet certainly he had moved toward this end. Only a dolt and an ass could have remained unaware of the calamity until it had fallen upon him.

He had lost Felicity and, he was increasingly sure, the old, easy friendship with her brother. Minor misfortunes had stood like signposts on the road he had traveled. Adam had ignored them all, though he could see them with glaring clarity now.

Gossip, like a pickpocket, had robbed him a bit at a time of his faith in Felicity. The suspicions of angry men had led him to distrust Justus. His perverse adherence to The Grants' cause had deprived him of his place in an established society and of the bulk of his inheritance. Why had he been unable to recognize till now how fatefully those adversities had led to the crowning, final loss.

Blunderers ascribed the evils that befell them to fate, yet it truly seemed that this land, where other men were laying hold upon a braver, better life had stripped him of purpose and ambition and had left him, directionless, in its cool, green limbo. Ahead of him, he could see no landmarks, no further trace of road. It was a desolate feeling. He despised himself for his aching throat, his smarting eyes.

Olin came and stood in silence by the stable door while his friend unsaddled. Adam offered at last with false jauntiness, "My mission was not a complete success."

Olin watched his toe scuff the litter and asked quietly, "Quarrel?"

"With Felicity."

"Oh!"

"Violently and finally."

"Certain?"

"I am. She seemed to be."

"A headstrong wench," said Olin, taking no visible satisfaction in his rival's discomfort, "who'll fight, these days, with anyone. Too pretty for her own good; that's her trouble."

"I thought—" Adam groped, watching the severe face.

"Ehyah," Olin nodded. "So did I; so I still do. Worked on me a plenty at Bennington, hoping to pull wool over my eyes and tie a knot in my tail. Learn her manners in my own good time. Don't figger in letting her make a fool out of me and neither should you, Adam."

"It's a little late to prevent that."

Neither of them ever had spoken so openly of the girl. As though tardily regretting his candor, Olin cleared his throat and said, "Someone's called to visit with you."

"Justus. I met him on the road."

"Not him. Came to make his peace with us, and I guess he did. Ethan Allen. He's up to the house now."

In the Roydens' rarely opened front chamber, Allen heaved himself out of his chair with a squeak of strained woodwork that made Mindwell wince.

"Gods of the mountains, Adam! I'd begun to fear you had vanished again as is your peculiar wont. Come outside, boy."

"Mine, Madam," he turned and informed Mindwell sonorously, "is a spacious and natural spirit, most contentedly at home amid the dimensions of the wilderness. Therefore, with your permission—"

He tramped from the room, clapping on his gilt-bound hat which now was further embellished by a green cockade wrought from the cloth Adam had seen Warner hacking into strips before the Otter Falls' mill. That building, Allen announced with prodigious satisfaction, had been remade into a blockhouse, had been garrisoned, and the Colonel Commandant himself was riding south next day. He paused and then proclaimed:

"It is my particular wish that you ride with me, Adam. Together we can accomplish mighty works for the confusion of the heathen and the utter blasting of our enemies, God consign them all to torment eternal."

264

"How?" Adam faltered, dazed by the vehement rush of speech, "Where?"

They were striding back and forth across the dooryard to the muted jangle of the great brass spurs. Allen sank his voice into a soft rumble.

The season, he confided, was too far advanced to expect further aggression by the hell-spawned forces of York, wherefore he looked forward to sheathing his sword and turning with true philosopher's zeal to the pen.

There was a monstrous amount of literature, the hard-reined voice explained, that must be accomplished. Allen purposed to compose for The Connecticut Courant further disquisitions to blast the implausibly begotten Tryon and to render the spines of sundry Grants malingerers, falterers, and trimmers stiffer than a slipshod deity originally had designed them. In these projects he needed Adam's help.

"Help?" the other echoed, unable to picture this violent behemoth in need of aid. Allen's squirm was like a miniature earthquake. His sanguine face grew redder still.

"Now I yield, sir, to no man in the dextrous accomplishments of martial or statesmanlike pursuits but, Jesus, Mary, and Stepfather Joseph, Adam! I still so grievously lack ease with quill, ink, and paper that I despair at times of ever gaining it."

There was urgency in the voice, appeal in the brilliant blue eyes.

"No plans that you may cherish, I swear, will as greatly benefit mankind as the post I now offer you, sir; namely and to wit, that of my secretary or, if a soldierly title suit you better, of my aide-de-camp, performing for me those services that made my late letter to Tryon so veritable a thunderbolt."

He paused, mistook Adam's amazement for refusal, and plunged on:

It was his intention, Ethan confided, to return to Salisbury, Connecticut, spending the winter there in the bosom of his family. Beside defamation of the deserving that cried for publication, Allen must undertake the compilation of advertisements for the land he and his relatives were in the process of purchasing on the Onion River.

"I pledge myself, sir, that you will live well and drink better, lacking nothing the deservedly renowned Allen hospitality can supply. Furthermore, no occupation you can contemplate to while away winter's rigor, whatever its nature, can be of so vast a benefit to your country."

Adam to his own surprise, found himself no longer fumbling for tactful refusal. The proposal had merits. He had been daunted by the emptiness that lay before him, and here was a remedy. Association with Ethan Allen would be counter-irritant to pain and loneliness. Pride that the swashbuckling chieftain should beseech him for aid, curiosity over the workings of the Allen household pushed him toward assent. His companion misread his hesitation.

"As for material compensation, Adam," his bluster ebbed and he stumbled on, ill at ease, "I can offer you no immediately negotiable honorarium, for every pistole I have been able to squeeze from friend or foe has been invested in that veritable Eden, that choicest jewel in The Grants' diadem now in the custody of the Onion River Land Company where—and may future generations sneer at the name of Ethan Allen, otherwise—our fairest city will one day rear stately domes and proud battlements.

"However, if two hundred acres in an earthly paradise, immediately adjoining those I have chosen for my own farm, be an inducement—"

The earnest appeal on the usually domineering face beneath the bizarre hat was at once comic and flattering. Adam rejected the memory of Sherwood's slurring comment on Ethan Allen as a self-seeking land gambler.

"I have no conflicting plans," he said. "I will serve you most willingly."

"Now damn," Allen cried, "till the twitching tail-end of eternity this talk of 'service,' Adam-boy. We shall fight shoulder to shoulder against the hosts of Belial, I supplying powder and ball, you properly charging the piece. Tomorrow we move against the Mammon of Unrighteousness."

The great bedizened figure rode away at last, after elaborate farewells to Mindwell and Delight. It seemed as though a portion of the clearing's brilliance departed with him.

Mindwell, later, stayed Adam as he passed through the kitchen. He could tell, despite her impassivity, that she disapproved of his

266

decision, though her speech circled widely about it. She had been relieved, Mindwell said, standing solidly with hands on hips, by Sherwood's call. She didn't like to be at odds with any neighbor, specially Justus. He and she had had a real good talk and she guessed she had misjudged him. He seemed to have done what he could, according to his lights, though it had been a sight less than Ethan Allen.

"Justus 'n' Felicity," the woman went on while Adam felt the calm eyes probing him, "figger on goin' back to Quebec 'fore the lake ices over."

"More schooling for his sister?" Adam asked with attempted indifference.

Mindwell shook her head. Felicity, Sherwood had said, was finished with school. Justus couldn't winter in New Haven; he hadn't made a crop.

"Wants Delight should go to school again, though, 'n' I want she should, too. Delight won't."

"Eh?" Adam was jolted out of his own dark thoughts by the grotesque picture of a pliant spirit again turned mutinous. Mindwell nodded.

"Ehyah. Contrary age, I wouldn't wonder. Mad for more learnin' last year. Now she holds she's got all she'll ever need."

"She should go," Adam said and wondered at his emphasis. Mindwell bobbed her head again.

"What I hold. Won't, though. Real sot."

"I'll talk to Delight," he promised incautiously and Mindwell looked relieved.

"Wish ye would; mebby ye can sway her."

Uncomfortable silence fell while the woman eyed him keenly and Adam felt that she had come to the brink of her chief purpose.

"Why ye leavin', Adam?"

"It seems best," he muttered, uncomfortable under the keen eyes' dissection. "I can't live off you forever."

"Ain't, yit," Mindwell told him. "Glad if ye did. Owe ye a plenty."

He felt the penetration of her silent look.

"Trouble?" Mindwell asked at length.

267

"Of a sort."

"What I figgered. Wal, mebby a change'll be good for ye. Miss ye, though."

She said no more, yet he had the feeling of knowledge shared and sympathy offered.

"I'll go talk to Delight," Adam told her.

He found her on her hands and knees among the garden sauce, thinning a row of young turnips.

"What's all this," he asked, "about your refusing more schooling?" and, seeing her face turn scarlet, regretted his abruptness.

Delight rose and brushed at her dress with intense care. She answered in a low voice, "I'd rather bide here."

She seemed so obdurate, yet appealingly meek, standing there with small, grubby hands clasping and unclasping, that Adam relaxed his purpose.

"Well," he told her with forced lightness, "I have executed your order, Delight. I have been to the Sherwoods as you bade."

He feared, meeting her gray eyes, that she was about to question him and went on hurriedly with false cheer.

"Justus and I met on the road. We're still friends."

"I'm glad."

Delight bent, carefully retrieved an uprooted turnip, and placed it in the basket with its wilting fellows.

"Since," Adam pursued with false gaiety, "I have performed your bidding, won't it be fair if you heed mine?"

The girl pushed pale hair back from her forehead.

"Is it about school?"

"It is. You used to like it. And your mother wants you to go."

"I can be of help to her here."

"You will be of more comfort to her, if you go to Quebec with the Sherwoods. Why won't you, child?"

Delight answered quietly, "I have all the schooling I'll need."

"That's the silliest thing I ever heard you say," he told her sharply. "Neither you, nor I, nor anyone can boast he has learned all that is needful. This frontier won't last forever, or you live on it all your life."

"Is it your wish that I go?" she asked him with a simple directness that, for some obscure cause, he found irritating.

"What I wish or don't wish has nothing to do with it. You, yourself, should want it. Child, you were made for something better than to stand, barefooted, in a turnip patch."

Delight looked down at her dusty toes and replied in a voice so low he could scarcely hear it, "I said I'd do whatever you asked of me."

Her submissiveness troubled him.

"I'm not your guardian; I don't command you, but while I am away this winter, it will be pleasanter to think of you at school than prisoned here by the snows."

She looked up.

"Will you be gone all winter long, Adam?"

"That is Colonel Allen's proposal."

Delight drew a long breath.

"Then I'll go, since you desire it."

"And since you truly desire it, too," he insisted.

"And since I do, too," she agreed and they both laughed as though a crisis had been weathered.

In midmorning of the next day, Allen, Baker, and their escort of a half dozen horsemen who wore green cockades arrived with a spare mount. Adam rode south with them.

They traveled at ease and in an almost perceptible glow of triumph. The escort, lolling in their saddles, chanted persistently an interminable ballad by Thomas Rowley of Danby, poet to The Green Mountain Boys. They roared one verse with the utmost vigor:

> "*We value not New York with all their powers.*
> *For here we'll stay and work; the land is ours,*
> *And as for great Duane, with all his wicked train,*
> *They may eject again; we'll not resign.*"

Chapter XXIX

IT SEEMED to Adam that barely a week had passed since autumn had laid on the Salisbury hills its first, hesitant color, yet now the slopes that lately had flamed were misted gray-blue by the hardwoods' bare branches. Mornings were fronted and noons steel-bright and over the stubbled fields of the Allen farm wind set gusts of leaves to leaping and fluttering like feeble, frightened birds.

This was early winter in the Year of Our Lord 1773 and Adam had been—he paused to estimate and disbelieve—one of a clamorous household for almost four months. Time in the Allen home traveled swiftly, as though Ethan's energy hurried it along.

His was a large house, ambitiously built, yet it wore a haggard look as though it were aging before its time. Adam fancied he found a like expression on the face of Mary, cousin to Remember Baker and wife to Ethan Allen, a drab and angular woman whose whine darkened the brightest tidings. She employed it with most relish in relating the symptoms of obscure afflictions to which she was hostess, as though there were not enough actual forever about her.

Mary Allen's four pugnacious daughters and their wan eight-year-old brother, Joseph, a spindling, wet-nosed child who seemed to despair of ever justifying his father's vast pride in him, filled the house from sleep to sleep with shrieks of glee or woe and ear-piercing trial by battle. The thunderclap of Ethan's voice never silenced them more than briefly.

The youngsters, whom their mother seemed to regard as the result of sharp dealing by nature and her husband, were only a fragment of the trials she recited on slight provocation in her de-

270

ploring voice. The house harbored a perpetual floating population, now larger, now smaller, but never entirely absent.

Baker and Sunderland were repeated visitors and Ethan's lathy, salty cousin, Ebenezer Allen, dry Sam Herrick, and the furious, red-headed Robert Cochran. Seth Warner appeared more seldom. All of them brought tidings from The Grants and rode back with their Colonel Commandant's intemperate orders.

John Brown, a ruddy, solid man, came down from Pittsfield to hold in Allen's office talks less uproarious than most such conferences. Thomas Chittenden, a tall, one-eyed Salisbury farmer whose face was enclosed in parentheses by rudimentary side-whiskers, called, merely to sit and listen in silence, and, day after day, some or occasionally all five of Ethan's brothers were sheltered by him.

None of them regarded their more famous kinsman with any trace of reverence. Each of them—the plump, bland youngest, Ira; Levi, fat and jovial; Heman, a smaller, more finely drawn version of Ethan; and the comparatively mild Heber and Zimri—was thirsty for punch or dispute and cherished in common with their host the belief that victory in debate was won by the loudest and most abusive voice.

This was their method of dispute and it was carried to extremes without any subsequent rancor as Adam learned when, at the end of a brotherly discussion, Levi appeared for supper, cheerful and unresentful, with a slice of beef bound over one eye.

"Ira," Allen explained, chuckling with delight, "threw a stool at him. Fiends of hell, all my five brothers, and my two sisters are like unto them. God's truth, Adam!" he roared, enraptured by the thought, "My mother and Mary Magdalen were the only women ever delivered of seven devils."

Adam continually marveled how his host could contribute so large a quota to the din and disorder and still possess the power to rise beyond it. Allen's energy was elemental and inexhaustible as a river's.

Dictation was not an enterprise the man could accomplish sedentarily. While Adam strove to keep pace on paper with the explosive speech, Allen charged about the room and bawled denunciation. On their first day of association, the secretary had learned to edit his principal's utterances without intrusion upon their salvos.

"The vicious, felonious, abandoned, indecent, and barbarous proposals of the so-called gentry of York," Allen had roared, "are paramount to slavery for freemen."

"Tantamount?" the other had suggested.

"Now, by the flaming hubs of hell," Ethan had bellowed, "that is your responsibility, Adam. Paramount, tantamount, catamount —set it down as it should be and cease this quibbling."

Sometimes Adam had the queer feeling that in these deranged surroundings he no longer was himself but a stranger who had never known the ordered life of England or the less studied luxury of Albany. The illusion made Felicity seem a figure in a dim, unhappy story.

There were instants when the memory of her ardent body, the scent of her hair, the pressure of her hands, dizzied and then angered him, but fresh uproar blasted memory and thrust the girl back into that remoteness where Mindwell and Olin and Sherwood and, to a lesser degree, Delight now dwelt. In his rare idle moments Adam wondered about the child and whether she was reconciled to the schooling he had forced upon her.

Sunderland came for still another conference with Ethan and brought to Adam a letter, soiled and creased by many hands. It was from James Duane, the recipient saw with sudden collapse of his hopeful excitement, and had been sent months earlier to the care of Morrison in Montreal, whence by devious ways it had passed into Sunderland's possession at Skenesborough. Adam went to his own room to read it.

The letter was as firm as its author's penmanship. Duane was writing at a venture because he felt the need was great. Adam had promised to return to Albany from Montreal but he had not appeared. If he were not dead or immersed in further Grants insurgency—Duane seemed to consider the former the happier fate— he might not be too lost to all responsibility to heed the counsel of his father's friend.

The writer urged Adam to come immediately and inconspicuously to Duane's home in New York. Genuine penitence and the exercise of influence might still save much from the wreckage.

"It is my duty," the letter ended, "to warn you that further association with a rebellion that is a stench to the nostrils of the respectable will bring down upon you and your accomplices condign punishment that your most earnest well-wisher will be powerless to avert or mitigate."

The smug piety of the reproof galled Adam. He found satisfaction in writing a brief response for Sunderland to bear on the first stage of its journey:

He had been engaged for the winter in a position of trust by Colonel Ethan Allen—Adam chuckled, picturing Duane's choler as he read this—but he might be able to do himself the honor of visiting his counselor in the spring.

Suddenly, it was veritable winter with whirling snow and swelling drifts. Adam sat on a day of storm with Allen's current guests in Allen's office. The punch bowl had its accustomed place upon the table and dispute over the management of The Onion River Company was rising as the liquor-level fell. The vessel was not passed from hand to hand, frontier fashion, but at intervals Ethan rose, collected the pottery mugs, and charged them afresh, continuing meanwhile his acrimonious argument with his brother, Ira.

Remember Baker, lately returned from a journey through Connecticut and Rhode Island in the company's interest, canted his head, lifted it, and drawled, "Might stop yellin' for a spell; ye got more comp'ny."

He padded to a window. Adam, peering over his shoulder saw snow-dimmed figures alighting stiffly from their horses.

In the hall Allen trumpeted for a man to take the visitors' mounts, for Mary to replenish the punch bowl, then flung open the front door with a bellow of welcome. A white gust blew in with the travelers.

Snow flew from Ebenezer Allen's shoulders as Ethan caught and shook them. He turned to wring the hand of John Brown whose ruddy face had been lashed to brilliance by the storm.

They sat together in a larger semicircle before the fire and Brown withdrew his nose from the steaming mug with a grunt of satisfaction.

"No day for man or beast to be abroad," he admitted with a smile. "I was minded to turn back to Pittsfield, despite the news I carried, when Captain Allen," he nodded at Ebenezer who looked from his emptied mug hopefully toward Ethan, "overtook me."

He paused. Joviality faded from his face.

"Gentlemen, there is further trouble in Boston town. The harbor is full of tea and none remains on the damned British tea ships."

He told his tale in quick bursts while his eyes grew hard.

"Wal," Baker offered when he had ended, "good riddance, say I. Tea's a puny drink."

The tip of Ebenezer's long nose twitched.

"All that tea 'n' the fort to boot. George ain't real lucky."

"Eh?" Ethan asked staring. "Fort?"

Ebenezer's narrow face spread in a grin of gratification.

"Mean ye ain't heered? Crown Point—kerblam! Barracks ketched fire 'n' up she went. Women was soap-bilin', folks say."

"Gods of the mountains!" The giant's mouth was creased by scorn. "A fine military establishment the king maintains! Well, as Remember has so cogently said, good riddance."

He drained his mug. Ira's luminous eyes were thoughtful. His lips were a thin line between plump cheeks.

" 'Fore you cry hosannah," he told his brother, "why'n't you think a mite? 'Good riddance,' eh? Wal, it's done us no real good. Fort was protection; a comfort like."

"Protection!" Ethan snorted, finding affront in the word. "To whom? The Canadians?"

"Onion River Company," Ira retorted.

"There's still Ti," Ethan said, gathering up the emptied mugs.

"Too far uplake," his brother answered promptly. "Folks'll know that."

Small wrinkles of distaste ran to Brown's mouth corners from the flanges of his nose. Adam liked the look and the dryness of his voice.

"Have you gentlemen thought that this—this tea party in Boston brings us one full step nearer war?"

Ethan at the punch bowl lifted his head. His brother retorted, "Bay Province, mebby; not The Grants."

The smugness brought more color to Brown's face and an edge to his voice.

"Not The Grants, eh? Then you'll have to dry up Champlain.

How were the old wars waged? Up and down the lake. If a new one comes, you'll have an army on your shore, to fight or to welcome."

The contempt in the last word turned Ethan from his replenishing task. He blared, "My battalion will tend to that. With five hundred men I can be in Quebec in a month."

Ira surged in his chair and spat like an angry cat.

"Gone completely mad at last? Plunge The Grants into war, you wild ass, and what happens to The Onion River Company and the folks we're trying to sell to? If the British come uplake from Canada, where'll our settlements be? Right under their bayonets. What ye got eyes for, Ethan? Just to see yourself a hero?"

"And what happens to The Grants," Brown asked, keeping his voice level, "if they turn against the provinces?"

Ira gave a violent, abolishing gesture. His mouth was tight with calculation.

"God damn all wars. We want no war. Let the provinces dress their own pork. We'll hold to peace."

The bang of Ethan's fist on the table made the laden punch bowl clatter.

"Now by the tailfeathers of the archangel Gabriel," he cried and his eyes were blue fires in a molten face, "we aren't swapping horses, Stub. We're talking about Liberty."

"I'm talking about property."

"Liberty and property, then," Ethan bawled. "There are worse watchwords, for if you maim the one, you hamstring the other. We've fought York for both. If you propose that I surrender either—"

"Oh, dear Lord!" his brother deplored. "Why do I waste breath on a bull-headed oaf? The Onion River land is in the path of war. Colonel Brown says so himself. So the best way, you hold, to prosper our purchases is to fight the British army. Any idea what the British army is, Ethan? You start to fight it and it'll go through The Grants like grass through a goose."

His brother ignored him, rose and assumed a pose.

"Colonel Brown, you may tell the worthies of Bay Province that the emulous spirits of my Green Mountain Boys ever are vigilant in Liberty's defense. They will uphold the cause of freemen as readily against Britain as against York and should the tide of battle," Ethan pursued, pointing a finger heavenward, "turn against us, we will retire into the desolate fastnesses of the Green Mountains and still wage war against all tyranny."

Ira muttered beneath his breath. Ethan, glowing, reseated himself and lifted his mug.

Grimed drifts were shrinking and where the late March sun dwelt longest, earth lay bare. On an afternoon so warm that he could enjoy the privacy of his own room, Adam made his decision.

When roads were passable once more, he was going home; home, with a prodigal's willingness to suffer reproaches and whatever punishment Duane's influence could not avert; home, to table and bed linen, to a seemly house with fair furnishings, to folk of courtesy and decorum. He was as hungry for these as for food daintily cooked and served.

He was not, he told himself firmly, running away from obligation or deserting his friends. He had engaged himself to Allen only until spring. He could serve that portion of The Grants' cause he still endorsed better in York than here. Certainly, he could advance it with no time spent in jointly extolling The Onion River Company.

Adam would not forget the Roydens when he had regained his fortune. He might send them, as earnest of his friendship, the rights to the Onion River land Ethan had promised him as fee. He could be of further material aid to Olin and Delight. As for the Sherwoods—

He had a pleasant vision of a stately dinner in the home to which he had been restored with honor. Distinguished men among his guests questioned him respectfully about The Grants. Women listened to his adventures with admiring eyes and with them sat Felicity, awed and beseeching his notice.

Now that his mind was firm, Adam could permit himself to be affronted by the noise that was welling up from Allen's office. Baker had arrived, blaspheming and mud-plastered to the thighs, just before Adam had come upstairs. Remember had been compelled to leave his spent horse at Sheffield and walk the rest of the mired way. He was closeted with Ethan now and a dispute, or liquor, or both, had set them to yelling at each other. He could separate Allen's clarion stridor from Baker's catamount snarl but the argument's cause was obscure. Adam picked up his pen, bent over the half-written page, but laid the quill down again and leaned back to weigh and fortify his resolution.

When he proclaimed it, Ethan would storm. Adam was proud that no person in the clamorous, perpetually disarranged household was aware how thoroughly distasteful the dwelling, its inmates, its very smell had become to him. In The Grants, he had seen the drama of revolt. He had lived now for a half year close to its seamed underside.

He had become unsure whether the once uplifting struggle for freedom was anything nobler than an exploitation by the greedy of the hopes of the Roydens, Strongs, and other of the stanch, aspiring folk. The leaders who bawled of York's tyranny seemed less intent on advancing liberty than in selling lots.

Adam had analyzed, sometimes with regret, sometimes with sour amusement, most of The Grants' notables who had come and gone all winter. Ethan Allen alone eluded classification. The personified hurricane who bombarded York with phrases he esteemed more for their resonance than their meaning, or trumpeted with equal disregard the virtues of Onion River lots, was charlatan, braggart, and something else that still was baffling. The evasive ingredient might be madness; it might just possibly be a touch of greatness.

Whatever Ethan's true stature, whatever the worth of his associates and their cause, Adam was turning back from the course that had led him toward personal ruin. He still believed in the freedom Ethan so vehemently extolled and his slick brother, Ira, regarded warily. James Duane might be a better servant of liberty—he would certainly be a more agreeable—than the woods-running, invective-shouting irresponsibles who came to this house.

The brawl endured in Allen's office. Juvenile competition began on the stair—shrill voices, squeals, a multiple bumping, and, hushing this smaller tumult, the deploring whine of Mary Allen. Adam, undistracted, stared at the further wall, framing the letter he would write to Duane, announcing his return.

He had chosen fresh paper and was reaching for his pen when

a door burst open below. Allen shouted Adam's name. It was impossible to pretend that he had not heard. He called upon his patience, responded, and went downstairs.

Ethan was pacing the office floor, watched with relish by Baker who sat straddling a chair with arms folded upon its back. Adam, at his employer's gesture, closed the door behind him and looked from the giant's suffused face to Remember's dry grinning. Allen was enormously overplaying a rôle or else it was no insignificance that disturbed him.

"The Bloody Law!" Ethan paused to roar at Baker. "So it is; so we shall call it henceforth. So 'twill reverberate through the smoky halls of hell and rouse Satan to envy that there be mortals so fiendish to compose it. Adam, by Jehovah, Jesus, and all the company of Heaven, we have driven Tryon to madness and the dog has bitten the Provincial Assembly, rendering it as rabid as he."

Experience had taught the colonel's aide that he would obtain enlightenment sooner by attentive waiting than by questions. The wrath of Ethan Allen, like a fire, flamed higher if stirred. He struggled now over an enormity that seemed too great to utter, striding the floor, pounding a palm with the other fist, while bits of volcanic blasphemy flew. At last in Adam's continued silence he regained partial composure and said in a trembling voice:

"Remember has brought tidings that lately came to Bennington. Billy the Butcher has opened his venomous jaws to consume us all."

"Wal," Baker demurred with a shade of jealousy, "wouldn't say that, exactly. Hungrier for you'n' me than for the rest of 'em."

He grinned up complacently at the stricken man whom rage again had partially strangled. While Allen wheezed and snorted, Remember turned to Adam.

"Tryon," he said, eager to spread his own news, "has set higher prices on our heads. Offerin' now hundred pound a piece for Ethan 'n' me."

He plumed himself and pursued:

"Costly, ain't we? Anyone bringin' in Seth or Rob Cochran or Sunderland or ye, Adam, gits only fifty pound. Mebby ye'll respect me more from now on. After seventy days, if we ain't s'rendered by then, we all are to be fair game, to be executed without trial."

"Who told you this?" Adam asked, dry-mouthed. Baker's grin spread.

"Seen the placard at Fay's. Real elegant."

"Nor is that all," Allen shouted, recovering breath, while Adam felt nightmare helplessness enfold him. "The blood-dabbled bastard of Beelzebub"—he paused to savor and approve the epithet—"and his accomplices in the Assembly have launched against us a law more iniquitous and despotic than I had deemed even York could contrive. We are denied all meetings or other gatherings, rioting is to be punished by death, and the murdering minions of York who maim or kill us in enforcing this damnible edict are to be deemed guiltless."

Adam laid a careful hand on the table top to steady himself.

Duane had foretold this in his letter and he in reply witlessly had jeered. Now, Tryon and his Assembly had struck. His own mind flew helter-skelter on a cold wind. His palms were clammy. There was sickness in his stomach.

Allen, staring at him, misinterpreted his look and was satisfied.

"I name it," Ethan proclaimed, "The Bloody Law, for it displays to an aghast humanity York's insatiable, avaricious, overbearing, inhuman, barbarous blood-guiltiness of disposition."

Again he seemed to file the utterance in his memory.

"By Moloch, Baal, Jehovah, and all other gods of blood, Adam we shall publish this iniquity to the world. We shall rub His Bloodthirstiness's nose in his own infamy, despite his bleatings for mercy."

"I had thought—" Adam began. His voice failed. Memory of his tardy intention was harder to bear than York's vengeance.

"You thought," Allen supplied acutely, "that spring was at the door and our labors were over. Adam, they have just begun. We'll answer His Excellency the Assassin, not cowering here, but from Bennington, boy."

"Figger on goin' there now," Baker offered, "ye'll foot it, crotch-deep in mud."

"The Philistines are upon us," Allen cried to the dazed Adam. "If you desert the conflict now, you'll regret it to your dying day

279

and"—he gulped over the confession—"I need you, boy, if I am properly to impale Tryon on my pen."

Adam's silence was not due to a weighing of choices; it was the hesitation of the suddenly blinded.

"If it be a question of remuneration—" Allen blurted. Adam shook his head.

"No, it is not that."

There was no other shelter discernible and he felt rage begin to melt his stupor and urge him to strike back at those who would destroy him. Still, he wavered and asked a tentative, secretly probing question, "What of the land company? You planned to write—"

"Now may the eternal flames of the nethermost pit consume its every acre," Ethan exploded, "ere I place property before liberty. We turn from trade, boy, to the nobler art of war."

"I will go with you to Bennington," Adam said slowly.

Allen struck his hands together with the sound of a pistol shot.

"Then by the great whore of Babylon and all her pimps of York, as soon as the roads have cleared we ride north to do battle against the hosts of iniquity."

Chapter XXX

"WE FIND in all York officials," Ethan Allen roared with a wide gesture that further uprooted his shirt, "insatiable, avaricious, overbearing, inhuman, barbarous blood-guiltiness of disposition and intention."

The denunciation had a familiar ring. Adam, while recording it, remembered where he first had heard it.

In the large room Allen maintained at Fay's Tavern as a combined office and lodging for his secretary, the Colonel Commandant was composing the defiant letter to Tryon which the convention of Grants leaders, meeting lately at Arlington, had empowered him to send. Amusement flickered in Adam's eyes on the rare instants when he was able to raise them from his task and .observe his principal.

Allen had shed his uniform coat and waistcoat as preparation for labor, and a few more waves of his arms were certain to bring his shirttails completely over his waistband. By the fury with which he tramped the floor, surging here, charging there, while he flung further invective, Adam was certain the Colonel in the heat of imagination pursued Tryon about the chamber and bellowed threats into his deafened ear.

"Come on," Allen shouted. "We are ready for a game of scalping with them for our martial spirits glow with bitter condemnation and consummate fury to blast their infernal projections."

He halted, wiped his sweating face on a shirtsleeve, and announced in a slightly hoarsened voice, "I prophesy that will fetch him."

"It should," Adam said dryly and Ethan gave the chuckle of a successfully wicked child.

"We have advanced only skirmishers, so far. We shall get our artillery into battery later."

He wiped his face again, picked up his waistcoat, and as he drew it on stopped and considered his companion before he asked abruptly, "You are contented? You are comfortable here?"

His gesture included the sunny room, chairs, table, bed, and the fire on the hearth.

"Why, yes," Adam answered with surprise.

"I want you should be," Allen pursued. "The laborer is worthy of his hire. You were belly-sick of it at Salisbury and didn't want much to come."

He grinned, shrugged on his coat, and clapped Adam on the back as he tramped from the room. His heavy feet pounded down the stair. His voice trumpeted a greeting to the taproom below and a dozen replied. Adam laid down his quill, flexed his fingers, and, staring through the window at the varnished maple buds, wondered whether lifelong intimacy would take away the man's ability to confuse him.

The winterbound Ethan Allen who dabbled in authorship had become a wearing and irksome person. The Ethan Allen who now actively led revolt was another being.

A dammed stream stagnated and scummed. Freed water followed its predestined course, roaring over obstacles, purifying itself by violence. Adam had watched with reluctant belief a like transformation of Allen.

They had ridden hither from Salisbury and then on to Arlington where delegates from a dozen towns that dared defy The Bloody Law were to hold convention. The man who chiefly had wrought their plight was not acclaimed when he swaggered into the meeting. Fright was plain on some of the faces turned toward the garish enormity; hostility on more.

Allen did not endear himself to the company or recommend Adam by presenting him majestically as "Captain Corlaer, my aide-de-camp." The delegates were in no mood to be impressed by the pompous instigator of most of their misdeeds, yet Adam, sitting alone and ill at ease, saw the timidly opened convention rouse when a glittering figure blared a reveille to valor.

Ethan's speech was not cast in the tight, sparse vernacular. His green, red, and gold uniform was a dissonance among the men in dull garments of towcloth and homespun, sagathy, fustian, and fulcher cloth, yet the brazen voice spread courage as a fire casts heat. The exhortations aimed at the convention, the invective Allen hurled like hastily gathered rocks at Tryon and New York, lifted courage and raised it to defiance.

Men were yelling when he ended with a flourish of his arms and a great climactic bellow, and Adam was surprised to find that he was among them. When the tumult had died, the convention that had met in apprehension threw Tryon's threat back in his teeth by declaring void all York commissions in The Grants and branding as public enemies those who persisted in holding them. With Ethan Allen still looming splendidly, with the mighty voice still ringing in their ears, what had men to fear? The meeting forthwith had commissioned him to write a letter to the governor, accepting York's challenge.

The rough draft of that missive lay before Adam now. He ran through its explosive periods with new respect. Its author still was braggart, poseur, and an infant in a soldier suit. He was also, now that veritable danger lowered, the captain of his people.

Those who had disparaged him spoke of him with awe. Elders, who had denounced him at Council meetings as an enemy to peace, sought him out and gained fortitude from his confidence. Adam, the surfeited, was finding in service with Ethan Allen, adventure, zest, and reviving faith in The Grants' cause.

He rose and opened a window, for the day's warmth and the fire were overheating the room. With his arms on the sill, he looked past the road's gouged and caking mud to the trees and the shriveled grass of the Green. Its attendant houses seemed less shabbily grim than when, still sullen and disheartened, he had ridden with Allen and Baker into Bennington. It might have been the spring, it might have been the glamour Ethan cast over The Grants and its people, that made the small, winter-soiled dwellings fair.

April's air was cool and sweet. Adam wondered, drawing it in, whether snow still lay in the woods about the Royden clearing. He was more intimately close to Mindwell, Olin, and Delight than when in Salisbury he smugly had planned benevolences for them. They and he and all freemen were following the same road now, wherever it led. It was a good feeling.

Sherwood would come back from Canada soon to plant his

crop. Even with the smell of spring in his nose, Adam found he could think of Felicity with no bitterness. Their quarrel had only hastened the inevitable, severing what Tryon's late proclamation surely would have broken. He wondered how the girl had spent her winter in Quebec and whether Wadman was prospering in his suit.

Resignation rather than jealousy flavored the thought. There was odd tranquillity in being an impoverished outlaw whom, when Tryon's days of grace ran out, the righteous were invited to kill on sight. Adam smiled as he turned from the window to copy Allen's letter to the governor.

Days that followed were filled with more than correspondence. Facing the violence that York's legislation presaged, the hopes and purposes of The Grants centered increasingly on Allen. Adam's responsibilities multiplied.

Alarmed settlers were seeing conspiracies in every movement of their Yorkish neighbors. These had been sustained in their loyalty by the Assembly's severity and predicted the day of victory was at hand. The Reverend Benjamin Hough was the most vehement of such prophets. Some elders in The Grants believed the Arlington convention had gone too far. Certain officers of The Green Mountain Boys were equally sure its action had been too mild and begged for immediate conflict. Beset by appeals, complaints, protests, Allen turned more and more to Adam for aid.

A book also was forming in the Colonel Commandant's spacious mind. It would be, he confided, only an indirect blow at York. Its prime purpose would be to explain to the world the divine justice of The Grants' cause. Only the title had been composed. Allen read it to his aide with modest pride:

"A brief Narrative of the Proceedings of the Government of New York Relative to their Obtaining the Jurisdiction of that Large District of Land Westward from Connecticut River Which antecedent thereto had been patented by his Majesty's Governor and Council of the Government of New Hampshire."

Word came that Tryon had gone to England, seeking more power to deal with rebellion, though Allen believed his letter had driven the Governor to flight. Cadwalader Colden, an older enemy, ruled in his stead. April ripened into May with shadblow and cherry afoam on the hills among the myriad blurred colors of unfolding leaves, and still the violence all men had expected withheld itself. New York's ferocity and The Grants' defiance seemed to have balanced each other. Allen, as the tension lessened, began dictating his "Brief Narrative." In mid-May, while he and Adam were at work, Justus Sherwood came to their door.

He was thin and haggard but his smile was so friendly, his handclasp so warm that Adam, meeting the candid eyes, once more felt a twinge of shame. The three sat by the table on which Joseph Fay, at Allen's thunderous bidding, had set a bowl of punch, and the others chiefly listened to the earnest flow of Sherwood's speech.

There seemed no room in the man's spirit for grudge. He was cordial toward Allen who had wrecked his efforts at compromise and picked up an old companionship as though Adam never had suspected him of treachery.

The traveler had come in haste from New Haven because of a visit Major Skene had paid him there. Skene was planning a voyage to England. He had reason to believe—Sherwood lowered his voice—that persons near His Majesty favored the erection of The Grants and the land west of Champlain into a separate government, the very project Justus and Ethan had worked for so hopefully in the past. In the light of New York's late savagery, the thing seemed possible.

Allen's breath whistled through his nose. Sherwood spread his hands in a gesture, half deprecation, half appeal.

"I am revealing this only to you"—again his magnanimity pricked Adam—"because it must be kept secret until the king declares the institution of a new royal province with all the Hampshire grants confirmed.

"Meanwhile"—he spoke more directly to Allen—"as you love this land, lead it into no further brawls."

Ethan sat up straighter.

"Lead it!" he echoed in a hushed bellow. "Brawls! Have you forgot that I am to be hunted like a buck, by Tryon's order, with a hundred pound, York currency, tied to my antlers?"

"I know that," Sherwood grinned at his indignation. "But if strife be unavoidable, let it be clear that York is the aggressor."

The chair creaked beneath Ethan Allen.

"Gods of the Mountains, Justus, I am a man of peace. If you wish peace yourself, quiet the scurvy, scaly, surreptitious, and altogether goddamnible Yorkers who make the trouble we must quell. Spencer we have abated, Munro we have mitigated, but there still remains that fiend in parson's form, the so-called Reverend Hough of whom daily we have complaints."

"I'll see him," Sherwood promised. "I'll try to—" but Allen still champed upon his grievance:

"He has been warned. His cloth will not protect him forever from a viewing. He spies for York and runs tattling to Albany. He goes up and down The Grants, preaching that Ethan Allen has a spiked tail buttoned inside his breeches while Tryon wears a halo under his wig."

"I'll see him," Sherwood repeated.

When the bowl had been emptied, Allen departed, leaving the others to talk with a revival of their old ease. Sherwood chuckled over Adam's account of his winter's labors. His own had been limited to advising General Carleton occasionally on the crisis in The Grants.

"We should have less trouble if he were governor of New York. He is a moderate man, earnest for peace and much concerned over the rebellion here."

If Sherwood's winter had been idle, Felicity's—he spoke her name lightly—had been gay. The Delaplaces had sponsored her—Justus wondered sometimes if they were not too indulgent—and had brightened Delight's last year at school as well.

"We all came uplake together," Sherwood reported. "Mrs. Delaplace and the children are staying with the Roydens while the Captain prepares proper quarters for them at Ticonderoga. He has relieved Anstruther, who was relieved indeed to be supplanted since neglect is accomplishing at Ti what the explosion wrought at Crown Point."

Adam found melancholy in his speech. The Sherwoods had turned one way; he had been thrust along another. Each reunion hereafter, he thought sadly, would only emphasize the wider space between them. Felicity, learning of Adam's state, would feel justified. He could not blame her and, thinking of her, found only mild wistfulness for a time irrevocably passed. Lest Sherwood think bitter longing had silenced him, he asked quickly about Delight.

"Well," the other reported, smiling. "And years older than when you last saw her. You would find great change in Delight. The Delaplaces urge her to come to Ti as companion to Millicent and governess for the children. They should have lodged with us, but our house is still at sixes and sevens and my crop is only half planted. Ride north with me, Adam, and help me get it in. No? I suppose not. Was there ever a time, I wonder, when the courses of lives changed more swiftly, and usually for the worse?"

He shook his head, regretfully.

"Captain Delaplace's subalterns," Adam asked, "have accompanied him to his new post?"

"Wadman has," Sherwood said with a grin. "He still pursues Felicity and she, the baggage, leads him on. He comes into his fortune, this year. Jocelyn Feltham is still in Quebec, where he courted Delight in his own peculiar fashion. There is talk of building a larger fort at Crown Point. That would bring more troops to the lake."

"That will comfort the Allens, since their Onion River lands border Champlain."

"Will it?" Sherwood asked shrewdly. "I am not so sure. I learned in Canada that His Majesty will close the port of Boston next month. That is a punishment long overdue."

"A sentiment," Adam said, tingling, "that a Grants outlaw can scarcely endorse."

"Yes, I know," Sherwood began, hesitated, and went on with more vigor, "Your situation is of your own choosing. For God's sake, my friend, why do you do it? You must have a motive. What do you believe?"

Adam met his earnest eyes.

"I still am not quite sure. Something is growing here—something that soon, I think, will reveal that all men can be free."

"With the wildman, Ethan Allen, as their governor?" Sherwood asked crisply. "A thousand years hence, there may be proper self-government, but only after each man has learned to govern himself. Surely The Grants' rebellion has proved that."

He looked hopefully into his companion's stubborn face, shrugged, and smiled.

"We still are poles apart," Sherwood said, rising and laying a warm hand on Adam's shoulder. "It is strange that though our minds run in such contrary fashion we should still be friends."

Chapter XXXI

DAYS grew warmer, golden-bright or murmurous with rain. Corn stood knee-high when July came in; the hay crop was heavy; the tall wheat blue-green and rich in promise.

"Good growing weather—so far," men told each other warily, as though the admission might offend fortune.

Summer, deep-breasted, open-handed, imposed its own truce upon the striving factions. In the north, the zealot Hough still preached calamity, and in Arlington a cross-grained physician, Dr. Samuel Adams, though he held land under Grants' title, declared for York, but elsewhere men worked their land in peace and the violence the spring had presaged never came.

In Adam's room in Fay's tavern, Allen dictated with continually fewer distractions while his pride in his performance increased, and the days marched by, each more placid than the last.

Sometimes, while working alone, Adam was beset again by the queer belief that he no longer was himself; that the man who industriously expanded the scribbled notes was in no wise the reckless and aspiring Adam Corlaer of a year ago. He wondered, leaning back in his chair and rubbing his pen-stiffened hand, if it were only through deprivation that one reached serenity.

All that he so eagerly had sought had been removed beyond his utmost reach. He needed only to recall Sherwood's visit to realize again how completely he had lost Felicity. Justus had spoken of his sister and her treatment of her suitor, Wadman, as though Adam never had known her. If Sherwood deemed his friend's courtship abandoned, how much more completely must Felicity have thrust Adam from her life. He no longer, for that matter, ached for her but thought of her with an agreeably romantic sadness.

Adam, by custom, worked upon Allen's growing "Brief Narrative" the better part of each day, exercised himself and his mare in the late afternoons, and in the evenings usually sat for a time in the taproom, always with Ethan, sometimes at a long, crowded table, sometimes with only Remember Baker or the engaging Dr. Jonas Fay, or the dry, brown Sam Herrick in attendance. Ira Allen came to squabble with his brother, vanish, and reappear, an increasingly complacent young man. In the illusion of peace the summer had brought, men were buying freely of The Onion River Company's lands. Chittenden, himself, had gone north to the new Allen-sponsored town of Williston, with his wife, four sons, and six daughters.

The new Adam Corlaer was finding a variety of contentment and, though he recognized its aridity, he accepted it gladly. An emotional desert was welcome after a winter spent in the Allens' house.

And Ethan, in the absence of flints to strike his steel, seemed also an altered person, less vehement in his bluster, less inclusive in his threats. Sherwood's appeal for moderation still dwelt in his mind. He worked industriously on his book, which he had begun to believe was worthy of standing with Plato, and broke away from daily dictation only once when, shortly after Sherwood's departure, he rode to Skenesborough to confer with its proprietor.

Ethan returned, so glossily smug, so steeped in mystery, that Adam judged Skene had promised him high office in the new province the major and he were trying to create.

"And by all the gods of the wilderness," Allen confided, "Skene may yet bring it off. He says that General Carleton greatly favors the project and is"—pride lit his face—"most eager to confer with me. Justus was right, Adam. We must hold The Grants from aggression. We must be wiser than serpents, who in truth are the most witless of creatures, and more harmless than doves, who can raise all varieties of hell in a man's cornfield."

Adam thought the colonel had belied his own sermonizing on the day when the apostate Dr. Adams was haled to Bennington. Robert Cochran, who possessed more than most men the ability to swagger in a saddle, and a half dozen Green Mountain Boys brought in the prisoner, a flabby, disheveled person, bound and straddling a led horse. Adam wondered whether the shallow glitter in the doctor's eyes betokened defiance or a deranged mind. Certainly the man's conduct, as revealed by witnesses at the hearing in the Council Chamber where Ethan Allen presided, was less than rational.

The physician had turned, overnight and for no clear reason, from a loyal upholder of The Grants' cause into the most vociferous of Yorkers. He had been warned and Cochran, calling with a further threat, had been obliged to strike a pistol out of Dr. Adams' hand.

The prisoner, when invited by Allen to defend himself, proclaimed his devotion to York in a contentious, rambling speech and announced, while his plump hands beat on the arms of the witness chair, that he would rather be hanged than retract a single syllable.

"Now, by the tears of Christ, sir," Allen exploded, "you shall have your wish. The sentence of this court is that you shall be hanged forthwith and, since we lack a gallows, from the scaffold supporting the emblem of this very hostelry."

Adam bit back his protest but a murmur of dismay filled the room. This was the overt act, the willful breaking of the implicit peace, against which Skene and Sherwood had warned and the now furious judge, himself, had preached.

He stood, immense and still, hushing the company by his ice-blue glare. Not until the room again was silent did Allen turn to the prisoner.

"Hanged at once," he threw the words again into the sickly, smirking face, "as a warning to other loose talkers; hanged as high as Haman in the chair you now occupy and there left suspended until you recant."

His grim mouth relaxed. Someone tittered and set off a great burst of laughter, half delight, half relief, overwhelming the prisoner's squalls of dissent. A rope appeared, seemingly out of the air. Men clustered about Dr. Adams, binding him fast in the chair, bearing him, still squealing, from the room.

Adam's was among a hundred upturned, mirthful faces. Midway between earth and the catamount effigy, the prisoner, still seated, dangled like an uneasy plummet. The wind swung and deliberately spun him. The chair tipped perilously when he stirred. The doctor, at first, had yelped defiance at those who informed him he would remain suspended a day, a week, until he resumed Grants' allegiance. He was silent now, still swinging, still slowly revolving. His face had turned gray, his eyes were glazing. Nausea was besetting the physician and he was in no position to heal himself. Adam began to back away. An amused voice said in his ear:

"Nice goin's-on for a grown man to share in."

He wheeled and looked into the grinning face of Olin Royden.

"Ethan Allen," Olin cried, nodding toward the human pendulum, above the whooping crowd, "can't be far off when things like this happen, and I've ridden far and fast to see him."

Adam closed the windows but the clamor of the hanging man's volunteer counselors still came into the room as though deriding Olin's tale. He scowled as he told it and spoke hurriedly as if, even to him, its taste was dubious.

Two young officers—Lieutenants Wadman from Ticonderoga and Feltham lately from Quebec—had come to Sherwood's home to fish and hunt. They had seemed queer folks at first but, when you got used to them, not too bad.

Adam was aware that Allen stared at him and wondered tardily what his face had revealed. Olin hastened on:

He had taken the pair to Champlain for bass and pike. Feltham had been often at the Royden house to see Delight. A few days ago, both men had sought Olin and had asked him to guide them to Ethan Allen. When he had refused, they had pledged him to secrecy and Wadman then had revealed that he had recently been with Feltham in Quebec where he had received the honor of a confidence from a highly placed personage. He was so distinguished and the mission he had entrusted to the lieutenant was so delicate that Wadman had not revealed the name or errand, even to Sherwood.

"Wouldn't tell me," Olin reported, still scowling, "who this 'personage' was, but maybe I can guess, always providing the whole thing isn't a fraud. Wadman holds the man wants to talk with you, Ethan, soon and secretly. He asked—maybe he ordered —Wadman to contrive a meeting. It's queer-sounding but—wal, I don't know."

He flushed as though the high yell that rose from the street were comment on his own report and fumbled in his homespun shirt.

"All their talk boiled down to this: Said I knew you and where I might find you and promised at last to carry a message. Here 'tis."

Allen broke the letter's seal and unfolded it. Adam heard the whistle of the Colonel's breathing and saw his eyes grow brilliant.

"Hah!" Ethan said, looking up. "By the foreskins of Shechem, I believe—"

He checked himself, grumbled in his throat, and passed the letter to his aide.

"Colonel Ethan Allen," Adam read, "commanding in The Grants. Honored sir: A Neighbor of yours in the North has done me the honor of making me the Bearer of his Request for a meeting with You to discuss the future Welfare of his and your adjacent Properties. I therefore most respectfully and urgently Request a discreet Interview to establish the Time and Place for such a Conference. Were I not wholly confident of your honourable Station and Willingness to observe a Secrecy that is my Mission's prime Necessity, I should not risk subscribing myself: Yours in Obedience and great Respect, George Wadman, lieutenant, H. B. M.'s 26th Rgt. of Foot."

Another burst of derisive yelling was like an amplification of Adam's own thought. He said sharply, in response to Allen's prompting glare, "You must recall this—gentleman," deliberately soiling the word. "We fought in this very tavern."

"Now did you, by God? Then I do know him. A high-spirited young man."

Adam shrugged and Olin, reading the slur in the gesture, said in his own defense, "I found him forthright and agreeable. Else, I wouldn't be here."

"And how," Adam asked nastily, "is his courtship of Felicity progressing?", but Olin could not be roused.

"Don't seem to me," he returned quietly, "that's what we're debating."

"Now this 'exalted personage' "—Allen blurted in waxing excitement—"must be, can be, no other than General Guy Carleton, himself. By the toenails of Jehovah—"

"If the 'personage,' " Adam broke in, "exists at all."

"Exists?" Allen echoed, portentous as a thundercloud.

"Olin"—Adam was surprised at his own vehemence—"already has hinted at fraud. Have you forgotten you are worth a hundred pounds to a kidnapper?"

Allen found reflection on his own intelligence in the query.

"Adam," he bawled, "you talk so like my brother Ira that sometimes—"

He swallowed the rest of it when Herrick pounded on the door and entered with a grin on his weathered face.

"Ethan," he said cheerfully, "if you don't aim to hang that bastard till he's tender, you might order him lowered. He has disavowed York, professed and reprofessed his allegiance to The Grants, puked twice an' is 'bout ready for another spell."

"Then let him down," Allen cried. "Bid him go and sin no more."

The interruption had cast Adam out of the path which otherwise, in obstinacy, he might have followed. He already was regretting his vehemence. It was not right that he should use his enmity to sway Allen.

"I spoke in heat," he admitted, when the door had closed on Cochran. "Olin is a better judge of these men's intentions than I. Yet I still believe," he persisted, "you should proceed with care."

"Wal," Olin offered, "he acts honest. That's far's I'll go."

"It must be Carleton," Allen thought aloud, "who has sent this Wadman. If the Governor of Quebec seeks a meeting with me, great things are in the wind. Jesus Christ and all his relatives, Adam, I cannot refuse! What reason have you to doubt the message?"

"None, save a personal dislike."

Ethan brushed it aside.

"In a matter so weighty, so ponderous with portent," he pursued grandiloquently, "discretion is of course required. Delicacy, too, is essential if General Carleton's wishes are to be respected and secrecy absolutely maintained. By God"—he banged upon the arm of his chair—"Adam, you shall ride back with Olin as my ambassador, confer with Lieutenant Wadman and, if you are convinced of his integrity, proceed with the protocol for a meeting."

"I am no more likely to be agreeable to Wadman than he to me," Adam objected, heartily unwilling to undertake the mission. "Besides," he pursued desperately, "what excuse would I have for appearing in Panton?"

"There are folks there who'd be real glad to see you," Olin pointed out. "You wouldn't have to explain a visit to our house."

"Which is already amply filled by Captain Delaplace's family."

"No," said Olin detestably, "they've gone on to Ti."

"The journey," Allen proclaimed, "will benefit you, boy. You've ink in your veins and sand in your hide. The book, since an even more momentous project intervenes, can wait your return."

Adam gulped.

"As you will," he said at last.

"Good," Allen bellowed and, recalling himself to statesmanship, pulled his triumphant face into extreme gravity. "All that remains then, Captain Corlaer, is to prepare your credentials as my ambassador extraordinary and minister plenipotentiary."

It had been almost three years earlier when Adam first had ridden toward Panton by the North Road. It had been little more than a trail then; now, it was assuming the aspect of a thoroughfare, with the larger streams bridged and many of the marshy stretches corduroyed. It had grown like an animate thing and the wilderness was retreating from it.

Despite the endemic rebellion in The Grants, a procession of settlers had used it and many had made their pitches beside it. Cabins were frequent and clearings let in sunlight where unbroken gloom had dwelt. The villages through which Adam and Olin passed had a look of new strength and confidence. Not until they got beyond Manchester did the veritable wilderness close in, and even here the old blazed trail was transforming itself into a road.

Adam, while his journey was only a few hours old, had begun to acknowledge the merit of Ethan Allen's prescription. It was good to be freed from a desk, with his mare between his knees and Olin for companion. It was good to be riding back to Panton. The Roydens' was the one remaining home where he still was serenely sure of welcome. He began, now that he was committed, to look forward to testing in Felicity's presence his fancied immunity.

He found he could endure without emotion Olin's talk of the girl, though he marveled at his friend's placid confidence.

"I look at it this way," Olin confided. "Farm won't yield enough this year for me to wed. Next year, she'll decide to have me. Surer of it, every day. Patience does it, Adam. You worried me more 'n Wadman does. If he couldn't win her among all the hoity-toities and macaronis of Quebec, where you might say he was in his own country, hardly likely he'll do any better in mine. He's as lost on a pitch or in the woods as I'd be in the army. Don't worry about me, Adam. I don't."

The benign summer gave them fair weather and they made good time. They were riding through the sunset light toward Chimney Point where they planned to spend the last night of their journey, when their sole adventure befell them. Olin said softly to his companion, "See who comes."

The shadow the Reverend Mr. Hough cast before him was scarcely darker or longer than he. Adam knew by the glare of the white-ringed eyes that the minister recognized them but he would have passed without a word on the strong, young steed that had replaced Abijah if Olin had not said acidly, "Mite out of your parish, eh, Reverend? You'll find few Yorkers this far north."

It was strange to see color come into so parched a face; more startling still to hear the vindictiveness in Hough's clattering voice.

"God," said he, reining in, "of a certainty has turned His face from a land when rebels presume to question His minister's comings and goings."

"Wal," Olin answered composedly, "God's probably a deal more concerned over where you've been and what becomes of you than we be."

Hough aimed a long, grimed forefinger like a weapon first at the speaker, then at Adam.

"The blasphemer and the robber still follow their evil paths, but the day of wrath is near, sirs; the day of wrath is near. God is not mocked, nor is His servant to be silenced."

"Now I wouldn't argue that," Olin said, grinning sideways at

296

Adam, but Hough pursued, leering as though he cherished some malign secret:

"I have been warned. Mine own eyes have seen how bandits afflict the loyal. The trimmer, Sherwood, has implored me hold my peace, yet I shall continue to preach God's justice and the rights of York in the ears of the iniquitous."

There was a demented look in the rolling eyes. Adam said to Olin, "Let's get along."

"Aye," Hough rattled. "Go. And take this text with ye: 'Whoso causeth the righteous to go astray in an evil way, he shall fall himself into his own pit.' Selah!"

He thrust his snorting horse past them and rode on, an elated, scarecrow figure. Adam, looking after him, said, "I believe he is a little mad."

"But real pleased over something," Olin said thoughtfully. "If I didn't know our folks, I'd say someone had just done Brimstone Benjy a big favor."

Chapter XXXII

THEY came at noon of the next day to the Royden house, standing in its new coat of red ocher and skim milk, sturdy and substantial as Mindwell who came to the door and smiled.

"Wal," she told Adam, " 'twan't the wild-goose chase figgered 'twould be when Olin went a-peltin' off. Come to stay a spell?"

"Not long," he answered and pursued uncomfortably under her searching gaze. "I was tired of service as clerk and eager to see you, so Ethan gave me a holiday."

"Ye're welcome, Adam."

The deception continued to gall him as he and Olin unsaddled, yet even this distress could not obscure the sense of healing ease the fields and buildings bestowed, as though truly he belonged here, as though this were homecoming. Mindwell told him when he returned to the house that she guessed Delight would be as pleased as she, when she got back from the picnic on which the Sherwoods had taken her with—the woman sniffed—the two young soldiers.

It was late afternoon before they heard laughter and the clatter of a cart. Sherwood already had halted his team before the house when Adam came out to suffer the scrutiny of many eyes.

The two young men who stood by the cart's tailgate stared at him and the taller spoke under his breath to his stalwart companion. Feltham and Wadman, Adam thought with amusement that eased embarrassment, had purchased in Canada costumes for their venture into The Grants' wilderness. In fringed and beaded deerskin, red sashes, and fur skullcaps they more resembled half-breed Hurons than Yankee frontiersmen. Sherwood had leaped down from his seat and was crying, "Adam, what on earth brought you here?"

His handclasp was warm. He turned and called to his sister, "Felicity, look."

Already, Adam knew, she was aware of his presence since for an instant their glances had crossed, yet her surprise was prettily portrayed and the smile she gave him flawless. He bowed deeply, fortified by the irritation her duplicity had quickened. Sherwood said, "You must meet our guests." He stumbled and added with a strained laugh, "I forgot you were old acquaintances."

The barbarically arrayed young men were advancing. Adam had scarcely time to deplore Feltham's precise gait when Wadman held out his hand and said earnestly, "I have wished to encounter Mr. Corlaer again so that I might beg his pardon so eloquently for a loutish offense that he might be persuaded to show me a certain wrestling hold in which he is adept."

"The hold, sir, is clearer in my mind than the offense," Adam replied with polite mendacity.

"Oh, I say now!" Feltham cried, enraptured. "Skin me, sir! A well-turned reply."

"Adam," a voice close beside him asked, "have you no greeting for me at all?"

He turned and for a long instant was silent.

The voice and the great gray eyes were familiar. While he groped for speech, Sherwood's comment at Bennington came into his mind: "Years older than when you last saw her."

The intervening months had tenderly remolded Delight, drawing childish angularity into new, sweet curves, ripening young breasts that lent beauty to the fulcher-cloth bodice, softening and granting luster to a fragile face, lightening a wistful mouth with mirth. She was, Adam thought wildly, fair and blithe as a wind-swept sapling birch. It was strange to see her laughing; it was a shock to know she was laughing at him.

"I'm still Delight Royden," she told him and held out her hand. "Had you forgotten me?"

"How could I forget," he replied, desperately summoning his wits, "loveliness I never had seen?"

"Well said!" Feltham acclaimed with his faint lisp. "And, having seen, can never forget again, eh, sir?"

He turned upon Delight pale, languishing eyes. She laughed and Adam, watching, felt a sense of loss. The coltish child he had known was gone and in her place stood this semi-stranger whose ease as she listened to what Feltham babbled in his damned, mincing voice left Adam deprived and lonely.

Sherwood was handing his sister down from the cart. By its tail, Olin and Wadman stood, talking in low voices. Felicity slipped an arm about Delight's waist and turned her toward Adam again.

"And what, sir," she demanded with the easy generosity of the rich, "do you say of our little woods mouse now? Is she not exquisite?"

In her own sultry brilliance, Delight seemed pale as the daylight moon. Resentment stirred in Adam.

"I am dazzled," he confessed, "and bewildered."

"And whose fault may that be, sir?" Felicity cried. "He neglects his friends for ages, doesn't he, Dee? And then complains that he is bewildered."

The provocation in her eyes irked him. Felicity, he thought bitterly, could no more refrain from enticing than she could cease breathing. He was grateful to Sherwood who rescued him by asking, "Will you be long here, Adam?"

"No," he answered, keeping his eyes away from Olin's and Wadman's conference. "I'm taking the brief holiday Ethan Allen recommended."

"If it be you who has kept him quiet all summer," Sherwood said with a sour smile, "I shan't urge you to stay. I wish I had been as successful in hushing Benjamin Hough. Come to New Haven before you leave, Adam, and see what has been made of the house we built together."

Feltham and Delight had withdrawn to stand beside the team. The girl threw back her head and laughed. The blithe sound increased Adam's undefined loneliness.

"Is she not the loveliest thing?" Felicity asked him, but her upturned face dared him to utter such heresy in her presence. Sherwood and Mindwell had moved away. Adam had no cause to curb his feelings and answered briefly, "I should be a prejudiced judge."

"You were not always so—scrupulous."

"No, to my sorrow."

She caught her breath and her eyes took a hurt look. They passed over his face like a caress.

"Sorrow," Felicity said softly at last, "is at least something."

"Was something," he corrected with a slight lift of his shoulders. "That, too, has passed."

She hesitated. Her voice throbbed.

"Bitterness does not become you, Adam."

"Nor does pretense adorn you, Felicity."

She gave a small, helpless gesture.

"Must we quarrel, again?"

"That is the question you always manage to ask me," he told her almost cheerfully. "Not 'again.' I shall be here too short a time for that."

He saw color spring into her face and admired the clarity of her laughter as she turned away. Sherwood called, "It's time to go if we are to get home before dark."

In the stir of departure, Adam found Wadman beside him and holding out his hand with a smile.

"May our future meetings, Mr. Corlaer," he said, "be increasingly pleasant," and, dropping his voice, confided, "We shall talk on the morrow."

In the supper candlelight, Delight's smooth hair shone like pale metal and her face was ivory, delicately carved. It was odd, Adam thought, that he who once had felt a child's surveillance should now be stealing glances at her. At last she caught his eyes and smiled. His face grew hot.

"I keep seeking," he told her, "for a little girl who no longer is here."

"Feltham," Olin laughed with brotherly candor, "seems satisfied with her successor. Goin' to be transferred to Ti, Dee, just to be near you?"

Her face was warmer but her voice still was cool.

"If you think—"

"I think," Olin broke in grinning, " 'twould be real seemly if you went to the fort. When the Delaplaces don't need you and Leftenant isn't soldiering, you could sit together and sew a fine seam."

"I won't," Delight told him with difficult gravity, "have you making fun of him. He's been very agreeable to me."

"Agreeable," her brother granted, "but real comic in those Injun clothes and not what I'd call hearty."

"Never," Mindwell offered, "was one to abide a lisper."

It was strange that a single year should teach Delight to smile so calmly; it was stranger that they should sit here, discussing her suitor. She could manage her life and her swains now without Adam's counsel. He found it a daunting thought. Mindwell, rising to clear away supper, told her daughter briskly, "Was I you, I'd make up my mind whether I was hirin' out to Millicent Delaplace or not. She won't wait forever."

"She said," Delight pointed out serenely, "that I had plenty of time to think it over."

Olin stretched and said with unconcern so large that Adam discounted it, "Early to bed for me. Riding over in the morning to Sherwoods to talk about his dam."

His eyes rested guilelessly on his friend.

"Come along if you've a mind, Adam."

"I'd be glad to."

"Oh," Delight said, "I thought—"

"Wal, what?" Olin asked at last.

"Nothing," she said and rose to help her mother bear the dishes away.

Wadman and Feltham were waiting, as Olin had foretold, a mile from the Sherwood clearing. They rose from the boulder where they had perched with fowling pieces across their knees.

"We are not," Wadman grinned, indicating the weapons, "highwaymen. There seemed no other way to get clear so I told our host we were off for a bit of shooting."

Feltham snickered confirmation. For all their appearance of ease, both men were taut, and Adam, dismounting, thought he understood why. In a chamber where eavesdropping was possible, they might have been confident but here their eyes shuttled from tree to tree as though each might hide a witness. Adam smiled and held a paper out to Wadman.

"My credentials, sir."

The other scanned the document and nodded. His voice was

hurried. Caution demanded this conference should be brief. If Mr. Corlaer—Wadman's eyes met Adam's squarely—had any doubts or questions, would he voice them? Wind stirred the tree-tops and Feltham flinched.

"Two questions," Adam said promptly. "First, is Colonel Allen to presume you are acting for General Carleton?"

Wadman hesitated, glanced toward the apprehensive Feltham, and nodded. "He may so presume."

"Colonel Allen," Adam pursued, "then is puzzled why this mission was entrusted to you instead of to Mr. Sherwood who is understood to be in the General's confidence."

Again, Wadman shot a sidewise glance toward Feltham who waved his hands impatiently and gabbled, "Oh, tally! Can't that wait? This is a cursed unpleasant place for bickering, sir."

"No, Mr. Corlaer is right," Wadman asserted but he himself rushed through his explanation. Mr. Sherwood, it was true, was considered entirely loyal but he had undertaken last year to compose The Grants' difficulties. His failure and Reid's anger over what had happened at Otter Falls had diminished Carleton's approval of him.

Quebec's governor, Adam reflected with mild amusement, had been scarcely more fortunate in his choice of agents. Wadman and Feltham were bad conspirators, advertising their rôles by stealth and apprehension.

"Then here," he said, willing to end their trial, "is Colonel Allen's proposal: A long day's ride south of here is a lake the French named Sainte Catherine's and not far from its upper end, a house, now unoccupied, that the Colonel's brother, Heber, has built. Colonel Allen will meet you at the lakehead, early in the morning, ten days hence, for futher conference."

"Oh now, flay me!" Feltham protested. "You expect us to find a damned lake through these doubly damned and monstrous woods?"

He tittered. Adam gave his answer to Wadman.

"Mr. Royden will supply you with directions, the name of someone with whom you may lodge, and a map. He also will find horses for you, either on the pretense of a hunting expedition or for an overland journey to Ticonderoga."

Wadman nodded, his eyes narrowed by thought.

"Yes," he conceded at last. "That seems a sound plan."

"Then if there are no further questions we shall so agree and meet at Lake Sainte Catherine."

"You," Wadman asked after hesitation, "will accompany Colonel Allen thither?"

"Probably; with no more than one or two others. The smaller the party, the less curiosity it will rouse."

"Then I approve entirely, sir. No one should be included who has not Colonel Allen's confidence. It has been a pleasure to deal with so forthright and farseeing a gentleman, Mr. Corlaer."

"And now," Wadman's smile was cordial and relieved, "if you will accompany us to Mr. Sherwood's, we have some prime Barbadoes rum in which to drink to—"

Olin spoke vigorously.

"No. We'll ride on alone, since I told Justus we were to visit him. You must not go back till later and you better shoot something, or at something, before you return. If we still are at Sherwood's when you do appear, remember we have not seen each other since yesterday."

He and Adam mounted. As they moved off, Olin looked back at the twin figures, incongruous and disconsolate in their fringed and beaded deerskins.

"And I wouldn't," he threw back, "venture too far from the road."

He chuckled softly. They rode on for a time in silence before he looked at his companion and prompted, "Wal?"

"It seems authentic enough," Adam said thoughtfully.

"And to me," Olin confirmed.

Chapter XXXIII

Justus welcomed his visitors happily and deplored Wadman's and Feltham's absence. Adam and Olin admired the flourishing crops with less than usual triteness, for Sherwood had devoted to his farm and more productively the energy he had spent last year in the king's service. He and Felicity led their visitors from room to room of the now furnished house.

Adam, ignoring the invitation in the girl's eyes, accompanied Olin and their host to the site of the projected dam but, after their return, when his companions had begun seemingly endless calculations of the timber and stone required, he found himself alone with Felicity in the dooryard.

He glumly admired the lightness of her speech which seemed as aimless as their strolling. His own responses were brief and stilted. The blue dress she wore was too dainty for housework. Her shining hair had been carefully arranged. Felicity had expected him, Adam thought with bitterness, and had prepared to enthrall him. Her confidence in her charm was a challenge.

She was looking at him with a wistful smile.

"Why are you so—remote, Adam? Why have you changed so greatly?"

"Why," he asked grimly, "do you never change? The eternal Felicity!"

Memory of his own misuse by her let him withstand her hurt, appealing look.

"I don't know what you mean," she whispered. "I only am sure it is not meant kindly."

"I mean," Adam informed her deliberately, "that I have grown rusty at swordplay. There are three on whom you may better exercise your skill—Olin, Wadman, Feltham. Employ it there. They will value it more highly."

For an instant she stood with her fingers pressed against her mouth as though to hide its trembling. Then she asked in a piteous voice, "You think I am a flirt? A wanton?"

"I do," he told her promptly, "and for cause. A betrayer, too, of a lover's confidence. You've overlooked that."

He saw her flinch and was glad. He was eager to sharpen the lately languishing eyes, to make still clearer the ring of metal in her voice.

"You find it worth while," Felicity asked slowly, "to come all the way from Bennington to insult me?"

"I came," he answered with imperfect candor, "to see the Roydens, with no thought of you at all. That is hard for you to believe, I know."

"But nevertheless you have come here," she told him, too angry to mark his momentary dismay. "Was there no more chivalrous way," she pursued, bending her voice to pathos, "to tell me all was over between us?"

"Oh, stop acting," he bade. "Ended? It ended a year ago. You know it. You ended it."

He was startled by the brilliance of her eyes, by the color that flamed up after momentary pallor. Felicity's small hands clenched and shook, but her words were clear as the sound of dropping coins.

"You came to mock me, then? And, of course 'to see the Roydens,' to leer at Delight. You will regret, Adam, that you chose me for your enemy."

He laughed, raised an invisible hilt to his chin, and swept his arms through exaggerated movements of the duelist's salute. The travesty infuriated her.

"And if you plan," she went on, while tears of rage shone on her eyelashes, "to console yourself now with little Delight, I'll take care to thwart that scheme."

He was alarmed to find how hotly his anger responded to the shabby taunt. He said in a low voice, for Sherwood's and Olin's steps resounded in the dwelling's hall, "What a detestable little vixen you are, Felicity!"

They rode away, after dinner, with Olin flushed and complacent from the fascination Felicity had spent upon him. Adam was grimly content. Let Olin have her, he told himself loftily and then, recalling the light in Felicity's eyes as she told him goodbye, retracted the vindictive assignment. His friend deserved better fortune.

Neither of the Royden children was happily entangled—Olin in his blindly confident fashion still pursuing Felicity; Delight, courted with whatever ardor the lisping Feltham was able to produce. Adam grew angry again at memory of Felicity's spiteful threat, nor was he soothed by further thought of Delight's swain.

Delight was gay and fresh as a mountain brook. Her fairness was a clear spirit at last made visible. If she lured the ineffable Feltham, why had not other better men courted her? What ailed the youth of Quebec? Where were their eyes and their hearts?

Olin, emerging from his rosy thoughts, asked suddenly, "Your errand is completed?"

"Eh?" said Adam, rousing. "Yes. You still must see that Wadman and Feltham ride south in time. I'll start back tomorrow."

"So soon?"

"I must," Adam insisted, half to his friend, half to his own thoughts.

Mindwell, when he repeated his intention at supper, looked at him a long instant before she said, "So short a stay for so long a trip don't seem wuth while, hardly."

Delight's face shone in the candlelight. Adam explained with what ease he could muster, "Ethan Allen's secretary has little time of his own."

"Hm!" Mindwell commented and pressed her mouth against further speech.

Restlessness drove Adam out into the dooryard when the meal was over. Delight's strange manner troubled him. His announcement had not openly distressed her; it had only muted her, so that she had sat through supper eating little, saying less. He wondered why he felt her placidity hid a hurt.

Delight could not possibly think of him otherwise than as an elderly relative. A jeering inner voice cried out that Feltham was at least his own age. He ignored it. The lovely creature the

307

engaging child had become deserved a more praiseworthy suitor than an impoverished outlaw.

His present distress was only the aftermath of his final violent passage with Felicity. He had berated her for saying what he now was thinking. It was well that he was riding away next morning. Still, he hoped he had not hurt Delight.

Once before, when he had lingered here in the dooryard gloom, she had come to join him. Adam's heart leaped painfully when the kitchen door opened and closed. He greeted Olin with an odd mingling of disappointment and relief.

They talked together in low voices, rehearsing all the details of Feltham's and Wadman's journey, and when it became clear that Delight would not appear, Adam went into the house.

Mindwell, alone in the kitchen, was setting bread. A flour smear was her face's most evident expression.

"Wal," she said in a dry, neutral voice. "Delight's made up her mind. Goin' to Ti."

"Is she?" Adam asked and dared not trust himself to say more. Mindwell bent over the breadboard.

"Seems sometimes," she offered, " 's if I was the only one willin' to bide here."

Adam, who had slept restlessly and wakened early, stole out through the silent house and to the stable. He saw flight in his haste and approved it. He was running away from an aberration that had spoiled his last evening here and had marred his night. If he fed, groomed, and saddled Allegra now, he could leave immediately after breakfast. Each mile he placed behind him would bring him further out of a ridiculous mood.

It was distrust of himself that bade him hasten. He was not in love with Delight, save as all men must be with the delicate and fair. The idea had been thrust diabolically into his mind by Felicity. She need not have promised to thwart his wooing. Delight had seen to that. She was going to Ticonderoga where her precious suitor was to be stationed and Adam, damned by The Bloody Law, dared not venture.

His mare laid back her ears and bared her teeth as he brushed her belly. He swore at her thoroughly and, incredibly, roused laughter. Delight stood by the stable's open door with milk pails in her hands.

"Isn't it," she asked in a shaken voice, "early to be in such a temper?"

"Sorry," Adam gulped, and because he thought he saw reproach behind her mirth, explained awkwardly, "Since I must leave so early, I am getting ready now."

Her amusement vanished. Her bright mouth stirred before she said gently, "I—we barely have seen you and now you are going."

She was still for an instant; then she added, "You show no great fondness for your friends."

Adam, watching her stand, not like a Grants' but a pastoral milkmaid, tried to break the perilous tension with a jest. While he sought and found none, he came from the stall, took down his saddle and heard himself blurt, "I show more than you."

"I don't know what you mean," Delight told him. He found himself comparing the honesty of her bewilderment with Felicity's coquetry.

"I mean," he said more carefully, "that you are about to go where I never may reach you."

Delight surveyed him with calm eyes.

"You profess a desire for my—our company, yet you stand there, holding a saddle, impatient to leave. Oh, Adam!"

"That is not the same thing at all."

Delight's question was so direct it unsettled him. "Are you asking me not to go to Ticonderoga?"

"I am asking nothing," he said sharply. "I only point out that, while I'm worth fifty pounds to the law-abiding, I can never see you there."

"Would you try, otherwise?" Delight asked and laughed at his confusion.

"The great privilege of seeing me," she persisted, eyes shining, "can mean little to you when you rise before chore time to leave the more quickly."

Adam hung the saddle across the stall's edge and turned toward her in exasperation. The look Delight gave him was so empty of pretense, so candidly expectant that for the instant it seemed the child she had been stood there. It was to her he spoke.

"I have told no one else. I am telling you because you know how to hold your tongue and because—"

She waited, cool and fair as the dawn, and he saw whither further explanation might lead. He checked himself an instant and pursued lamely, "I had a mission to accomplish for Ethan Allen. I must go back to him at once. That is why I'm leaving. It is not," he added with feeble sarcasm, "because I am sick of being with you."

It seemed for a moment that sunlight touched her face. Adam's voice ran away with him, "I never have been weary of that, Delight. I never could be."

His throat was dry and tight. The girl dropped her eyes, then raised them again to meet his.

"I'm glad," she said, "because I never could be, either." She added, still more softly, "I've always known that."

The faintest quaver marred her voice but the eyes fast upon his did not falter. He saw her mouth tremble ever so little and heard himself ask hoarsely, "If I come back, as soon as may be, will you wait till then?"

He drew a quick breath, knowing how happily impossible it was for him to stop now. Alarm crossed her face. Her sharp movement checked him.

Olin, still frowzy from slumber, grinned at Adam and demanded of his sister in mock alarm, "Don't tell me the milkin's done a'ready and me barely awake?"

"No," Delight told him quietly, "I've just—come out."

She slipped away. Olin squinted at his friend.

"You look queer," he said at length.

"Early rising never pleases me," Adam told him and turned to pick up his saddle.

He had had no further opportunity to speak alone with Delight when, an hour later, he mounted before the Roydens' door. Adam said to them all, "I promise I'll come back in a fortnight."

The girl, standing slender and glowing beside her stalwart mother, smiled up at him.

Chapter XXXIV

"WERE General Carleton," said Ethan Allen, rolling the name upon his tongue, "not so insistent upon secrecy, it would be my pleasure to go in a state befitting his position and mine with a large escort and a personal suite."

He considered the prospect wistfully. Ira, who had been summoned from Fay's taproom to hear Adam's report, looked at his giant brother with pious patience and moved his mouth reflectively across his teeth.

"Ye ain't," he said with faint acidity, "goin' to see Carleton at all, this trip. No cause to swell up—yet."

He endured calmly the hushed blare in which Ethan demanded, "Is it a matter of no concern that the king's own governor wishes to confer with me? Stub, by the south chamber of hell, I—"

"Concerns us a plenty if ye make a good trade. Mebby you haven't figgered out what a dicker with Canada could do for us. You get assurance from Carleton that our property'll be safe, an' we won't have a dribble of customers; we'll have a flood."

"Christ's stepfather!" Allen shouted, his face twisted by what Adam believed was honest affront. "Your mind is lower than a bug's belly. It is my purpose to serve The Grants, you mercenary poop; not to make profits for you."

"And you," Ira amended composedly. "Don't see ye scornin' any."

"Now, had I not so high a respect for our mother," Ethan informed Adam, "I would swear that she smiled once too often on a Connecticut peddler nine months before Stub was born."

"What bought ye that big white stud that'll kill ye yet?" his brother inquired. "Two Burlington shares that wa'n't worth a pistole, this time last year."

"Kill me, eh? I'll ride him north, gentle as a lamb. That's a Narragansett horse; a superior animal and you know it."

Adam was weary of bickering and surfeited, too, with Ethan's praise of his new stallion. He offered aridly, "We should leave by Tuesday if we are to reach Lake Sainte Catherine on time."

"True," Allen cried, "and I already have planned who is to accompany me: You and Stub, who needs enlightenment in the procedures of statesmanship, and Baker, even though he will dress like a squaw-diddling woodsrunner—"

"It was urged for secrecy's sake," Adam intruded, "that the party be small."

"And I shall limit it. Rob Cochran is the only other."

"Shall I wear my uniform?," Ethan went on hopefully, but when both Ira and Adam shook their heads, announced, "I must at least take a packhorse with provisions and ingredients for a proper punch."

The departure from Fay's tavern was not attended, Adam saw with amused despair, by the concealment Wadman and Feltham had recommended. The stallion squealed and reared; his rider bawled commands and the led horse, infected by the excitement, bucked until his burden gurgled. Ethan led the company out at last, loudly explaining to onlookers that they were off on a deer hunt.

The white stud set so sharp a pace that, contrary to Adam's expectations, they reached the trysting place the morning of the appointed day. Wadman and Feltham were not there. Cochran and Baker rode on with the baggage animal to Heber's empty house in Poultney. The others picketed their horses in a swale above the water and sought an elm's shade.

Ethan lay prone, a basking monster in butternut homespun; Adam settled down with his back against a boulder but Ira prowled about, considering the land with calculating eyes, pacing off the open space, estimating the surrounding trees, and stooping now and then to sample and taste a pinch of the soil.

The sky hung close. A breeze ran fitfully along the forest-bordered glade and rippled the sere grasses. They were the hue, Adam thought, of Delight's hair. In only a few days now, he would see her again.

His mind continually had swung, since the hour he had left her, from despair that his moment of enlightenment should have ended so emptily, to rage at the stupidity that so long had kept him blind. Delight was, he thought solemnly, nursing his knees and watching the shimmering grasses, all that a man could hope of woman, and more—tender and fair, gentle and understanding.

Adam damned himself once more for the irresolution that had let him ride away empty-handed. He had been so dazed by the sudden illumination that he could not tell, even now, whether Delight had seen its faintest glimmer. Once she had loved him. He had clung briefly to that assurance and then, remembering it had been Felicity who had said so, had rejected it.

Here, in the quiet glade, he could see Delight by the stable door, milk pails in hand. Whatever had transformed her face, whether it had been expectation or pity, understanding, he knew, had been part of it. Understanding was a certainty in Delight.

Ira returned to lie, plump as a basking seal, beside his brother. His dry voice granted that the land was sightly but worth little, poor soil that would scarcely repay the cost of survey. Ethan responded with indifferent grunts. The white stallion and his dark companions grazed uphill among the waving grasses. Insects sang thinly when the fitful wind died and Adam could hear in the distance small waves unrolling upon gravel.

The world was a fairer place because Delight dwelt there. His own life, whatever her feeling for him, was richer for her presence.

Baker and Cochran came back, reporting the house opened, provisioned, and ready for guests. Remember broiled salt pork which they ate with their journeycake. When the meal was over and the elm's shadow stretched eastward, they did not follow it but let the sun melt the stiffness of the long ride from their bodies. Only Ethan withstood the somnolent spell. He grew restless and demanded at last, "What in the seven levels of hell has become of them?"

"Lost, most likely," Baker droned.

"Lost? On the road from Panton?"

"Seen as many Britishers as me in the French wars, ye'd know a regiment could git lost in a three-acre woods."

Cochran gave a hawking, scornful sound. The sun sowed sparks in his cropped red hair. Ethan, lying prone with his chin on folded arms, said in a voice from which the heat had wilted a measure of its vehemence, "Cursed from cradle to coffin. In England some soft-handed superior forever leads them. God damn all kings, princes, lords, governors, and their fat-livered like."

Ira raised himself on an elbow.

"Figger on recitin' that piece to Carleton's folks?"

"It'll be dinned in their ears, soon or late," Ethan retorted with more vigor. "A new breed is coming out of Grants' beds. Babes who learn as they toddle to find their own way will throw pups who in turn will own themselves and to hell with all rulers."

"Git it all off your stomach before your guests come," Ira counseled, welcoming in idleness the diversion of another dispute. "Start rantin' at them an'—"

"And we may loose our property," Ethan mimicked his brother's twanging speech. "By the whiskers of Jehovah, I'd yield every acre if The Grants might be free of York and British troubles for a generation."

"Under Ethan Allen," Ira supplemented sarcastically, "monarch by the grace of God—"

The quickening voice rolled over his. "Under none and above none; each man, white or black, red or blue, owning his property and himself; hard men, bold men, free men, by God."

"But," Ira nagged, "a mite deficient in government, wouldn't ye say?"

"The best government is the least government," Ethan Allen replied. "It is in my mind that, potentate or prince, convention or congress, no government should do for men what they decently can do for themselves."

The sunlight drugged them all. The little wind failed and the insect voices clamored. Above them on the slope, the white stallion screamed, standing with tether taut, tail and neck arched, muzzle proudly lifted. His companions continued to graze, unheeding. The stallion stamped and screamed again.

"Now if it be," Ethan said drowsily, "that the dead come back, it would be my wish to return as a white stud, ranging Grants' hillsides in the summertime."

Adam found solemnity in the profession, but Ira jeered, "With a herd of likely fillies—"

Remember who had lain with his head canted, slapped the earth sharply with his palm.

"Hush," he bade and after a pause said briskly, "Yes b'God. They're comin' at last."

In the silence Adam finally heard the sharp, faint sound of metal on stone.

"That ain't the way from Panton," Remember chuckled. "Got themselves lost, like I said."

The other horses had turned to stand with lifted heads. The stallion whickered and trotted about his picket pin. Adam, scrambling up, went forward to meet the drooping figures in deerskin who rode down into the glade.

Wadman's teeth shone in a grin of relief that Feltham's babbling interpreted. They had missed the proper trail and had ridden too far east and, when set aright by a traveler, had cut across country to the lake.

"Your horses are spent," Adam said, noticing the lathered girths and pulsing flanks.

"We hastened," said Wadman briefly but Feltham implored:

"Pity us, sir, rather than our creatures. Scourge me, sir, if after this I ever accept transfer to a horse regiment."

He continued to chatter as Adam let them toward the group that waited by the elm.

The wind that had come out of the north before sunset blew so keenly that those in the long, low kitchen of Heber Allen's lonely house were grateful for the fire. Ethan, returning with the emissaries from the front chamber where they had been closeted, proclaimed that supper should be accompanied, not by punch but warming flip.

His manner, the trumpet note in his speech as he himself brewed the draught in a battered pewter bowl, employing a heated poker for lack of a loggerhead, revealed his satisfaction in the outcome of the conference. Flip increased his elation. He glowed, he beamed, and by waxing voice power abolished the rigidity his own companions had assumed and the British visitors had abetted.

None of the formality that lately had chilled the company now remained. Adam, receiving the bowl from Baker, drank, passed it to Ira at the table's end and leaned back, warmed as this latest draught took hold by a catholic fondness for all his companions.

He surveyed approvingly the faces the twin candles' light lifted out of the shadows. Ethan was a jovially smoldering mass at the board's far end with Wadman beaming darkly on his right and Feltham holding his sides in laughter on the other hand. Beside Adam Remember Baker was mumbling genially to himself, and across the table Cochran gravely beat time for his own inaudible song. Adam felt fondness for them all, even for Ira, sitting composed and watchful like a woodchuck before its burrow. They were good comrades, except Feltham with his shrill voice and distracted, rabbity air.

Wadman caught Adam's eye, smiled, bowed, and toasted him. Feltham, receiving the depleted bowl from Ethan, reeled slightly as he raised it and made only a pretense of drinking. A belated precaution, Adam thought with amusement, and leaned over to mutter in Baker's ear, "Your neighbor won't be with us much longer."

Remember squinted, as though trying to see a dim importance, discerned it, and demanded in a low, blurred voice, "Where was they for God's sake? Tell me that?"

"Who?"

"Airs 'n' Graces here 'n' his mate yonder."

"Trying to find us," Adam replied patiently. "They left Panton only yesterday morning."

"They left day 'fore yest'dy," Baker retorted, dropping his voice still lower. "Feltham let that out a while ago. Where they been, I say? Could crawl here from Panton in two days."

"They probably got lost oftener than they'll admit. You said the British had a gift for it."

Remember, face hidden by the bowl, gave a gurgling snort. Adam barely wet his mouth with the dregs of the flip. Baker's chronic suspicion irked him. If Wadman and Feltham had started their journey, not one but two days earlier, obviously they had been retarded by some blunder too glaring for them to confess.

His irritation rose when Remember gripped his knee sharply. "Hark!"

316

Ira had twisted about to stare toward the door. Wadman and Feltham looked doubtfully at him and then at each other. For an instant, in the still kitchen, Cochran's low chanting droned like bagpipes.

"Now by all the powers of darkness," Ethan demanded with enormous sarcasm, "what ails you, Stub? Be the Philistines upon you?"

Ira's liquid eyes were unabashed. He told his brother quietly, "Something moved beyond the door."

"A horrendous quill pig? Gird ye, Samson, and go forth to combat. Perhaps it was a bloodthirsty deer."

"Oh, if it was a dear," Feltham cackled, beating upon the table in rapture, "by all means seize her and bring her in. All that we lack is a dear for each of us, eh, Colonel?"

Baker had relaxed and was mumbling to himself. Ira listened an instant longer and seemed reassured. His brother had risen to loom above them all.

"A toast," he bellowed, "that all true men can drink whatever their politics. Rob, cease your braying and use your long ears. To—"

He stared into the bowl with dismay.

"Here is no proper draught. Adam, like a good lad, brew more flip."

A kettle still hung above the crumbling embers and the poker lay among the coals. On a bench stood a small rum cask, maple sugar, a flask of vinegar, and a jug of cider brandy. Adam, accepting the bowl from Allen, bent to his task.

His head swam. The noise at the table—Ethan's rumbling voice, Cochran's defiant singing, Feltham's wild laughter—confused him. He assembled the ingredients with intense care, lifted the kettle from the crane, measured hot water into the mixture, and, poker in hand, paused.

Something had hung in the night just beyond the small-paned window and now was gone—a pale, oval something that could have been only a human face.

The darkly shining glass was blank. Could drink have tricked his eyes? Adam hesitated, unwilling to risk Ethan's derision, yet his alarm grew and, with it, certainty that he had seen a dim face peer in and melt away, like maple sugar in flip.

Ethan was roaring with laughter and Wadman's dark face grinned. At a single loud knock upon the door, the lieutenant half rose and with a quick double motion blew out both candles.

In darkness that stunned him, Adam heard the door slam inward, yelling, and the rush of many feet.

The crimson oblong that wavered in the void was the heated end of the poker. This was the first certainty his overthrown mind regained.

Faint light from the dying fire scarcely reached beyond the hearth. In the blackness, voices howled and trampling shook the room. Above the din Ethan's bellow rose. A high screech soared and abruptly ended in a crash and the chime of falling glass.

Air puffed against Adam's cheek and a missile, smacking the fireplace behind him, peppered him with fragments. He leaped out of the light, felt hot liquid drench his feet as the bowl overturned, and stood at last with the wall's firm pressure across his shoulders.

Here, momentarily, he was free from the blind violence that boiled in the kitchen; the whooping, the crash of falling chairs, and, dominating the tumult, Ethan's enduring roar.

A blurred, paler oblong against the darkness was the open doorway. Blacknesses that reeled across it was grappling men. Out of the uproar, Adam now found himself able to fish a single word.

"Yield!" the invaders were crying. "Yield!"

Adam's respite ended. The thing that clawed across his face was, he knew, a hooked and groping hand.

"York?" a voice bawled so close to his ear that he flinched. Arms, savagely clamped, pinned his own. A boot, hard swung, kicked his feet from under him. . . .

Sound rose and fell like a fitful wind. The emptiness in Adam's head faded; the anguish in his throat increased. The throttling fingers burrowed deeper. He gripped bony wrists and wrenched.

"Yield!" his captor screeched and, when Adam still resisted, drew his head up and smacked it down upon the floor. The blow set off an explosion in his skull. Strength went from him; the avid hands squeezed tighter.

"Yield," the harsh voice bade again.

318

Adam was drifting into darkness filled with tendrils and whorls of flame. His hands fell away from the iron wrists and metal burned his palm. He was melting like the face at the window, but the poker was in his fist. Through the false fire, he saw a cherry-red point stir and rise.

"Yield," his tormentor cried once more from far away.

Adam's free hand found the merciless wrists. His other pressed the poker's tip against them.

His throat was free. Inrushing air scored his lungs. He jabbed his weapon at the body still covering his. It wailed and vanished. A black wave broke and rolled over him. . . .

Adam sat by the table in the disrupted kitchen. The candlelight hurt his eyes. He could hear the words his friends spoke but his mind no longer could link them into coherence. Baker, his face battered and his torn shirt falling away from his furred chest, grinned down at him and asked, "All right?"

"All right."

Baker accepted the echo for reassurance.

"No idea who any of 'em was? Not even him you burned?"

Clearly, these were questions but Adam could not understand them. Baker, still garrulous with excitement, rattled on:

No one yet knew the identity of the raiders. In the darkness, they had shouted "York?" and, lacking response, had grappled. Remember had struggled with two but had got free by jamming his thumb into the eye of one and his knee into the crotch of the other. Wadman and Feltham, when the lights had gone out, had leaped upon Ethan Allen who deftly had stunned them by cracking their heads together. They had been still senseless when the invaders had fled.

"Poured water on 'em both," Remember said with relish. "Now Ethan 'n' Ira's questionin' 'em in t'other room. Maybe they'll larn something."

"Learn something," Adam repeated with difficulty.

Cochran limped around the table, a tin cup in hand.

"Laddie," said he, "ye're still dazed. This'll revive ye."

The rum burned Adam's abused throat and made him cough. He thrust the cup aside.

"Rob, here," Baker said loudly, "might have fared worse 'n'

you. Nigh kidnapped him, but he broke free when the rest of 'em fled. You burned one of 'em. Ethan threw another square through the window."

He grinned toward the ruin of splintered glass and dangling sash.

"That Ethan!" he said in admiration. "Must ha' been a dozen of 'em."

Adam wished the incomprehensible talk would cease. The door of the front room burst open. Ethan strode into the kitchen, thunderously raging. Ira, following, carefully closed the portal behind him.

"Now may God condemn me," the giant implored, "to some other hell than that reserved for the British army. No," he bawled, forestalling Baker's question, "they won't tell who their accomplices were or from where. They admit they plotted with certain others to gull and take me and that"—his face grew redder still—"the tale of General Carleton and his wish to confer with me was bait, nothing more. Christ's sweat! A pretty enterprise for gentlemen who are so choice of their honor."

He snatched up the jug, rested it on a crooked elbow, and decanted it into himself, as though to wash away a foul taste. Ira, watching him, said dryly, "Forget, don't ye, that ye're outlawed; fair game for all? I'm the only one," he pursued with complacence, "not worth taking. Rest of ye'd bring a total of three hundred pounds, delivered in Albany."

"Wherefore, you did not resist," his brother sneered, "but hid beneath the table."

"Calmer there," Ira answered, unabashed. He paused an instant and then prodded Ethan, "Wal, what now?"

"What now? What short of hanging, for gentlemen who deem it beneath their honor to reveal their fellow kidnappers?"

"Mebby Sherwood had a hand in it," Ira suggested hopefully. Ethan shook his head.

"No. Both swear he knew nothing. They'll tell who didn't, but not who did."

"They can hear your every word," Ira said, tipping his head toward the closed door. "Best move 'em while we debate."

"I'd already resolved on that," Ethan snapped. "Rob, you and

Remember and me best carry General Carleton's high and mighty agents"—his mouth twisted over the sarcasm—"outside. They're trussed reasonably tight. Maybe a night in the privy will loose their tongues."

The scrape and shuffle of burdened footsteps sounded in the hall. Ira sat still, mouth unduly tight with calculation, eyes fixed dreamily upon Adam, who had folded his arms on the table and had laid his empty head upon them. Cochran, returning, nodded toward him.

"Let me wield that hot poker of his for a spell," he proposed hopefully, "and I swear they'll talk."

"Once more, in the morning," Allen promised, "I'll offer them freedom if they confess. Otherwise, Satan torment me through all eternity if I am not inclined to hang them both."

"Plenty of rope," Cochran acclaimed, his hard face lighting. "And a stout maple beyond the privy. Marked it just now."

Ira said quietly, "You can't do that."

He endured his brother's glare and pursued, "Never yet killed an offender. Been your boast, eh, Ethan? Hang two officers and where d'ye think the British army'll be? Not far behind us, however fast and far we run. Haven't you enough enemies now?"

"Then on this I am resolved," Ethan thundered. "If the rascals remain silent, they shall be taken to Bennington, there tried by our laws, and flogged at the public whipping post."

Cochran and Baker murmured assent but Ira said again, "You can't do that, either. Flogging," he went on smoothly, "would insult officers worse than a hanging."

He endured their indignation and seemed pleased with himself. Baker asked, "Release 'em, kiss 'em, 'n' send 'em home with thanks? That your idee?"

"If ye must have a hangin'," Ira informed him, "I propose we hang Rob to that maple he praises."

He looked with enjoyment from one to the other of the wrathful faces before him.

"Now," he said, drawing out his satisfaction to the utmost, "if the kidnapping gentry remain silent in the morning, we separate them. Thereafter, we inform each that we have voted him free but that his companion must hang."

He paused. Cochran still glared in bewilderment and Baker scowled, but Ethan's mind had seized the plan and his eyes were kindling.

"By God!" he said almost reverently.

"Ehyah," Ira grinned and preened himself. "We put a rope under Rob's arms and over a limb and haul him up. We then set Feltham free, bidding him hasten to Ti on peril of his life. From a distance, he sees Rob at half-mast and deems it is Wadman. An hour later, we elevate Rob again and in the same fashion release Wadman. He rushes to Ti, believing that Feltham has been hanged."

"And the two reputed corpses meet at the fort!" Ethan snatched the explanation away from him. "Each has been proclaiming the other's murder. Ira, you devil incarnate—"

He smote the table and guffawed.

"The garrison," he gasped, "will split its sides. The jest will run through The Grants. Eh, Rob? Eh, Remember? Eh, Adam?"

But Adam did not stir and, when Ethan clapped his shoulder to rouse him, tipped over and slid gently to the floor.

Chapter XXXV

WIND among leaves made a pleasant sound, soothing Adam's dim memories of pain and heat and jolting movement, of ghastly recurrent nausea. It was good to lie, knowing dimly that these miseries had passed, and to be lulled by the wind.

It would be unwise to open his eyes lest, with sight, the late, confused anguish return. Adam lay a long while between sleep and waking, steeping himself in the blessed consciousness of safety.

He cringed at the sound of heavy feet that moved toward him with a vain attempt at stealth. Could this be the late malignance, blurred yet terrible, returning with fresh torment? With great caution, he raised his eyelids.

Sunlight struck rainbows from his lashes and through their dazzle he discerned a shadowy, looming figure close at hand.

"Adam?" Ethan Allen's voice ventured with unwonted gentleness.

Greatly comforted, Adam closed his eyes. It was too sore an effort to reply but he tried to smile and slept once more.

It was dark when he woke, yet he knew in some unperceived fashion that he lay in his own room at Fay's tavern and that, truly, his ordeal was ended, though the broken memories gave him no understanding of its whole.

His hands felt sharp and thin as the framework of a fan. For an alarmed instant, he thought of claws that somewhere, somehow, had dug into his neck. His fingers were so fragile because he had been ill. Food would restore them. He found that he was hungry. That was a good sign. He sighed and fell asleep.

Sunlight painted the room again but it was not Ethan who bent above him now. Dr. Fay's firm brown fingers were fast upon his wrist. Adam was dismayed to see how like a peeled stick his own forearm seemed and was puzzled by black marks upon the shrunken flesh.

"Well!" Fay released his hold and smiled as he pulled up the blankets. "You fooled me."

"What—happened?", Adam whispered.

"That'll keep," the physician told him briskly. "Think you could manage a spoonful of broth with a drop of rum stirred in?"

"A joint," the other murmured. "Underdone."

"All in good time. I'll fetch broth now."

Jonas sat on the bed's edge, spooning a nectar whose sole defect was its scarcity. Adam could feel parched tissues sponge up the strong, hot liquid and send it through his body. He licked his lips and was startled.

"How long," he managed to ask, fingering the beard stubble, "have I been here?"

"A fortnight tomorrow," the doctor said and smiled. "Didn't judge when they hauled you out of the straw in Abe Jackson's cart that you'd last so long. Fever, delirium, severe concussion that I thought was a fracture."

"I'm grateful."

"No cause to be. Guess you were too obstinate to die, though I did spend on you most of what I've learned, short of amputation. Bled you"—Fay ran a finger over the black marks on Adam's forearm—"blistered, purged, clystered, and drenched. Maybe it's a miracle you survived."

Adam, with an effort, lifted his drooping eyelids.

"When can I get up?"

"Go to sleep," Fay bade. "That is still a long way off."

A sharp recollection brought Adam fully awake that night but he still was too deep in exhaustion for it to trouble him greatly. Whatever the delay before he could return to the Roydens, Delight, he was sure, would wait. He heard solid snoring in the next room. Voices were loud in the road below as the last of the taproom's patrons departed. Peace and sustenance more reviving than another bowl of broth lay in thought of Delight.

He was so refreshed next morning that Fay, who had driven Allen from the room on the previous day, relented and admitted him. His voice shook the chamber: "By Jesus, Lazarus, and Jairus' daughter, Adam! I would not have wagered a half joe, two weeks past, that I ever should talk to you again in the flesh."

The invigoration of a high wind accompanied him as he strode about the chamber and told to still another new audience and with undiminished relish the outcome of the ruse inflicted, by Ira's prescription, on Wadman and Feltham.

Each had been told that the other must hang. Each, upon his own release had been permitted a distant glimpse of Cochran, dangling from the maple and swearing proficiently beneath his breath.

"This lackadaisical popinjay, this Feltham, wept consumedly when we drove him forth, bidding him hasten to Ti and spare not. Wadman cursed us when we served him likewise and swore we all should hang in due course. Gods of the Mountains! I would willingly have paid the price on my head to have been at the fort when the pair arrived to find each other alive and unharmed."

When he had done with laughter, Allen pieced together for Adam the interval that his memory still refused to span. He had been half senseless, stirring only to vomit. They had fashioned under Baker's direction a litter for two horses to bear and on this had brought the stricken man over the hills and down to Deacon Abraham Jackson's clearing in the town of Wallingford.

There, since Adam had begun to rave and it had become increasingly difficult to hold him in the litter, they had borrowed the Deacon's oxcart, had contrived a harness, pole, and neck-yokes and, employing the horses Wadman and Feltham had ridden, had hurried on to Bennington and Dr. Fay's ministrations.

"And thereby saved my life," Adam completed.

"After imperiling it in a wild-goose chase," Allen retorted and, by the rush of crimson to the fierce face, Adam knew the lieutenants' imposture still galled. Ethan asked hopefully, "You have no suspicion who their accomplices may have been?"

"Only that one has hands like talons and a burned wrist," Adam returned at last. Allen tossed his head in despair.

"We can't learn who they were. I should have sworn there were not a dozen in The Grants who could keep a secret so straitly."

He squinted at the ill man and got up suddenly.

"I have wearied you," Ethan said with uncommon penitence, "and I promised Jonas I would not."

The room shook as he left it on tiptoe.

The maple tree beyond the window wore a tentative splash of scarlet and the hearth fire decreed by Dr. Fay to counteract the noxious vapors of illness had become more endurable. Adam, though still fretting over the slowness of his recovery, was able to sit up in bed without dizziness when, one day toward sunset, Allen stormed into the room.

The convalescent guessed that he bore further news from Philadelphia. The proceedings of the Continental Congress there already had profoundly excited Ethan but now he shouted, "Justus Sherwood is here and wishes to see you," and, giving Adam no opportunity to assent, rushed on, "He has ridden posthaste from New Haven solely to assure me that he had no part in Wadman's and Feltham's damnable machinations. A needless mission, for I deemed him guiltless, yet a gracious."

Allen scowled and shook his head.

"Sherwood, Adam, opposes much that I most earnestly uphold, yet I find myself unable to hate him as I should."

Traces of the indignation with which he already had protested his innocence still marked Justus Sherwood when he sat down at the bedside. His jaw was set, his voice crisp.

" 'Tis a bitter return for hospitality by those I presumed were officers and gentlemen."

He smiled apology for his vehemence and went on with weary humor, "When rogues are so plentiful, it should not affront me, I suppose, to discover them even in His Majesty's uniform. It is no thanks to Leftenants"—he adorned the title with irony—"Wadman and Feltham that they did not kill you. I wish I could discover who their fellow ruffians were."

He drew breath and pursued in a low voice more impressive than bluster, "Of this much I am sure: I have no knowledge how far Leftenant Wadman has engaged Felicity's favor, but I am resolved no sister of mine shall wed a man so lacking in principle. I should rather see her the bride of Olin Royden, despite his politics."

Adam asked and wondered at his indifference, "You are not certain where her affections lie?"

The warmth and pride with which Sherwood always spoke of his sister were in his smile, "I should hazard they extend over The Grants and Canada and rest most heavily on all personable males Felicity can bring to heel."

His mouth turned grim, his eyes severe: "I have been indulgent with her, unduly perhaps, remembering that my own mother was wed against her choice and the unhappiness this brought. When she and then my father died, leaving Felicity a child for me to rear, I vowed that she should have the gaiety and freedom our mother was denied. I shall never tell her whom she must wed. I can and will instruct her whom she may not."

He looked alarmed, then abashed, as though his tongue had run away with him and smiled at Adam again in half apology.

"That is more than I have told anyone of me and mine, my friend, since first I came to The Grants. I should not have confided, even in you, if Allen's account of the hoax and the brawl had not so deeply shocked me. Felicity shall learn my will the instant I return."

Adam swallowed the impulse to ask how far the girl would obey her brother and said, instead, "She did not come with you, then?"

"No, I left her with the Roydens, for I rode in haste."

The question the bedridden man repeatedly had asked himself was difficult to utter now. He inquired at last with what unconcern he could assume, "Delight, I suppose, has gone to Ticonderoga?"

"No," Sherwood replied, "she is still at home and, when I saw her, more interested in the barnraising the Pangbornes plan than in a journey to the fort."

Adam lay back upon his pillow. The depth of the sudden peace made him aware how great had been his anxiety. It would be easier to endure his invalid state, it would be a happier enterprise to get well, now that he knew Delight still waited at his trial's end.

"Do not think," Sherwood pursued, worrying his grievance like an angry dog, "that I shall let the matter of Wadman's and Feltham's misbehavior rest. I intend to go to Quebec straightway and lay the affair before Governor Carleton himself."

Adam looked at the rigid, hard-breathing figure an instant before he said dryly, "You forget The Bloody Law. It is no crime; in fact, it is an estimable enterprise, to hunt down outlaws like Ethan, Cochran, Remember, and me."

"Nevertheless," Sherwood persisted, "I shall go. It is an offense to use the royal governor's name as a bait and so, I hope, General Carleton may deem it."

He rubbed his forehead and there was weariness in his voice: "At a time when loyalty is becoming a crime and the damned Philadelphia Congress is accusing the British of all the sins in the Decalogue, it is no small thing to have even the least of the king's officers merit condemnation."

He misunderstood the look on Adam's face and rose quickly.

"I'm tiring you," Sherwood said with an apologetic smile. "Have you any word for me to carry north with me tomorrow?"

"I was thinking of that," Adam explained and, after hesitation, ventured, "I should like to write a message to Delight."

He felt his face grow warm.

"I think that could be managed," Sherwood assured him gravely and turned toward the littered desk to hide the amusement in his eyes.

It was difficult, Adam discovered, to write, half prostrate, with only his knee for a desk. It was harder to compose a love letter to a girl still unwooed. He scribbled at last, in desperation, while Sherwood looked intently through the window:

"Justus who will bear this to you, will tell you of my Plight. I wish I might ride north with him. As soon as may be I shall come to beg your Forgiveness for so much of Vanity and Madness, to implore you to let me be what, despite Illfortune and Thwarting, Blindness and great deserved Distress, I know now that I have been in Verity since my Birth: Your humble and devoted Adam."

He was truly weary when he had folded the page and surrendered it to Sherwood who bore ink, pen, and paper away and, igniting a splinter at the hearth, sealed the letter with wax.

"You have not addressed it," he said mildly.

"There is no need," Adam returned, flexing his stiff fingers, "since you will bear it."

He grew red at a memory and more fiery still when he saw that his friend was sharing it.

328

"In the matter of letters," he said awkwardly, "I have far more reason to trust you, Justus, than you me."

Sherwood laughed as he moved toward the door.

"Rest now, Adam. We shall hope for you soon in the north."

Adam, waking before sunrise, heard Justus ride away. The hoofbeats quickened his own heart. Knowledge that his message to Delight moved toward her restored a measure of yesterday's relief and peace.

He scorned himself for his late fretting. He need never have doubted Delight. Wrought of patience and faith, she would wait for him when his letter had reached her, constant as a star. Thought of her seemed to spread her own clear radiance about him.

If Delight in truth loved him, and surely her continued presence in Panton warranted his hope, no worship he could accord her could repay her trust, could atone for his own infatuated disregard. Through all the years ahead, he thought with reverence, his spirit must kneel before Delight.

The new strength and courage remained with him all day. On the morrow, it let him endure, unwearied, a visit from Ethan and Ira Allen and the usual consequent brawl, Ethan professing to discern in the meeting of Congress the flush of millennial dawn, Ira decrying its effect on land values in The Grants.

Adam sat up briefly the next day and Allen, entering and finding him chaired, spoke hopefully of resuming work upon the book.

"I have in mind, Adam-boy, a chapter so excoriating to the pretensions of York that Colden and his accomplices will wail for mercy, while the gentry of the Honorable Continental Congress will cease to consider only British outrages against liberty."

"Before all else, when I am able to mount a horse again, I must go north," Adam said firmly. Allen's explosive objections that gave way to outright pleading failed to shake him. Ethan went away at last, still grumbling. Adam smiled as he wavered back to bed, strengthened by the belief that even now Sherwood might be delivering his letter to Delight.

Chapter XXXVI

FELICITY SHERWOOD watched her brother dismount before the Roydens' door. Her heart's violence filled her throat and wet her palms, yet her face and her voice were clear as she said, almost gaily, "I felt sure you would be back to-day, so I stayed as housewife while the others went to the barn-raising."

Justus's smile was so slight that her alarm grew. She did not try to evade the danger, but pressed forward to meet it.

"What did you learn, brother?"

His eyes that had brightened unwillingly at the fair sight of her grew dull.

"Much. The truth is worse than the tale we heard."

He recited grimly the story of the conspiracy, of the night assault and Adam's injury, of the brutal deception imposed on Wadman and Feltham. Felicity listened with wary composure.

"This," Justus ended savagely, "is the jest at which the whole land is laughing. I can find no mirth in it. Two officers are made welcome in our home. They hoodwink me, conspire beneath my roof, and with accomplices descend to the violence I have ever deplored. You have strange friends, Felicity."

"But," she objected, wide-eyed, "they are your friends, too. I don't understand your anger. Haven't you railed against the self-styled Colonel Allen and his fellow bandits? Aren't they all outlaws, even Adam Corlaer?"

"Felicity," her brother bade in acid amusement, "stop acting the innocent. I have lived with that guileless look too long to be impressed by it."

His comment roused her easy laughter. His hard voice checked it.

"You know as well as I that for officers and reputed gentlemen to hatch in their host's house a plot that endangers him and lays him open to reprisal is a shameful thing. They have comported themselves not like soldiers but like raiding Mohawks or thief-takers who trap men for hire."

The girl observed his disgust a long instant before she said penitently, "I'm certain they never saw it in that light, and neither, till now, had I. It seemed to George and Jocelyn only a gallant adventure, a gay escapade. They—"

She grew aware of his look and her speech failed. Sherwood asked slowly, "Then you knew what they planned?"

"Oh, no," she said in haste. "Oh, no, Justus, indeed no. That is, only a very little. If they did confide in me a trifle, what could I do, brother, but keep the small secret they had entrusted?"

Sherwood's movement jerked so sharply on the bridle rein that his weary horse flinched.

"It was wrong of me," Felicity hurried on. "I see that now, but then it seemed only a high-spirited prank. I'm truly sorry, Justus."

"Who were the other men—Wadman's and Feltham's accomplices?"

"I don't know. Indeed I don't. Believe me, brother. They never were even mentioned."

It troubled her to see her contrition had only half convinced him. Sherwood stood for a still moment before he said more to himself than to her, "It is my own fault. I have indulged you too much."

She was on familiar ground now. She tried to lead him further.

"I know, brother. I am worldly and vain and so many wicked things, but I never mean to distress you. You are too good to me. No maid ever had a—"

"I have curbed your amusements less than a responsible guardian should. I have wanted happiness for you. Now, I am telling you my will: You will encourage Leftenant Wadman no more, Felicity, granting that you encounter him again. I shall never permit you to wed him."

He saw her cheeks flame and prepared for a storm that did not

break. Her mind, as always, was fleeter than his. She said with uncommon meekness, "Yes, Justus."

The victory was so easy that he distrusted it and pressed on, "I
have told you I never should oppose your choice, provided he
was a man of honor. I say so again."

"Yes, Justus."

Her ready submission baffled and irritated him. He pursued still
more severely, "You no longer are a child, though I and all other
men still contrive to spoil you. A woman has duties to match her
privileges. I have thought much on my journey from Bennington
of Adam Corlaer and of my onetime hope that he would wed
you."

Felicity caught her lower lip in her teeth.

"I have wondered, too," her brother went on, "how much your
vanity and trifling brought him to his present plight. He is still my
warm and valued friend, Felicity. I do not think he is yours."

Her face for an instant had gone white, but her recovery was
swift and her laugh flawlessly fond.

"Justus, I beg you, have done with mournful preachings, like
—like the Reverend Hough. Put your horse away, dear brother,
and let your penitent congregation feed you. You're tired, poor
man."

"I am, and not from travel alone."

He paused, uncertainly, flicking his open palm with the rein's
end.

"When," he asked, "do the Roydens return?"

"Soon, I should think. I am cooking supper now."

"I must ride to New Haven," Sherwood said with weary decision, "get a change of clothing, and then go on to Quebec."

"Quebec? And am I not to accompany you?"

He shook his head with decision.

"You will stay here, or with the Everests if your presence dis-
commodes the Roydens, until my return."

"I am to be punished then?" she asked with an edge to her
voice.

"No," he said with dry humor. "It is too late for punishment,
though it still might benefit you. I am not pleasure bound, Felicity, and shall travel fast."

He braced himself for argument and, surprised when it did not come, slipped the rein over one arm and held out his hands to her.

"Goodbye, sister, and take what I said to heart."

"I know what a trial I am to you, Justus," she murmured as he kissed her forehead. Sherwood pinched her cheek softly.

"A better guardian," he told her, "would have birched you oftener."

He climbed stiffly into the saddle.

"My greetings to the Roydens. Oh—" He was smitten by recollection as he gathered up his rein and, releasing it, twisted about to unlatch a saddlebag. "Here is a letter for Delight. Do not fail to deliver it."

Felicity stood with the missive in her hands and watched her brother out of sight before she stamped her foot with a shrill little moan. There was plentiful fuel for the rage that flamed in her.

She was angry with herself for revealing even so little of all that George Wadman had confided, and with Justus for his parental airs and pompous commands. She was revolted by the prospect of further imprisonment here. Delight's serenity, Mindwell's earthy candor, and the arrogant courting of Olin were insipid substitutes for her late association with young men of spirit and fashion. Her brother's reproachful citation of Adam had been the final affront.

It was like Justus to bleat mournfully over the one man who had presumed to flout and defy her; against whom she had declared enduring enmity. Felicity stamped her foot again and the rush of her anger wavered and was checked. She stared, as though she never had seen it before, at the letter she held. Justus had told her it was for Delight, yet it bore no address. She was dashed, when she turned it over, to find it uncompromisingly sealed.

She laid the letter on the kitchen table, served the fire, and turned about to stare again at the blank oblong. Who else but Adam Corlaer could be writing to Delight? Why, in his illness, should he be sending a message to her, unless the taunt Felicity had cast in their final quarrel were fantastically true; unless having thrown her, the irresistible Felicity Sherwood, aside, he were turning now for comfort to milky-mild little Delight?

The possibility was tormenting. Ignorance of the letter's contents was harder to suffer than any possible fact it might disclose. Felicity ran her thumb over the waxen spot, but the seal was tight.

333

She pressed upon it. A chip flew off and her nail gashed a small tear in the paper.

She thought with relief that she was past withdrawal, now. Her face was hot and throbbing. It would be plain, even to Delight, that she had tampered with the letter. It was better, then, to open it completely.

Pride in her acumen was Felicity's first thought when she had finished reading. The message was precisely what her intuition had whispered it would be. The lover who had rejected her— though only an instant before she had intended to discard him— had taken her warning lightly. This justified her in whatever reprisal she now might launch.

She reread Adam's scrawl, moved purposefully toward the fire, and halted. Mere burning of the letter would be a dull revenge. Her eyes sparkled as she reflected how she could most resourcefully employ the weapon her enemy had put into her hands by failing to address his message. She gave a blithe laugh as she thrust the letter into her bosom.

Felicity was more than ordinarily gay when the Roydens returned from the barnraising, Mindwell and Delight weary, and Olin slightly blurred. She admired the deftness with which she told of Sherwood's return, softening his tale of the kidnapping attempt, dealing lightly with Adam's mishap, casting over the whole an air of triviality.

She was winsomely grateful when Mindwell and Olin said how welcome she was to stay till Justus's return and was still more encouraged by sight of Delight, sitting white and silent during supper.

When Felicity and she had entered the bedroom they shared, Delight asked in a taut voice, "You're sure he is all right? Justus said so?"

"Right?" Felicity echoed with bewilderment. "Who, child?"

Beyond the tallow dip's small flame, Delight's distress was so candid, so childlike that the other felt mild disappointment at the ease of her task.

"Who?" Delight said as though the question were ridiculous. "Who else but Adam?"

334

She was, Felicity thought, rather attractive in her anxiety, with eyes great and dark in her pallid face.

"Dee, my dear, it is silly to worry. If Adam is well enough to write me a letter, he surely is not perishing."

"A letter?" Delight asked with an odd mingling of relief and dismay. "Did he, truly?"

"Indeed, he did." Felicity withdrew it from her bodice.

"Oh!" said Delight.

Her roommate laid the message upon the table beside the dip and sat on the bed to pull off her slippers. Delight's small, worn hands strove with each other.

"Adam, my sweet," Felicity said idly, "isn't worth concern. Men are strange, Dee, as you too will discover. They all are so certain that, though they offend beyond measure, they can be absolved by a mere plea for pardon."

She sighed and shook her head.

"I sometimes wonder whether spinsterhood is not the only enviable lot. Its members, at least, do not have to deal with the pompously vain and selfish."

"Adam," Delight said quietly, "is neither."

"Why, Dee!" Felicity exclaimed in gentle raillery. "It was of that very outlaw-gentleman that I was thinking."

"I don't believe you." The hands that had chafed each other were clenched. Felicity's reproof was fond.

"Why, my dearest child, it can't be that you've been letting yourself grow sentimental over our Adam? If so, forbear. He isn't worth the effort, Dee; yours or mine."

"Adam is—" Delight began and choked.

"If you truly wish to know how infantile a man can be," Felicity counseled lazily as she rose and let her loosened gown fall away from her lovely body, "read that letter. You need not hesitate. I know him too well to believe his pleading."

She sat down again and, bending to draw off her hose, smiled at the crackle of paper. Delight's face was inclined above the opened sheet. Long lashes hid her eyes but the soft lips trembled and then were tight-pressed.

It was like Delight, Felicity thought with amusement, to lay the letter down at last, never commenting on the missing superscription, and, still in silence, to turn about and hastily undress.

"Do you understand now, Dee, what I mean about the childishness of men?"

The fair head nodded. Later, Delight said as she blew out the dip, "Good night, Felicity."

She lay far to her side of the bed in so complete a silence that her companion knew she was stark-awake. How long she remained rigidly still, Felicity never was sure, for warm satisfaction brought her quick slumber.

Chapter XXXVII

THE maple beyond the window had flamed and flaked away to an ash-blue skeleton before Jonas Fay released Adam.

"And you are not," he warned when his patient had nagged him into permission, "to ride as though the devil was after you, or vice versa. A little at a time. You'll live longer and I'll have one less affliction."

Adam made ready for his journey in solemn elation. It was as though Fay's dismissal had closed one volume of his life and another, braver, was opening. Trial had ended and before him lay a future brighter and more tranquil than the late October days.

During his convalescence, he had managed to finish the task he had undertaken with Ethan Allen, who straightway had rushed off to a Hartford printer with the completed manuscript and loud predictions of apocalyptical consequences when it burst upon the world. Adam's employer had bestowed upon him before departure not only the promised rights to land in Burlington but others to land in Colchester and Hinesburg, as well. Immediate sale of these, Ethan had confessed, would bring no great return but they would, if retained, yield in time unbounded wealth.

Adam now was rich, in verity, with land of his own, most of the cash he had brought back from Montreal, returning health, and, at the end of this journey through the bronze and crystal autumn, the respite and the surety that were Delight. All these treasures he counted over as he rode sedately north through the bright weather past the new clearings, the more frequent dwellings, and the sturdily growing little towns.

He was leaving behind him the strivings and difficulties, the hatreds and the clashes of factions. His future, once so daunt-ingly blank, was clear as the sunlight because of Delight. She was the true beginning and, by God's grace, the faraway ending of life for him. A plan that at first had been only a possibility grew firmly outlined as he rode.

Before the snows came, Adam and Olin would journey north from Panton to find and estimate the new properties. On the best of these and on Champlain's shore, they would choose the site for a house. Materials and skills bought with Adam's money would make it the fairest dwelling north of Major Skene's. Its owner's labor would be spent on it without stint, as feeble ex-piation for his earlier blindness. Not until the house was complete, within and without, would he bring Delight to her home by the water, far from fear or discord, deep in the peace of the wilder-ness.

There, they would begin their lyrical life together. Each mile of the deliberate ride gave the intention new solidity, increased the grave sense of fulfillment that accompanied Adam. On a cold, bright noon he rode out of the forest and toward the red house that stood in the sunlight's pale blazing.

The thump of his heart thickened Adam's breathing. There was assurance of welcome in the chimney smoke that rose, thin and blue on the still air. As he advanced, he watched the kitchen door.

From a field where he piled a red-gold pyramid of pumpkins, Olin whooped and ran. Adam raised an arm, with a trace of dis-may. His imagination had not included witnesses to his and De-light's meeting, yet he got warmth into his voice when he had dismounted and Olin, having wrung his hand, beat him upon the shoulders.

At the sound of the doorlatch, Adam turned away quickly from a fusillade of questions but it was Mindwell who stood before him. The wrinkles were deep about her eyes.

"Wal," she said. "Longer gittin' back 'n' ye figgered, eh, Adam? Mite puny, too. Tired, I mistrust."

"Stronger and better with every mile," he boasted gaily above the singing of his heart.

The odd shyness that had come down on him must have laid its spell on Delight, too. She was lingering in the house, postpon-

338

ing till the last exquisite instant that moment henceforth to be theirs. All their days, they would share the memory of a severe brilliance sharpening every twig and frost-shriveled grass blade, of pumpkins glowing in a tan field, of the intense, cloudless sky, and, at last, the eloquent meeting of their eyes.

Olin was undoing the saddlebags and the portmanteau strapped above them. Their owner said to Mindwell in forced jest, "All my worldly goods. I have come for a long stay."

"Good hearin'," the woman told him. "Felicity's still here."

"Is she?" he said in dismay. Mindwell blinked.

"Justus'll be back from Canady soon. Then there'll just be you 'n' Olin 'n' me."

"You and Olin," he repeated and then asked sharply, "But where's Delight?"

"Gone," her mother told him without expression. From far away, Adam heard his own voice echo:

"Gone?"

"Ehyah," Olin confirmed. "Gone uplake to live with the Delaplaces at Ti."

"I see," Adam said at last.

It would be like this. He should have known the importance of his hope had doomed it. He was destined, for the amusement of some malign power, to see whatever of virtue or excellence he tried to build fall about him into ruin. Adam's body felt hollow. His mind offered nothing more than dazed scorn of himself.

He lifted Allegra's rein and turned her toward the stable.

"Olin'll tend to her," Mindwell told him. "Best come 'n' rest a mite. Ye look spent."

Adam surrendered the mare.

"Yes," he said vaguely. "I'm more tired than I thought."

He lay on the bed in his old room while corroding amusement invaded him. Hope so wholly overthrown, confidence so completely blasted, merited nothing more dignified than bitter mirth. He had been comic in his smug certainty.

He had no reproach for Delight. His own complacence had wrought disaster. He could see it now with scathing clarity.

What reason had he cherished to think Delight loved him? Only Felicity's half-malicious assurance and that, long ago. Adam plied the lash without mercy. He had ridden away with no word from

Delight to support his fatuous belief. Thereafter, he had hung all the weight of his future upon one, uncertain thread.

He groaned, recalling the presumptuous letter he had sent; he who thitherto had spoken no single word of love to Delight. She had no cause, knowing of his earlier infatuation for Felicity, to esteem his ardor. Adam flinched, remembering the future he loftily had planned. He despised himself for the moisture that smarted on his eyelids.

He heard Mindwell call Olin to dinner and rose to join them. He would not add to his ignominy by wallowing here in self-pity.

"Where is Felicity?" he asked, secretly relieved by her absence.

Felicity, Mindwell informed him, had chosen that morning to ride over to New Haven to make the house ready against her brother's return. She had said she might not be back by noon, so there was no need to wait for her. As she spoke, the woman's eyes strayed to her son who plunged with haste into talk of Wadman's and Feltham's plot, and its farcical ending over which The Grants were still chuckling.

"John Strong saw Wadman at Crown Point, t'other day. 'Lef-tenant,' says John, 'neck trouble ye much?' Wadman pretended he didn't hear."

Olin laughed and pushed himself away from the table, saying he must get back to the field, but he held Adam's shoulders down with firm hands when he too would have risen.

"No. Get some brawn on that carcass first. Rest the journey stiffness out of you. Let Ma nurse you a spell."

Mindwell sat like a weathered, wooden effigy for a moment after her son had gone.

"Don't like it," she said at last and Adam knew she spoke of Olin and Felicity. He waited, unsure in his own wretchedness what comfort he could offer. The woman watched her horny fingers twirl a pewter spoon and then went on, "Don't like her, for that matter. Ye know that. She's up to somethin' I can't see. Feel it, though."

"With Olin?"

"Who else? Only wish there was other game handy. Ain't like herself. So mild, butter wouldn't melt in her mouth. Don't want they should wed, Adam."

The anxiety in the honest eyes drove him to say, "Olin told me he couldn't afford to marry for at least another year."

"Eh? Wal, hope she lets him hold to it. Real glad when Justus is back 'n' his sister's off my hands."

Adam cleared his throat and disciplined his face and voice. "I shall miss Delight."

"Ehyah. All will, I guess. Better for her, though, than stayin' here."

"When did she leave?"

"Why now, lemme see. 'Twan't more'n a few days ago Dela-places come downlake to Chimney Point for her. Made up her mind right after Justus come back from Bennington."

There was no ground for error. The girl's flight had been her response to the effrontery of his letter. Why had he written and frightened her away? Otherwise, she might be here; Delight with the bright, pale hair and the clear eyes and the calm that was like faint shining! Mindwell was saying:

"Always was different from Olin. He jumps at things 'n' mebby can be hauled back. She's quiet 'n' biddable, till she makes up her mind, sudden, 'n' then all the powers can't sway her. Real surprised when she decided to go."

"I know," Adam said.

If he had had delicacy or decency, Delight still would be here. Deference, deliberation might have won her; at worst, they would not have driven her to take refuge where she knew he could least easily reach her.

"Adam," Mindwell bade suddenly, "go lay down a spell. Way ye look, rest won't do ye no real harm."

He had been certain he would not close his eyes but he woke from so deep a sleep that, for an instant, he was lost. Then, sunlight on the west windows told him the afternoon was waning and he heard the voices of Mindwell and Olin in the kitchen. Adam was so drugged by slumber that it was a long instant before he got himself, blinking and befuddled, from bed.

Olin, standing by the outside door, turned and grinned at Adam, but a scowl still hung above his dark eyes. Mindwell explained, "Gittin' late 'n' Felicity ain't back."

"Shouldn't have been let go alone," Olin offered. Adam heard in his voice an echo of earlier dispute.

341

"No need," the woman said sharply, "for her to go at all, 'n' you 'n' me had enough to do here."

"Back 'fore this if nothin' had happened," her son persisted.

"Guess she didn't heed the time. She ain't real—reliable."

"I'm going to find her." Olin's voice was defiant.

"I'll ride with you," said Adam.

"Wal, mebby"—Mindwell tried vainly to hide her relief at this arrangement—"ye better."

They had gone far along the shadowed way to New Haven before Olin's grievance burst from him.

"Ever since she came, Ma's been cross-grained as a she-bear in spring. Guess"—he grinned crookedly—"I'll have to build another house before I wed."

Adam made sure of his voice before he asked, "Then it's—decided?"

Olin chuckled sheepishly.

"Always has been, far as I'm concerned. Guess," he pursued with pride, "you could call it decided, lacking Justus's consent. Since his precious Officers and Gentlemen tricked him, maybe that won't be too hard to get. Felicity as much as consented this morning. She's mine, like I always thought she'd be."

There were precincts barred to even the closest friendship. Adam deplored the priggish sound of his voice.

"I wish you all happiness."

Olin's laugh was at once embarrassed and complacent.

"Told you long ago I'd win her. Patience and independence did it, like I was certain they would. Girl's likely to take finally the one man she never could fool."

He scanned the gloomy vista with waxing anxiety.

"Thought we'd meet her long before this. Maybe she's been—"

The rest of the surmise was left unuttered. He kicked his horse into a swifter pace.

The last of the sunlight still dwelt on the shorn fields and the tall tents of shocked corn in the Sherwood clearing. It gleamed on the tarnished clapboards of the house. Justus, Adam thought as he surveyed the well-tended precinct, had farmed to good purpose.

Olin had galloped on ahead and now was dismounting before the dwelling's door. He thrust it open, called, and entered. As

Adam drew rein, his friend reappeared and shouted, "Felicity!"

Long ago, in a like moment, the same mocking echo had cast back Delight's name. There was contagion in the alarm that creased Olin's face.

"She's not here. Horse gone, too, unless maybe she stabled him."

The thought sent him running toward the barn. His friend turned to follow, then paused. The house might hold tidings Olin in his haste had overlooked. It began to utter them as soon as Adam entered.

Dust filmed the stair and blurred its rail. Clearly, Felicity had not got far with her cleaning. Marks on the treads proclaimed that someone lately had visited the second floor. Felicity's room was upstairs. Adam's footsteps were loud in the silence.

He paused, breathing hard, at the chamber's open door. The disorder within was due, he recognized with ebbing alarm, not to violence but haste. A gown and petticoats lay in a mound where Felicity had stepped from them. Hose had been flung nearby. Open doors revealed the wardrobe was empty. So were the gaping drawers of a chest. Upon its top a sheet of paper lay.

It was queer to be reading now, for the first time in his life, a message from Felicity.

"Lieutenant Wadman waits for Me below. Before Anyone reads this, we shall be far away. Before we could be Overtaken, we shall be Wed. Tell Justus his Anger must cool before our Return, for George has his Inheritance and his Leave and we plan a long and lovely Wedding Tour."

Adam went slowly down the stair toward Olin, who cried from the doorstep, "Her own and another horse were in the barn, hours ago. Their tracks lead toward the lake road."

He saw the paper in his friend's hand and clutched at a straw. "Is it from Justus? Did he return and take her away? If so, he—"

"No," said Adam, and handed him Felicity's message.

Chapter XXXVIII

MINDWELL ROYDEN sat, thick forearms folded on the table, and watched her son pursue his task with an intensity that shut him away from her and from Adam, who stood irresolutely before the fireplace.

Olin had taken his musket from its pegs above the hearth and had drawn the old charge. He cocked the empty weapon now and pulled its trigger. With a double click, the hammer fell and the frizzen flew up, baring the pan. Olin muttered and, turning a screw, readjusted the flint. It was no darker or harder than his eyes. He tried again, nodded at the stronger flash of sparks, and, picking up powderhorn and ramrod, began reloading. His mother offered mildly, "Best bide till daylight, Olin. 'Tis full dark now."

He drove wadding down upon the powder charge with cold violence.

"Ride tonight, maybe I'll find 'em 'fore morning."

"They must be a long ways ahead."

His voice had the sound of a saw driven through hardwood.

"Bed somewhere, won't they? Why else has he taken her? To wed? With the left hand. That's the pretty way of Officers and Gentlemen, God damn them all."

He emptied the bullet pouch into his palm and chose a ball with care. Only his quivering hands betrayed his fury. His swarthy face was still, his mouth a darker scar across it. Adam had seen this baleful immobility come down upon his friend.

After his first brief raging when he had read Felicity's message, Olin had spoken less and less, as though gradually he had recognized the emptiness of words. He and Adam had tracked the elopers' horses across the Sherwood clearing and along the trail that led to the lake shore. Olin had railed then, with a zest for self-torment, over his own stupidity and Felicity's craft.

"Gulled me," he had groaned, "from the day she came. Took a deal of pride in it, I wouldn't wonder. And 'twas this morning she said she'd wed me."

He had been tricked into believing, the scalding voice pursued, that the kidnapping plot had turned Felicity toward him. Under her spell, he had seen no significance in the presence of Wadman at Crown Point, nor had he been suspicious when twice the girl had ridden alone to New Haven, ostensibly for fear some ill had befallen the house.

" 'Twas only this morning I reset her horse's shoes. Didn't seem to need it, but she wanted I should. She'll ride farther today, thanks to me. Can't go fast enough or far enough to outrun me."

The tracks they followed turned south at a crossroads. Olin spoke again, "Wed her, by God! Why would he? He's got her. Another conquest for him and Feltham to snicker over. I've heard 'em."

He gave a strangling sound. After an instant, he went on, "Justus ought to be real proud of his lickspittle raptures over the goddamned officers of His goddamned Majesty's goddamned army."

Dusk was falling when they drew rein where the way to the Royden farm forked from the North Road. Adam dismounted and bent over the fugitive's tracks.

"A full half day ahead of us," he said, breaking long silence. "We'd best go home."

"Ehyah," Olin replied slowly. "For my firelock."

It had been dark when they had reached the house. With no further speech, they had tethered their horses before it. Adam, entering before his companion, had told Mindwell of Felicity's abduction. It had been as well, he thought as he watched Olin complete the musket's reloading, that her son had not seen the justification and relief that had burned on the woman's face.

"Wal!" Olin now exclaimed grimly. He weighed his weapon.

Mindwell said, "If ye're set on craziness—"

"I be." The words were final as a door's slam. "Justus ain't here. This black whore's bastard has seduced his sister."

"Let me git a word in edgeways, Olin. Best bait the horse 'n' yerself, if ye figger on travelin', hadn't ye?"

"Ehyah," he said, roused from brooding by her tart speech. "Guess you're right, Ma."

He strode heavily across the kitchen. The look on the woman's face impelled Adam to call, "Feed the mare, too; I'm riding with you."

Olin paused an uncertain instant, nodded, and clumped out. Mindwell rose, went quickly to the hearth, and bent over the fire. She said without turning, "Neighborly of ye, Adam, feeble as ye be."

"I'd forgotten that I was," he said in all honesty. "If I rode here, I can ride back."

Mindwell's face was rigid but the worry in her eyes smote him. "Never seen him like that before. Deep-wounded, I guess. Mebby ye can ease him, Adam. Glad it come about, if it don't lead to killin'."

"I'm going to make sure it doesn't. That's Justus's problem, not Olin's."

Her hand caught his arm in a brief tight grip. He smiled down at her and, kindling a dip at the hearth, went to his own room to pack his saddlebags.

In the cold night, the stars hung close. The horses, standing before the open kitchen door, breathed out gusts of steam. The frozen earth rang beneath their hoofs. Adam, looking back, saw Mindwell stand, an oblong darkness against the glow.

They rode for a time in silence, following the lighter streak in the gloom that was the road.

"Armed?" Olin asked at last.

"No."

"Good. Settlin' this is my task."

Increasingly, as the night wore on, Adam was grateful darkness imposed so slow a pace. Otherwise, considering the aches already invading flabby muscles, he could not have ridden long with the frenzied Olin who was so fixed in his belief that Wadman had

346

taken Felicity solely to debauch her that he demanded repeated assurance that the fugitives still were ahead of them.

This entailed halt, blind scrabblings at the roadside for inflammable materials, the ignition of these with flint and steel, and identification by the resultant flickering light of the heavily caulked hoofprints of Wadman's horse.

"They'll bed when they think it's safe," Olin swore again and again. He talked wildly of slaying them both with a single bullet. The night wore on. The blundering pursuit continued. It seemed to Adam he had been thrust out of the world to wander through frigid, black eternity with a madman.

The forest shut away the stars' faint light and they groped through darkness so solid that the horses snorted and flinched, so cold that Adam's hands grew numb. Olin's animal stumbled and almost went down. He cursed it savagely.

Adam's mind amplified an abused body's protests, decrying a pursuit that crept blindfolded; proposing fantastic attacks upon his obsessed companion whereby Olin would be overcome, disarmed, and led docilely homeward. Why did he not speak up in the chill and muffling darkness, proclaiming truthfully enough that he was exhausted, and let his companion go on alone?

He fumbled with the idea and deliberately let it drop. It was Olin's sister, not Olin, who kept him steadfast. He could atone, by restraining her brother from violence, for the offense that had driven away Delight. By guarding Olin, he also protected her.

Olin's voice said suddenly, "Joe's gone lame." He dismounted. Adam thankfully drew rein and heard his companion grunt and swear.

"Sprained a foreleg when he stumbled, seems," he reported at last.

To Adam, hearing the subsequent, drawled profanity, came the bizarre impression that Olin's own spirit was returning to a lately usurped body. The leaden quality had left the voice that asked, "Wal, what now?"

"Break off," Adam ventured, "and turn back?"

Olin offered dryly, "Ride this horse 'n' I'll ruin him; don't figger I can walk back home. I'm all pulled apart."

"And I."

"Ehyah"—with contrition—"you must be." He added after a brief silence, "Ought never to have let you start."

"You should," Adam told him through chattering teeth, "never have started, yourself."

"Would you have had me—?" Olin began with vehemence. He gulped and ended, more mildly, "That don't settle what to do now."

"Unless day is never to return, dawn can't be distant. At least, that will show us where we are."

"We can't be too far from Castleton. We'd best push on to Zadok Remington's tavern."

Adam's first sensation when he woke was relief to find himself whole and sound. Weariness like renewed illness had accompanied him to Remington's inn. There had been a stupefying emptiness within him that the alarmed Olin had tried to dispel with rum. After the consequent nausea, they had carried the victim upstairs. He had fallen into bed with sickness heavy upon him.

Adam took pride, as drowsiness ebbed, in the stamina that had mended and revived him, though Olin, beside him, still snored. Quickening memory lessened complacency. Adam had not, like Olin, walked the miles to Castleton, leading a limping horse. Neither had Adam suffered the frenzy that wasted his friend.

The sunlight in the bare little room proclaimed that it was past noon. Adam stretched and winced at his muscles' protest. He could hear movement downstairs and, below the window, voices and laughter. It would be pleasant to lie indefinitely, between sleep and waking, if his stomach were less voracious. His bedfellow's snore was a homely, reassuring sound. Here, in the sunlit chamber, yesterday's violences, Olin's enveloping rage, the irrational pursuit it had launched had a dreamlike quality.

The man who lay with dark face relaxed beneath a mop of hair bore faint resemblance to the maniac of yesterday. The fury had gone out of him; already, the wound was healing. He had rid himself of the worst of his anguish in one wild paroxysm. Perhaps, Adam thought, that was the better way.

Olin had known betrayal by the woman he complacently had believed he had won. Olin had not found, at the end of blindness, a shining creature into whose small, toil-hardened hands he had longed to entrust the remainder of his life, only to have her flee from the tardily offered tribute.

Women were Circe-like creatures. One had transformed his friend into a murderous madman. Another, by her implicit rejection, had changed Adam from suitor into servant. He had undertaken a mad, black journey in her brother's company for Delight's sake. He and circumstances had saved her from tragedy. It was a sustaining thought.

Olin's snore checked and broke into a mumble. He sat up rubbing his head while Adam watched competence return to the dazed and blinking eyes.

"God!" said Olin. "Thought I'd killed you."

"I take a deal of killing."

Adam saw his friend's mouth go white as memory smote him. Olin hesitated, then swung himself from the bed. He peered through the window and without turning, said gruffly, "Obliged to you, Adam. Stark crazy, wa'n't I?"

There was pathos in the resolutely light voice.

"I know," Adam ventured awkwardly. "I know her, too. She's not worth it, Olin."

His friend nodded and, after the way of his breed, clapped a lid down upon emotion.

"Late, isn't it? Should have tended to Joe's leg long since."

"Before anything else we'll breakfast, unless you want to be devoured à la Iroquois."

They fed well on Champlain salmon, cold pork, pumpkin stewed with maple syrup and rum, and drank Mrs. Remington's spruce beer from wood-bottomed horn cups, while their chubby host debated Joe's injury with Olin and suggested a variety of remedies.

In the scrubbed and sanded taproom, with November's pale glare beyond the small-paned windows, yesterday seemed to Adam a half-remembered nightmare, yet he saw when their host at last departed the pallor return about Olin's mouth.

"A bowl of punch?" Adam suggested, thinking it might ease his friend, but Olin shook his head with a crooked smile.

"Drunk enough, yesterday, on no liquor, wa'n't I? Don't figger on startin' again."

He paused and stared into the wide, shining road before the inn.

His voice when he spoke again, twanged dryly, "Tricked me. Maid's privilege, wouldn't wonder. Not Wadman's, though. He fooled me, too. Wal, I'll pay him, some day, if I storm Ti to find him."

His mention of the fort pricked Adam.

"A precious pair, you and I," he offered, wondering whether he sought to comfort his friend or himself. "Jilted and mourning together."

Olin's dark eyebrows lifted.

"You said—I believed—" he groped and bogged down.

"That it was finished between Felicity and me? It was, long ago."

He looked down for an instant at his tightly clasped hands before he met his friend's stare.

"It was Delight I came to Panton to see, Olin. If she had—been there, I should have asked your leave to address her before now."

The other's silent amazement unlocked Adam's speech. There was relief in confiding the sorry tale.

"But," Olin faltered when he had ended, "why should she run away from you? God, I thought Delight was real fond of you, not"—with a sour laugh—"that I'm judge of any maid's feelings."

"Nor I. She's taken herself beyond my reach, and yet"—he lifted his horn cup and was a long while draining it—"and yet," he began again, meeting his companion's puzzled eyes with shamefaced defiance, "I want greatly to see her, if only to beg her for forgiveness."

"There'll be a way, Adam. Maybe she'll tire of Feltham's prancings and come home. Maybe John Strong, who travels much by lake, would bear a letter to her."

"I have lost faith in letters."

"Ehyah. Turn things upside down, don't they?"

By his parched look Adam knew his friend's mind had swung back again to Felicity and her message. Olin rose and went to tend his horse. Perhaps it was better to leave him alone. Adam, who had started to follow, turned and passed through the tavern toward the blaze of sunlight before it.

The little houses on either side the ambitiously broad road were nested in leaves, piled about them for winter protection. The still, cold air smelled of smoke and frost. While Adam paced to and fro, working stiffness from his legs, his mind made no greater progress with a problem he had hoped to solve.

He must return to Panton, since most of his belongings still were there. He would be welcome, yet he had no cause to stay now and the place would be haunted by Delight. There was no greater reason, he considered wretchedly, for him to go elsewhere. He knew the anger simmering within him was childish, since it had no more creditable object than his own emptiness, yet it waxed as he tramped to and fro.

Was frustration truly his ordained fate, the home port to which, whatever the voyage and its purpose, he must always return? He recalled, inconsequently, how trout had surged this way, darted that, foiled by the tension of his rod and line. Was this his destiny? Did a malevolent Fisherman find sport in Adam's struggles upon adversity's hook?

The rhythm of hoofs roused him and, looking up, he saw a black, familiar figure come riding. There was sweat on the tall, strong horse, yet he was not spent and fretted when Benjamin Hough drew rein.

"A good day to you, Mr. Corlaer," the minister rasped in uncommon geniality. "Now here is a strange thing! Tell me, sir, is the ruffian, Olin Royden, with you?"

"He is," Adam replied, vexed by the covertly gloating air.

"Then God moves mysteriously, sir. Would you believe that I was told only a few hours ago that I probably should encounter you both on the road?"

"By God?" Adam inquired, knowing the question would offend. Hough's eyes rolled, ringed with white.

"Who is this that speaketh blasphemies?" the shattered voice demanded. "Behold he that pursues evil, pursues it to his own death."

He was angered by the other's grin, as Adam had hoped he might be, and wielded his tidings like a weapon.

"Mrs. Wadman was the prophetess, sir; Felicity Sherwood as was; sister of him who lately warned God's minister to refrain from preaching what the Almighty had bidden him to utter."

Adam shrugged, determined to favor the expectant eyes with no sign of surprise or alarm.

"Did she or her seducer claim she was wed?"

"Ahah!" Hough cried in angry glee. "Not she or he but the Lord. Leftenant Wadman and Felicity Sherwood came to me last night. I sent them on their way this morning, one in the eyes of God and man."

This snapping of tension, this trite ending to drama, robbed Adam of breath. He wondered whether Olin would be enraged or comforted by Hough's news and managed to say with indifference, "Man's eyes may not be as tolerant as God's, Reverend. There's the matter of the law."

"Grants' law?" the minister asked with sepulchral zest. "There is none that I honor. They were properly wed, sir, under York statute, since the banns have been cried in my church on successive Sabbaths. And what say you to that, eh?"

The elopers had planned thoroughly. The knowledge woke in Adam an anger kin to the frenzy that had overcome Olin. Felicity was not one to sell herself at a bargain and her bridegroom already had proved his facility as a plotter. Wadman's and Feltham's tardy arrival at Lake Sainte Catherine, months ago, might have been the aftermath of a secret conference with Hough. Adam's temper was not improved by the parson's death's-head grin.

"What do I say to that, Reverend? What many others already have told you. You are a meddler and a troublemaker and one day will find yourself viewed, despite your cloth."

"Say you so?" Hough rattled, his face muddy with wrath. "The times indeed need mending when rebels and outlaws presume to threaten God's minister."

He raised himself in his stirrups to tower, black and menacing.

"I am, sir, the Lord's and York's servant and I keep my covenants. Even now, I journey to Governor Colden with pleas of the afflicted in hope God will move him to scourge an iniquitous land. Tell that to the profane and profligate bandit king, Ethan Allen."

He gathered his rein in one brown, clawlike hand and leveled a bony finger.

"Warn that arch-blasphemer and his crew that the evildoer shall be cut off but that those who wait upon the Lord shall inherit the earth. To him and his and you, young man, anathema maranatha!"

Hough, shaken by rage, raked his spurs. Adam gathered himself and leaped for the bridle. The horse shied from the clutching fingers. For an instant, as Adam reeled, he saw above the frantic animal the minister's contorted face.

Hough screeched. The horse leaped forward and struck Adam down. Hoofs trampled, then rang through the stillness. Their sound dwindled, was gone.

Adam pushed himself up from the road. There was grit in his mouth and on his face a plastering of thin mire the sun had thawed from the frozen earth. He got carefully to his feet and blinked at Olin and Remington who were running toward him.

Chapter XXXIX

Z ADOK REMINGTON, innkeeper, veterinarian, tooth-puller, blood-letter, and bonesetter for Castleton town, followed Adam and Olin to their chamber where, after prying and prodding at the victim, the volunteer physician pronounced him no more than bruised. Adam had told only half the tale of his meeting with Hough when Remington moved purposefully toward the door.

"Goin' down," he said grimly over his shoulder, "to reprime m' firelock."

"Eh?" Olin asked.

"So's to be certain," the landlord explained, eyes snapping, "she don't misfire when that psalm-singin' York son-of-a-bitch rides past m' tavern again."

He left, still mumbling. Olin blurted to his friend, "Lend me your mare and I'll go after Hough."

Adam shook his head.

"He has a fresh horse and a long start. If he is not pursued, he may return—and I want greatly to meet him again. You might as well hear this now, Olin."

He told his companion with merciful brevity of Felicity's and Wadman's marriage and wondered while he spoke how anyone who had been maniacal a few short hours earlier could look so wooden and inert, now. There was a silence when he ended that Olin broke with a laugh, grim and curt as a pistol shot. He wheeled about and strode to the window where he stayed a long moment before compelling himself to turn toward Adam again.

"Wal," he said with a resolute smile, "gulled complete 'n' proper, wa'n't I?"

354

"I know," Adam muttered. "She—"

Horses stopped before the tavern and voices clashed. Adam, watching his companion's desolate face, proposed, "Best take Allegra, Olin, and ride back home. I mean it," he insisted when the other demurred. "Your mother'll be anxious; you've work to do before snow flies. Come back when Joe's leg is mended and bring me the gear I left in Panton."

He met Olin's stare with a sour grin.

"Why bring them? Aren't you coming home?"

"No. I should be—lonely there and I may be needed here."

"Needed?"

"Exactly. As witness, if they catch Hough."

Olin scowled. Adam pursued in a low voice and with secret excitement.

"It's because of what happened today. When he pointed at me, I saw—"

Remington beat on the door and thrust it open before either could respond.

"Thar he is, boys," the landlord proclaimed, "an' eager, I mistrust, to see the Reverend as you be."

He thrust the grinning Peleg Sunderland into the room, stepped aside for Ira Allen to follow him, and went away, closing the portal behind him.

Mud lay on the visitors' clothing and they had the sagging look of men who had ridden long and hard. Sunderland said with over-gravity.

"Looking for one Benjamin Hough. Any idee whar he might be?"

"Five miles, at least, west of here," Adam told him with equal solemnity, "and bound to complain to Colden of you bandits' misdeeds."

"Don't doubt it," Ira said and seated himself while Sunderland's mild drawl explained their presence.

Word had been brought to Ethan Allen at Bennington that The Grants' most fanatical Yorker had stolen back to his home in Clarendon. Peleg and Ira at once had been detailed to take him. They had missed their quarry by a bare hour—Sunderland professed the belief that Hough was in league with the devil instead of the Deity—and on weary horses had been unable to overtake him.

"Been wonderin'," Peleg pulled his long face into an uneasy grin, "what Ethan'll say when he larns he got away again. Bound to be memorable."

"Why do you want Hough?" Adam had the dismayed feeling that treasured knowledge had been snatched from him.

Ira, squat and observant, blinked lambent eyes and offered, "For more'n enough. Should have viewed him long since. Told Ethan so."

"He'll reach too far; we'll catch him yet," Sunderland promised.

The solid little man frowned.

"By then, he'll have hatched more hell. Know who helped Tryon dragoon the legislature into passing The Bloody Law? The Reverend Hough. We learned that lately. Who is encouraging that Scottish glutton, Colden, to issue more York patents? The Reverend, again."

Anguish tightened his voice.

"Better than three hundred thousand acres has Colden bestowed on the York gambling gentry since last spring—three hundred thousand acres of our land!"

He brooded over the enormity. Sunderland asked, "That enough reason for taking him?"

"I think," Adam said, "I know a better"—and paused to enjoy the bewilderment of his companions.

"There is," he said at length, "a red scar on Hough's hand."

"Eh?" Sunderland asked without comprehension. Adam drew out his triumph.

"I think it is the mark of a burn, a burn that might have been dealt by a poker to a hand at my throat."

Ira had come out of his weary pose and his eyes were bright.

"Adam, are you real sure?"

"Sure enough to be run down in an attempt to halt him. Hough wed Sherwood's sister to Leftenant Wadman this morning."

"Sherwood's, eh?" with a revival of the old suspicion.

Adam answered sharply, "He knows nothing of it. It was an elopement, long-planned. I think Wadman and Feltham and Hough plotted together to seize us at Poultney."

356

Ira moved tight lips across his teeth.

"Peleg," he said finally, "hereafter, a detail watches Hough's farm, day and night."

He turned thoughtful eyes on Adam.

"Where you figger on goin'?"

"I—don't know," Adam replied with a shrug and a crooked smile.

"Real helpful," Ira offered, "if you bide here a spell till we trap Hough."

"There is no reason I should not," Adam answered slowly.

Ira and Sunderland left at daybreak and, a little later, Olin unwillingly departed, urged on by Adam who, when his friend had left, regretted his own insistence. Fortune's abuse had left him scant patience or philosophy. There were desperate moments when he felt that a pursuing malevolence had broken off his life and that this was its ending. There were black hours when the Royden farm, steeped though it was in memories of Delight, appeared a pleasanter haven than this frontier tavern.

Adam tended Olin's horse, applying the remedies Remington supplied. He rode his own mare occasionally toward Clarendon and trysts with Sunderland whose men still watched Hough's dwelling fruitlessly. There was much remaining of each day for grim brooding. As time crawled by, Adam found his bitterness centered on Benjamin Hough.

The score he owed the gaunt minister grew heavier as he considered it. Hough had aided Tryon in the passage of The Bloody Law that was designed to destroy, among others, Adam himself. It had been Hough's assault that had injured Adam and had led to his loss of Delight. Hough had conspired with Wadman and Felicity to blast all Olin Royden's complacent hopes. Hough came in time to be the embodiment of all ill fortune.

Adam, nursing his grievances against the man, took sour satisfaction in the thought that he was not an entirely abject victim. Already, he had struck back against his enemy. It had been he who had seen the damning red mark on Hough's hand; it had been his evidence that had intensified the hunt for the Yorkish parson. Adam used this knowledge to keep despair from drowning him.

He was receiving, almost imperceptibly, further comfort

357

Gradually, he became aware that Remington's and his lean, tireless wife's warmth toward their guest was something more than innkeepers' professional hospitality. The woman saw, at mealtime, that Adam was well fed. Her husband presented him with pride to taproom frequenters. These were tributes, Adam appreciated at last, to his importance.

He was Ethan Allen's associate. He also was one of The Grants' foremost outlaws. The Remingtons, in wordless, Yankee fashion, were expressing their gratitude to a defender. The knowledge was heartening to an embittered, thwarted man.

Perhaps Adam's career had not been as vain as it had seemed. Here, close to the frontier and far from the trimmers, moderates, and placators of every shade in Bennington, the pattern was simple, cast in the absolutes of white and black. The settlers' straight minds saw their neighbors without reservation as patriots or traitors, and among the former Adam was a distinguished personage. Perhaps, reviving self-respect hazarded cautiously, there were higher achievements than material accomplishment.

There still were moments when his own aimlessness bore Adam down into despondency's pit but the Remingtons were patient rescuers and when Olin returned from Panton, their guest greeted him with a new cheerfulness.

Olin bore with him the remainder of Adam's belongings and tidings that he confided while punch thawed him. Sherwood, returned from Canada, had accepted the news of his sister's elopement with what Olin had considered less than satisfactory dismay.

"Truth is, Adam, Justus has been oiled so slick by Carleton he swallows King George and Lord North, too, with never a hiccup. Tighter things get, more of a Tory he becomes. Talks now of selling his pitch. He'll go back to Canada; see if he don't. Better he'd never settled."

They talked of the completed harvest, of Mindwell's concern over Adam's mishap, of whether this calm, warm December presaged a rigorous later winter, before the punch had warmed Adam sufficiently for him to ask, "And Delight?"

John Strong, Olin reported in an impersonal voice, had brought downlake a letter from Delight. She was well, the Delaplaces were kind, and their children not too difficult.

"Don't think she'd heard about Felicity. Didn't mention it, anyway."

Olin drank deeply from the bowl as though to wash away embarrassment and ventured, "Come home, Adam, and we'll figger out some way for you to see her. Maybe she'll be back 'fore the winter ends. Maybe if the lake stays open, we can travel up to Ti, you staying hid on the boat, me bringing her down to meet you."

"When Hough has been taken," Adam conceded gruffly, touched by his friend's concern. Olin grew red. He said awkwardly:

"I've told no one, not even Ma, about you and Delight."

"Thank you," said Adam, less heartily. "It is not a tale for a man to take pride in."

"If this war talk comes to anything, Delight'll be home to stay. British are aiming to build Crown Point fort again and Sherwood says there's talk of sending two regiments to Ti."

They sat that night in the shining taproom while a peddler from Massachusetts spoke darkly of the tension in blockaded Boston, the militia companies that drilled daily in the outlying towns, and the probability of hostilities before the Continental Congress met again in May.

Olin rode away next morning on his own horse and in the succeeding days Adam spent more of his waking hours debating Grants' affairs with Remington, listening while the tavern's patrons chewed solemnly on the cud of rumor.

They were dry men with weathered faces, eyes meshed in wrinkles by sun and wind, and well-considered, pungent habits of speech: Ephraim Buell who had cleared, single-handed, one of the first pitches in Castleton; Gershom Lake whose four-year-old apple orchard was the earliest in the town; James Kilbourne, the tanner; and others like them, with the torment of pioneering over and a brave hope before them.

When they had gone home, Adam was kept awake by questions the slow talk before the fire had roused. He could feel in the darkness the stir of dim, vast forces, grinding upon each other, moving inexorably onward.

The seed already lay in the American earth and the next spring would bring it forth. Adam felt those who nightly exchanged unqualified opinions in the taproom were as aware of this as he and readier to meet the test. Their cause would be Freedom's. There was no uncertainty in their level minds.

Ira Allen, for all his urgent talk of neutrality and negotiation, had ignored the nature of the people whom he wished to guide for their own, and the Onion River Land Company's, security. The sublimated horsetrading he had advocated was prudential, and impossible, since the men he must sway already and at great price had become Freedom's devotees.

Seeking Freedom, they had come to The Grants and had found space in which to grow. It was unlikely that these slow, tough pioneers, with shoulders bent by toil and hands permanently half closed by use of spade or axe, would entrust their freedom to any one man, however astutely persuading. They had grown to distrust, here in a free land, all leadership but their own.

For this ideal they had opposed, were still opposing, New York. In Freedom's compelling name they were willing now to ally themselves even with their New York enemies in her defense. Ira Allen, Adam thought with amusement, would find it a hard task to bend these drab zealots to the devious ways of compromise.

He took pride in this certainty. The folk in Remington's taproom saw further and more clearly than he. They had discerned a distant splendor and were moving toward it. Liberty was implicitly part of the farms they cleared and the mills they raised. They had inhaled, living intimately with wilderness, its own strong essence.

Theirs was a still, contagious passion. Adam found his empty spirit turning with new affection to the land through which he had stumbled from misfortune to misfortune. It was a fair land, a land of still unrealized promise, a land to which an empty man might worthily accord loyalty and service. It was Delight's own land.

It snowed on the day after Christmas, which Remington's wife said foretold a winter of twenty-six storms, and on the following afternoon Ethan Allen burst in upon the tavern like another tempest; bawling greetings, bellowing orders for his stallion's care, beating the grinning Remington on the back, painfully wringing Adam's hand and turning to bow to Mrs. Remington and volley flattery that broke her severe face into simperings. Vigor, spreading from him, enlivened and warmed the tap-room, as the punch he straightway ordered heartened Adam.

"I give you a toast," Allen trumpeted, lifting the bowl aloft. "To all true sons of Liberty and confinement for the ages of ages in the nethermost boiling backhouse of hell to trimmers, moderates, Tories, and Benjamin Hough."

He loomed that night before the hearth, a glowing, apocalyptical figure that spoke to the company, not of grants and shares or the iniquities of York, but of Boston's plight and the king's malevolence and the strange red dawn the provinces would see with the coming of spring.

"By the brazen buttocks of Beelzebub, neighbors, the Continental Congress will reconvene in Philadelphia, come May. Not the Bay Province or the Virginia congress, not the York or Jersey or The Grants—The Continental Congress. Do you grasp what that means?"

Adam, watching the rapt faces, the eyes that glittered in the chamber's uncertain light, felt a lump in his throat and new lightness in his heart.

A fire had been kindled in the tavern's largest bedroom and when, at last, they went upstairs, Allen drew Adam in with him.

"Have you plans of your own," he asked abruptly, "that keep you here?"

"Only the desire to requite Benjamin Hough. No other purpose holds me, if"—with faint bitterness—"I were needed elsewhere."

"You will be. Ready yourself for a journey, Adam, a month hence."

Ethan stole ponderously to the door, jerked it open upon emptiness, and, returning reassured to his chair, spoke in a hushed voice.

Delegates from Canada had been invited to sit with the new Congress. John Brown, Allen's Pittsfield crony, had been ordered by the Massachusetts Committee of Correspondence to bear its persuasions north. He had applied to his friend for guides.

"He seeks James Morrison, whom you know," Ethan confided. "You and Sunderland will conduct him, as soon as the lake be frozen."

"Willingly," Adam said after an instant's silence. His companion grinned and laid a great hand on his shoulder.

"Good lad," he approved and added, "you hesitated because of Hough and your score against him, eh? Rest easy, Adam. We'll have the creeping, sanctimonious, nefarious, bloodthirsty, treacherous, and altogether abominable traitor before then. We then shall see whose blood The Bloody Law brings forth."

He subsided into rumblings like a spent thunderstorm: He should have moved against Hough earlier, but he had been unwilling to break the informal truce and shock the pious, with whom he considered The Grants were oversupplied, by arresting a man of God.

"My belief in divinity is lessened, Adam, by the men of God that God chooses."

Stars slid across the black windowpanes as the two talked. Allen girded against his trials in Bennington with the timid and the placators who, as tension grew, clamored more loudly for compromise, and with the vindictive who could see in the looming crisis no greater enemy than York.

"Some cry for liberty while others bewail the peril to their property, their weevily minds ignoring that neither can be secure without the other. Liberty and property! There are worse slogans for a new nation, a-borning."

He forgot his indignation in praise of his "Brief Narrative" which, he insisted, wholly demolished New York's claims against The Grants. All fall, he had gone up and down New England, a prophet-peddler, vending the book at the ridiculous price of one shilling and sixpence.

"I verily believe, Adam, that since Jesus was sold for thirty pieces of silver, no one has purchased so great a bargain."

Allen rose at last and stood a long moment at the window.

"It is past midnight," he said, turning, "and you are tired. Come back with me to Bennington, Adam. There are great works ahead."

The molten look came suddenly to his face and the blue eyes blazed. His voice had muted clangor.

"Great works, Adam, with freedom to gain; with The Grants in the forefront of the battle and Ethan Allen leading the hosts of The Grants."

362

Chapter XL

ADAM had been a week in Bennington when word came that Hough had been taken. Sunderland brought it. His long, narrow face was scarlet with cold and wore a mournful look to conceal great pride. The minister with the boldness of long immunity had walked into the trap set at his home. There, Sunderland and a detail of Green Mountain Boys had overwhelmed him; there, they still were holding him pending orders from Allen.

"Nobody hurt," Peleg reported as though he deplored it, "without ye count damage by the Reverend's language. Can't rightly call it swearin', I figger, when a parson uses it. If quarter of what he promises should ever happen, no hope for me 'n' the Boys—or for you 'n' The Grants, Ethan."

He stared aggrievedly at his chief, baffled to find only a stony expression where he plainly had expected disheveling jubilation. Allen looked past him in silence that Sunderland broke with determined irreverence.

"Wal," he inquired hopefully, "what happens now? Burn his house 'n' seal him thorough; mebby hang him?"

Allen drove his reply over invisible obstacles.

"No. This is no time for riot. He shall be tried and, in the court's judgment, sentenced and punished."

Peleg and Adam stared at the giant, so uncommonly rigid of demeanor and voice. Adam asked, "Try him? Here in Bennington?"

His incredulity stung Allen, whose violent gesture batted away the question.

"Body and blood of God!" he demanded. "Has neither of you

foresight or awareness? We burn the house and seal Hough with the beech twigs of the wilderness. How then will we appear to the provinces who, tomorrow, must be our allies? Like Mohawks, like the veritable banditti that York proclaims us. Benjamin Hough is a hell-deserving scoundrel matched with whom a skunk has the sweet savor of frankincense and myrrh, yet he must be duly tried."

"In Bennington?" Adam asked again.

Allen shook his head like a pestered bull.

"Not Bennington. We must not make a Roman holiday of Grants' justice and I know the seven varieties of flaming hell that would burst forth were Hough brought here."

He grinned, contemplating the prospect, and then bade the dazed Sunderland, "Ride back to Clarendon, Peleg. Convey Hough with great care to your own house where we shall hold a judgment seat, according to Grants' law."

Peleg left, still stupefied. Ethan glared at Adam, who inquired mildly, "Grants' law?"

"The conventions," Allen said with dignity, "have proclaimed that we are to be governed by the laws of God and Connecticut. These we shall employ until we can establish better."

They tried The Reverend Benjamin Hough, on a dark and bitter day, in the kitchen of Sunderland's home in the town that bore his name. The handful who attended—Allen and Warner who sat as judges; Adam, Herrick, Cochran, Dr. Fay, and Peleg's men who guarded the prisoner—crammed the chamber, yet the court had dingy dignity.

It sat briefly. Adam, drafted as clerk, had little to write and more opportunity than he wished to watch the ravaged face of the defendant who was flanked by awkward young men with drawn swords.

Adam wondered again, as Hough's eyes rolled above the blackness of his unshaved beard and he cast back shrill answers to the court's ponderous questions, whether in truth the man was not mad. The prisoner made no attempt to deny the single accusation brought against him. Allen, at Warner's urging, had agreed that Hough should be tried only for holding office, against convention statute, as a York justice of the peace.

364

"Save a deal of scandal and washing of dirty linen," Seth had said and had added heavily, "Not a pretty chore at best, though it must be done."

Hough defiantly admitted the charge against him. The absence of a proper court's state and trappings, the clumsiness of the prosecution, transformed his defiance into rankling condescension, as though no penalty worthy of dread could be inflicted by so shabby a tribunal.

The prisoner's clattering voice ran ahead of the slow questions. He proclaimed himself a duly commissioned justice under York law. He insisted he could be tried for misconduct only by a New York court. While the judges fumbled, Hough blinked complacently, licked his thin lips, and challenged, "I call upon any man to say that I have misused my office," and when none broke the silence, leered about him in triumph.

"We do not charge you with that," Ethan told him gravely. "Your crime lies in holding office," and Warner, nodding confirmation, added, "I would as lief have you judge me as any man."

The smirk of confidence the admission brought endured until Allen, after conference with his fellow judge, rose and proclaimed the verdict.

"The court," he intoned, "having heard the evidence in the case of Benjamin Hough does hereby adjudge and declare him guilty and sentences him to banishment from the district known as The Hampshire Grants and furthermore does sentence him to two hundred lashes."

Adam saw the derisive face go slack. A pity stirred that sight of the red mark on the hand Hough clapped to his mouth could not dispel.

"Ye dare not," the prisoner croaked, "chastise a servant of God."

"If He won't train His help, then we'll oblige," Cochran replied cheerfully. "This way, Reverend."

A beech tree stood before Sunderland's house and to this they bound Hough with his emaciated arms about the smooth gray bole and his half-naked body pressed against it. The sky was leaden and the small, sharp wind that cried through the colorless world bit at Adam as the first of the four chosen executioners stepped forward. He was a burly young man with a vindictive face and a thatch of hay-colored hair, and he gripped a length of rope, doubled so that its ends hung free.

Adam flinched as though it were his own body the scourge smote. Cochran counted grimly:

"One."

The rope ends sighed and struck with dull, slapping sounds. Beyond the house, where Sunderland's hounds were kenneled, one lifted its voice in eerie wailing.

"Four," said Cochran and then, "five."

Warner's oxlike calm, Ethan's ability to turn his face into a mask were beyond Adam. No one else in the small group of witnesses, standing silent to see the sentence fulfilled, betrayed sympathy or glee. They watched with wooden gravity. Even the flogger swung his scourge with more industry than passion. In all the self-possessed company, Hough alone displayed a horrid vivacity.

Across the bold grating of the victim's ribs and the sharp knobs of his spine, welts were weaving a crimson pattern. At each sibilant thwack, Hough gasped and surged against the embracing tree trunk with orgastic rhythm.

The hound still keened. A voice that Adam did not recognize counseled the flogger:

"Milder, Obed."

"Twenty-six; twenty-seven," Cochran droned. Adam's stomach could endure no more. He stumbled headlong around a corner of the house.

It was over when, shaking and clammy, he returned to the kitchen where impassive men watched Dr. Fay spread ointment on the prisoner's humped and glistening back. For an instant, Hough's eyes met Adam's emptily as though memory had been beaten from him, then slowly filled with still, dark bitterness.

Fay looked up and said briskly to Allen, "He is not badly hurt; he is well enough to travel."

At Adam's shoulder the first executioner mumbled resentfully, "Rest of 'em plied easier'n me."

Hough, sitting straighter, was saying to Ethan in a wasted, yet still contentious voice, "Then I demand a passport from you, sir, lest I fall again among—thieves."

366

He stabbed with the epithet but Allen only nodded and, marking the wan Adam, grinned.

"Able to hold a pen?"

"I think so."

"Then write," Ethan bade, "a safe conduct for Seth and me to sign," and when Adam was seated, dictated:

"This may certify the inhabitants of the New Hampshire Grants that Benjamin Hough hath this day received a full punishment for his crimes committed heretofore against this country, and our inhabitants are ordered to give the said Hough free and unmolested passport toward the city of New York or to the westward of our Grants, he behaving as becometh. Given under our hands this day and date aforesaid."

Adam stood in the doorway and watched the minister depart. Two men helped him into the saddle. Hough's eyes, as he looked about him, were stagnant pools, abrim with hate.

The exile moved slowly away, a bent and beaten figure, sullenly foreboding as the wintry land.

"Gettin' off too light," Sunderland mumbled in Adam's ear. "Wouldn't have straddled a horse for a week if the Boys up north had viewed him—Olin Royden, John Strong, 'n'—"

He broke off to stare and fumble in his leather coat while he swore proficiently.

"Been carryin' a message for ye," Peleg faltered, producing a crumpled letter, "for must be ten days now. Bore it clear to Bennington 'n' back to Clarendon again, scatterbrain that I be. All this hurly-burly made me forget it till now."

He stole away shamefacedly while Adam still was staring at the address:

"To Mr. Adam Corlaer at Remington's Tavern in Castleton by the hand of John Strong. To be sent on at opportunity."

He broke the seal.

"She will be home," Olin had written, "until January's end. I send this at a venture in hope it will bring you here."

Adam stood a long instant, holding the message. His impulse was to rage after Sunderland whose forgetfulness, for a moment, seemed a graver crime than Hough's.

"January's end!" And today, the 30th, found him three full summer days' journey from Panton.

He was dazed by the swift turn of his thought from the recent violence to the distant Delight. Malevolence had stooped again for his undoing.

Adam drew breath. January was not yet spent and Delight's return to Ticonderoga might be postponed. He would be laggard and craven if he did not try to reach her, even now. He would not surrender to the futility that once more was threatening to abase him. If snow lay no deeper in the north, he still could force his way through. A vain attempt was better than another meek submission.

He weighed the manner of his departure, the excuses he must offer, as he went into the kitchen. Warner, Cochran, Herrick, and Sunderland approvingly watched steam rise from the flip Ethan Allen was concocting. He raised the bowl, sampled, nodded, and on impulse thrust it toward Adam.

"Gods of the Mountains, boy, you look as though your need surpasses ours. Drink, Sir Doloroso. You'll need all warmth you can acquire where you are going."

His apparent insight halted the bowl below Adam's gaping mouth.

"Christ's stepfather!" Allen bawled. "Are we to die of thirst while you goggle? It was no incantation I uttered. Peleg reports Champlain frozen and I have sent John Brown an express, bidding him come as soon as may be. Had you forgotten you were guiding him to Canada?"

"No," said Adam with a dreary feeling of surrender. "No, I had not forgotten," and raised the bowl.

Chapter XLI

J OHN BROWN, when they moved north through the winter-locked world, surprised his guides. Sunderland at the outset had regarded him doubtfully, deeming the man's florid bulk a handicap and his joviality certain to wither quickly on the trail. Brown had more durability of body and spirit than either companion had suspected, never faltering, whatever the rigors of the day's travel, and carrying through the cold and the drifts, the searching winds and the storms, his original calm cheerfulness.

With a less resolute person they might have turned back, for the snow's depth compelled them to leave their horses at Remington's tavern in Castleton and still another, wilder storm held them a day and a night in a lean-to set up in the wilderness. When the downfall ended, flakes were so light and soft beneath their racquettes that they were forced to abandon their plan to go overland as far as Panton and were driven out onto the easier footing of the lake.

Here winds had packed long, white ridges or had swept Champlain's surface bare so that they marched with their snowshoes strapped between their shoulders. As the lake widened, the blast, running free across a piebald desert of snow and black ice, acquired new edge and the three men plodded in silence, swathed to their streaming eyes.

The harsh blue sky was no emptier than the world. The arctic immensity dwarfed them all, making their enterprise puny so that Adam, narcotized by exertion, could feel only dim disappointment that the weather had barred them from Panton and the Roydens' home where it was faintly possible Delight still lingered.

Bound to the rhythm of march, camp, and further marching, Adam nursed a sense of doom; a feeling that irresistible forces had caught and controlled him. He, Sunderland, Brown, and all other men were puppets of powers that in their own time would disclose their purpose. Meanwhile, with the groaning ice below and his breath's frost on his face, sluggish fatalism sustained him.

Brown, in the brief intervals between their camp-making and when they bedded, huddling close, spoke fragmentary auguries.

He sat by the fire Adam and Sunderland had built on the windscrubbed tip of Colchester Point and looked at the glimmering of Champlain's greatest width. The ice boomed in the cold and the sound pulled Brown's chapped mouth into a crooked smile.

"The ghosts of old battles," said he, "or the harbingers of new."

He toasted his hands while he peered north toward where snow-smothered islands melted into the dusk.

"If Canada rises," he went on, as much to himself as to his companions, "if Canada marches with us, that door will be barred."

"Hey?" Sunderland asked.

Brown waved toward the lake.

"When—if, war comes," he went on and Adam marked the hasty correction, "yonder is a fair road for armies, by winter or summer, unless our Canadian friends prevail and bar the way."

"Bar the way?" Adam echoed. "With British troops already at Ticonderoga and Crown Point?"

Brown hesitated, cleared his throat, and smiled again.

"I think Ethan Allen has a remedy for that. Unless," he added thoughtfully, "the British do reenforce the garrisons."

Sunderland remained at St. Johns, professing a higher admiration for the ale of the tavern than for Montreal and its inhabitants, and Adam guided Brown the remainder of the way to Morrison's counting house. He left his companion there, having no wish to endure the questions Morrison would ask, but had no more than reached the street where bells on the small French sleighs enlivened the bitter air than a breathless clerk overtook him and begged his return.

Morrison rose from behind the desk on which Brown's dispatches already were spread.

"My word, Mr. Corlaer, it seems ye are over-cavalier wi' old friends."

Adam forced a smile and accepted the bony hand.

"Ye turn up," Morrison pursued, "like—like—"

"Like a bad penny?"

" 'Tis not the comparison I sought but I beg ye to consider a coincidence. Not two months ago, Mr. Duane was in this verra office and much disturbed about ye."

"Wouldn't 'scandalized' be the better word?"

Adam was irked by the airing of his sorry affairs before Brown. Morrison's dry voice ran on:

Duane was worried, like all men, by the ominous drift of affairs. He also possessed far more influence with Colden, the acting governor, than he ever had had with Tryon and lately had learned that Adam still was in The Grants.

"A Leftenant Wadman and his lady, whom Mr. Duane has met, assured him ye were still whole."

"And doubtless," Adam amended silently, "profoundly deplored it," then listened with more interest.

Duane, Morrison reported, was extremely anxious to confer with Adam. The waxing crisis had magnified the importance of The Grants' rebellion in the eyes of York's landed gentry. Duane before leaving Montreal had talked wistfully of compromise and of his eagerness to help his former protégé recover his forfeited station.

"As yer father's old associate and yer own late man o' business," Morrison urged, "I recommend that ye go to New York town. 'Tis in my mind that ye'll benefit thereby."

"Thank you for your counsel," Adam said after hesitation and withdrew.

He wondered, walking aimlessly through the frigid little town, what had reinspired Duane's interest in him and had little doubt the urgency was financial.

He was no longer concerned, Adam told himself stubbornly as he floundered over the packed snow, with James Duane's fortune, or even in his own. He had made his choice. If the war Brown and others seemed to think inevitable actually should break, his loyalty lay with The Grants. Ethan Allen's was a more satisfactory patriotism than the gentry of New York were likely to display.

371

It was hard to picture Duane endangering his capital by the attack upon Ticonderoga that Brown had hinted Allen was ready to undertake.

Adam was defiantly unwilling to exchange his lot for any station Duane's influence or Colden's clemency was likely to gain for him, yet a York pardon—the impact of the thought halted him —would abolish a barrier.

If he were no longer an outlaw, if he won the acting governor's absolution and Duane's support, Adam might go in safety to Ticonderoga; he might seek out Delight and, at worst, end the uncertainty that endured like a low fever. Face to face with her, he could learn whether, actually, she was to remain forever beyond his reach.

A man, hurrying by, jostled him, but Adam paid no heed. He could lose nothing by obeying Duane's summons; he might, through compromise, recover all that he drearily had considered lost. He felt as though at last he had found the key to a long-locked door.

He was unaware that the man who had collided with him had halted, had stared at him uncertainly, and now came toward him, smiling and holding out a hand.

"Adam," Justus Sherwood said. "I hardly knew you."

They sat together in a tavern over mugs of brandy flip and, now that the warmth of greeting was spent, talked with unnatural care. Sherwood's questions were so elaborately unconcerned that Adam found himself weighing each reply. The universal tension, he thought with bitterness, was pulling old associations apart.

Justus abandoned unprofitable inquiry to rattle through an account of himself. He had quit The Grants, permanently, unless an infatuated people turned from the ruinous path along which Ethan Allen and other madmen drove them. He had obtained responsible employment under Quebec's governor and was as contented as anyone might be in the mad state of the world.

"I have done with divided loyalties," he said with a challenging air, "and am satisfied to be at last where truly I always have belonged, in the humble service of my king."

He paused as though expecting retort and, when Adam offered

none, said in a gentler voice, "Where you, too, would be if I might only clear your eyes. Few things would please me more."

He submitted with slight lifting of his shoulders as Adam shook his head. After a moment's silence, Sherwood asked idly, "And what brings you to Montreal in the dead of winter?"

"A friend who needed a guide," Adam answered briefly.

"From The Grants?"

"No."

"A man that I know?"

"Now this is a strange thing," Adam answered with a grin of derision, "but at the moment I have wholly forgotten his name or his errand."

Sherwood blinked, then chuckled, and lifted his mug in a saluting gesture.

"Good shot. I deserved that."

He drank and proposed suddenly with his old, pleasant smile, "Shall we cease fencing, abandon politics, and talk henceforward as good companions?"

"Very gladly."

"Then since we are agreed," Sherwood pursued, matching Adam's lately mocking grin, "let me in friendship refresh your mind. John Brown is the man whom Sunderland and you guided hither and he will be closeted with James Morrison sufficiently long for you and me to fill ourselves comfortably with flip."

Adam's expression roused him to silent laughter.

"You will find," he said at last and wiped his eyes, "that the king is better served than you rebels believe. You will find, too, whatever spring brings forth, that Canada will remain loyal to the Crown. Tell Brown so, if you wish. It will save him time."

Sherwood, having enjoyed his triumph, led the talk away from controversy and questioned his friend concerning Hough's trial and punishment.

"Deserved, perhaps," he granted when Adam had told the story, "but ill advised. The Reverend is a vindictive man. Allen has made another enemy."

"They already are so many that one more or less will not matter greatly."

Sherwood nodded and then spoke with unexpected moderation of his sister. It was plain he already had forgiven her defiance and her husband's iniquity and was taking pride in her marriage to an officer of the king. He had not seen Felicity since the elopement but he had had an appeasing letter and had obtained later tidings of her and Wadman during a visit to Ticonderoga.

"They are spending the winter in New York town where Captain Delaplace tells me Felicity has become the rage. George's inheritance, his own parts—and his wife," he added smugly, "should carry him far."

The complacence galled Adam, yet he held his peace. Nothing was to be won by reminding Justus of his late denunciation of Wadman. Sherwood, like most men as the crisis neared, had cast away hampering compunctions to embrace more intensely the cause he had chosen. He doubtless observed a similar zealotry in Adam who asked hastily, "You have been to Ticonderoga? Then you saw Delight Royden?"

Sherwood smiled.

"She is an abiding comfort to Captain Delaplace and his lady. Indeed"—he paused and cleared his throat—"I think I have seen no fairer, sweeter maid than Delight."

"Yes," Adam acknowledged.

"Leftenant Feltham," Sherwood pursued, "is her veritable slave, yet Delight remains immune to his wooing. I fancy, when the garrison is reenforced, there will be a different tale to tell, unless all young officers have been bereft of their senses."

"Yes," Adam said again.

His friend hesitated, fumbled, and ventured, "I thought, even hoped, last summer that you were drawn to her and she to you."

"You were only half right, it seems," Adam told him and drank deeply.

"I am sorry. I would not have said so much if I had not recalled the letter I bore to her from Bennington."

Adam asked, keeping his voice level, "Do you recall, too, what she said, how she looked, when she read it?"

Sherwood shook his head with a sympathetic smile.

"She was away and I was in haste. I left it in Felicity's care."

"I see," said Adam slowly.

March was well advanced before John Brown completed his mission and joined his guides at St. Johns. Adam had gone there, days earlier, as though his accomplishment of this first stage of the homeward journey might hasten its completion.

Sunderland repeatedly prescribed heavier dosages of ale to cure the impatience that afflicted his friend. Fretting, pacing about, and swearing, Peleg pointed out, only lengthened each day. Nothing sped time more swiftly and pleasantly than a belly full of malt, particularly when the price thereof could properly be charged to the Bay Province's Committee of Correspondence.

Adam could not acquire this thrifty philosophy. His uncertainty was a torment not easily borne. Until he had seen Delight, it must be his fate to swing without end from hope to despair; from the certainty that Felicity had never delivered Adam's letter to the conviction that she, however great her hatred of him, never would stoop so low.

Only Delight could quiet the doubt. Only Duane could clear Adam's way to her. Meanwhile, he was prisoned at St. Johns until Brown's tortuous mission ended. When, toward mid-month, the wind got into the south and blew with clammy mildness, Sunderland contracted his companion's impatience. If Brown did not come soon, Peleg said darkly, they would creep home miserably through slush and snow water. His prophecy was fulfilled when the emissary finally appeared, his patience frayed by Canadian evasion, and the southward march actually began.

Pools that the waxing sun and the warm, wet wind spread over Champlain's ice drove the travelers ashore to plod through sodden, sticky snow. Drifts were dwindling and free water cried from every gully when the mud-plastered three returned to Bennington. There, Adam immediately addressed a letter to James Duane.

April was half spent when the reply came. Next day, Adam rode his mare toward Albany.

Chapter XLII

THE sloop's brown sails filled and the Hudson gurgled beneath her counter. Albany's hillside houses slid by while Adam reflected, with an unlikely mingling of relief and resentment, that he might have been a disembodied spirit for all the heed his native town had paid him.

The caution of his return seemed ridiculous now. He had waited till dark to ride into Albany and had sought humble lodgings in The Bull Tavern, but the face of the hostler who stabled his mare was familiar and the landlord, Adam discovered with alarm, was an old acquaintance. Neither had accorded him more than routine heed.

Teunis Duycking, the stout, red skipper of this sloop, had been equally indifferent when Adam had applied for passage, though they once had been dame's school classmates. Teunis had blinked and dickered and finally had taken him aboard as though he were inanimate cargo. Now, as the craft gathered headway, Adam sardonically questioned the necessity of this journey. If Albanians failed to recognize him, he surely could enter Ticonderoga with a specter's immunity.

The sloop heeled at the river's bend and the wind, spilling overside the reek of baled furs and smoked whitefish that were her chief cargo, bore to Adam's nose for an instant the sweet smell of April. Duycking shouted to his crew, a gnarled Dutchman who stood vigilantly in the bow, then leaned against the tiller and grinned widely at his sole passenger.

"Wager ye feel better, eh, Adam, now the town's behind ye?" His smile broadened and pushed his eyes shut.

"Then you do know me?" Adam managed at last.

"I'm not blind," the skipper snorted. "Neither am I wishful to have some informer sell an old friend for fifty pound."

"I'm grateful," Adam told him gruffly. "I still don't understand."

Duycking thrust against the tiller.

"Did ye ever consider how little governors' proclamations and the like utter what plain folks believe? There's something astir this spring, Adam. Maybe ye've felt it. Now, the gentry, even them that oppose the king, hold that liberty must belong only to the best people. That's one reason us lower classes"—he mouthed the phrase—"are partial to Grants folks. Seems there's enough freedom there for every man to have a helping."

"That's why the landlord at The Bull ignored me?" Adam marveled in a warm daze.

"That's why more folks than ye know did. That's why ye're here. The Sons of Liberty have a real active lodge in Albany."

The south wind's blast retarded their passage but brought the spring upstream to meet them. The lawns of the patroons' riverside mansions were green. The softness of unfurling leaves lay upon The Highlands, and in their shadow men were staking shad nets.

The warmth and the sense of promise trembling on fulfillment's verge belied the animosities of men. Here were only the lap of small waves, the creak of yards, the flutter of canvas as the sloop tacked and tacked again, and the soothing incantation of the wind. They could not dispel Adam's restlessness; the craving to have done with his errand and to be journeying north again.

April and Delight were so alike that it was torment to experience one in the other's absence. He found echoes of the girl in the tranquilly waking earth, the bright water, and the tender sky. He spent long hours in the sloop's bow, as far as might be from her penetrating smells, and, lying half asleep, felt himself drenched by sunshine and the warm, deep need of Delight.

A worshipful quality had come into his yearning. It was better to love Delight unrequited than to win another maid. The world always would be fairer because she dwelt in it. Adam could not look upon lovelinesses, great and small, that the river revealed, without wishing to double their worth by sharing them with Delight.

He was bound to her whether she would have him or not and, as the days passed and more miles came between them, he could feel the strain of a tether, excruciatingly stretched. When the fog of an early morning burned away from beneath The Palisades' brown wall and disclosed the smoke and shining roofs of New York, Adam felt relief that the pull would slacken when he turned back toward Delight again.

Duane welcomed his guest with warmth so great that Adam knew it did not spring alone from fondness. His host summoned his lovely wife to rejoice with him in the wanderer's return and outstripped even her in hospitality. Adam must lodge with them. Duane cried for servants to prepare the Blue Chamber and bear Mr. Corlaer's belongings thither. Had he dined? A cold collation could be served at once. Would he drink? Then, if he had no immediate wants that it would be Duane's great delight to supply, would Adam accompany him to his office in the mansion?

The raptures that had overwhelmed the guest modified as they sat in the tall, cool room with the noise of the town a distant windy sound. The flanges of Duane's heavy nose twitched; his smooth, white fingers tapped his snuffbox lid.

"Scripture," said he, dryly, "omits to mention it, but no doubt the earlier Prodigal was equally redolent of his late companions."

He smiled in pretended great relief when Adam, red and flustered, attributed his aroma to the sloop's cargo.

"I feared, my boy, that it might be Liberty's very scent. My experience in the late Congress at Philadelphia has taught me that those most vehement for the rights of man were least particular over their own ablutions."

The smile died out. Duane took snuff and, flicking his nose with his kerchief, said earnestly, "You have come at a critical moment, Adam, like an answer to prayer. Where is Ethan Allen?"

"He was not at Bennington when I left," Adam answered cautiously, "but he can be reached there."

"Can you reach him on my behalf?"

"I—think so." Adam hesitated and then asked bluntly, "Why?"

Duane nursed one silk-sheathed leg and spoke urgently: He believed America to be in great danger. The fires the British orig-

378

inally had kindled and radicals, equally wrongheaded, had fanned at any moment might get out of hand. Once released, they might sweep away all the country had built in a century. A spark would ignite Boston. The Grants was another open magazine and Ethan Allen—Duane obviously and with some difficulty swallowed the epithets he usually attached to the name—still was scattering gunpowder about.

The speaker's jowls were redder but his voice was admirably controlled as he pursued:

"When New York's fate, indeed the fate of all the provinces, hangs in the balance, men of foresight, perforce, must be willing to suffer loss for the sake of the public weal. We are eager to remove the causes of the reckless actions to which this"—he swallowed again—"Ethan Allen is dedicated. If my associates and I are willing to make sacrifices, then so should he be, for our common country's safety."

He looked hopefully at Adam who asked carefully at last, "What sacrifices and in what degree?"

"Let us defer that till tonight," Duane proposed with increased confidence. "Certain patentees of Grants' land will be invited to dine here with us. Allen is well known to you. Can you induce him to confer with me and others?"

"Possibly; even probably."

"Excellent, my boy. I said you came at an opportune time."

"I have," Adam said stoutly, "an interest of my own."

"I know, I know." Duane waved his hands. "You need not worry unduly over your own property if you can bring Allen and us together."

"That is not my concern, sir." Adam felt his face grow hot. "I require safe conduct into Fort Ticonderoga."

Duane jerked as though he had been pricked. His plump hands slapped down loudly on the chair's arms. The ruddy face, lately beaming, was hard and the eyes were narrow.

"Ticonderoga, forsooth! And why must you go there? Eh, sir?"

"Because," Adam retorted, careless of the other's alarm, "the maid I wish to wed is companion to the commandant's wife and I cannot visit her in my present outlawed state."

"Oh," said Duane. The internal pressure that had stiffened him eased away as he stared at his defiantly glowering companion. "On your honor, that is your sole purpose?"

He breathed deeply in relief and fumbled for snuff when Adam nodded.

"There should be no great difficulty in obtaining safe conduct for you. I was startled because of rumors that have lately come to me respecting Fort Ti. A Leftenant Wadman and his bride—well, sir?"

"I started," Adam explained, "because I know them both."

"Indeed? A handsome young woman. She and her husband rode north only yesterday. Before she left, she informed Governor Colden that Ethan Allen is projecting a mad attack upon Ticonderoga."

"The lady," Adam chose his words delicately, "was not well informed. There has been discussion of such an assault in the event of war; nothing more."

"Now damme, sir," Duane burst, his face crimson, "that is what makes the villain, Allen, so great a menace. Nothing so surely leads to war as such boasts. An attack upon Ticonderoga, though foredoomed to failure, would be a firebrand flung into an open powder barrel, blasting all hope of compromise."

He wiped his forehead with a desperate gesture.

"If there were fewer Adamses, Henrys, and Allens in our world, there would be greater hope for enduring peace."

The servant who had unpacked Adam's portmanteau had pressed his blue broadcloth suit. Its owner's nose was so inured to the sloop's smell that he could not tell whether the fabric also was tainted. Further airing would do it no harm.

He rang for a tub and bathed, luxuriating in the half-forgotten joys of hot water, white soap, and fleecy towels, and then, since his host had gone to summon his associates to dinner, left the house and breasted the clamor and crowd of The Broad Way.

The street's turbulence sent his lightened spirits higher. Ballad vendors cried at him and hawkers shouted their wares in his ears. He moved toward The Bowling Green through a press of ponderous Dutch burghers, dark sailors with gleaming earrings, merchants, drovers, dawdling macaronis, and a scattering of iron-faced Indians, and because the sky was silken with April and the wind blew warmly from The Battery imagined Delight walked beside him.

One day, Adam promised himself in gay, new confidence as he picked his way over the muck of a crossing, Delight and he would view the lusty little town that had neither Boston's settled dignity nor Philadelphia's metropolitan stature but its own rousing vitality. He turned in on impulse at a goldsmith's and, after much uncertainty and debate, bought a ring, not without qualms lest his daring revive fortune's animus. He drove away compunction with the picture of how the heavy circlet would adorn a small, brown hand.

In a few days, he told himself, as he came out with his purchase, he would be on his way to Delight, armed by Duane for a personal storming of Fort Ticonderoga. He was so lost in that bright prospect that he collided with a solid person who straightway wrapped thick arms about him and acclaimed the miracle of this meeting.

Teunis Duycking was more than creditably drunk for this hour of the afternoon. His sloop's cargo, he announced, weaving and grinning, had been whipped out of her and another was being put aboard. He would sail at midnight with the turn of the tide and he implored Adam to forsake a town where liquor was ruinous in price and water-mild in effect and accompany him upriver. When at last they parted, Duycking shouted after his friend:

"Coenties Slip, Adam. Stroke of twelve."

The table had been cleared. The candles' flames set their reflections deep in the sleek mahogany, and a silver-chased decanter was making its clockwise passage from Duane to his grave, patrician brother-in-law, Robert Livingston; to John Kempe, the attorney general, with his stubborn mouth and unpowdered hair; thence to Goldsbrow Banyar, provincial secretary, whose face, even in repose wore a startled, foxy look, and from him to Adam on his host's right. Duane stood and raised his glass:

"To His Majesty the King! May his wisdom and mercy prevail over evils wrought by his ministers abroad and his enemies here."

Chairs scraped as the company rose and drank in silence. The body and fragrance of the Bual Madeira spread balm on Adam's spirit. Earlier, he had felt alien in his worn broadcloth among those soft-voiced, soft-handed gentry, so confident in their grace, so fine in satins and lace. He had been suspicious, too, of the purposes of the entirely male gathering, from which even Mrs. Duane had been excluded, and vigilant lest in some undiscerned fashion his companions seduce him.

Adam had discarded these rigidities now. The polished ease of the conversation; the crystal, silver, and delicate chinaware; the succession of savory dishes daintily served; the sound wines that had accompanied them, all had been eloquent welcomes to a returned exile. The dinner and the company belonged to a world from which his senses cried he had been too long absent.

When the obligatory toast had been drunk and the company had reseated itself, Adam, with a sudden tightening of his attention, saw that Duane approached the dinner's purpose. It had been, the host was explaining pleasantly to his associates, good fortune for them all to have Mr. Corlaer appear out of the wilderness. His experience in The Grants had been intimate and active enough—Duane smiled broadly—to win for him a proscription at Governor Tryon's hands. Mr. Corlaer had agreed to act as emissary to Ethan Allen, for a consideration—his host cocked an arch eye at Adam—that shortly would be forthcoming. The question now was just what the approach to Allen should be.

Livingston stirred as Duane ended. He asked gravely, "You know Allen well, Mr. Corlaer? Exactly what does he want?"

Adam weighed his reply, knowing it would ruffle this sleek, composed company.

"I think, sir, that his prime purpose is—liberty."

Livingston shrugged but Kempe frowned and grumbled, "Liberty, indeed? Something that everyone cries for in these disjointed times—and few deserve."

"I should have gone further, perhaps. I should have said liberty for the people of The Grants."

"Oh, come!" Banyar barked. "He is surely less the pure spirit than you picture him, since his strivings for 'liberty' have included making extremely free with land that is, under law, our property."

His acidity smarted. Adam filled his glass before he replied, "I don't believe land, as such, is important to Colonel Allen."

"No?" Banyar returned with a foxy leer. "How many thousands of acres does his tribe claim in The Grants?"

Duane, seeing Adam's face grow rigid, said with dignified haste, "The question of The Grants land titles can best be left to the forthcoming Congress to which Mr. Livingston and I have the honor to be delegates. We are considering expediency, not law. We wish to dissuade Mr. Allen from his defiant pose, since we recognize that his further rebellion, in the country's present plight, might disastrously run into revolution."

Livingston nodded. He said complacently, "I have reason to know that many respectable persons in The Grants deplore Allen's activities."

"Some may confide this to you, sir," Adam conceded. "They will not profess it publicly in Bennington, or elsewhere."

"Because," Kempe advanced unpleasantly, "they fear a villainous bully?"

"No," said Adam, holding fast to his temper, "because Grants folk in general have a peculiar patriotism you gentlemen overlook."

"Now damme, sir," Banyar broke in with heat, "we yield to none in patriotism. Our motives in trying to appease this—this land pirate are above self-concern. We seek a settlement for our country's sake."

"Before," Adam retorted, tingling, "I admire such altruism, may I ask you the question lately put to me: How many thousands of acres do you gentlemen claim in The Grants?"

In anger's light, he matched the smoothly groomed personages about him in this stately room with the grimed folk who had offered him unstinted hospitality in the smoky kitchens of The Grants. Kempe intervened, while Banyar colored: "Tell me this, sir: Is it not true that, with Ethan Allen appeased, The Grants in all likelihood would grow tractable? Yes? Then, sir"—he leaned forward earnestly—"if we four, and possibly other patentees, were to offer to buy the Allen holdings at a fair price, what would his response in likelihood be?"

"I cannot pledge him but I believe he would refuse," Adam replied, not liking the canny glitter in the attorney-general's eyes.

"Refuse!" Banyar yapped. "What manner of man is he? Charlatan? Extortioner?"

Adam ignored him and said to Kempe, "I do not think he

would sell his holdings to New York purchasers. I do think him less than sordid. You have heard of his intentions against Ticonderoga, if war comes. No man who thought first of his own fortune would risk that venture, since the Allen properties are close to whatever counter-attack Canada might launch.

"Furthermore," he went on, his voice gathering strength as dislike for his sleek companions mounted, "you will find that, Allen or no Allen, nine-tenths of the frontier people have owned themselves too long to submit to any other proprietor."

The butler had come on tiptoe to whisper urgently to Duane, who now rose and went quickly from the room. Kempe, who had been watching Adam, raised his glass and said cynically, "Liberty, like Madeira, should be reserved for those who can appreciate it."

"Or, like Madeira," Adam said quickly, "liberty, once enjoyed, turns any alternative insipid."

Kempe surveyed him more thoughtfully. Banyar said with a barking laugh, "Perhaps we should drink to Mr. Allen's designs on Ti. An attack would abolish our problem by destroying him."

Duane entered in soft haste and closed the door behind him. His taut look hushed them all.

"Gentlemen," he told his associates, "the Committee of Safety has had an express from Boston."

He paused, drew breath sharply, and caught tight hold of his chair's back.

"It has begun, gentlemen, for all our efforts to avert it. Massachusetts has been fighting the regulars at a place called Lexington."

Chapter XLIII

SOMEWHERE in the silent house a clock cleared its throat and struck eleven. Dampness, entering as Adam softly opened the front door, cooled his face. He peered into the blackness, heard church bells toll and the voice of a distant watchman proclaim that all was well. It seemed as Adam went down into the street a sardonic assurance.

Fog magnified the sound of his own quick footsteps. His haste was almost flight, as though he dreaded that the qualms he lately had cast aside might follow and drag him back. Only a few windows still shone high in The Broad Way's dark walls. Twice he passed other hurrying men. Otherwise, the town slept, spent by earlier frenzy.

While Adam had prowled about his bedroom, striving to re-order the mind Duane's tidings had roiled, he had heard distant cheering, the blare of horns, and a desultory popping of firearms. Word of the fight in the Bay Province was spreading swiftly.

The thing that most men had predicted, yet few truly had believed, at last had happened. The incredible had come to pass and the lives of New Yorkers, of all night-bound Americans, had been changed.

Adam thought enviously of Duane and his friends, debating expedients in the Committee of Safety. He gladly would have exchanged places with anyone in the crowd that celebrated a dark uncertainty. Instead, he paced his chamber with doubt and fear for companions.

"My boy," Duane had said, hastily linking the throat of his cloak, "this dire news must excuse a host's inattention. Ring for a servant if you have any need. I find Mrs. Duane has retired.

Good night to you, Adam. God knows at what hour I shall return."

He and his friends had left, talking in hushed, excited voices. Already they had forgotten Adam. Pride had kept him from crying after them, "What about my own plans? What will this do to them?"

Yet the questions had ding-donged at him and had driven him at last from the empty dining room's desolation to the Blue Chamber where in solitude he had groped for enlightenment. Nothing his stunned mind could offer had the least validity. The unquenchable fire finally had burst forth.

There had been fighting at Lexington. There would be fighting in York, in Pennsylvania, in Virginia. Adam turned from the disaster's glare to inspect his own situation. Realization that the derisive force, once again, had brought him face to face with futility numbed his brain.

The acting governor, a loyalist, would be unlikely now to honor requests from James Duane, delegate to the rebel Congress. It was ridiculous to imagine that Colden would waste time on a semi-penitent outlaw; it was fantastic to think he would grant Adam safe conduct to Ticonderoga.

News of the strife in Massachusetts must soon penetrate The Grants. Adam had a lurid picture of how Ethan Allen would receive it. He would be deaf to inducements from Duane and his fellow patentees. Even now, the giant might be bellowing defiance, bawling orders, cramming himself into his preposterous uniform, preparing with martial pomp and fury to execute his threat against Ticonderoga.

Adam's fate had seen to it that he should be far away when the crucial hour came. There would be ample time before he possibly could return to Bennington for the fort to be assailed. Ethan, Baker, Warner might be dead before he could reach The Grants; possibly Delaplace and Feltham as well. And how many more? Delight!

The thought was like a blow against his midriff, taking his breath, smearing him with sweat. Delight was at Ticonderoga and in peril. At best, if an attack were launched, she would learn much of terror. At worst? The room he paced became a trap and Adam its frantic prisoner.

Delight was in danger and he impotently was fuming here, five days' journey at the least from Bennington where even now Ethan Allen might be mounting his attack. Adam groaned and wiped his clammy face. He could only wait and cling to the hope that Duane, through Colden or the Committee of Safety, might still accomplish the unimaginable and allow him to reach the fort in time to save Delight.

For an instant, it seemed that the girl stood actually before him, gravely sweet, serenely fair, with the lacerating look of trust in her eyes. While he flinched and groaned again, he heard, like an echo, Duycking's farewell: "Coenties Slip, Adam. Before twelve."

Adam checked his pacing, looked dazedly about him, and then began frantically to pack. He thrust aside the protests and alternatives that, almost at once, his treacherous mind began to offer, pointing out the insanity of departure, asking scornfully what he could accomplish by hastening back to The Grants, warning that Duane's influence now was his only dependence.

He stonily withstood his own persuasions. This impulsively undertaken venture might lead only to another failure. There was, nevertheless, decency in action. He would not abandon it. Just possibly, if he could reach Bennington in time, he might prevail upon Allen to withhold assault until Delight had been got clear of the fort. Whether he succeeded or not, he thought as he crammed belongings into his portmanteau, he would have tried his desperate utmost. Adam had scribbled a hasty note to Duane and had stolen down the stair.

Now, as he hurried along The Broad Way, he thought of himself as a ghost, roaming the darkness of a dead town. Panic stirred when he lost himself among the warehouses that bordered crooked, black streets. Salt air, cutting through manifold stenches, led him to the waterfront. An ever more frantic search among shoreward-thrusting bowsprits brought him at last to Coenties Slip and the squat shape of the Duycking sloop with master and man stumbling about her deck.

Teunis helped him joyously overside.

"So you have not fallen victim to the rumpots, fleshpots, and sireens of this damned town?"

"I have business in the north that will not wait," Adam panted.

387

"Call me an Abenaki," Duycking proclaimed, "if I do not set you ashore in Albany, four days hence."

They were twelve days making the passage. Off Spuyten Duyvil, the tide turned and the following breeze that Teunis had promised would grow with the dawn, failed entirely. They waited becalmed on water sleek as oil until an unseasonable thunderstorm, evoked by the precocious heat, brought wind that drove them as far as Yonkers, and deserted them again.

The days that followed were to Adam a torment of shining water and delusive breezes so brief they hardly warranted the hoisting of the sails. He tried with scant success to imitate his shipmates' fatalistic patience and might, he truly believed, have lost his mind had not contact with craft the outgoing tides drew sluggishly downstream reassured him. It was news the boats failed to bring that sustained him.

Every crew had tidings, more or less fantastic, from Boston, but none had knowledge or even rumor of activity in The Grants. Gradually, as the sloop crept toward Albany, a sense of anticlimax oppressed Adam, a feeling that he again had been duped, this time by a practical joke the hot, windless days, the shimmering river, and his own headlong haste had played upon him. He felt he had aged a year when the sloop reached the end of her voyage.

There was a report in Albany that Ethan Allen would take The Green Mountain Boys to join their fellow New Englanders in the siege of Boston. This relieved Adam yet increased his scorn of his own hysterical haste. He spent the night at The Bull Tavern, still ostensibly a stranger to the landlord, and in the morning rode Allegra toward Bennington.

Midway to the Hudson ferry, he overtook a small, ambling cavalcade. He had come abreast of the mounted servant who led two baggage nags before he recognized the man and woman who rode at a leisurely pace before him. It was too late to obey the alarmed impulse and drop behind for, even as it rose, the masked woman in the long dark habit and the gaily feathered hat glanced back then hastily bent toward her companion. Wadman twisted about in the saddle and stared from beneath lowering, black brows.

388

"Adam Corlaer!" he exclaimed and drew rein, blocking the way. In the black silk mask, Felicity's eyes shone. Adam halted his mare. Behind him, the servant cried, "Whoa!" to his charges.

"Good morning, Felicity," Adam said coolly. "Good morning, Leftenant."

He was watching Wadman's swarthy face and got satisfaction from its indecision. Felicity gabbled, to end the tension, "Adam! Fancy! Wherever did you drop from, and where are you going?"

Allegra snorted and sidled. Wadman uncompromisingly barred the way. His eyes, sliding toward his servant, bore an unuttered command. Felicity's babbling ran on. They had been till this morning guests of the Ten Eycks in Albany and were traveling now to Skenesborough.

"Poor George must report on the tenth. Our lovely wedding tour is almost at an end."

The servant sat gaping, unable to read his master's unspoken bidding. Irresolution swayed Wadman. Adam said briskly, "By your leave, Leftenant, I shall pass. I am in haste."

The other scowled, cleared his throat and offered in a surly voice, "I seem to recall that there was, or still is—"

The accusation hung. Adam jostled the slow mind by completing it. "A reward for my capture? True. That is why"—he smiled widely, leaned forward and unlatched his saddle holsters—"I go armed, perforce."

Still smiling, he drew and displayed a pistol, not leveling it but weighing it on his palm. "I have no intention of being taken. And now, if you will allow me the road, sir."

After an instant's tight silence, Felicity begged in a low voice, "Please, George!"

Wadman pulled his horse aside.

"Thank you, Leftenant. A pleasant journey to you both."

"I trust, sir," Wadman groped for his shattered poise, "we shall meet again."

"And I," Adam returned.

He would have ridden on but Felicity fluted, "It is vain, I suppose, to look for you at Ticonderoga. Have you any message," she pursued with sugary spite, "that I may take to our little Delight?"

The barbed question filled Adam with unscrupulous wrath. He bent low in the saddle and smiled. "Thank you deeply, but I think not. I have learned how unwise it is to entrust a message—or even a letter—to anyone."

The mask screened her face, yet he saw color stain her throat, justifying his suspicions, confirming his half-belief. He was sure now that Delight never had received his letter. Adam laughed, saluted Wadman and his wife, and put spurs to the mare.

The solemn gaiety that possessed Adam was worth the otherwise empty journey. He followed through the quickening spring some still undiscerned way to Delight. The roadside, bright with the blossoms of bloodroot and windflowers; the chime of small, brown sparrows fitted his mood. The blithe serenity was broken, late in the day, when he ran, full tilt, into ambush.

Under the muzzles of the muskets leveled by four grim men who stepped suddenly from the underbrush, he slowly raised his hands.

"Dismount," the rawboned spokesman ordered, " 'n' then, ye'll —Hol' on. Know ye."

"You should."

He had been one of the escort that had brought Hough to Sunderland. Now, he grumbled, "Guess ye can pass, though orders is to take all travelers."

"Why?"

The other blinked. "All I'm s'posed to know. Ain't tellin' what maybe I kin guess."

Adam rode on, but the incident and the mystery that clothed it continued to gall him and not even the tranquillity gathering dusk had laid on Bennington Green nor the cheer of lighted windows could dispel irritation.

He found the tavern taproom uncommonly empty for this hour. Stephen Fay shook his head when Adam asked for Ethan Allen. The Colonel, the landlord said with unsatisfactory brevity, was absent, but Ira was upstairs.

Ethan's youngest brother sat at a paper-spread table and the face he raised as Adam entered belonged properly to an older man. There were lines in his forehead and about his traplike mouth, and in the candlelight his eloquent brown eyes were haggard.

"Wal," he said in acid accusation. "Ye've heard, eh? Real pleased, too, wouldn't wonder."

"Heard what?"

Ira assembled the scattered papers before he made indirect answer. There was anguish in his dry voice.

"Been summin' up what we stand to lose. Sold, so far, sixteen thousand acres. Company still holds sixty thousand all close to the lake and worth at current prices maybe sixty thousand pound. That's all," he pursued with irony. "Sixty thousand pound! That's what the devil gave me for a brother is imperiling."

"I have just returned from York," Adam told the fuming little man. "I still don't know what you're talking about."

"By rights," Ira chewed on his grievance, "ye shouldn't be here at all, since Ethan's ordered all roads closed to travel."

Adam started to speak and then kept silent, feeling explanation would come more quickly without his further inquiry. Ira's compressed lips moved across his teeth. He complained at length: "Curbed him all I could. Rampin' an' pitchin' like that damned, half-broke stud of his ever since news come of Lexington. Kept tellin' him he'd no authority to act 'n' that sort of held him down."

"Then"—the sour voice grew still more strident—"they came an' kicked the pail over. Mott an' Bull an' other God-blasted Connecticut men with Easton an' that damned fire-eating John Brown from Pittsfield and some hay-foot milishy they'd picked up on the way. Wanted Ethan to raise the Boys an' be lord high leader of 'em all."

The normally composed young man's gesture was shockingly wild.

"So," Ira shrilled, "that's where the lunatic's gone an' that's how the Allen family will be beggared."

"Gone? To Boston?"

"Who said aught of Boston? To Castleton, to marshal the Boys there and"—he gulped over the enormity—"and storm Ti."

"Ti?" Adam repeated blankly.

Ira relapsed from frenzy into calm despair.

"Ehyah, Ti. If the garrison's been reenforced, or even if it hasn't an' they get word, Ethan an' all his bedlam are dead ducks."

"When," Adam asked slowly, "is this to happen?"

The other shrugged.

"How do I know when? The high, exalted Lord of Hosts didn't unbend sufficient to inform me. Where," he asked more sharply, "are you goin', for God's sweet sake?"

"To borrow a horse from Fay," Adam threw over his shoulder, "and get north to Castleton."

Chapter XLIV

ADAM, riding his weary mount down the last slope toward Castleton, laid the faint tumult in his ears to fatigue. His body, he reflected, had cause for mutiny. He had eaten little and slept less since his departure from Bennington yet, save for the enduring murmur, he felt no sign of exhaustion. It was as though the vitality of The Grants' atmosphere had sustained him.

He had been conscious of this sparkling quality when first he had ventured into this land. Now it hung, intensified, like the ominous, rousing air that broods before a thunderstorm. Each breath he drew had stirred Adam. He had seen the reflection of his own excitement in the settlers' faces, had heard it in the taut voices.

"Bound north, be ye? Wal, Isaac 'n' Uriah, they left yest'dy. Somethin's afoot, b'God. Give the bastards what-fer, whoever they be."

A spasm of exultation shook Adam as he rode down through the spring-scented forest toward Castleton. Something native to this country and its people was moving, strong and full-statured, toward consummation.

The trouble with his ears was not internal. The hivelike humming had waxed into an uneven brawling sound. He emerged from the woods and in the distance saw its source. Horses were tied to every possible projection about Remington's tavern and the dark mass of men that filled its porch had spilled out into the road to eddy and fray and convulsively reassemble with clamor lanced by whoops and wolf yells that surged briefly into cheering.

It was the crowd's endeavor to force its way into the already crammed taproom. A minor riot simmered at the door where men were hauled from within and flung aside, only to recover, return, and do their earnest best to serve their late assailants likewise. One parched aspirant reached in and pulled a drinker bodily through an open window. They grappled, fell, and amid shouting rolled off the porch while four others struggled to enter the aperture.

Within the packed chamber, a fiddle's voice twisted through the clamor and led a strong chanting:

> "*Come all you laboring hands that toil below*
> *Among the rock and sands, that plow and sow*
> *Upon your hired lands, let out by cruel hands—*"

The more composed, or less thirsty, fringe of the crowd broke away as Adam approached and encircled him, gaping, squalling inquiries and tarter comments on the stranger's appearance, probable morals, and infamous ancestry. It seemed to the deafened newcomer that all the able of The Grants had assembled here, well-oiled firelocks in hand—barefooted men, skin-clad and fur-capped; spurred and booted men with the dust of their journeys still upon them; men from the settled south, decently habited in homespun or towcloth; lean, harsh, untrammeled men whose faces shone with glee and sweat, whose eyes were level, whose voices bellowed.

Through the din, the chorus in the taproom tramped on:

> "*For who would be a slave that may be free?*
> *Here you can have good land, just come and see;*
> *The soil is deep and good, here in this pleasant wood,*
> *Where you may raise your food and happy be.*"

The reek of alcohol and heated bodies was sharp in Adam's nose. The comments smarted in his ears.

"Hoss thief, Seth, if ever I see one. . . . No sir; so pretty in them fancy clothes, hoss stole him. . . . Where from, friend? . . . Bennington? Started real late, didn't ye? . . . Hell, started on time but dallied with our gals all along the way. . . . Hol' on, boys; I know him. 'Tis Adam Corlaer. . . . Do tell? Wal, all the wust Grants' rascals is present then."

The clamor altered direction and swelled into derisive cheering as a file of dusty horsemen rode up to the tavern.

"Here's Neshobe, boys. Last in the fight 'n' the fust to leave it. Whar you Neshobe folks been? Bring any rum? Wal, go back 'n' fetch some. Ye'll git none here. Them fellers in the taproom are makin' a pitch thar."

Two men carried a helpless third from the tavern and a bellowing dozen tried to force their way in. A wrestling match that promised to include mayhem drew away the last of Adam's admirers. He rode toward the stables. They were filled and Remington himself, hoarse and streaming, waved the newcomer off.

"No room," he croaked. "Got eyes, ain't ye? Wal, b'God, 'tis Adam!"

He gasped and wiped his eyes on a sodden sleeve.

"Mebby I can smuggle ye a bait of oats but ye'll have to take yer horse elsewhere, secret-like, to feed him. Damn near cleaned me out a'ready. Rum's gone, beer's dwindlin', 'n' cider ain't too plentiful. If Ethan don't take 'em away pretty soon— Hey, ye dinged fool!"

A whooping crowd was gathering about a man who swung a scythe with a mower's rhythm at the legs of his companion who, at each sweep, yelled and leaped, skip-rope fashion, over the steel.

"Higher," he screeched. "Higher 'n' faster."

"My best blade," Remington moaned and strove to force his way through the massing spectators. A burlier figure, preceding him, wrapped an arm about the scythe-wielder and pulled his weapon away. The deprived man's snarl faded as he looked up into Seth Warner's solemn face.

"Cap'n," he protested with dignity, "we was settlin' of a wager, nothin' more. An', by God," he bawled at the panting jumper, "one more sweep 'n' I'd a got ye, Zed."

Warner, grinning, restored the scythe to its owner and turning saw Adam.

"Boys a mite playful," he chuckled, wringing the other's hand. "Ethan? He's not here."

"Not here?" Adam repeated dully and Warner chuckled again.

"Moved out to Bentley's farm when the Boys got so loud he couldn't hear himself holler."

He cleared a way through the press for his friend's horse but came closer after Adam had mounted and asked in a low, concerned voice, "Did you hear aught in New York of reenforcements for Ti?"

Adam shook his head.

"We've had reports," Warner confided. "I wish I knew."

Renewed yelling followed Adam as he rode away. Through the tumult, he heard still another snatch of the taproom's savage song:

> *"We value not New York with all their powers,*
> *For here we'll stay and work, the land is ours."*

Allen's white stallion grazed in a rail-fenced field beside the Bentley farmhouse. The sentry who sat on the doorstep with his musket across his knees unfolded as Adam approached and, learning his errand, shouted into the dwelling, "Here's another, Colonel."

He stood, clumsily barring the way with his firelock, until steps sounded in the hall. Sam Herrick's dour brown face creased slowly into a grin.

" 'Tis sorcery," said he, "no less. Colonel was speakin' of ye, a moment ago."

He led the way into a chamber where Ethan Allen overflowed a chair on which his brassbound coat was hung. He raised his head from the papers before him, flung down his pen to their detriment, sprang up, and bellowed, "Gods of the mountains, Adamlad! You could not have come more opportunely."

His great hands caught the other's shoulders and shook till Adam's teeth clicked. The brazen voice pursued, "I wallow here in an inky swamp—muster rolls, requisitions, vouchers, and the king of hell knows what else. Sam has been aiding me, yet we have been close to foundering, windbroken and spavined. Now you, who are familiar with such things drop from the sky. Sam—"

He remembered decorum and began again, "Captain Herrick, my compliments to the Board of War and my invitation to gather here to meet a new member."

None of the board, Herrick's twanging voice reported, was present. Captain Mott had gone with Captain Warner to arrange for commissary transport; Colonels Brown and Easton had ridden to view Champlain.

"Hah," Ethan cried, glowing. "Determine then if there be a

sufficiency of rum in the kitchen to contrive a punch for this re-union."

Herrick saluted, grinning, and left. Allen, with the air of one forever renouncing clerical work, put on the uniform coat that seemed to increase his stature. He loomed above Adam. Pride suffused the rough-hewn face and set the blue eyes ablaze.

"Christ's great-grandfather, boy, what a day this is and what a fanfare of fame history henceforth will accord our names! We shall bring a mighty fortress lower than Babylon. You have seen the host I am assembling. The continent boasts no better troops."

"They seem spirited," Adam commented briefly.

"Aye, sir. Vigorous lads and unbridled in their ease, but by the sword of the Lord and of Gideon, you shall see them over-whelm Ticonderoga, however many regulars they summon to defend it. I wish—"

He clamped his teeth against further speech but his frown lin-gered. Adam asked, "When do you attack?"

Hidden concern had muted the lately vainglorious blaring.

"Another company is assembling at Shoreham. We shall join forces shortly. The Board of War will decide tonight when the assault is to be launched.

"I wish—" Allen said again, bungled and then went on dog-gedly, "I wish I knew whether the garrison had wind of our plans. The damned Yorkers—I mean the British—have talked of strength-ening and reenforcing Ti, but I have no sure word of the present state of the fort."

He scowled at his ink stained fingers before he confided further, "We find a scarcity of boats on this side of the lake. That is a bad sign."

His epaulettes gleamed as he shrugged and Adam, seeing how worry beclouded the rocky face, felt a throb of sympathy.

"Such doubts," Allen admitted with a crooked smile, "twist, I'll hazard, all commanders' bowels. I will reveal to you, Adam, that there are moments when I almost regret my derision of the Lord God Jehovah who, if he should in truth exist, is unlikely to grant me the aid he is said to have accorded Gideon. By all the deities in Palestine, I'd give an eye to know the true situation at Ti."

"I can save you an eye." Adam kept his voice steady. "I am bound for Ticonderoga."

In the silence, they could hear the faint echo of the tumult in Castleton. Adam withstood the harsh scrutiny of Ethan Allen who asked, finally, with a sound of distant thunder, "Have you lost your wits, entire? You bound for Ti?"

"I have returned from New York for no other purpose. Delight Royden is there. I intend to bring her away before the attack.

"I ask permission, sir," Adam pursued, hoping military precision would appease the glowering giant, "to conduct a reconnaissance."

Amusement puckered Allen's eyelids.

"Have you forgotten that you were at Poultney, Adam, and shared in our entertainment of the leftenants there? Once they clap eyes on you, madman, you'll end in a cell."

"Perhaps not, Colonel." Adam was encouraged by Ethan's willingness to argue. "Wadman, I know, is on leave. Captain Delaplace is an easy gentleman, much influenced by his wife. Surely, the risk is worth the intelligence I might bring back."

"With the pretty, little wench, eh?"

"Surely not without her." Adam knew his face was red.

"Now it might possibly be," the Colonel said portentously and largely to himself, "that Jehovah, recognizing virtue to his own great discernment, will perform a miracle for Ethan Allen's sake. Look you"—Adam felt the odd yet familiar shock as the blazing blue eyes bore upon his—"you are determined in your madness to attempt this thing?"

"I am." It was hard to get words past the sudden triumph that filled his throat.

"When?"

"Now, if time presses. I would leave at dawn tomorrow, otherwise. I have not had much sleep, lately."

Allen glowered at the littered table before him and rumbled like a distant thunderstorm.

"Then you have my permission," he began and, seeing the glee in Adam's face, held up a warning hand, "if first you bring some semblance of order to this nauseous and God-despairing mess before me—by the Trinity and all its appurtenances, sir; hold your peace until I am finished!—and providing furthermore that you tell no one—no one, mind you—of your purpose or that I have sanctioned it. Should anyone learn that I have approved so harebrained a scheme," he added with bitterness, "I should not be deemed worthy to command a file of goslings."

"Agreed," said Adam. Allen's great hands caught his shoulders and shook them gently.

"You will run all the risk," he warned fondly, "of a powder keg set down within the brazen gates of hell, yet if by some prodigious chance you were to get into Ti and out again, I do admit that your information would be most welcome. But no one must know; no one, lest I be considered as demented as you."

He dropped his voice and spoke more quickly. Adam must ride westward to the riverlike upper lake, swim his horse across where the water was narrowest. On the further shore, he would find a trail that led to the fort.

"And the Lord have mercy on your soul, Adam—and on mine for letting you go."

For an endless time, Adam worked over the papers that had so confused his commander. His eyelids smarted for lack of sleep; each bone had its separate ache of weariness. It was twilight when he ate hastily and alone in the kitchen and at Allen's suggestion crawled up into the Bentley hay mow to find slumber. It came reluctantly and was troubled by dreams in which Delight wept piteously and a jeering voice proclaimed that time was short.

He woke at last in utter darkness and found he could sleep no more. From the door of the mow, he looked out upon the black mass of the Bentley house and the stars that marched toward dawn. The faintest light was bleaching the east when Adam stole down, found his unwilling horse in the pasture, saddled, bridled him and rode away. His own body was stiff and mutinous but excitement, like strong drink, set his heart to pounding joyously.

The sun was high and hot and the overridden horse was becoming increasingly rebellious when Adam came down at last to a reach of turbid water, stained an unmerited blue by the bright May sky. His mount shied and snorted as they moved along the lake's marshy edge, seeking a likely place to cross, and flies the warmth was spawning swarmed up from the reeds.

Where the riverlike lake pinched in, Adam forced his animal through the sucking, smacking mire to its brink—where fresh affliction joined the flies' bloodthirsty cloud. The horse balked and, when its rider dismounted to test the water's depth, plunged, whipped the rein from his hand, and scrambled in a flurry of mire up the bank where, finding solidity, it trotted away, heedless of Adam's yells.

Adam abandoned brief pursuit, stripped off and bundled his clothes, while the flies fed well, bound them to his head and launched himself into the roiled water. His burden was almost as wet as he when he crawled up the steep, further shore. He worked himself into the sodden garments and, moving inland, almost at once found the trail.

He followed the narrow track toward Ticonderoga, pausing dutifully at intervals to rest, then trotting on again, while the day's waxing heat beslimed him and fleshy cloud masses slowly came over the ridges in the west.

He was wet, wilted, and the brisk jog had dwindled to weary plodding when the trail led him past a tree-broken glimpse of wider water to the north and, curving, set Ticonderoga before him. A bright stream that was Lake George's outlet flowed into murkier Champlain at the base of the hill the fort crowned.

Adam forgot his weariness. He stood at last on the threshold of his goal. It was not alone the slanting sunlight that spread glamour upon the squat, compact stronghold. Those gray stone walls, the red-tiled barracks roofs with a flag hanging limply above them, were Delight Royden's dwelling place.

It was right, he considered reverently, that beauty so serene and clear—majestic hills; wide, untroubled water; the benison of the afternoon's low, long light—should enfold Delight. His eyes could span the distance between them now.

He saw the trail led on into the forest but directly before him a finger of land thrust out into the outlet's slow current, pointing to the fort. He walked toward its end. He would be still closer to Delight there.

He marked, as he neared the tip, ripples dilating across the still water. He crept forward, seeking the disturbance's source. The fort loomed almost above him, close enough for him to see sun flash from a sentry's bayonet. Brilliance, nearer at hand, drew his eyes. A few rods off the point, a man in a red coat fished from a

400

blunt-ended boat, so absorbed in his enterprise that Adam could inspect him, unobserved.

The bare head, cropped for a wig, was downy yellow as a new-hatched chick. Mild features had been sunburned to the uniform's hue. China-blue eyes squinted at the water. The fisherman jerked his pole violently and mumbled as he rebaited his hook. A trout broke water close beside him.

Now that he had reached Ticonderoga, Adam thought with amused dismay, he had no clear plan to carry him further. All his faculties had been bent to accomplishing the journey. Perhaps the relenting fortune that had brought him hither offered him further aid in this absorbed angler. Adam stepped out upon the narrow beach. He said:

"Hello."

"Gaw!"

The soldier's rod fell with a clatter. He recovered it, gagged, and demanded with hollow hostility, "Now where the bloody 'ell did ye come from?"

"Skenesborough," Adam replied at a venture and pursued, improvising swiftly, "Bound downlake, but ran my canoe on a snag. It sank, nigh drowning me."

"Aye?" asked the soldier, absently. He spat on his bait and threw out his line, with a double splash of sinker and hook.

"Can I get lodging for the night at the fort?"

" 'Tain't my gawd-blasted fort."

Another trout leaped, close at hand. The soldier swore.

Inspiration touched Adam.

"Catching many?"

"Now 'oo the bloody 'ell told ye to awsk me that, eh? That dog, Corporal Mason?"

There was desperation in the scarlet face.

"Because," Adam pursued, "if you're after trout, you're doing everything possible not to catch them. They're feeding on the surface. Take off your sinker, man, and troll."

Both bewilderment and hope were in the grunt.

"Troll," Adam repeated. "Draw your bait slowly along on the surface."

The soldier obeyed sulkily. A swirl wrung a yelp from him.

401

The stout pole bent, shook, and derricked a stalwart trout into the boat, where with whimpers of excitement, the man fell upon it.

He sat up at last, his face a full shade brighter, and gabbled of the late derision of his squad mates and the sixpence he now had won from his corporal.

"Wagered I'd catch nothing, Corporal did. I'll 'ave this beggar for me supper. Rare change 'e'll be from sow-belly, to be sure. Ow!"

He swung in a still larger fish. When he had dispatched him, he did not cast again but stared at Adam in grateful awe.

"If they'll not give ye a bed at the fort, sir, ye shall 'ave me own or I ain't Private 'enry Grant."

"Perhaps," Adam suggested, "when you've finished fishing, you'll ferry me over."

Grant, without other answer, drew up the anchor and put his boat ashore at his tutor's feet.

"Step in, sir," he said worshipfully. "I'll set ye across, and welcome. Wait till Corporal sees them fish. Fair stricken 'e'll be—and sixpence the poorer."

"There is no haste," Adam told him craftily. "Anchor again. We'll humble Corporal Mason further."

A dozen trout lay at Grant's feet when at last they rowed toward the fort. Joy beyond measure reigned in the mind of their proprietor and new confidence possessed his companion.

Adam had been amply paid for his lecture on the rudiments of trout-fishing. He had learned in return that none of the promised reenforcements yet had reached the fort; that Captain Delaplace, his family, Delight, and Lieutenant Feltham, for whom his informant seemed to cherish no high regard, had gone downlake that morning on a picnic; and that Private Grant had become Adam's awed and aboundingly grateful debtor.

"Never in all me life 'ave I 'ad such luck, Mr. Curler. Not that I get much chawnce to fish in a garrison filled with crocks and invalids and Corporal Mason forever chivvying me. If ye'll do me that honor, sir," he proceeded humbly, "we'll 'ave a tankard in the barrack room at 'is expense, though 'twill be naught but spruce beer, worse luck."

402

The mild, sunburned face was radiant with devotion. Adam asked, "Is that the best His Majesty supplies you?"

"There's rum," Hopkins replied grimly, "for sergeants and the like who can pay commissary prices. Poor, bloody privates must content themselves with spruce beer."

"Now I think I can afford," Adam said slowly, "to stand a bit of rum for you and your friends."

Solemn glee was lifting him. Fortune at last had become his ally. Private Grant surveyed him with reverence that perceptibly curdled into doubt whether so benign a personage could be genuine.

"Might I awsk, Mr. Curler," he stumbled, "where ye come from and whither bound? New York town to Canada?" His relief was immense. "Then ye're not of these Grants' bastards, begging your pardon, sir. Ye'll 'ave to excuse me prying, but the blighted farmer we 'ave for commander—"

"Captain Delaplace?" Adam asked maliciously. "I know him."

"A hexcellent farmer, too," Grant said in haste. "I 'aven't a doubt. Ye cawn't blame 'im for the attention 'e pays 'is stock, good 'ealthy cattle and sheep, with a doddering garrison like ours on 'is 'ands. A dozen proper men, sir, in all fifty of us, granting of course that ye consider Leftenant Feltham a proper man."

"I know him, too," Adam acknowledged and eased his companion's anguish by adding, "and like him probably less than you do."

Grant sighed.

"Gaw," he said solemnly, looking down again at his catch, "this is a fortunate day for me, sir."

"And for me," Adam confirmed.

Grant hauled his boat well ashore beside others on the point beneath the fort, chained it to a tree, and burdened himself with his string of trout and the oars.

"Captain's orders," he explained sourly. "All craft must be well secured each night now against the thieving Grants' folks."

He led Adam uphill along a deeply worn path. It joined another from the north and then climbed further between shoulder-high, moldering walls of stone.

"The covered way, this is," Grant panted. "Covered against gunfire, not by a roof as ye might think from its name, sir."

He paused for breath where fallen masonry of what had been a gateway had left a jagged hole in the fort's south wall.

Beyond the shining of the lake, the forests of The Grants lay in the golden peace of late afternoon. Nothing discernible stirred there. Only a small darkness of ripples, roused by air that wandered through the hot stillness, troubled the bright water.

Adam looked up at cannon muzzles, sagging drunkenly in their embrasures, and the limp flag on its tall pole. His heart tried to break through his ribs as he followed Grant through the gap in the wall.

Beyond the counterscarp, the iron-studded portal to the building-enclosed parade ground was shut, but a slovenly sentry guarded the wicket gate let into the massive door. He gaped at the trout and grinned at Adam as Grant passed him through.

Chapter XLV

CORPORAL MASON who first had looked upon Adam as Private Grant's accomplice in a plot to defraud him of sixpence, now was singing. His thin and lately peevish face shone ruddily in the barrack room's smoke while he chanted to the unprecedented number of Grant's friends Adam's rum had produced. About the table in the low-ceiled chamber sat most of the garrison not then on duty. They seemed, despite the brilliance of their yellow-faced, scarlet coats, a most unsoldierly assembly.

Many of the faces that drink was enlivening were elderly; some were wan with recent illness. Adam did not envy Delaplace the quality of his command or blame him for his preoccupation with farming. He thought of the hard-bitten men he had seen uproariously assembling at Castleton. The report he would take back to Allen, with Delight, would be encouraging. It was strange that he should be sitting here with the fulfillment of his purpose still undetermined.

" 'Tis a good song," Corporal Mason proclaimed with firm self-approval. "All together now, lads."

> *"We'll all drink out of the gallon, boys,*
> *We'll all drink out of the gallon.*
> *The gallon, the quart, the pint, 'arf a pint, quarter-*
> *pint, nipperkin, h'and the brown bowl,*
> *We'll all drink round as the sun goes down*
> *And we're off to the barley mow."*

Adam sang loudly, lest anyone mark anxiety that nagged like an aching tooth. It had been almost dark when the company had gathered. He could not be certain whether Delight and her companions had come back and was still less sure what his further course should be. He must in some undiscerned fashion enlist the support of Delaplace and his wife as antidote for Feltham's justified enmity.

"Pass a boll," Corporal Mason ordered and weaved slightly. "Now lads, another verse."

> *"We'll all drink out of the quart, boys,*
> *We'll all drink out of the quart—"*

They were singing more lustily now; wasted faces lit by specious vigor. Grant, at Adam's elbow, met his benefactor's eyes and drank to him with devotion in his own.

"A toast," Corporal Mason announced, filled with the rum of human kindness, "to the most comradely provincial that 'as entered this post in my time 'ere. May 'e never lack a drink—or a song. Sing another verse in 'is honor, now."

> *"H'and the brown bowl—"*

The long note was cut in half by the entrance of the sergeant who grounded his halberd and looked about him grimly.

"Leftenant Feltham," he warned, " 'as assumed command, pending the Captain's return and is bloody well likely to be less patient with the 'ell ye're raising than I 'ave been. I've a bit to say to ye, meself: Guard changes in an hour and if one of ye palsied defaulters as much as stumbles, there'll be a proper flogging for 'im on the morrow. Mind that, now."

His stern eyes dropped from the rigid faces to dwell with a wistful glitter on the array of black bottles. As he wheeled, Adam said on impulse, "A tot for yourself, Sergeant Anderson, before you go."

"Now that was kindly said indeed, sir," the other acclaimed, unbending. "A drop, thankee; no more."

He leaned his halberd against the wall and slid into the place Adam made for him on the bench.

"Good 'ealth, sir," he said and drank while the company sat and primly looked down their noses.

406

"Now this," Sergeant Anderson confided ruefully to Adam, relinquishing the mug, "might be worth me stripes in a stricter post. Don't 'old with drinking with rankers, meself, but ye need what cheer ye can find in this filthy 'ole, so ye do."

"A drop more?"

"Ye're very good, sir. Ye may understand that I need it, with the fort left in me 'ands all day. Service ain't what it used to be, sir; not with Leftenant supping in Captain's quarters instead of properly taking over and Captain himself too troubled lest one of his blasted cows don't calve according to regulations for 'im to return till it's done. Can you wonder, sir, that I deem rum a blessing and a saving grace? No; no more, thankee."

He rose with dignity, pulled his coat into place, resumed his halberd, and tramped away. Voices and mugs were raised as he departed. The dismay that had afflicted the company fell from them to mass upon Adam.

Sooner or later, the lackadaisical Feltham must learn of his presence within the fort and, if Delaplace remained preoccupied with his cattle, would have a free hand in dealing with an enemy. Adam turned on impulse to the admiring Grant and asked in a low voice, "Can you take word unperceived to Miss Royden for me?"

The mild blue eyes blinked but their devotion was not abated. "I can try, sir."

"Then tell her Adam Corlaer begs her to wait for him, as soon as may be, at the foot of the stair to officers' quarters."

Adam had not need to force urgency into his voice.

"No one," he warned, "but you must know it is she I truly came to see. Leftenant Feltham in particular must be kept in ignorance."

"That ain't 'ard to do," Grant said and grinned.

Adam admired the aimless fashion in which his messenger rose and strolled from the barrack room. He returned before the strain of waiting through further verses of Corporal Mason's interminable song became unendurable.

"She'll be there," Grant murmured, reseating himself, and pursued as though his tidings had not turned Adam breathless. "Encountered 'er in the 'all, sir. Supper's just over."

Adam leaned toward him with desperate inspiration.

"Grant," he breathed, "help me get her away. She must not marry Leftenant Feltham. That is why I came here."

"Wot ho!" the other said softly and a grin split his red face. "Any way I'm able, sir."

"—H'and the brown bowl," the company chanted, rocking to the rhythm.

> "We'll all drink round as the sun goes down
> And we're off to the barley mow."

It was difficult, Adam found when he rose, to appear at ease with nerves wound tight and the pulse in his throat half choking him. It was hard to stroll with an idle air toward the door when knees and elbows were weak. He closed the portal on the din and moved a shade unsteadily across the dark parade toward the lighted windows in its west wall.

A slice of moon hung in the heat haze and he could hear above the thudding of his heart the tumult of the outlet's rapids.

Long before he could discern the stairs that slanted up the wall, he knew Delight waited at their foot. He could see nothing, yet in a strange way he was certain she was there.

"Delight?" he whispered, stealing closer and she answered quietly:

"Yes, Adam."

He swallowed and struggled with his breath. All the splendid utterances he had rehearsed in loneliness evaded him. He could only say in desperate brevity, "You are in danger here. I have come to take you away. Will you go with me, Delight?"

His clumsiness appalled him.

"Yes, Adam," she said again, without hesitation. "When?"

He could have knelt before her unquestioning trust. Instead he asked in haste, "How soon can you leave without attracting notice?"

"Come back for me," she whispered, "in ten minutes."

He heard her feet tap lightly on the stair. The door at its head opened and, in the instant before it closed, he saw her, slender and sweet in her homespun gown. He heard the laughing ease of her response to a question from within.

Adam fought, as he stumbled back toward the barracks, against intoxicating pride and passion. He must form a plan that would justify Delight's clear faith, yet he could lay hold, for all his frantic scrabbling, only upon Grant's promise of aid.

Grant must get oars and guide them down to the tethered boat. Without his help—

He was close to the barrack door, beyond which Corporal Mason's chorus still was singing. Adam must get hold of himself, enter unobtrusively, and, calmly as possible, make his appeal to Grant.

Someone came with crisp steps across the parade. Adam flattened himself against the building wall. The man went past with a peevish muttering and a whiff of drink. Before Adam could stir, the latch clicked and the barrack-room door was thrust open. Outrushing light blazed and glittered on Jocelyn Feltham who gabbled:

"Eh, what's this, now? You, sir, skulking there; stand forth, d'ye hear me? Stand forth"—the reedy voice grew shriller—"or I'll run you through."

Adam looked down the fiery line of the bared sword and obeyed. Feet slurred and pounded across the floor. Feltham cried, "Stand back from the door there; stand back. Let me have light on this rascal."

Adam saw recognition stir the girlish face.

"I thought so," Feltham said with relish. "Stand quite still, Corlaer, and give an account of yourself."

He continued to smirk while Adam, stunned and destitute, limped through his tale of the journey to Canada and the foundered canoe. Feltham tittered when he had ended.

"Now claw my vitals, this is a fortunate meeting for me but a damnibly unfortunate for you, sir. I find an outlaw prowling about His Majesty's fort in a time of rebellion. Stab me, sir, I could have you shot, forthwith."

"Not hanged?" Adam asked, heedless of the taunt's probable cost, satisfied to see color flood his captor's face.

"Ho," the lieutenant called. "Guard! This way."

A shout and the clatter of feet poured from the low archway. Grant's and other faces gaped in the barrack room. Dark figures stood at the lighted windows of the officers' quarters. Adam wondered dully whether one of them was Delight.

409

"You find me in command here, Corlaer," Feltham told him pompously, "during my superior's absence. I shall give you the lodging for the night you say you seek."

He giggled as a panting corporal and four men came out of the darkness.

"I am not indifferent to the rites of hospitality, Mr. Corlaer. Permit us to escort you to your bedchamber."

He bade the corporal, "March this man to the punishment cells."

An iron door clanged; a lock rasped and clicked. The lieutenant's face grimaced through the barred wicket as he raised a lantern high.

"Delightful to have you as a lodger, Mr. Corlaer. George returns to duty tomorrow. I vow he will be as pleased as I."

Feltham found, as he followed the cellar corridor into the fresher open air, that his mirth was hard to curb. He had drunk heavily of the punch that had enlivened the picnic, hoping that it might fortify the ardor Delight always seemed able to blight. In his captain's absence, he had made free at supper with his superior's wine but chiefly he was intoxicated by glee.

His capture of the Corlaer person was a long-delayed revenge for the jest Allen's coarse louts had inflicted upon him and Wadman. The prisoner had not been chief of the perpetrators but he was, nevertheless, an outlaw and a henchman of the detestable Ethan. His downfall—since Feltham had taken the villain practically single-handed—already was cleansing the lieutenant's self-respect and surely must elevate him in the Royden maid's esteem.

Since that wretched time when he and Wadman each had been tricked into belief that the other had been hanged, he had detected a covert amusement in Delight's manner. Surely, she would view him more respectfully after tonight's exploit.

Someone stood at the foot of the stair to officers' quarters. The light of the lifted lantern shone upon Delight's face.

"Lord!" Feltham marveled, enraptured by this new stroke of fortune. "Whatever are you doing here?"

After a brief interval, she answered, "I heard the guard turn out. I thought Captain Delaplace was returning."

He tried to stretch this rapturous instant.

"No. I summoned them to imprison a great scoundrel I myself apprehended prowling about the post, a leader in The Grants' rebellion, your own onetime acquaintance, Adam Corlaer."

"Oh."

He was dashed by her indifference, but his voice ran on, "He will cool his heels in punishment cell till tomorrow when the Captain and I will decide what is to be done with him."

"I wondered," Delight said at last, "what caused the alarm." She turned to the stair. He tried to lay hold again upon the confidence that even in this high moment the girl had snatched from him.

"Will you not stay a little while?" he begged. "Does heaven grant me so many opportunities to see you alone that you must cruelly take this from me? May nights, surely, were made for—"

Even while he spoke, Delight was climbing the stair.

"Millicent," she told him from the landing, "will be needing me. Good night."

In Feltham's chamber, his servant was drowsing when the lieutenant entered and cursed him waspishly. Delight's indifference had marred a triumph. Sometime, Feltham promised himself rancorously, he would humble the hoity-toity maid as deftly and finally as he lately had abased the Corlaer ruffian.

Feltham swore again at Delight and, in a measure, at himself. The girl's indifference was a slur upon the amorous repute of the officers of the 26th Foot. It was intolerable that not the least of these should be kept so ignominiously at a distance by a peasant whom the Delaplaces perversely had befriended.

"If you have left me any of my brandy," he snapped at his man, "pour me a bumper."

The draught brought water to his eyes and clarity to his mind. This dwelt on the lack of *noblesse oblige* displayed by his captain. It was a pretty thing that an officer of His Majesty's service should disregard the garrison entrusted to his command to attend a horrid cow's accouchement. It was not impossible that an individual of such debased inclinations might, when finally he did return to his post, free the blackguardly Corlaer from the cell where he deservedly suffered.

That, the brandy-fortified spirit of Lieutenant Feltham resolved, could and would be prevented. He must see to it that his captive remained in duress at least until Delaplace offered his subordinate good reason for the villain's release.

"Go to Sergeant Anderson at once," Feltham ordered his servant, "and tell him I wish the key to the prisoner's cell."

The messenger, returning, observed with bereavement that the brandy bottle now was entirely empty and that his master, having removed both coat and waistcoat, was fumbling with his stock. Feltham stowed the key in a breeches pocket, sat down heavily, and thrust a gaitered leg at his man.

"Off with it," he bade. "I am for bed and am not to be disturbed unless Captain Delaplace sends for me."

Chapter XLVI

DELIGHT had survived fright's great dark hand that had covered and almost borne her down. She had managed to hide her terror from the gloating Lieutenant Feltham but when she had fled to the Delaplaces' quarters her face was so stricken that the Captain's wife immediately had been infected with dread.

"Blessed child," she gabbled, "Dee, my own sweet, what has happened?"

Sympathy broke the fortitude that had enabled Delight to endure Feltham's malicious glee. She wept, standing like a child with streaming face and twisting hands, until she was enfolded in her friend's billowing, perfumed embrace. The girl's sobs shook them both.

"My pet," Mrs. Delaplace begged, swayed by the contrary insistences of condolence and curiosity, "calm yourself, I beg of you. Tell your Millicent what has happened."

"Leftenant Feltham—" Delight gulped and could go no further.

"Jossy," her comforter gasped, at once scandalized and thrilled, "has—assailed you? Darling, I can scarcely believe—though he has been heated all day by drink. Sweet, compose yourself and tell me. If Jossy has so much as laid a finger on my own dear—without your encouragement, of course—you safely can leave the matter in my hands. Billy-boy shall call him to account, the moment he returns. But really, darling, I cannot picture poor Jossy overcome by passion, however tipsy. Tell Millicent, my pretty. Millicent can manage, as you must have learned by now. Now, now; no more, I pray. Dry your tears."

She lent a handkerchief to the quaking girl and bathed the stained face with cologne water.

"There; tell Millicent," she urged, alternately rocked by pity and curiosity.

Delight, reviving, saw and laid hold upon this avidity. Millicent Delaplace's chronic yearning for romance, the power she indirectly wielded over the whole post, gave the girl a thin hope.

This was no time for scruple. To win Adam's release, Delight was willing to be ruthless and, at need, downright sinful. She spoke shakily with a new, hidden resolution, selecting whatever facts her knowledge of Millicent told her would be persuasive and adorning them to suit her friend's taste with downright falsehood. Instinct, deft and sure, dictated her opening:

"You must," Delight faltered, "never, never, as long as you live, tell anyone. Promise?"

"Darling, of course; need you ask?"

The captain's wife laid both hands on her bosom and rolled her eyes heavenward.

"Adam Corlaer," Delight told her, "is here. He is in a cell where Leftenant Feltham has thrust him."

"Adam Corlaer? Adam Corlaer?" Millicent repeated, frowning. "I seem to know that name."

"I have never spoken it to you, because"—Delight plunged into mendacity's dark waters—"we have long been plighted lovers, with all the world against us."

"You poor dears," Millicent said absentmindedly, then clasped her hands and cried, "Adam Corlaer! But, of course, I know him —the tall, handsome young man with the gallant manner who came uplake with Billy-boy and me long, long ago."

"He remembers you so well," Delight assured her, "and has spoken of you so often."

"A dear boy!" Millicent sighed and then asked crisply, "And Jossy has imprisoned him? How dared he?"

"Because he is jealous and vindictive," Delight confided with a woeful air, "as all the world is toward Adam and me. He knows we are lovers and always will be, no matter how cruelly fortune uses us.

"His family and mine," she pursued, wide-eyed and obviously suffering, "oppose our union. That is why my mother and brother sent me here. They thought even he would never dare follow me to Ticonderoga."

414

"And he has," Millicent cooed. "How sweet, my pet! But why shouldn't he?"

"Because"—Delight's conscience groaned, but she declined to heed it—"because Governor Tryon has outlawed him at the instance of Adam's wicked uncle who wishes him to wed a maid of great property in Albany."

"Oh, my sweet," the other murmured, enraptured. "How beautiful! Oh, how you must have suffered!"

"I am used to suffering now." Delight's smile was sad and world-weary; her mind was increasingly hopeful. "But Adam could bear to be parted from me no longer. He has risked his all for me, and now is in prison."

"Risked his all," Millicent repeated, eyes shining. "What a truly delightful young man!"

"Leftenant Feltham, knowing York's governor has offered a reward for Adam and loathing him as a rival, has cast him into a punishment cell."

The tears that blurred Delight's eyes were in part a tribute to her own hitherto unsuspected gift for drama. Mrs. Delaplace was wiping her lashes while her bosom surged. The girl pursued, brokenly:

"I saw him only a precious instant, after these long, empty months. He urged me to elope with him. I—I didn't know what to do and bade him wait. I could not bear the thought of leaving you, Millicent."

"You should have gone, my pet, my sweet," her friend proclaimed in a stifled voice. "Love, darling Dee, should not be denied."

"I know," the girl acknowledged desolately, "and now he is imprisoned, and I am powerless as he."

"Delight, my treasure"—the other's tone was deep—"that is not so. Have you forgotten your own Millicent?"

"No; no, of course not, but whatever can we do?"

"I will prove to you," the woman promised, rising majestically, "that even in the absence of Billy-boy, Mrs. Captain Delaplace is not without importance in the post her husband commands. What can we do? Send at once to Sergeant Anderson my order that the poor, brave boy be released and brought here."

She strode into the front room where her husband's orderly

waited and, after dispatching him on the errand, returned triumphantly.

"How can I thank you?" Delight asked in a tight voice and was rewarded with a smile and a pat on the cheek.

"By never doubting hereafter your friend, your own, true, influential, if I may say so, friend."

"Oh, Millicent!"

They embraced.

"Poor child," Mrs. Captain Delaplace whispered, "how you must have suffered and never a word to anyone, you faithful, gallant girl! My pet, if only you could see how radiant you look."

That could be so, Delight admitted soberly. Her face might be illuminated by the winning of a victory beyond her hope's furthest reach, but her Yankee inheritance would not allow her to accept this unimagined triumph without qualms.

Never before had she resorted to barefaced lying to gain an end and her dexterity with falsehood alarmed her. She supposed, with a stirring of penitence, that it was like a bent for liquor that, indulged, demanded further indulgence. Once Adam was freed and safely away, Delight promised herself, she would never employ her lately discovered aptitude again.

"Love," Mrs. Delaplace sighed to the mirror before which she was powdering her face and reordering her hair, "conquers all. I shall see to it that Billy-boy rates wicked-wicked Jossy soundly for his assumption of authority. Captain Delaplace is most particular that no subordinate of his preempts—"

At a knock on the door, she crossed the chamber like a ship under full sail while Delight felt her own heart flounder in her throat. The orderly announced nervously, "Awsking pardon, m'am, Sergeant don't 'ave the key. Leftenant Feltham took it."

"Then," the captain's wife bade with a regal air, "present my compliments to Leftenant Feltham and inform him that—"

"Awsking pardon again, m'am, but Leftenant 'as retired, leaving orders 'e was to be disturbed by none but Captain, 'isself."

The orderly waited in apprehension and departed with relief when all his commander's lady said was, "Very well."

Delight watched, with a faint nausea, while Millicent sailed the length of the room and returned.

"Outrageous!" she muttered. "Intolerable! Oh, if I only were a man! Jossy's retirement was sheer maliciousness, my pet, nothing more, depend on it."

She marked how despair blanched and wilted her friend and said with forced cheer.

"I dare do nothing more now, darling. Further interference by me would surely anger Billy-boy. We need only wait till he returns. He is bound to be in good spirits over the new calf. I shall have no difficulty in freeing your lover then, I warrant you."

Adam had been in great haste. Adam had spoken of danger and time was passing. Delight found herself returning, drunkard-like, to the mendacity she lately had renounced.

"But," she ventured dolefully, "Captain Delaplace may stay away till morning. He has, before. And—and Adam looks so worn and ill, with a frightful cough. A night in that cold, damp cell may—destroy him."

Mrs. Delaplace was irritated by the gloomy hazard and her recent check.

"Really, my dear, I can interfere only so far with discipline. I can't order the sergeant to wake Jossy and certainly you can't expect me to rouse him myself."

"It would do no good," Delight said wretchedly. "He would never yield the key. He has imprisoned Adam to torment us both."

"Don't," Millicent begged, deeply affected, "don't cry like that, my darling. I vowed," she pursued through Delight's soft lamentation, "that I would save your Adam. Mrs. Captain Delaplace does not renounce a pledge. Wait, pet; stay where you are. Let me see what still can be done."

She went in great stealth from the room. Delight, listening intently, heard a small stirring in the hall, a muffled cough in the chamber where the captain's orderly waited, a thin, metallic squeak, and then, long, excruciating silence. It was broken by the return of Millicent in such haste that Delight for an instant believed an inflamed Lieutenant Feltham was in pursuit.

Mrs. Captain Delaplace burst into the room, clutching a wad of white fabric to her breast, closed the door, and leaned against it, palpitating and pale. For an instant, neither spoke while terror faded from the older woman's face and she, marking Delight's fright, suddenly was struck helpless by laughter.

417

"Oh, Lord!" she gasped. "Oh, my pet! What have I not risked for my Delight? I have stolen Jossy's"—she choked over the word and expelled it in a whispered squeal—"breeches."

Her hands, extending the bundle, let it relax into the indubitable outline of Lieutenant Feltham's late, intimate clothing. She sank into a chair and, still shaken by mirth and fright, gabbled wildly.

She had listened at Feltham's door and heard him snore. Quite against her will, the latch had lifted noiselessly under her hand. The candle, still burning at the lieutenant's bedside, had revealed to Millicent no trace of the key.

"I was possessed, that I vow," she related, wiping her eyes. "It can have been nothing less. If someone had marked me, stealing into Jossy's bedchamber at this hour! Suicide alone would have served me. Then I saw Jossy's"—she delicately refrained from naming the garment and shuddered as if again she endured the ordeal—"on a chair, close by."

"I lifted them," Millicent pursued in a dramatically hushed voice, "and at the very instant I felt the key's outline, someone below shouted for the guard."

She shuddered, and then smiled at Delight over the dangling breeches.

"My dear, for an instant I was stricken, truly palsied by terror. The next thing I knew, I was back in the hall, still holding—these."

Wild laughter once more overcame her. Delight asked anxiously, "The key?"

"Oh, yes," Millicent gasped, subduing her frantic mirth. "The key, of course."

Hesitantly, as though the breeches still contained the veritable person of Jocelyn Feltham, she explored a pocket.

"Here it is, darling," she breathed, extracting the key, "a guerdon of my devotion to you. Now," she pursued, resolutely rebundling the garment, "these must be returned at once. Fancy"—again laughter strove to overwhelm her—"what a rout there would be if Jossy were to wake and find them missing, or Billy-boy, returning, should discover a most compromising piece of his subaltern's attire in my possession."

"Millicent?" Captain Delaplace's voice called from the front room. "Millicent? Where are you?"

Delight gasped, hid the key behind her, and stared speechless at Millicent who for an instant seemed smitten as dumb as she and paralyzed as well.

"Millicent!" the captain called again.

"Here, Billy-boy," his wife responded in a peculiar voice and, reviving, thrust the incriminating raiment beneath her and settled herself upon it.

"Lover," she prattled with forced gaiety as her lord entered, "Dee and I were just debating whether to wait longer for you or retire. Has the cow been—ah, safely delivered, darling? Is it a pretty, pretty calf, Billy-boy?"

She twisted while she spoke, as though the breeches were smoldering. Delaplace was too occupied with his own grievances to notice the agitation or his wife's unusual interest in his avocation. The irascibility upon his normally agreeable face was proof against Millicent's frantic smile.

"A very pretty calf," he answered with culminating bitterness, "an excellent calf that would have made a fine heifer, if it had not been born dead, despite my best efforts."

"Oh Billy-boy!" his wife gasped, less smitten by his tidings than by his mood. Delight, turning away, thrust the key into her bodice and wondered how the Captain could fail to see each heartbeat shake her. She moved an indifferent step toward the door. Delaplace's intemperate voice stayed her.

"I learn from Sergeant Anderson that Jocelyn has been comporting himself like the Great Cham of Tartary during my absence. Who is this 'Curler' he has arrested and why has he presumed to lock him up?"

Delight found his indignation encouraging but Millicent was not heartened. She twisted in her chair and glanced down to assure herself that what she concealed still was safely hidden.

"Billy-boy, I haven't the least idea. Don't worry about that now. Poor dear, you're tired. A glass of port, my love!"

She half rose, remembered, and sat down again in haste.

"By God, Madam," her husband told her with the unscrupulous wrath of a generally amiable man, "I mean to let a number of persons discover, however painfully, that I command this post. I shall neither rest, drink port, nor pursue whatever further irrelevant suggestions you persist in making until I find out on what grounds Leftenant Feltham has presumed to arrogate to himself authority that properly is mine. Where is he?"

"Abed, I think," his wife faltered, with a convulsive movement that Delight, edging again toward the door, interpreted as another barely checked impulse to rise.

"Damme, he shall get up instanter. Orderly—"

"Billy-boy, no!" Millicent begged, aghast at the thought of the nightmare that would ensue were Feltham awakened. "I implore you. I mean, lover," she limped on in frenzy, aware by his clouded regard that his wrath was turning toward her, "that Jossy is not at all well. Quite ill he seemed, didn't he, Dee?"

"Sick," the captain snorted, "from the punch he swilled today, nothing more."

"But you are wrong, oh, dreadfully dreadfully wrong, indeed, you are. And don't shout so, Billy-boy. You will wake the children. They—they seemed unwell when we put them to bed. Delight feared so, too. Isn't that so, Dee?"

Delight, with a hand at last upon the doorlatch, wet her lips to reply but Millicent's voice ran on without pause, "It's the vapors of this wretched place that cause the trouble, I'm positive. They —they infect us all."

Her husband looked at her more carefully. She suffered his regard with a feeble smirk.

"What ails you?" he asked in an altered tone. "Are you certain you are quite all right yourself, Millicent?"

"I don't know," she said with sudden languor, eagerly grasping this small handhold. "I do feel—a little strange, Billy-boy. You know how delicate my nerves are. It's been an exhausting day and you were away so long, lover, and now all this tow-row-rowing is making my poor brain dizzy."

"You should not have waited up for me," he told her and laid a hand against her cheek. "Your face is hot, my dear."

"It is late, isn't it?" she said faintly. "We all should be abed."

She pulled his head down and as she whispered in his ear, Delight saw the captain's face grow pleased and red.

"Can't discipline wait till morning?" Millicent begged softly. "Please, Billy-boy. I so want—I mean, it is so very late."

"Very well," he granted. "A glass of port first and then to bed, my love."

"Yes," Millicent agreed with soft ardor. "Will you fetch it, darling?"

Captain Delaplace, the devoted husband once more, moved away. Delight as she opened the door saw her friend rise at last and with a quick movement cast Lieutenant Feltham's crushed breeches under the bed.

The orderly, lingering impatiently at the stairhead, gaped at the girl as she passed.

"It is so close and hot," she told him serenely, "that I shall walk about a bit before I go to bed."

The coolness of the air as she moved across the parade told her how feverishly flushed her face must be. She should not hasten, but stroll, apparently idle and unconcerned, lest the orderly's or other eyes follow her through the darkness.

Delight lingered an instant at the entrance to the cell corridor, then slid through like a shadow.

Adam, sitting in the apathy of despair on the edge of his pallet, heard through the dank stillness the light sound of feet and a soft voice speaking his name.

"Delight!"

"Hush. Be quiet and quick."

Iron clinked on iron. The key turned in the lock. Out of the void, Delight's groping fingers came to find and cling to his.

"Hurry," she breathed.

Before he obeyed, he bent and kissed the hand that was lodged, small, strong and urgent, in his own.

Chapter XLVII

THEY came from the dead cellar air into cleaner, lesser darkness. A light burned in the barrack room but elsewhere the buildings' walls were black and a somber sky hung close, a lid clamped down upon a breathless world.

Delight's hand stirred in Adam's and, when he would not release it, lay still. The small submission set pulses beating in his temples, yet at the same time her ready yielding troubled him. In some undiscerned fashion, she had won his freedom. Now, she was surrendering leadership to him and he was empty of resource. He had come from his cell only into a larger prison that was the fort.

Adam winced as gravel stirred beneath his careful feet. He whispered, "Where shall we go? How best can we get clear?"

"Only the wicket gate stands open at night. All other doors are locked," Delight answered serenely. The depth of her trust dismayed him.

"A sentry is posted there?"

"Yes."

She impelled him to say with hollow valor, "Come, then; we'll try."

He had thought that danger's tension had been tricking his eyes so that they falsely had seen the imminent sky throb and flicker but now a wavering glare shook it and he recognized the reflection of far-off lightning. Somewhere beyond this pressing, damp stagnation, a storm was on the move. Adam went forward more hastily, wondering whether in the wan illumination they had been seen by sleepless eyes that might be peering from invisible windows.

His throat was dry; his heart was thudding like a Mohawk dance drum when they paused before the long, low archway and saw at its far end, the open wicket, faintly outlined by some obscure radiance. Adam released Delight's hand. He murmured in her ear, "I'll scout the sentry. Don't stir till I return."

He went forward with intense care, testing each step as though the blackness of the passage were water. It seemed endless time before he reached the wicket.

The bells and tambors of frogs throbbed above the roar of the rapids and air, wandering freely beyond the stronghold's walls, soothed Adam's face. The gate creaked as he leaned out, striving to find the source of the weak light spilled across the pavement. A horn lantern sat beside a bench that bore a dim figure. This stirred and Private Grant's voice said mildly, "Eh, now! Oh, 'tis you sir?"

"It is." Adam drew a deep breath as Grant rose with a clatter of accouterments to gape devotedly through almost visible rum fumes. The sentry seemed neither puzzled nor alarmed. He clearly accepted Adam's presence as a normal miracle in the career of a miraculous person. Grant inspected by lantern light the hour-glass that had stood on the bench beside him, replaced it, and inquired, "You'll be goin' now, sir, you an' the leddy?"

"Yes."

Adam still was pulled about by hope and doubt. Grant shouldered his musket.

"Then, by your leave, sir, I'll pace me beat. If me back is turned, I can swear on honor I never saw you pass."

He went away into darkness. To Adam, hastening with Delight toward the break in the south wall, came a disembodied voice, softly chanting, "*H'and* the brown bowl!"

The walls of the covered way guided them downhill. Lightning ran over the sky again and, after a space, came the mutter of thunder.

In the bright instant, Adam had seen Delight's face. She moved beside him, invisible again, yet more intimately near. Reverence for her faith unsettled him. He thrust the rapture away. They were not yet safe. They had come only a little way and the obstacles before them were tall.

Somehow, he must free a boat and put the lake between them

and the fort. Dawn, he thought fearfully, could not be far off. There was no time now for anything but flight.

Delight uttered a faint cry as Adam stumbled and almost fell. "That ledge!" she said penitently. "I forgot to warn you."

He muttered, "You know the way. Can you take us to the point?"

"Willow Point? I'm sure I can. Give me your hand."

It seemed her fingers closed about his heart. It was strange that this small contact should make explicit all the wonder of her dear body. He said hoarsely, "I spoke to you of danger. Allen is planning to storm Ticonderoga."

"And you came for me?"

She pressed his hand more tightly. Tenderness, welling within him, loosened his knees and made his head swim. Harsh radiance fell on the path before them and turned the half unfolded leaves of brush to points of green fire. Thunder boomed.

"It will storm," Delight said.

"Rain will wash away our tracks."

If a bolt were to consume him now, he thought solemnly, his life would have been justified by this brief dark communion.

Wind, cool and wet-smelling, came over the hill behind them, bearing with its own sound the stronger clamor of the distant rapids. The way was longer than Adam had thought. Light, diamond-brilliant, blazed and revealed before them a grimed, stone structure on one hand, a sagging shed on the other. The thunder boxed their ears. Adam asked, alarmed, "Are you sure this is the way? We did not pass these when Grant led me to the fort."

"The charcoal oven," she said confidently. "Willow Point is only a little further."

"Willow Point," he forced himself to ask, "thrusts into the outlet of George, just below the fort?"

"No. It is downlake and reaches toward The Grants' shore. I thought—"

Her voice failed. He said lightly, "Willow Point may serve us better. Are there boats there?"

"I fear not. I thought you had your own. I—"

"We have come by the wrong road," Adam said with resolute cheer, belatedly recalling the forking trails below the covered way, "and the fault is mine. You led us where I bade you. We must go back and take the other path. We—"

His voice died. He stood, staring upward.

Aloft, a point of light shone, crept across the darkness, vanished, reappeared.

"They have discovered our escape," Adam said slowly. "They are searching for us at the fort."

"It may be only the guard changing," Delight offered with no conviction.

"Unless we were sure," he told her at last as the light winked out, "it would be madness to turn back now. We must try Willow Point and—"

The hill leaped out of darkness as lightning clawed the clouds. Haze was enveloping the fort. A cold drop struck Adam's cheek. A sighing came downhill.

"There is shelter ahead," Delight cried.

The storm drummed tamely on the shed's roof. Lightning shook the rain's silver tapestry. Thunder rolled clumsily across the sky. Adam and Delight stood in silence while the languid downpour waned. It was difficult, he found, to keep his mind on their plight.

Men might be following them. Beyond, lay the lake's barrier. They were in the open jaws of a trap from which his energy must snatch them.

He could not accept the reality of peril when Delight stood so close that he imagined he could feel the sweet warmth of her body. The fancy quickened heat in his own. He drove speech through a tight throat, "We have scant time for talk, but one thing I must know: Was it the letter I wrote that sent you here?"

"Letter?" she repeated in so odd a voice that his heart grew heavy.

"A letter," he pursued, "I sent you by Justus from Bennington. It was presumptuous, I know, but I was ill and could not come myself, though I had promised you."

Delight said slowly, "I have had no letter from you, Adam, in all my life."

He knew his laugh had a wild sound.

"By God," he babbled, "it was as I suspected, then. Justus entrusted it to Felicity to deliver to you. She destroyed it."

425

"No," Delight said, in a strange voice. "She showed it to me."

"Oh."

"She—she boasted you had written it to her."

After an instant's silence, Adam said, "She warned me of her enmity. She boasted—and you believed her?"

It was bitter-clear as the lightning's brilliance. The letter, lacking address, had been a weapon in a malicious hand. Through the murmur of the rain, Delight's voice came again, "I did believe her—and I came to Ticonderoga."

"She promised," Adam said with difficulty, "to turn you against me."

"She never could have done that."

The calm voice made him tremble.

"She never could," it pursued, "because—"

He felt his own throat close. He heard while the paroxysm endured, Delight stir beside him. Her hand fumbled along his sleeve and found his own.

"Because—" she tried again and halted with a sound that might have been mirth or tears.

"Have you no mercy?" she begged suddenly and frantically. "Will you stand there, wooden, while I tell you I have always been yours, if ever you had wanted me, oh, Adam, indeed whether you wanted me or no?"

He groped and found her. The earth tipped. They were joined, long-parted halves of an entity. He had the delicious belief that they fused and flowed together, quenching, yet firing, rousing by their seemly intimacy a wind, too great for sound, that whirled them upward through flame-shot darkness.

Far away, dim and distraught through the ringing and the rhythmic clamor in his ears, he heard his own voice, repeating like a litany, "Delight, Delight, Delight!"

She stirred in his arms, not seeking release but closer union. Her hands lay, hot and firm, upon his cheeks, slid upward through his hair, clasped and pressed his mouth down on hers. So they clung, while time stood still. . . .

"You laughed," she murmured drowsily. "Why did you laugh, Adam?"

"For joy and wonder," he whispered. "How could you know?

426

Where did you learn, my darling? Never in school at Quebec."

"I began to learn," she answered, her mouth close to his ear, "the first hour I saw you. All the rest of my days, I still shall be learning, Adam, my dear, my only love."

After a space, she ventured, "The rain has ended."

"We shall never end," he told her, "you and I."

Later still, it was she who laughed.

"It must have been the guard's light we saw. Else, they would have found us before now."

"I know," he said, by great effort turning to the world again. "We can stay here no longer. It is too late to go back now; we had best press on."

They moved, hand in hand, in the warm, wet darkness. By the scent of resin and drops deliberate falling, he knew they groped through forest. Anxiety pursued and overtook him. He asked with what indifference he could summon, "You are sure there are no craft of any sort at Willow Point?"

"I only know that Captain Delaplace has ordered all boats secured in the outlet."

Her serenity, born of trust, smarted in his mind, drove it frantically ahead. If they could find no means of passage across the lake, they must return to the fort. He could not expose Delight to privation he himself might endure. He must take her back and surrender, yet he quailed at the shameful prospect.

If there were nothing that would float them at Willow Point, he would leave Delight and, as a last desperate measure, seek the outlet and try for one of the boats there, bringing it, if he succeeded, around to the point. It would be a perilous errand.

"You're worried."

Delight's hand clung more closely to his.

"No," he lied. "But if—"

"Adam, what is it?"

He halted. Now he whispered. "Wait. Listen."

He heard only water, dripping from the trees, Delight's tight breathing, the drum of his own heart.

"I thought," he began, "that I— No. Hark. There it is again."

The splashing sound was plainer now, too rhythmical for leaping fish. Beyond the blackness the forest cast, a boat was moving. Searchers from the fort must be coasting the shore. They were close. Adam heard low voices, the thump of oars on thole pins, and beat down the impulse to wheel and run. It was wise to remain hidden in the woods. If men sought them by water, others hunted them by land. It would be wiser, still, to creep forward and determine the stature of the peril.

"Come," he whispered.

Delight's face was a faint shining in the darkness now and, looking up, he saw trees vaguely outlined upon the sky. Night was almost spent. Presently, as they advanced, he could see a dark gridiron of trunks against water's dull glittering.

Adam stopped again. He heard the growl of gravel beneath the prow of a beached craft, furtive clatter, the rasp of cloth on wood, the splash and thud of disembarking men. They were closing in. His worst fears had not encompassed this. He and Delight were to be hounded, driven, and run down. For her sake, prompt surrender was best.

A second craft ground upon the beach. An oar rattled loudly and through the hushed confusion, a muted voice blared, "Crucified Christ! Did I not impose absolute silence?"

The furious question was like a blow, rocking, half-stunning Adam. Doubt was his first clear response. Surely his ears had tricked him.

"Fall in," the voice commanded. "Gods of the Mountains, fall in! I have a word to say to you."

Adam laughed softly and, bending, kissed Delight.

"Sweetheart," he said, "yonder is Colonel Ethan Allen."

He led her toward the muffled tumult and the brazen voice that, having stilled it, ranted on.

The trees gave way. In the fading night, Adam saw the gleaming of the ripple-shaken lake and the gravel strand to which the trail ran down. Darknesses thrust out into the water were the beached boats. The black mass before their prows was men, close-huddled, whom the ferocious voice harangued. Adam and Delight slid down to the shore. As they hurried forward, the conclusion of Ethan Allen's fantastic oration reached them clearly:

"—and, as it is a desperate attempt which none but the bravest men dare undertake, I do not urge it on any contrary to his will. You who will undertake it voluntarily, poise your firelocks."

It was like Ethan, Adam thought with a peculiar blending of

amusement and dismay, to spend precious minutes of the remaining darkness in exhorting men who, if they already had not been committed to the enterprise, certainly would not have crossed the lake. Clattering rose as muskets were lifted high.

Allen's voice broke loose again, "There is said to be a trail to the fort from Willow Point. Where is it? Not yet found? Now by the cinders of Eblis, Gehenna, and Tophet—"

Adam called, as softly as he might and still halt the objurgation, "I am here to guide you, Colonel. Corlaer, lately from Ticonderoga, with his mission accomplished."

He heard the babble his announcement roused. He saw a dark form break away from the massed men and bear down upon him.

"By God and Very God, by angels, principalities, and powers —!"

Adam's ribs were dented by the brass buttons of his assailant's coat. He was swung off his feet in a half circle and released to be beaten on the back and shoulders by a vast palm.

"You come," Ethan clamored, "like Jehovah to Joshua in his time of sorest need. And lately from the fort, you say? From the courts of the ungodly? Now do I know that we shall smite the Amelekites shrewdly, hip and thigh."

Neither Adam nor he was aware of a slighter form that had advanced to the giant's elbow until a sharp voice intruded:

"I make so bold as to ask, Colonel"—under the surface courtesy, anger crackled—"whether plans for this—ah, water picnic still include an advance upon Ticonderoga?"

Allen gulped loudly.

"Colonel Arnold," he said in haste, "I have the honor to present my aide-de-camp, Captain Corlaer, who has just reconnoitered the fort."

"Eh, sir?"

Benedict Arnold's scorn vanished. He fired, while Allen stood by, fuming, a fusillade of questions concerning Ticonderoga. Adam replied as briskly, warming against his will to the man's enthusiasm and military knowledge. Ethan managed at last to intrude with inquiry of his own.

"Can the fort, in your judgment, Adam, be taken by a handful of heroes?"

"It is a shell, sir, with only some fifty, mostly elders and invalids, for garrison. Your three hundred can take it by storm. A few score might capture it by surprise."

"A few score, eh? That is as well, Adam"—Ethan dropped his voice ruefully—"for the truth is that, what with the scarcity of boats, we have barely eighty here."

"If I might suggest, Colonel," Arnold offered caustically, "it would be wise if the boats returned for more of your men."

"Colonel Arnold," Allen informed Adam, without acknowledging the counsel, "had been empowered by the Bay Province to capture Ti, but, arriving at Castleton without his force, he has accompanied us as an observer."

Arnold, with a hiss of impatience, wheeled and strode away.

"And by the brazen, bare buttocks of Belial," Ethan confided, in a voice that might have reached the retreating officer's ears, "he is the most contumacious bastard with whom it has ever been my misery to associate."

In the bleaching east, the mountains of The Grants were black and sharp.

"Time we were marching," Allen muttered.

Adam glanced toward the slight figure that had waited, silent and observant, behind him and laid his hand upon the colonel's sleeve.

"Delight Royden is with me," he said quickly. "It is thanks to her that I am here. I wish passage for her across Champlain."

"Madam," Ethan proclaimed with flourishes of hat and voice, "you shall be wafted over with the most distinguished compliments of my command and me."

He strode away, hastening the formation of the column with sulphurous expletives. Adam turned to Delight. She said quietly, "I won't go."

Her hands were clammy in his. She turned away.

"Please," she begged, "please don't send me away when—when I only so lately found you, Adam."

He lifted her and said in her ear as he bore her toward the nearer craft, "You will be more secure; I shall feel safer, too, with the lake between you and what may take place on the hill yonder. Wait for me on Champlain's far shore if you wish. I shall come to you as soon as I may. Dear heart, don't cry. It is only for a little while."

430

"Adam!" Ethan cried in hushed impatience.

Adam lifted Delight over the gunwale. His cheek was cool with her tears as he helped spectral figures shove the boat clear, then turned and ran to the head of the shadowy column, where Allen waited with Arnold beside him. The giant drew and waved his sword.

"Forward!" he bade in a steamy whisper.

Chapter XLVIII

IT MIGHT have been a host of shadows Adam led, so silently moved the woodsmen of The Grants. It still had been night when they had entered the forest. Wan light that had no source was flooding the world when they emerged. Here was the squat, black charcoal oven; yonder—Adam's breath left him —was the shed that had sheltered him and Delight.

A murmur rose from the column like a brief, sharp wind. Before the marchers, clear against the dark west, Ticonderoga rose studded with guns, ominous in its silence. A single cannon, well served, could blast away the little column before it reached the height. Adam felt a knot draw tight in his belly while he watched for the gush of smoke.

The men moved steadily, three by three, over the muddied road. It climbed steeply now. Allen's bared blade was no harsher than the face he turned aloft, less brilliant than the rapt eyes. Arnold, dwarfed by his companion's bulk, strode beside him, brave in the red-coated uniform of Connecticut's Foot Guards, a sneer on his darkly handsome face.

Behind the strange pair, solemn and drab and awkward, plodded the men of The Grants—the transformed wild roisterers Adam had seen, flushed and whooping, at Castleton, following their colonel now toward a still wilder enterprise.

All his life, Adam would remember the raggedly slanting firelocks, the uneven files, the grave, upturned faces with the silver light of dawn upon them.

It was strange to retrace his steps over a way he had followed earlier in darkness. The column moved like mist past the grass-covered mounds of two ancient redoubts and below a cliff washed by daybreak. Adam drew breath and felt taut muscles ease. The rock face was continued upward by the fort's east wall. They were directly beneath the stronghold. No cannon could reach them now and before them the trail turned into the covered way.

Their goal was close and still there was no stir of life beyond the funereal ramparts. The molten look had come to Allen's face and Arnold's black eyes blazed. The east was quickening. Robins began a wheezy caroling. Adam dropped back and, walking by Ethan Allen's side, pointed out the crumbling breach in the fort's south wall.

"There should be a sentry above," he muttered, shamed by his shaky voice. "If he be drowsing, we may reach him before he can close the wicket gate."

Arnold would have leaped ahead but a beamlike arm, outthrust, spun him back. Allen went up with great strides over the broken masonry.

"Stand!" a voice quavered. "Who goes—"

"Forward," Ethan trumpeted. "Forward, boys! No quarter! Slay and spare not!"

Wild voices caught up and multiplied the shout. The column broke apart and surged up, bellowing, into the fort. Adam, scrambling to the counterscarp, saw the sentry stand, dazed and wavering, beside his bench while a caparisoned monster bore, roaring, down upon him.

"Yield," Ethan blared and hacked the air with his sword, "yield or you are pork!"

The sentry raised a wabbling musket. Sparks twinkled from the lock but no report followed. The soldier shrank from the charging giant, cast his misfired weapon from him, and fled, wailing, through the wicket while Allen's boots thundered and his blade whistled a bare yard behind.

Adam leaped through the gate and after him, with ear-piercing yells and a trampling din, poured the men of The Grants, filling the low passage with clamor that seemed to overwhelm and thrust him out upon the parade.

The walled quadrangle, brimming with grave light, was a sardonically tranquil stage for violence. Allen had paused midway across the parade to whoop and wave to his screeching followers. A soldier, appearing from nowhere, bore down upon him with bayoneted musket. The man's pale face was twisted by rage or fright. His lunge was half-hearted. The giant in green and gold leaped aside and struck his assailant down with the flat of his sword.

A bellow deafened Adam. Ethan, stooping, snatched up his victim. A hat skittered across the parade, a wig flew far as Allen, shouting questions, shook information from the captive and then flung him toward the cavorting invaders. The Colonel's sword was an arc of light. His voice burst through the clamor and roused brazen echoes, "Yonder is the barracks. Break in the door; seize and bind. Some of you follow me."

The column poured out upon the parade and dissolved into a swarm of demons who yowled of massacre. Most of them ran, still screeching, for the barracks. The rest, with Adam, followed Allen and Arnold, who had stood aloof, regarding with scorn the unbridled conduct of Ethan and his men. Now, he raced for the officers' quarters, determined to share in the actual surrender, but when he reached them Allen already was pounding up the stair to Jocelyn Feltham's door.

The Colonel's fist beat like a sledge. His vast figure seemed to expand in the quickening light; his voice was the sound of trumpets fiercely blown.

"Come out. Come out, d'ye hear me?"

He canted his head at some indistinguishable reply and bellowed louder.

"Who is it? Come out and see, you skulking bastard, or, by Christ and the Twelve Apostles, I'll break in the door and haul you, feet first."

Arnold, lips pursed, laid a deterring hand on Allen's arm but he did not heed and, after listening briefly to the voice that yammered beyond the portal, cried, "For the final time, come out, or—"

Wood groaned under the thrust of a great shoulder. The door gave, then flew wide. Feltham came out delicately to meet his captor.

The lieutenant's face was scarlet, his eyes faintly glazed. The radiance of daybreak dwelt without mercy on his red coat, its yellow facings, the silver gorget, and white waistcoat.

Someone behind Adam muttered, "Jesus!"; someone else guf-

434

fawed. Only then did he realize that the cringing man, correctly clad from the waist up as a lieutenant of His Britannic Majesty's 26th Regiment of Foot, wore below that splendor only the original pale covering of Jocelyn Feltham.

"Gods of the Mountains," Allen blurted, momentarily dazed by the spectacle, "you had done better to clothe your other end first, sir."

Arnold intruded.

"Leftenant, I am—"

Allen's voice swept his aside.

"Sir, I demand the immediate possession of this fort and all the effects of George the Third."

Rhythmic pounding across the parade ended in a crash as the barrack door went down. Maniacal howlings rose. Feltham jerked convulsively. He smirked and then, standing knock-kneed with his hands modestly before him, gabbled, "I do not command here. Captain Delaplace's quarters are yonder. I beg you, sir"— his voice scratched and squealed—"to permit me to retire."

The men below, who gaped and grinned called suddenly, "Here's another, Colonel."

Delaplace, in shirt and breeches, stood at his own open door, staring with a stunned look at the fierce, upturned faces. His eyes moved toward the sound of a mammoth dogfight that raged in the barracks and came back to Allen's prodigious figure.

"In—in whose name, sir," the captain demanded in a dazed voice, "is this—this outrage committed?"

Arnold stepped briskly forward and bowed.

"Colonel Benedict Arnold, sir, of Connecticut, at your service. I demand—"

Allen's bellow drowned his voice and filled the fort.

"In whose name? In the name of the great Jehovah and the Continental Congress."

Dazed soldiers were stumbling from the barracks, jostled and hauled by apparent savages who promised them dismemberment and worse. One prisoner broke away and ran in blind terror toward Adam with two joyously screeching fiends in pursuit.

"Oh, sir," Corporal Mason gasped, flinging himself upon this possible protector. "I yield, I yield. Quarter, sir, oh, quarter."

He involved Adam in a species of impromptu dance, desperately whirling him about, striving to keep his body a shield between himself and his tormentors. Adam had difficulty in extricating himself and more in convincing Mason that he was not to be flayed, roasted, or cut into thin slices. Before the corporal's late pursuers led him away, he gulped, blinked, and stammered:

"Servant, sir. I've seen ye somewheres, it seems."

"*H'and* the brown bowl," Adam replied and left the prisoner in still graver mental confusion.

Here on the fort's east rampart, there was a variety of quiet. Adam sighed, seated himself on a gun carriage and leaned against the ornately chased breech of a brass twelve-pounder. His mind was too weary to arrange the violences of the last few hours.

The tumult that had ebbed, after the officers had been locked in their quarters and the garrison had been disarmed and confined to barracks, now was boiling up again on the parade ground. Cheering had been succeeded by more tangled uproar, pierced by wolf yells. Allen's men were celebrating victory in a fashion that Benedict Arnold, by the light of his earlier disapproval, was bound to deplore. Adam marveled at the durable vigor of The Green Mountain Boys.

Their intemperate conduct, though it had won Colonel Arnold's scorn, had served the enterprise well. A more orthodox attack might have ended less fortunately. These pretended barbarians who, like their commander, roared, raged, and bellowed ghastly threats they had no intention of fulfilling had taken a stronghold with injury to none, save a few elderly soldiers frightened temporarily out of their wits.

Adam yawned and shook his empty head. In time, when sleep had restored him, the immediate past would lose its dreamlike texture. Now, his dulled mind retained only a single, imperative purpose. Beyond the distant water, ablaze in the early sunlight, Delight was waiting. He must seek and find her, never again to let her go.

The uproar on the parade was increasing. Two tall, brown men swaggered by, hats tilted, firelocks jauntily slanted and one called out, "Rum's being broke out within, friend. If ye don't crave your share, might deed it to Hosea 'n' me."

A musket banged and the sound was followed by another burst

436

of cheering. Adam, turning, squinted at the lake's harsh glitter. He thought with humility of Delight, whose wonder no imagination could compass; Delight, the valiant and gentle; Delight of the pliant, responsive body; Delight, his own, ordained love, and, looking about, saw Ethan Allen approaching. The low light was splendid upon him. It transformed the bold face and glorified the tawdry uniform.

"Adam," Allen shouted. The vitality he spread was as actual as warmth from a hearth. "By the left hind leg of the throne of God, man, why are you moping here in the hour of triumph? No taste for the spoils of victory? There are food and drink within for weary warriors. The Boys are enjoying them."

He leaned upon the cannon and looked down at his companion. Fires still burned in the blue eyes. When Ethan spoke again there was awe in his voice.

"The sun this morning," it rumbled, "seemed to rise with a superior splendor. I deem it an augury. A great day has dawned, Adam; a braver day, a freer day for the new-whelped nation and I and the men of The Grants have hastened its delivery."

He lounged against the gun, strong chin propped by a palm, scowled and said at last, still thoughtfully:

"It is strange that now I should be so bedeviled by thought of life's brevity. I wish I might endure another century to view the man the new babe will become. Life is too short, Adam. We do not see the flowering of the best seed we sow."

He shrugged, laughed, and clapped his companion on the shoulder.

"Come drink a bowl with me to the babe and his midwives and wet nurses in Philadelphia. I must apprise them—"

"Colonel," Adam broke in, "I have but one need."

"By God, name it then and—"

"My—my betrothed"—utterance of the word thrilled him—"is on the lake's far shore."

"And you wish to go after her, snorting, with tail held high?" Allen completed, frowning. "I feared as much. Adam, I need you here. There are dispatches to be written. You must help me deal with this black-a-vised bastard, Benedict Arnold. By Jehovah's chin whiskers, flay me and steep me in brine if he is not the most supercilious, arrogant, contumacious, altogether—"

He broke off in mid-objurgation with a groan of martyrdom and then said grimly, "Here he comes."

Arnold's uniform blazed but his face reflected none of its brilliance. Beneath the surface courtesy of his address, Adam sensed affront fermenting into hate. The newcomer stood stiffly by the lounging giant and met his gaze with bitter, black eyes.

"Colonel Allen, I must protest again and in the strongest terms against the unsoldierly conduct of this—this mob of yours, sir, that defiles the most sacred standards of civilized warfare."

The rancid voice ran on, reciting in detail the offenses of Grants' men—insubordination, defiance of duly commissioned officers, malicious mischief, widespread plundering, and waxing drunkenness.

"These savages have broken into the commissary, sir. They have stolen what Captain Delaplace assures me is no less than ninety gallons of His Majesty's rum."

"Well," Allen told him coolly, "I hold the king shouldn't grudge the Boys a few drops, when all his garrison is left unharmed. The Boys aren't regulars, Colonel. They're—"

"They are most villainous bandits, sir." Arnold bit sharply upon each word. "One of them, Christopher Hawley by name, is a flagrant mutineer. He—he shot at me a few minutes since."

Wrath that was not soothed by Allen's broad grin strangled him.

"If Hawley fired and missed you, sir, he didn't mean to hit you. Chris is a close shot. The Boys have an appetite, Colonel, for—"

The thunderclap shook the fort and almost overthrew them. Arnold staggered and snatched at his hat. The breeze spread a reek of powder smoke. Allen laughed.

"By God, sir," Arnold bawled, "if that was the magazine, you shall answer to—"

"No, sir." Ethan still shook with mirth. "That mad Irishman, Matthew Lyon, asked permission to fire the largest mortar as a salute to liberty. The Boys, as I was saying, have an appetite for revelry."

Arnold glared, wheeled about, and strode haughtily away.

"Gods of the Mountains," Ethan whispered, "I wish he'd go home before someone shoots at him in earnest. That would be indeed a breach of discipline. I'd best go reason with my command."

438

He took a determined stride, hesitated, and turned to blurt like a small boy:

"Don't leave me now, Adam. There are dispatches that must be written to the august and great. They should be couched in a style befitting a mighty victory if I am to appear worthily on history's pages."

The pleading tone was more difficult to withstand than the usual blustering vehemence. Adam wearily gathered himself to resist and paused to look down over the parapet at a line of men that plodded up the covered way. They grinned, but the heavy face of their leader lowered. Seth Warner had brought the rest of Allen's host across Champlain and grievance sat so heavily upon him that when he met his superior before the now wide-open gate he ignored military strictures for the unbridled freedom of a family row.

"Wal," said he with ponderous resentment, "you done it, hey? Fewer to share the credit, since you left me behind."

"Someone had to be left," Ethan returned with unwonted mildness.

"Shan't forget 'twas me. You take Ti, Sam Herrick sends word he's got Skenesborough with all the Major's family, while I cool my behind on the sand of Hands Cove. I owe you something, Ethan. You'll get paid."

Adam watched anger in Allen wrestle with the responsibility of command. His face was dusky but his voice when he replied was admirably calm.

"The lake is not freed from British dominion, Captain Warner, while Crown Point still stands."

"Wal," Warner admitted grudgingly. "Better than nothing, maybe."

On the parade voices were raised in unsteady song:

"We value not New York with all their powers
For here we'll stay and work; the land is ours."

The chant collapsed into laughter and wild shouting. Ethan grinned.

"Best enlist your force while there still are men with their legs under them."

439

While the two debated the project in low, appeased voices, Adam cautiously moved away. Matched with his purpose, the downfall of another of the king's forts was of no moment. Delight still shone, bright and compelling, through the haze of fatigue. He clung to thought of her when Ethan's reproachful glare stayed him.

"You are determined still to go," Allen blared, "with tidings of a victory that will shake the world still unproclaimed?"

Adam found it great effort to clothe his thought with words.

"I have served my fill," he said, a trifle thickly. "I have scouted Ticonderoga, have guided you hither, have been imprisoned and parted from my betrothed. Let someone else shake the world, sir. I intend to rejoin Delight Royden and take her home."

His truculence pleased Warner who, for the first time, seemed aware of his presence.

"I bear you a message from your maid," he smiled. "She bade me say she waits for you in Hands Cove."

Allen's great laughter was deafening.

"This is mutiny," he cried, "mutiny crass and most foul, Adam. In punishment I sentence you to immediate exile from this stronghold. By the ass beneath Balaam's, boy, find her, wed her, bed her, and have done with it. And whom Ethan Allen and God hath joined together, let no man put asunder."

Adam shambled down the covered way past groups of clambering men whose faces swam, whose questions could not penetrate his mind.

If it were not for Delight, he would not be driving a leaden body onward; if it were not for Delight, he would seek the nearest shade and fall asleep; if it were not for Delight, his torpid brain informed him, he would not be here, or of Ethan Allen's soldiery, or, possibly, even part of the rebellion that the fall of Ticonderoga would invigorate.

The capture of the fort was a lesser thing than the knowledge that Delight was waiting for him, steadfastly, ardently. Never henceforth would he be parted from her without that certainty. It was a reviving, clarifying thought.

He could see his present as the epitome of his past. He was

breasting obstacles, evading persons who sought to distract him, toilsomely moving onward to Delight. Adversity and peril, the malevolence of Felicity Sherwood, even the vehement persuasions of Ethan Allen had failed to thwart him.

Adam turned out to pass a group that, halting, had filled the way. Weariness so nearly merged reality with illusion that he accepted without surprise the sight of George Wadman standing pale and scowling in the center of argument, with his wife, incongruously fair, beside him. Adam halted, blinking, when the lieutenant called his name but before he could reply, the foremost of the debaters turned, squinted, and then asked:

"Cap'n Corlaer, ain't ye? Wal, then, what do we do with these here folks?"

He jerked his head toward the Wadmans and, while Adam groped for competence, explained in an acid voice:

He and his men, by Warner's orders, had scouted up the outlet and had captured the lieutenant and his wife as they had disembarked at the foot of Lake George. Now, they did not know how to deal with them or where to take them. It had been more than enough trouble to march them this far.

Adam looked from Wadman's surly resentment to Felicity's anger-brightened face. He could find no satisfaction in his enemies' downfall, only gnawing irritation at this delay.

"Take them to the fort as prisoners," he bade.

"Prisoners!" Wadman burst. "Gad, sir, prisoners of whom? Of what?"

"Of the great Jehovah," Adam replied lightheadedly, "and the Continental Congress."

He turned away. The lieutenant protested, "You, a—a gentleman intend to leave a lady with this rabble?"

"She will be quite secure," Adam promised. "You will find that Colonel Allen will care for your wife with the utmost courtesy."

Again, he turned. Felicity said, her voice clear, her color high, "With more than you display, I trust."

A vindictive spark shone briefly in Adam's brain.

"You can be sure of it," he replied. "You have never had a letter of Colonel Allen's entrusted to your care."

He saw her face go white. He wheeled and plodded on.

441

Adam sat in the galley's bow and let exhaustion's agreeable torpor overwhelm him. His shipmates who had launched the craft and willingly were plying the oars were temperate men who, with or without sanction, were returning to their farms and clearings. However the world ran, it was May and there were grain to sow, gardens to plant, and trees to fell.

The wind blew laughter and voices across the water. Adam's thoughts were haphazard as the spray that burst before the plunging bow.

Something had ended; something mightier and nobler had begun. His numb mind could not span it. It was wrought of the tempestuous spirit of Ethan Allen, of the wind and the lake and the august hills. The men who returned from the taking of a fortress to spades and plows and axes were of its essence.

The galley's bow dipped and recovered. Adam's head nodded in concert. He was weary to the marrow of his bones. Something had been born. Ethan had said so. Adam had stood at the bedside.

In the tide of drowsiness, his thoughts eddied and swirled. He could almost see Duane's prudential smile and Mindwell's keen regard, Baker's hard grin and Ira's tight-lipped stare. Here was Private Grant with his sixpenny trout; there was Corporal Mason with his endless song; and Feltham, quailing unbreeched; and Arnold's bitter face and speech; and Allen's summons filling Ticonderoga with thunder.

They met and merged and fell apart, irrelevances to be dropped behind like foam that spun from the galley's passage. Confusion and futility were over. Out of great travail there had been born—

The boat lurched and shook Adam awake. He squinted across the sun-smitten water. Yonder were trees, whipped by the wind and, nearer, a beach where waves broke into froth and, just beyond the white, uneven line, Delight, waiting with her arm uplifted.

Adam stood and raised his own.